Feather and Blade

Rachel Taylor Thompson

To Edward's Oak, Tanglewood, and a childhood playing under a very old tree.

ONE

The first time the witchcraft struck, Emrie Das sat on a turquoise pillow in her private foyer. She blamed the tingling in the pads of her fingers on her needlework. She was supposed to be embroidering a scarf for her elder sister. It wasn't going well.

She shook out her hands and returned to stitching.

The second time the witchcraft struck, Emrie was alone in her dressing chamber re-plaiting her hair after her matie servants overtightened her braids, making her scalp ache. This time the tingling swirled from the tips of her fingers up to her knuckles. It wasn't painful, just odd and uncomfortable in its singularity. Maybe she was developing a palsy?

When her maties returned, she asked for a salve.

A case of the witchcraft seemed unlikely. Witchcraft didn't happen to genteel, obedient, sensible Second Daughters of the First-ring Houses of the blessed city-oasis of Pol-Thiri.

The third time the witchcraft stuck, Emrie sat at a wrought iron table on the Breakfast Patio. A canopy of flowers fluttered over her head, and her father's tiny Juju birds chirped out a pleasant song from their cage. Fresh berries and nuts waited on the table for her dining pleasure, as did a cup of chilled tea to fortify her against a day promising to be miserably hot.

The scarf lay next to her meal, a mess of uneven stitches, puckered fabric, even a slight snag. Gifting it was supposed to be an excuse to visit her sister, Noemi, to ask for a boon, but anything to do with Noemi left Emrie tense and her mind weighted.

As Emrie picked up the scarf to see if there was any way to save it, tingling spread from the pad of each finger outward, this time pressing and coiling with a painful intensity. The feeling pushed through her knuckles into her palms and then her wrists. Emrie stiffened in her seat. Her hands splayed wide with the strength of the feeling, and she shoved them as far from her body as possible.

Emrie gasped for air at the intensity of the pressure, her breath coming in short, shallow thrusts. Then the twisting, racing pressure receded to her palms, her knuckles, and just the tips of her fingers before fading. Emrie slumped forward, bowing her head and propping her useless arms on the table. There was no possibility she had a palsy.

"This cannot be happening."

Only it was.

The punishment for having the witchcraft was the removal of one's fingers. By sword. Under the Renoa Tree. With the population of the city-oasis as witness.

Before Emrie had time to do more than acknowledge the severity of her situation, the rug between the patio and House Das flew open and someone walked out. Distinctive off-cadence footfalls said it was her father, Brunau Soen Das, Lord of House Das and Fourth Adviser to the Sovereign.

He must not find out. Emrie took every thread of horror and panic about the witchcraft and buried it behind a lifetime of etiquette training. She straightened her spine and folded her traitorous hands decorously in her lap. She forced her mouth into a pleasant smile.

The Juju birds burst into loud singsong chirps. Delicate arrows of emerald, sapphire, and glossy pomegranate feathers shot between the leafy branches of their cage, a cheerful cacophony of color. Her father gave a brief Blessing-of-the-Air in the birds' direction and dropped seeds in their feeders from a pitcher left for his use. He turned to face the massive field with the blue-leaved Renoa Tree at its center to speak the full Blessing of That-Which-Is-Life.

Emrie waited, silent and proper, trying not to think of all the things that could go wrong. Not that her father would ever betray her should he find out about her hands. He'd do nothing that would cause a loss of Status for the family, but Emrie would lose Status in his eyes either way, and that was unsupportable.

Once her father's devotions to the Renoa were complete, he limped over to kiss Emrie on the top of her head and give his usual affectionate tug on one of her rose-brown braids. Emrie patted the back of his silken sleeve with wooden fingers, praying the movement wouldn't bring the witchcraft. It didn't.

"All is well?" Emrie asked, her voice high. He was clothed from shoulder to heel in a laptevi tunic and formal overdress in royal blue. Something important must be happening.

Her father didn't answer but eyed her with a look that might've been disapproving if one didn't know him well. He had a face fit for the crags of the Kidji Hills. Long, jutting bones with a beak of a nose and deep indentations on each cheek, all made to look that much more severe by his shaved head.

"Have you seen your brother?" he asked in his quiet, gravelly voice.

"I haven't. Perhaps he's attending morning practice at the Barracks." More likely, Ahrens was still asleep.

Her father straightened slowly, protecting his bad hip.

"Ahrens won't have left House Das. The First Heir called for a full procession for the arrival of the river caravan from Gir-Tosaq."

"The caravan arrives today?" This was the point of boon she'd hoped to ask her sister. This particular caravan carried the Daughter of a Sovereign of one of the city-oases that lay southward along the river, the girl being a potential wife for the Sovereign of Pol-Thiri's eldest son. Emrie wanted an invitation to participate in the procession. She'd reached the age of majority more than a month ago, and it was tradition that all-important family members ride on the family's oxen-drawn barge.

"At any moment." Her father glanced back at the house, his attention already elsewhere.

Reality crashed in, bringing a wave of stomach-twisting fear with it. She lowered her gaze to her traitorous hands, still folded in her lap. There was no way she could take part.

"I'm happy to find Ahrens for you," she said, keeping every ounce of emotion banked and hidden. "Perhaps he's in the Central Garden."

Her father turned his back and limped back to the house without replying. Emrie's words fell to the ground with silent thuds. She flushed with humiliation, but said nothing, as was proper.

Her father paused outside the door rug and turned to look at her. The blue of his laptevi tunic and overdress contrasted against the thick white walls.

"Go to Noemi. She'd like to speak to you about a duty."

"I . . ." Emrie stumbled for words. Noemi rarely called for her and never, ever through their father. It was unheard of, nearly broke etiquette. And what was more . . .

A day ago, any moment previous to right now, Emrie would've been thrilled by such a bidding, by what it might mean. But if Noemi invited her to ride on the barge, Emrie would have to find some way, somehow, to refuse without revealing the truth of the witchcraft.

She'd never refused her sister in her life.

"Yes, of course. I'll wait on Noemi presently."

Two

There were stories of the disasters the witchcraft caused—wars between the Houses, the Status of entire families destroyed, Lords and Ladies turned into dictators that perpetrated evil on those around them. They were old stories. Tales of the early days of the Renoa Trees, when the peoples of the city-oases weren't fully civilized.

Nothing like that had happened in a thousand years. Only once in Emrie's lifetime had anyone even had their fingers removed, and that person had been a criminal from the outer-rings.

But it would happen if she got caught. The Laws of the Renoas were not trifles.

None of the old stories specifically said what the witchcraft did nor how it worked. Nor could Emrie ask, not even in a general sense. One didn't speak of these things, regardless of how badly one needed to know.

Most especially, she couldn't ask her sister. The safest way to talk to Noemi was to stay silent unless unavoidable, always speak exactly what Noemi wanted to hear, and keep to every aspect of etiquette.

At least the previous witchcraft attacks had occurred hours apart. Hopefully, she had a window of relative safety if she went right now.

Noemi's suite was in the wing of House Das reserved for the Lord and Lady and First-borns. Emrie asked a matie servant to let Noemi know she was on her way. Then she tidied her knee-length laptevi, patted her hair into order, tucked her hands into her sleeves, and offered several full Blessings that she wouldn't do anything to embarrass herself.

As was custom, the walls of Noemi's suite were pure white and unadorned in deference to the Renoa. The floor was tiled in jewel-green. Fabrics in bright shades draped one after the other from the ceiling, creating an overhead patchwork of color. Tidy large-leafed plants in glazed pots filled the corners, and silver-plated lamps on poles provided soft light.

Emrie found her sister in her dressing chamber, unwinding a scarf from around her intricately looped braids of brown hair. Noemi was the most magnificent girl in

Pol-Thiri—tall, slender, with flawless skin, dark eyes, and graceful features. She also excelled at anything she put her mind to, most especially being First Daughter, running House Das, and overseeing the family's Mining Guild.

Sometimes Emrie wished her sister was a little less perfect and a little more human.

"Come in, Sister," Noemi said in a serene voice. "May the Holy Renoa give you welcome."

Emrie buried her hands even deeper in her sleeves.

"As the grace of the Sacred Grasses do to you." She gave a respectful bow.

Noemi took a seat at a small table facing a mirror in a carved wooden frame.

"There are two things of which we must speak. First, we're to have a houseguest. The Daughter of a cousin from Kye-Boehlke. Her stay is to be extended."

This was highly unusual. Such trips usually implied a marriage contract, like with the First Heir and the Daughter from Gir-Tosaq, but the only person their House had available was Ahrens. It seemed unlikely that Noemi and her father would want Ahrens to marry a distant cousin. Even though it was Noemi who would inherit the role as Fourth Adviser and Head of House Das, Ahrens's Status as First Son wasn't a role without power and prestige.

Emrie pressed her lips together to contain all the things she wanted to ask but could not. Curiosity never worked in her favor.

Noemi hummed in the back of her throat and examined a row of clay crocks on the dressing table. She opened one, taking her time about it, dipped in a cloth, and began removing the kohl from around her eyes.

"Ahrens met this cousin once while on guildwork. He says she has no graces nor idea of how to behave in public."

Definitely not intended for Ahrens, then. The girl sounded like trouble, the last thing Emrie needed more of. She pasted a pleasant look on her face.

"I can help. Keeli and Lianjit will as well. She'll be our project."

"She isn't a member of your friends' Houses." Noemi dipped another cloth into a pot of liquid salve and stroked it into her luminescent skin. "I'll have to do it. We can't let this girl embarrass us. I'll make time in the mornings to teach her etiquette. You'd better come as well."

"I'm happy to learn etiquette."

Noemi sent her an unfriendly glance in the mirror, her brows lifting into perfect arches. "We both know your manners aren't lacking. Sometimes, Emrie, you're too obliging. You'll never be a person who matters by begging for it."

Emrie winced. "I didn't mean—"

Noemi raised a hand to silence her. "You'll attend in order to model for this girl how to behave. Between my work with the Mining Guild and the House, my shoulders are full."

Emrie nodded, accepting the orders for what they were.

"Which brings me to the second item." Noemi stood, and the cushion of her stool fell to the floor with a soft thump. Emrie stepped out of her way. "The Daughter of Gir-Tosaq," Noemi stated, "is already proving herself a challenge. There was an incident on the river this morning that is causing talk." Noemi looked toward the window and the outline of the Renoa Tree watching over Its Field and the First-ring Houses. "It would be best if I didn't attend the Ceremony of the Thousand Gratitudes tonight. Would you like to attend in my place? With Father, of course."

"I . . ." A flutter of anxiety twisted through Emrie. This wasn't the same as riding in the procession. This was . . .

Second Daughters only attended social functions with the Firsts when they intended to go courting or be courted. Emrie wasn't ready for that. Even more, a Ceremony meant socializing with large quantities of people she didn't know, something Emrie struggled with at the best of times. Not a single one of her friends, who were also Second or lower Daughters, would be present.

"Are you certain?" she managed to get out.

"Of course, I'm certain." Noemi glared at Emrie, her voice tinged with annoyance. "Don't be coarse. And don't worry about others thinking you're courting. You're on the young side to do so. I'll put out a rumor that Father requested your company. It's the perfect excuse."

For Noemi. Noemi wanted an excuse to cover her own absence. This wasn't an invitation. It was another order.

One Emrie couldn't refuse, even though the thought of attending made her legs feel weak and her stomach ill. She rested a hand on the frame of Noemi's mirror for balance.

"I'll have Mati Dechta find you something appropriate to wear," Noemi continued, walking over to a shelf stacked with fresh scarves.

Emrie's fingers tingled. Just the barest tips of the pads, but she gasped anyway and jerked her hand away from the wooden frame. The tingling spread quickly this time.

Much quicker than it had before, up her knuckles, into her palms, and then her wrists and arms.

"You'll stay in the background," Noemi said without looking up from what she was doing. "Present, but not expected to accomplish anything." She selected a raspberry-red scarf.

The witchcraft swelled stronger, pressing, coiling, expanding under Emrie's skin, making her arms feel like they were on the verge of exploding. Even worse, this time the pressure had a presence to it, an awareness. As if an enemy invader was inhabiting her bones and frantically seeking to push itself free through her blood and sinew and skin.

Emrie's lungs stalled. She fought for breath. She needed out of here, to double over and gasp for air. Since she couldn't do that, she glanced wildly around for something, anything, that might cause a distraction so that Noemi wouldn't notice her distress.

"There is one thing I'd like you to do tonight." Noemi tied the scarf neatly over her braids, still facing the other direction. "Monitor the Daughter from Gir-Tosaq for me and report back if you notice anything unusual." Noemi started to turn. "Especially between her and the Heirs because—"

Emrie lurched sideways into the dressing table, intentionally knocking one of her abused hands into an open crock. It clattered sideways, spilling golden liquid onto the tabletop, the floor, and the front of Emrie's laptevi.

"Apparently, you need the lessons in grace and etiquette after all," Noemi stated, her voice filled with irritation.

Emrie would've liked to have pointed out that she wasn't ready for such a great honor anyway, and that being dismissed from the invitation would be a relief. Not words she could utter, though, especially as the witchcraft's pounding under her skin forced her jaw to clench.

Noemi stepped away, the fabric of her laptevi rustling as if she were waving her arm at the door.

"Go to your rooms and clean up. You will attend tonight in my stead, even if your ability to show grace is currently lacking. It's still the simplest solution. Just make sure not to do anything to embarrass the family."

THREE

Emrie fled for her own suite of rooms on the far side of House Das, Noemi's words burning in her ears. She was likely to pay for her pretend clumsiness for seasons, and if she let herself think about it too much, she'd likely become ill. It was all so very, very wrong.

But at the same time, Noemi's words reminded her of something.

Don't embarrass the family. Noemi said such things regularly, but once, years ago, as part of a lecture on familial duties, she'd told Emrie that should anything disturbing ever occur to Emrie that might *embarrass the family*, Emrie should write a letter. Emrie had thought little about what that meant at the time. But now . . .

What else could Noemi have been referring to other than the witchcraft?

Halfway to her rooms, Emrie ran into Mati Dechta, the head of House Das's matie servants and the person who had raised her and Ahrens in their infancies after their mother died. She was tall and thin and wore the traditional beige laptevi of the matie class.

Mati Dechta looked at the golden liquid dripping from Emrie's hands and down her front and grimaced.

"Made a mess of things, I see." There was also no softness in Mati Dechta's voice.

Emrie shook her head.

"Well, let's clean you up then so that you don't embarrass the family."

Noemi's words yet again.

Mati Dechta ushered her along to her suite, which was identical to Noemi's with white walls, green floor tiles, and draping overhead fabrics, if not as spacious and more cluttered. Once there, Mati Dechta cleaned Emrie's hands herself before calling for Emrie's maties to change her laptevi.

The moment they all were gone, Emrie hurried to the nook where she stored her books and pulled out her copy of the Das family lineage. Noemi's instructions would have been about writing to a family member. The matter was too sensitive to involve anyone else.

Most extended families lived together in the family House, but that wasn't true for House Das. It was relatively empty, with most wings closed off and unused. Her father's generation had scattered over several city-oases to better serve the Mining Guild. Only Aunt Calys, the First Lady of House Das, and Uncle Otto, Emrie's father's brother, had remained, along with their spouses. Emrie ran her fingers down the names carved into the parchment, trying to trigger the original memory again.

She paused at Omert Das of Kye-Boehlke, her father's cousin. The upcoming visitor would be related to him. None of the other names in his line were familiar, though, nor brought back that distant memory of Noemi giving her instructions.

She turned the page and then several more until she found her parents' marriage, her mother's death, and the births of Noemi, Ahrens, and herself. She followed several other Das lines to the current generations, but most of the individuals had died or were so far removed that Emrie had never heard of them before.

Then she had another thought. Of someone whose name wouldn't be written in the book because she wouldn't be considered a Das. Their mother's twin sister. Aunt Poercha.

Aunt Poercha lived in Ter-Ramachat and had not once come to visit during Emrie's lifetime. Emrie couldn't specifically remember Noemi mentioning their aunt in connection with a letter, but it would make sense. Noemi stayed in contact with her. Aunt Poercha was the logical conclusion.

Unfortunately, a letter to Ter-Ramachat would take a handful of seven-days to arrive and the same for a return reply. Even if Aunt Poercha was the correct person, she could not solve Emrie's immediate problem of the witchcraft and tonight's Ceremony.

Emrie went in search of her writing tray and settled on a cushion in front of a low table anyway. "*Dear Aunt Poercha,*" she carved, listening to the scratch of the stylus as she etched each word into the parchment. Once a word was complete, she dipped the tip of the stylus into the ink cup and filled the indentations of the letters with blue-tinted, silvery ink. The easy part of the letter done, she stared at the words, not knowing how to ask for what she needed in such a way that wouldn't betray her problem if Aunt Poercha was not the correct individual.

"*May the Blessings of the Renoas' fall upon you and your House,*" Emrie wrote. It was a standard greeting. Emrie included several more, just to be polite. She was just about to add a line complimenting Aunt Poercha's wisdom when the witchcraft struck yet again.

She rode it out, her face tight, her lungs even tighter, a small flame of anger igniting in her chest. Why couldn't it just leave her alone?

The moment it was done, she returned to the letter. Almost immediately, the witch-craft returned. She rode it out a second time, but instead of anger, it was curiosity that flickered inside of her. Was it possible that using her hands to carve and ink the letter was causing the witchcraft to attack?

She hesitated a long moment, not wanting to do anything that might invite the pain. But there was no other way to confirm her suspicions. She picked up the stylus and started a new line of text.

Three characters in and the witchcraft returned. This time, excitement undercut the pain of the attack. She'd been right.

Every other time the witchcraft struck, she'd been using her hands, too. Embroidering the scarf, plaiting her hair, grabbing onto Noemi's mirror, carving and inking the letter. If she wanted to make it through the Ceremony that night, all she had to do was not use her hands.

FOUR

The city-oasis of Pol-Thiri was built in a series of quasi-circular rings around the Renoa Tree's Field and the Sovereign's House. The seven most powerful families lived in alabaster homes edged in blue tile built against the field. Each home was flat-topped with garden roofs containing water cisterns and arching and vining plants that cascaded over the walls. The inner-ring Houses created a stunning tapestry of white, blue, and green.

The farther one traveled from the Renoa Tree, the less impressive, less white, and less decorated were the homes. The buildings in the outer-rings by the farmyards, growing fields, and river were more of a mottled yellow-brown.

The Ceremony of the Thousand Gratitudes was held in the Hall of Guests, which was connected to the Sovereign's House and thus part of the Renoa's Field itself. By the time Emrie and her father were poised at the top of the staircase of the Hall, Emrie had worked herself into a giant case of nerves.

The witchcraft had attacked four times while she carved and inked the shortest letter of her life to Aunt Poercha. But once she'd finished, the witchcraft had disappeared and not returned.

Her current fears were related to the large group of strangers.

The room below them was flooded with people in colorful dress, the smell of roasted delights, and the beat of drums. The musicians were to her left. To her right was a raised metal dais for the priests and the members of the Sovereign's House. Remembering her sister's assignment, Emrie's attention went there first.

The Sovereign was a large man, made to look that much larger by the layers of blue and green robes he wore over his laptevi. He appeared hale and healthy from a distance, but it was rumored he was quite ill. With him on the dais were his two Sons. And there, just beside the older Son, stood the Daughter from the city-oasis of Gir-Tosaq.

She was a tiny thing, but other than that, Emrie was too far away to form an opinion.

Emrie's father tugged her down the last of the steps.

"I'll find you when it's time to leave," he said.

"But—"

He walked away into the crowd. As much as Emrie would've liked to have chased after him, she knew better than to do so.

"I don't see anyone I know," she finished weakly.

The original contract with the Renoa obligated the Firsts of each House to participate in the Ceremony of the Thousand Gratitudes and the Lighting of the Thousand Lamps once every seven-day, but in the many millennia since the contract had been made, practicality and impatience meant that the Ceremony occurred between the Sovereign and the Priests of the Renoa only. The rest of the Houses honored their obligation by sending their Firsts to bask in the light of the lamps and enjoy food, drink, and company until the fuel was spent. It was going to be a long evening.

"Emrie of House Das? That is you, isn't it?"

The voice came from behind her. Emrie didn't recognize it but swung around, grateful to have been noticed. A girl in a vivid grape laptevi watched her, a thin-lipped smile across her face. Taspin Kolera, First Daughter of the Seventh Adviser to the Sovereign. Which was pretty much all Emrie knew about the girl in grape, other than that there were several centuries of bad feelings between House Das and House Kolera. Not her first choice for company, but she wasn't about to be picky.

"It *is* you," Taspin drawled. Her voice had a twang to it as if she found speaking mildly exhausting. Behind her were two other girls. Each offered the ritual bows of someone of inferior Status greeting someone of higher. Emrie had no idea who they were other than not First-ring based on their behavior. If Emrie's friend Keeli were here, she'd have been able to draw out their names and Status with no one realizing she was doing so, but Emrie had no such skills. Instead, Emrie made the same bow to Taspin, since Taspin's Status as a First Daughter was greater than Emrie's, even though Emrie's House outranked hers. Taspin accepted the bow, and the two of them went through a brief formal greeting, exchanging compliments on each other's Houses, Guilds, clothing, and devotion to the Renoa. Once complete, Taspin took Emrie by the arm.

"Noemi asked a few of us to help you feel comfortable."

Emrie hadn't realized Noemi and Taspin were close. Then again, there were few high-Status Firsts of similar age, so it made sense.

"I'm very much obliged. It's all overwhelming, isn't it?"

"Only on your first visit. The rest of us find it tiresome." Taspin turned, beckoning Emrie and the other two to follow her through the crowd.

Taspin's formal laptevi had a high neck in the front but cut deep in the back to show off her spine before folding into a cowl at her hips that was more decorative than functional. Her hair was in piles of braids and loops with a matching grape thread running throughout. Taspin's outfit was divine, and Emrie made mental notes of the details to share with Keeli, who loved clothing. Emrie's own dress was a pale yellow with a higher back and more modest design.

Taspin led them to where a grouping of potted trees created an alcove of semi-privacy. A matie servant offered cuts of crisped fruit. Emrie shook her head, not wanting to risk doing anything with her hands.

"Tell us about Noemi," Taspin said in the same drawling tone. "She isn't ill, is she?"

"Tired only," Emrie replied.

"So kind of you to come in her stead." Taspin's words were more question than statement. She seemed to be fishing for information.

"I'm grateful to be in such distinguished company," Emrie replied politely.

Before Taspin could ask anything else, they were joined by several more girls, each bowing to first Taspin and then Emrie, although they must all be close friends of Taspin's, as no one offered a formal greeting. Taspin threw several more probing questions Emrie's way, which Emrie answered as blandly as possible. Since Emrie had no idea who the other people were and none of them showed any additional interest in her, she was pushed to the background. It was all awkward and uncomfortable, and anxiety slithered up her spine.

She turned her attention toward the Sovereign's dais just to give herself something to do. Maybe in this, at least, she could please her sister.

She was closer now and had a better view. The Daughter from Gir-Tosaq had a chirpy, cheerful look about her, with wide eyes, a pert nose, and glossy lips. Her hair wasn't in braids like all Pol-Thirian girls but wrapped around her head in a bird's-nest-looking crown. And the color was different, too. Still brown, but thicker and streaked with gold in a way that was not Pol-Thirian at all. She wore a laptevi tunic not unlike Emrie's own, fitted through the bodice and falling loose to her knees with leggings underneath. The peach color varied from what was produced in Pol-Thiri and her laptevi had no cowl, which was odd. Keeli would have lots of opinions about that.

Next to the girl stood the First Heir, tall and wide-shouldered in comparison. His hair fell free down his back, its burnt-rose Pol-Thiri color rich with contrast, thick and heavy.

He was a younger version of his father, serious and stoic, the male ideal of the city-oasis. He seemed a mismatch for the delicate, perky-looking Daughter from Gir-Tosaq. Then again, what did Emrie know about these things?

The Second Heir waited behind the trio, an oddball accessory as usual.

Even more girls joined Taspin's group and brought with them several boys. Emrie shifted several paces back to make space, putting herself outside of the ring of friends. In doing so, she stepped on one of the many cooling grates set into the floor, and as if in response, the grate puffed out three breaths of chilly air against her slippers.

Her fingertips tingled as if touched to ice.

Emrie shoved her arms across her chest in a panic, burying her hands into the crooks of each elbow as the tingling built. Not now. She hadn't been doing anything at all with her hands. Please, please, not now.

"Are you cold?" Taspin asked, turning her full attention to Emrie. "We can't have that." Taspin stepped in close, too close, and Emrie backed away as if chased. Her hands felt like they were going to burn right through her laptevi at any moment, as if the alien presence was working especially hard to make Emrie's life difficult. Emrie fought to keep her face still and the rest of her as relaxed as possible against the horror of it.

"I'm fine," she managed to get out through a gritted jaw as the tingling pinnacled.

"Come, let's get some drink. That'll help."

The witchcraft subsided, and Emrie was more than happy to find somewhere to go, away from the grate. She didn't know for sure it had caused the reaction, but it seemed too much of a coincidence to be unrelated.

Taspin escorted her to the nearest matie with a tray decorated with the Sovereign's crest. Emrie hesitated to take a goblet, not wanting to touch anything, even though her prior theory hadn't been correct.

"Don't be shy," Taspin said, sounding amused.

Emrie took the goblet. Nothing happened, and she gulped down the wine in relief.

"Come," Taspin said. "You must meet one of my dearest friends. He's the Son of a Ninth-ring House and very handsome."

"I'm not here to court," Emrie said quickly, but Taspin had already turned away. Even worse, Emrie's fingers tingled again.

If it was possible for wine to curdle, the stuff she'd just downed did so. She could feel another chilly breeze, but not from under her feet this time, just in the room. A pressurizing of air as if the floor grates all pulsed at once. She wrapped her fingers around the goblet, clutching it hard against her chest, her whole body rigid.

The conversation didn't go well. Emrie mumbled out a few yaes and nays to his polite questions about the health of her sister and enjoyment of the evening while she tried to keep her body's reaction to the witchcraft as unnoticeable as possible. This meant Emrie became very stiff, and Taspin carried the bulk of the conversation. When the witchcraft subsided, Emrie tried to engage more, but the damage had been done and the boy looked down his nose at her.

"You didn't like him," Taspin said, leading her away. "Let's see if we can find someone more to your tastes."

"I'm not here to court," Emrie repeated, trying to sound firmer.

"Of course you aren't, but we mustn't let you miss an opportunity to consider your options." Taspin grabbed her by the arm. Emrie left the goblet on a matie's tray as she was tugged along.

Right as they approached the next boy, the room flooded with cold air and the witchcraft struck. The chat went about the same as with the first boy. Taspin introduced her to a third boy and halfway through that conversation, the witchcraft returned again. Emrie began to predict it—the grates made a subtle noise, a chill of air lifted into the room, the witchcraft reacted. Her stomach rolled and her face flushed with every rustle of movement from the floor.

"You're a reserved one, aren't you?" Taspin said after five boys and twice as many bouts. Emrie'd given up on being chatty or impressing anyone. She just wanted to go home and collapse. Her entire body ached with tension, and all of these people must think her a lunatic and an embarrassment.

Taspin turned away for a moment as if looking for another boy, and Emrie was left with a view of the Sovereign's dais. A circle of cushions had been arranged for the Daughter of Gir-Tosaq's comfort, and she sat chatting with several other women. The First Heir paced back and forth along the front edge of the dais as if guarding the space. The Sovereign was surrounded by Advisers. The Second Heir stood off to the side, looking inscrutable.

As if he felt Emrie watching, the Second Heir turned her direction. Emrie darted her attention back to the Daughter, who stared at the Second Heir with a mix of longing and come-hither on her face. The blatancy of it made Emrie shift backward uncomfortably.

Emrie knew little about the Second Heir. He was more refined than his heavily boned and muscled brother with silky midnight hair, sharp-edged features, and a whip-cord build. His mother had been the Sovereign's concubine from Vin-Yonekur, and he was disfavored because of it. Well, that and because he'd spent several years living in Vin-Yonekur and was said to have returned with a difficult personality.

He was also not the brother the Daughter of Gir-Tosaq had come to Pol-Thiri to potentially marry. Which made the Daughter's look the exact thing Noemi would want Emrie to note.

The First Heir swung around to face the Daughter, and the Daughter's expression went blank. The First Heir reddened, his lips curled into a sneer, his hands balling into fists. Clearly, he'd caught where she'd been directing her attention.

The floor hummed. A burst of cool air entered the room. The witchcraft tingled Emrie's fingers. She pushed aside any interest in the doings on the dais and crossed her arms over her chest once again. Taspin took that moment to offer her a biscuit topped with soft cheese. Emrie shook her head, hoping her refusal appeared more gracious than it felt.

Right as the witchcraft rose to its peak, there was a universal gasp from those in the Hall, followed by an awkward pause in the drumming and woodwinds, as if even the musicians had been startled into silence. Then the rumbling of voices.

"Did you see that?" Taspin whispered loudly.

"What?" Emrie mumbled, still focused on hiding her tension.

"The First Heir punched the Second Heir in the face. Blood flew. He went down." Taspin sounded thrilled.

Emrie gave a small shake, trying to hurry the last of the witchcraft away. "The First Heir?"

"The Second Heir. Didn't you see it?"

Then before Emrie could reply or ask for details, her father was at her side, taking her by the arm and insisting in his rumbling voice that it was time for them to leave. Right at that moment.

***

Deriek Costa Valiyard, Second Son of his father, the Sovereign of Pol-Thiri, fought to control the dark, roiling steam building under his skin. He'd repressed a thousand responses in the moment he'd been punched, all of which would've left his brother flattened. Deriek now paid for the restraint.

A string of maties followed him as he threaded his way through a servants' section of his father's House. One of them waved a damp cloth over his shoulder. Deriek took it and wiped at the blood smeared down his chin. It'd been years since his brother had hit him, and the reasoning behind today's actions was beyond ridiculous.

Recognizing that didn't curb the blistering anger that made him want to explode.

He couldn't do so, though.

The people of Pol-Thiri needed to see a detached, aloof Second Heir, and thus Deriek slowed his pace and forced an outward appearance of nonchalance. A matie pressed a cup into his hand. Deriek tried to down the contents, but it was both sickeningly sweet and made his split lip sting like he'd pissed off an oversized hornet. Which wasn't inaccurate. He spit the whole of it into the nearest potted plant. The matie didn't show any disapproval of this, and within a few breaths, Deriek's lip went numb. He nodded to the matie in acknowledgment of the good deed and kept walking.

He craved open space, stars rather than a ceiling, fresh air rather than that shared with a thousand other bodies. Somewhere he could react without an audience. He rounded a corner, the maties still following, and found the Third Adviser of his father blocking his way. She was known for dealing fairly, and Deriek might've stopped had she not had a sympathetic look in her eye. Maybe it was genuine. Likely not. She raised a hand, asking him to pause.

"I would speak to you."

Deriek bowed in her direction without stopping. He did so with an extra flourish, dipping his head near to his knees. It was a mocking behavior, one that was effective because no one but him employed it. He straightened just in time to see the briefest glimpse of irritation on the Third Adviser's face. Not genuine then.

"As the bird of prey hunts the mouse, I don't have the time." Let her puzzle that for a while. Deriek stepped around her and kept going.

She likely wanted to discover his intentions toward the Daughter of Gir-Tosaq. As if he'd have any intentions. Deriek hadn't spoken a word with the girl outside of the Receiving Ceremony, which had occurred in front of no less than two hundred people.

Deriek was also well aware that any type of entanglement between himself and another person, whether it be through a marriage contract, romance, or even friendship, would leave a gaping hole in a rather necessary shield of defense.

He arrived at a side door used for late-night messages coming to and from his father and paused there to dismiss the maties so that they wouldn't be forced to stand there waiting for his return. It wasn't their fault his life was a mess.

As he exited, he greeted the norie servants guarding the exterior of the door.

"I'm off to Gennant's Tea House," he said, giving his usual excuse. Whether they believed him, he had no idea, but it was a signal that he wanted privacy as the backrooms of Gennant's were known for having brishka strong enough to knock an ox insensible in two cups. Deriek wasn't stupid enough to do that, but no one ever questioned him.

Once he was away from the Sovereign's House, he turned neither toward Gennant's nor toward the river where people and lamps worked round the clock this time of year and trouble or companionship could usually be found. He headed in the opposite direction, toward the gate where the desert minerals and iron and such were hauled into the city. There was a door there, a place where he might leave unobserved and, after a bit of a hike, leave the city and his problems behind for a while.

He was halfway to that gate when he realized someone was following him. It wasn't the first time this had happened, and the person wasn't skilled at stealth. Which either meant his father had sent a norie servant or another Adviser was making an attempt at conversation.

He was in the middle-rings now and the streets here were narrower. He ducked into the nearest alcove, pressing into the shadows of a sidewall where he couldn't be seen. He wished he'd brought a sword or at least a knife. Not that he'd likely need to defend himself as Heirs were untouchable under the Laws of the Renoa, but it would take the edge off his temper to scare the color out of whoever dared follow him. He decided to do so even without a weapon.

The person took forever to get close and Deriek grew impatient. Hopefully, it wasn't anyone that would complain later of what was about to happen.

He waited until the person was right in front of him and then eased out, taking the third position of Tenkiantemir's Fourth Dance of Swords. He got a glimpse of a young male face, one he recognized but couldn't place. Hair braided back. Eyes gone wide in surprise. For just a moment, Deriek hesitated at how vulnerable the boy looked. Then he launched forward.

And was caught from behind by an arm around his neck. The arm tightened, cutting off his air. Deriek didn't panic. He relaxed and twisted sideways.

A second person he couldn't see caught his arms. And then a third swept his feet off the ground. Deriek realized not with fear but with a fury ten times what his brother had created that he'd been ambushed. And by skilled soldiers. His brother must've finally had enough.

The boy, the bait who'd gotten him caught, stuffed a rag in Deriek's mouth with a gleeful look in his eyes and then shoved a hood over his head. Deriek's rage dissipated and was replaced instead by a dark humor. So, this was how it was all going to end. Such an ignominious death. Such a disappointment. His father would be pleased.

FIVE

"And then the First Heir punched the Second Heir," Emrie said as she walked with her two best friends, Keeli and Lianjit, through the blue-cobbled street of Pol-Thiri. They headed toward the Artisans' Marketplace. It wasn't the only market in the inner-rings, but it was their favorite and thus their usual destination. "From what I heard, the Second Heir went down without fighting back."

"Likely he didn't know how." Lianjit clasped both hands together and made a sweep as if slicing an invisible sword through the air. Her single, plain cue of hair swung against her back. She was the shortest of the three of them but made up for it by being sharp-edged and having solid strength. "I've never seen him at Barrack's Practice or with a weapon in his hand. What kind of Heir doesn't learn to defend his home?"

"Lianjit," Keeli said in the disapproving tone she always used when Lianjit went too far. "You shouldn't say such things."

"Keeli," Lianjit said, imitating Keeli perfectly, "you don't like the Second Heir, either. He could be the city's greatest swordsman if he just practiced once in a while. Besides, what we all want to know is what happened to the foreign Daughter."

"Also," Emrie said to Keeli, "you were mothering once again."

Keeli made a humphing noise and lifted her chin in pretend offense. Keeli had a strong mother hen mindset.

Emrie had been the one to suggest they go out this morning. She hadn't wanted to do so, but there was no way her friends wouldn't demand to hear what Emrie had witnessed. It would be easier to hide any bouts of the witchcraft on an outing.

The witchcraft had disappeared the moment she'd left the Hall and hadn't reappeared since. Not even when she'd pressed her fingers to one of the cooling grates of House Das. She didn't trust that it wouldn't, though.

"I wish I'd seen more," she said with a glance toward Keeli. Emrie hadn't even seen enough to please Noemi who'd replied to Emrie's request to visit with a message about already having what she needed from elsewhere.

Lianjit nodded. "Thank the Tree that Keeli needs more hair baubles. She'll get us the rest of the story."

"Don't be rude," Keeli said, even as she patted the convoluted loops and braids that were indeed wound through with many colored threads and several jeweled pins that matched her heavily embroidered apricot laptevi. She turned to Emrie. "And you, don't fret. You did the best you could."

Emrie smiled her gratitude, even if Keeli was mothering again. Lianjit rolled her eyes.

The road they followed widened into a maze of fabric-walled stalls that was the Artisans' Marketplace. There were already plenty of people and voices and the smell of someone roasting nuts.

"Who can we find from a House that isn't closed-lipped?" Lianjit asked.

"Just let me handle it," Keeli insisted, which was of course what Lianjit was trying to get her to do. Lianjit was not long on patience.

The center of the Marketplace was filled with a massive copper fountain of the Holy Renoa. The fountain was good luck, and the stalls closest to it had the best wares. Keeli led them to a seller of hair threads. Usually, Emrie would've joined her in riffling through the spools, but today she stayed back with Lianjit who grumbled that Keeli wasn't taking her need to know what happened seriously enough.

Keeli snickered at that.

"You're tormenting us on purpose, aren't you?" Emrie called to Keeli.

"Not you, just Lianjit." Keeli showed her a spool in vermilion that had a metallic shimmer to it and then turned to pay the vendor. "Let's go look at fans, and then maybe I'll see what I can unearth regarding gossip."

Lianjit sighed.

They didn't make it to the fans. They were skirting their way around the fountain when a girl their age came hurrying over, a huge grin on her face. She hailed Emrie with a respectful bow and was greeted by Keeli by name, who then made a point of mentioning that she was of House Ayre and a Fourth Daughter. After a formal greeting ceremony handled by Keeli, the girl jumped into why she'd come over.

"I just heard the most delicious tale," she said in a conspiratorial whisper. She gave a quick glance at Emrie as if asking for permission to speak.

"Do tell," Keeli said, as she knew very well Emrie hated public deference.

Not unexpectedly, the girl launched into the same story about the Heirs but with many exaggerated details. Such as the Daughter of Gir-Tosaq throwing herself bodily at the Second Heir to protect him from his brother and the First Heir drawing a sword and nearly taking off the Second Heir's arm. Keeli nodded along as if this was the first time they'd heard any of it. Lianjit folded her arms over her chest and sent Keeli a this-is-the-best-we-can-do? look. They'd just reached the part where the Second Heir had to be carried out by nories because he was too injured to walk when Emrie's fingers began to tingle.

Sun, Wind, Soil, and Rain, did it have to happen now?

Emrie took a casual step away from the others. In doing so, she bumped into the stone rim of the fountain with the back of her calves. She turned to pretend to study the fountain while the Fourth Daughter described the Daughter of Gir-Tosaq begging the First Heir for mercy for his brother on her knees.

Emrie fought to keep her body still, her face relaxed. The fountain towered above her head, its copper trunk and leaves weathered into a teal blue that leaked fat droplets of water much like the afternoon rains. To appear normal, Emrie shoved her aching, twisting hands out to catch the drops in her palm and shake them back at the trunk in a Blessing-of-the-Water. The moment she did so, the witchcraft surged and the tingles intensified as if the water urged the presence inside to split her skin and burst forth to freedom. Emrie repressed a scream of pain, barely.

The girl dropped her voice. "Then the Second Heir returned to his rooms, packed a trunk, and left Pol-Thiri."

"I thought he was too injured to walk," Lianjit pointed out.

Emrie jerked her hand out of the water and scrubbed it down her laptevi, removing the dampness that had worsened the feeling. With the motion, the witchcraft disappeared. It happened so suddenly Emrie went off-kilter and stepped to the side to rebalance herself. She stared down at her hand.

"His maties fixed him up," the girl explained. "They say he was so angry and humiliated that he's sworn to shake the dust of Pol-Thiri from his feet and return to his mother's people."

"Let him go," Lianjit said dismissively.

The fingers of Emrie's other hand still swirled and ached as the witchcraft receded. She scrubbed it down her front as well. The witchcraft there disappeared just as fast.

"Lianjit, don't say such things," Keeli said.

The Fourth Daughter continued. "The Daughter of Gir-Tosaq is so impressed by the First Heir's strength and leniency that she is on the brink of agreeing to a marriage contract."

Lianjit snorted.

Emrie continued to stare at her hands.

"Is something wrong, Emrie?" Keeli reached over to touch Emrie's arm. Lianjit and the other girl were staring at her as well. "Have you injured yourself?"

Emrie grinned, including them all in her smile, even the Fourth Daughter with the outlandish tale. If rubbing her fingers made the witchcraft go away, living with it wouldn't be so bad after all.

"I was offering a Blessing-of-the-Water. I think it might've worked."

SIX

Over the next several seven-days, Emrie's ridding herself of the witchcraft became second nature. The moment her fingers tingled, she wiped them on her clothing and the feeling disappeared. She was in control, and with that, she gave up caring about what made it trigger. It just didn't matter. All she had to do was wait for Aunt Poercha to send instructions, and she'd rid herself of it permanently.

She resumed her regular life, even letting Keeli drag her to several visits with other Houses where there was plenty of gossip to be listened to, much of it about the House of the Sovereign. As the Season of Water wore on, the difficulties of that House had her father and Noemi running ragged even if nothing specific was ever mentioned on Petal Nights, when each House dined formally as a family.

It was a pleasant surprise when late one afternoon, a matie came to find her, asking her to join her father in his private chamber. She went immediately as was proper. Her father had only called for her a handful of times in her life, and at this moment, she had a good guess as to the reason. Aunt Poercha must have replied sooner than expected and her father wanted to hand-deliver the letter.

She'd always liked her father's private chamber. It was only one of two places in House Das with a wooden door, the other being the formal front entry. The door to her father's private chamber was intricately carved with hawks diving for a kill, desert cats downing gazelles, and wide-open crocodile mouths. The chamber beyond had no windows nor other ways to spy on the Fourth Adviser. Where every other chamber in House Das had silk hangings draped to cover the ceilings and potted plants rotated in and out daily, here the ceilings were plain blue tiles and the room was empty except for lamps on poles and the line of family swords along the back wall. Her father sat behind a stone table so that the row of swords were behind his head. There was something reassuring and right about him surrounded by the history and might of their House.

He nodded toward a bench on the far side of the table. "Please sit."

Emrie did, rubbing her fingers lightly on her laptevi out of a newly born habit.

"Emrie, I have a request of you. Something I wouldn't ask if I felt it could be avoided."

He looked so grim that Emrie's heart thrilled with love. Perhaps Aunt Poercha had sent an invitation for Emrie to visit. It would be an unusual thing to do, but if she was right, her father was saying he'd miss her when she left. She'd miss him, too.

"I'm happy to do whatever must be done. And . . . it'll be alright."

"I hope so," he said. "As you know, the Renoa blesses Its people through order."

"Order begets responsibility which begets Status," she said, repeating her father's favorite adage. Not what she would've expected him to bring up at this exact moment, but she knew this lecture well. "The Guild is tied to the House which is tied to the Family. The outer-rings swear fealty to the middle-rings who swear fealty to the inner-rings." But none of it existed in any tidy, hierarchal way, more like the chaotic branching and crossing and combining of the Holy Renoa itself.

He nodded and went into a drawn-out description of the rivalries between the Houses that surrounded the Renoa Tree's Field. How the First Adviser's House had no children this generation and was likely to fall from its position. How the Seventh House hoped to embed their Sons into the Third House in order to increase their standing. How too many of the Houses were shrinking in terms of progeny and the Second-ring families were trying to push their way in, even as they, too, were lacking in children. Emrie listened attentively, doing her best to follow the generations of marriage contracts and alliances and betrayals as he seemed to expect. She knew all the names and could put a few of them to faces, but that was it. This was her father's world, Noemi's world, and even Ahrens's. Not hers, as her visit to the Hall of Guests had proven.

"The goal is influence. Power. Status for the House. And the finest jewel, the trunk of the tree so to speak, is controlling the Seat of Judgment itself." He looked at her, a solid, straight, expectant weight in his gaze.

"I don't understand," Emrie said since he seemed to want some response. "What does this have to do with me?"

"Yesterday, the body of the Third Son of the Fifth Adviser was found dead in the outer-rings. He was murdered by sword."

"You think Ahrens is in danger?"

Her father shook his head, his habitual frown deepening. "Did you hear what I said? The goal is influence."

Emrie tried to puzzle through what he was telling her but made no connections. What it didn't seem to be was related to her aunt.

"You saw the First Heir at the Ceremony. You know what he's like."

"He's unkind?" she asked, confused.

Her father stood abruptly, sending a flutter of uncertainty through Emrie. Nothing about this felt right.

"He's a monster," her father said, his voice serious. "He ignores the Advisers, he mocks the Sages, he blasphemies against the Renoa. He killed the Third Son for asking after his missing brother."

"The Second Heir is dead then?"

It was against the Law of the Renoa to kill the Sovereign or the Heirs. Their House was sacrosanct. If one of them was murdered, the Renoa got involved and enacted punishment, which was swift and gruesome according to the old stories, and left the offender in small pieces.

Her father came around the end of the stone table. Emrie stood to meet him, and he cupped her cheek in his palm. When he spoke, it was in a whisper as if his words were so dangerous not even this protected location was safe.

"The Second Heir is alive. I need you to keep him that way."

The tiny hairs on the back of Emrie's neck tightened as if hit by a cold, fearsome breeze. If it was anyone else, she'd have looked away, resisted. But this was her father and even if she still had no idea what he was inferring, she only had one option.

"I'll do whatever you ask."

His gaze became piercing, the brown of his eyes dark and deep.

"Of course, you will." Then he smiled, and he was once again the father she loved and trusted. He released her cheek to tug on her braids. "You're a good Daughter, Emrie. I've always known that."

"What would you have me do?"

He collected a book wrapped in linen from the table, holding it by the tips of his fingers. "You wrote your Aunt Poercha asking for assistance with a problem you're having."

"I . . . yes, I did," Emrie replied, both surprised by him bringing that up now and again utterly confused.

He smiled as if enjoying her reaction. "As Head of this House, I know what it means when a Daughter or Son writes such a letter. I haven't heard from your aunt yet, but when I do, I want you to reply that you'd like to wait a season. Perhaps two. Your aunt is likely to invite you to visit her and it would be hard on Noemi for you to be gone right now. She's under a great deal of stress, and we have a house guest about to join us who'll need your guiding hand."

For a moment, Emrie just stared at him.

He knew? About the witchcraft?

And he was smiling and just continuing on?

None of this, absolutely none of it, made any sense.

"I'm happy to help," Emrie agreed slowly. "I'll tell Aunt Poercha."

"That's the simple part. The difficulty is twofold. First, I know where the Second Heir is being held. I'll take you to him. After that, feeding him, caring for him, keeping him alive will be your duty."

Emrie took a sharp breath.

"You can tell no one what you are doing, not even your sister or brother. The boy himself can't know who you are or which House owns your allegiance."

"But—"

He put a finger up to halt her questions. She had plenty. This made no sense. Why her? Why not pretty much anyone with a better knowledge of politics or people or even caretaking? A faithful matie would be a better choice than her. But it was also the first time her father had entrusted her with something important.

"Once I show you how to get to him, you can never speak of your caretaking again. Not even to me. Our House, our lives, not just yours and mine, but Noemi and Ahrens and everyone else's, depend on it never getting out that you kept the Second Heir alive."

But why? What did caretaking even mean? Who was trying to kill him? She held her tongue, knowing by the look on her father's face that he wasn't finished.

He handed her the book wrapped in linen.

"Take it."

Emrie did, being as careful as he was even though it felt like an ordinary book.

"It belongs to House Das and is now yours. Hide it, keep it as secret as your assignment, for this also will get you killed if found. The only way I can see of keeping the Second Heir alive and not getting caught is you using this book to learn the witchcraft."

***

It had to be the most disconcerting moment in Emrie's life, worse even than the arrival of the witchcraft. She felt like she was standing on the edge of the river, being asked to jump in, and trying desperately to explain that not only did she not know how to swim but also she'd just seen the sharp blade of a predator's fin cut its way through the water.

She walked through the halls of House Das carrying the book as far from her body as possible. Once in her rooms, she detoured past the sumptuousness of her cushions, the length of open doors leading out to her patio, and the massive sleeping dais waiting behind gossamer curtains. She went to the chamber where she stored her clothing. In the center of that room was a wooden chest that held the few items she'd been gifted by her mother. Ancestors' belongings were sacred, so no one, not even the maties, would open it, let alone rummage through it. Emrie dumped the book inside but didn't close the lid.

Learning to command the witchcraft was forbidden.

Apart from the danger and the old stories, the witchcraft was also a direct affront to the Renoa. In the writings of Sage Thormas, the Holy Renoa was described as a continuing story where each person was tied into the Tree for their lifetime as were the leaves and branches and bark. The Renoa brought life to all Its parts and together they grew the tale of the city-oasis. Intentional use of the witchcraft was a breaking away from the Renoa's story. It was declaring oneself a Tree of one's own. Emrie had always thought that the Renoa liked her, found her charming. She didn't want to do anything to change that.

What if she opened the book and the witchcraft took that as an invitation? What if it reacted the same way it had at the fountain? What if that happened and she couldn't make it stop?

And then there were the old tales of what would happen if she got caught. The Judgment wouldn't just be her having her hands cut off. House Das would lose Status. Her father would be removed from his office as Adviser. Her family would lose their home. Emrie shuddered. The lid of the trunk felt painfully heavy.

Yet she couldn't turn away from a duty that had been laid specifically on her shoulders. One didn't refuse a request from one's Head of House.

Her father was willing to risk the dangers. He seemed confident she could protect their family. What he was trying to accomplish was for the good.

Right?

Besides, her father had asked her to postpone communications with her aunt, not cancel it. Once the Second Heir was out of her care, Emrie would still go to Aunt Poercha. Emrie closed the lid of the chest. She wouldn't look at the book for now. Her father had said he'd show her where the Second Heir was being held later that evening, and he wouldn't be using the witchcraft to do so. She'd wait to see what was needed and then decide about the book and the witchcraft in the hopes that maybe she could fulfill this duty without it.

SEVEN

Pol-Thiri felt a different city after dark with the colors bleached to shadows and the stars glaring down.

Her father took her through the city streets to an alley that led toward the Renoa's Field. They stopped halfway down at a metal door in the outer wall of what she guessed was one of the First-ring Houses. He pulled out a ring of four keys, using one to open the door. It released a burst of cold air that ruffled Emrie's hair.

"Take this," he said, handing her a lamp and metal pail. "The pail contains his food and water. You'll need to bring such to him every night. Pass through so I can lock the door behind us."

She obeyed. The other side wasn't a room but the top of a stairwell. To the cooling caverns? Must be. Considering what had happened at the Hall of Guests, it seemed somehow fitting.

Her father took the lamp back but left her the pail.

"It only spreads light toward the front." He turned the lamp to show her, and it was so bright all she could see was the glow of the wick. Her father, the walls, everything else disappeared. "As long as the light points toward him, he can't see you. When you leave, you must back away. You'll remember that, Emrie? It's important. If you back away, he can't see your face."

"I won't fail you." Her voice came out more whisper than words.

"I believe that," he said and led the way into the dark. Emrie gripped the pail tight and followed. She knew little about the cooling caverns. She'd been underneath House Das only once, with a tutor who'd been trying to teach her about the physics of it. Something to do with the chilled air originated deep in the earth and how the roots of the Holy Renoa and the workings of one of the Guilds moved the coolness up into the buildings. She'd found the tour to be frightening.

She fought against the same feeling now. Rough-hewn steps led downward. The air tasted like wet dirt.

Her tutor had said the cooling system went deep into the earth, and the staircase did seem to go on forever. Finally, it leveled out and her father's silhouette led her forward. The breeze of the moving air continued to tease at her hair. Unlike the aboveground winds brought by the Renoa in the Season of Air, it was steady and even, seeping through the seams of her clothing.

Pathways broke off to either side of the underground hallway they followed, but their course remained straight, and the witchcraft didn't react as they walked what felt like the entire length of the House above.

Her father stopped and motioned for her to step up next to him. His lamp reflected against steel bars running from floor to ceiling with hinges on one side. A gate between one House and the next.

A tremble of alarm stole up from the bottom of Emrie's feet to the crown of her head. This was much worse than just frightening.

There were stories from the early days of assassins and thieves using the cooling vents to sneak from House to House. For that reason, each side of the gate would have a lock, the key kept possessed by the Head of the House above. Her father pulled out his keys again and showed her two more that matched to glyphs on two locks, one on each side. She knew suddenly where they were going and gave a small gasp. As if he were expecting it, her father patted her on the shoulder reassuringly.

Her father didn't speak, and when he showed her how to open the locks, he did so moving slowly and silently. Noises from the cooling system could echo to the chambers above, and breaking into the space under someone else's House was a crime. Breaking into the cooling caverns under the Sovereign's House was treason. No wonder her father had warned her that no one could know what she was doing. No wonder he trusted no one but a family member to do this.

The metal gate swung open on silent hinges. Her father patted her on the shoulder a second time and led her forward.

The feel of the breeze increased, building until she shivered. Her father stopped again. This time in front of a door made of wide slats of wood. Someone had put a wooden door down here? It was ugly and uncarved, bound with steel and forbidding in a way she'd never seen wood used before. It seemed sacrilegious.

Her father showed her the ring of keys again, holding up the last key. A moment later they were on the other side, facing another stairwell, this one going up. Her father shut the door behind them. Silently.

"You'll have to go the rest of the way alone," he whispered into her ear. "My limp will give me away."

"I—" she started, but he put a hand on her back, pushing her forward.

"You must."

She hadn't been going to refuse. She understood her duty. She just didn't understand why.

"Follow the steps. At the top, turn to the right. Once you see him, push the food through the bars. Don't leave the pail. And don't be afraid. Even I can't unlock his prison. He has no way to hurt you or get out."

She nodded even though he couldn't see. Her father always spoke the absolute truth. "He can't hurt me unless he sees my face."

He handed her the lamp and then pulled up her cowl so that it covered her head.

"You won't let that happen." His voice was final and heavy with authority. Not the voice of her father, but the one he used as Fourth Adviser. She would've preferred something more personal.

Regardless, Emrie sucked up the cold air and her limited courage and turned to go. The first step felt huge. The second, even more so. Almost immediately, she lost any feel for her father behind her. She was alone in the dark with the lamp and the sound of her own footsteps.

She pictured the Second Heir as he'd been on the dais, the enigmatic look on his face. Hopefully, he wouldn't be too difficult now.

This stairwell wasn't as long as the previous one. She was at the top before she was ready. The silence became a solid, threatening thing. The dark, too dark. She felt a childish need to yell or scream or break out into one of the silly ditties Mati Dechta used to sing to her and Ahrens when they were children. Instead, she followed a short hall into a chamber and flashed the lamp side-to-side.

Directly opposite was an iron wall of bars set a hand's-width apart. To her right was a burned-out torch, abandoned by the Second Heir's guards perhaps. The space beyond the bars appeared empty at first, but she could smell him. The acrid tang of a human body left too long unwashed. Wafts of feces and vomit and who knew what else. She blew out through her nose, wishing she had a free hand to pinch it closed.

Only then did he move, and it was more of the turning of a pile of rags and tangled hair. An arm pressed against what must be his forehead, shielding his eyes from her lamp. He was twenty or so paces back from the bars, hunched or crouched or something so that he looked more beast than the third most important person in the city-oasis. Terror clawed up her throat, one barb at a time. The light of the lamp shook with her tremblings. She searched the mound of rags for some glimpse of the boy she'd seen before, someone she might recognize as human. She tried to remember her duty to her House. All that fled before a nearly irrational terror.

"Water?" His voice was so hoarse the word was barely understandable.

Emrie broke. She rushed to his door, dropping the lamp on the ground and going to her knees. She jerked the top off the pail and pulled out wafer bread, cooked roots, and cheese. She shoved everything as far through the bars as she could, piling the food onto the dirty ground and then tugging her hand back as fast as possible. He made no movement in her direction.

"Water?" he begged.

She took a bladder from the pail and shoved it through, too. Then she grabbed the lamp and pail and bolted. Backward, so there was no chance that creature would see her face.

***

Emrie didn't stop running until she was back to her father. He gripped her shoulder in question at her distress, and she took several gulping breaths before whispering that she was unharmed. He nodded and took the lamp. Neither of them spoke until they were back in the alley aboveground.

"What happened?" her father asked.

"I was frightened of him." Her voice trembled against her will. She hated her father seeing it but couldn't stop.

"You mustn't be, Emrie," he said quietly. "There isn't anyone else I can ask to do this."

She looked up into his face, framed in a patch of light. Lines of worry and exhaustion deepened the usual crevices.

It shamed her.

"You must return to House Das alone," he continued, "as I need to be seen in public to cover our disappearance. Make your way along the edge of the Field."

"The Renoa's Field?" Surprise stilled her nerves. No one did that. Ever. The Renoa's Field wasn't for mere passage.

"Skirt the Field and stay up against the buildings. The first-floor patios will be deserted by now, and you shouldn't be visible to the upper balconies before moonrise. As long as you're quiet and use no light, you won't be seen. That must be how you come and go from here."

"Yes, Father."

"Good girl." He reached over and tugged her hair. "Enter House Das through the Patio of History. The lock on the door there is broken and won't be fixed. You understand you must feed him each night, yes? I can't return here."

"I understand." The words brought on the flood of panic once more. How was she ever going to do this again?

"It's upon you to solve any difficulties. You and I must never speak of this. It must be as if I don't know what you're doing."

"Yes."

"Do what you must to keep that boy alive and bring Status to our House." He opened the gate, turned her shoulders so that she was pointed toward the Field, and gave her a gentle push. "You've always been an obedient daughter."

The walk itself was uneventful, even if it took her much longer than it should've to creep around the edge of the Field as she scurried from shadow to shadow while sending apologies for her impiety toward the Renoa every few breaths. The moment she was back in her rooms, she stashed the pail, keys, and lamp in the chest next to the witchcraft book. Since she didn't want the maties questioning her arrival home without her father, she changed into her sleeping tunic herself. Then she parted the gossamer curtains surrounding her sleeping dais, climbed in, and buried herself to her chin in her rose-scented blankets, knowing she wouldn't sleep. Instead, she stared at the nighttime skyline beyond her room. When the moon arrived sometime later, she had a perfect view of the Renoa Tree, an opalescent ghost in the distance. It was so beautiful that she offered the Blessing of That-Which-Is-Life out of respect and then more apologies for the turn her life had taken. A night bird hooted in reply.

It was then she realized she'd made a mistake.

Her father had told her to return with the pail, and she had, but she'd been in such a hurry she hadn't thought of the bladder. When the Second Heir's guards saw it, they'd know he'd had a visitor.

***

By the time the racing footsteps of his new caretaker had faded, Deriek had already downed the water, shoved the food in his mouth, and was feeling the ground for any crumbs he might have dropped. As he searched, the small part of himself that was still himself raged and screamed and berated the rest of him for weakness. He had one way out of this prison. He'd thought he'd found it when his old caretaker had disappeared, but his body was winning over what was left of his mind.

He went face-first onto the floor to lick the spilled water drops. Then he crashed onto his back, banging his head on the stone floor in a way that should've hurt but didn't. His stomach churned and twisted, trying to refuse the food and water. Even there his body betrayed him; the sustenance stayed down.

He lay motionless, staring at the walls that felt like they were closing in on him. Stone blocks set flush against each other. At the top, a single window gazed down at him, his only access to air and light.

His fingers were scabbed, his nails shredded, from trying to reach the window. He'd succeeded a single time, only to find that the bars across it were thick and solid. No matter how he'd attacked them, they wouldn't bend or break.

Deriek stared up at the window, hating both how close and how far from freedom it made him feel. The sliver of night sky teased him by its very existence, and black, roiling anger flooded him once again. Anger at the walls, at the window, at the girl who'd given him the food and water that would keep him alive.

It was definitely a girl. Her breathing had been high-pitched and her movements female.

He imagined all the things he should've done rather than beg and grovel. He should've thrown the food back at her. He should've screamed at her to leave him to die.

A remaining fragment of his rational self suggested he should've asked for help.

He blocked that out. Betrayal was too regular a companion. He should've reached through the bars, grabbed her by the neck, and wrung all that nervous, sniffling breath out of her. That would've been satisfying.

It would've been easy, too, even weak as he was. Then, in retribution, her family would've let him starve. As he wanted.

Eight

There was an old saying that originated long before the arrival of the Renoa Trees, the teachings of the Sages, or the drying of the lands into the desert. It went back to when the people had ridden around on four-legged creatures and great herds of animals roamed wide plains. Back in those times, it was said that if there came a day when one had no kills to feed one's family, that was bad. If on the morrow, one's bow broke or spear dulled, that was worse. But one shouldn't mourn those losses for surely on the day after, a storm would arrive, flattening one's tent and spoiling one's grain.

All of which was how Emrie felt the next morning when she rolled out of bed at the urging of her maties. She'd spent half the night praying the Second Heir would think to hide the bladder himself. She hoped so. He *was* supposed to be clever.

"I'm tired," she mumbled to Mati Sarta and Mati Ereana, but they weren't accustomed to her sleeping half the morning, and she disliked making their lives difficult. She let them bully her into dressing and redoing her hair with mint green threads to match her laptevi. She was too exhausted to invite conversation.

Once she was presentable and had offered her morning devotions to the Renoa, they prodded and poked her into going downstairs. Mati Dechta met them in the main hall, looking displeased.

"You're late and your braids look slept on."

"I just woke," Emrie admitted.

"Well, there isn't time to do anything about it now. Hurry, hurry. First Daughter Das called for you ages ago."

"Noemi?" Emrie asked, suddenly wide awake.

Mati Dechta didn't answer, just herded her toward the Central Garden of the House.

"Someone important has come to visit?" Emrie asked.

"Obviously." Mati Dechta gave her a push through the gate.

The Central Garden was encircled by House Das in all directions, open to the sky, and spacious. It held her father's pond of Nashua fish along with three tame gazelles, a grassy field for them to graze, and a rotating forest of potted plants. To the side of the pond was a stone dais, guarded from any hint of sun by a crimson awning with silver tassels. It was only used for receiving guests in the most important of situations.

Normally, Emrie would've been thrilled to be invited to the Central Garden. It was an honor. But not right now. She closed her eyes for a moment, wishing she could return to her rooms.

Then she opened them and stepped into the sun, pulling her cowl over her head for protection. Three people sat on the dais—Noemi, a stranger, and the foreign Daughter.

"Sister," Noemi said, her voice dripping courtesy. "I'd like you to meet our friend Imjin Beatrica Flaust, the Daughter of the Sovereign of Gir-Tosaq and House of Flaust. Imjin, this is my sister, Emrie Joleyn Das, Second Daughter of House Das." Noemi launched into one of the longer greeting rituals.

Emrie tried to find some excitement for the moment. Anything. She should be thrilled to see the Daughter of Gir-Tosaq up close. Keelie and Lianjit would be all over themselves in jealousy.

All she could come up with was a vague hope that she wouldn't do or say anything that might cause embarrassment.

The Daughter of Gir-Tosaq made a fluttering motion with her hand as if it were a tiny bird taking off in flight.

"I give permission to call me by Imjin, my Simple Name."

"I'm honored," Emrie replied carefully. "And you must call me by Emrie, my Simple Name."

Up close, Imjin looked just as Emrie remembered, tiny, feminine, and lovely. Her voice was high and cheerful as she offered a Blessing on their new bond of friendship.

Emrie settled onto the cushion nearest the pond, hoping to stay out of the way. A lime-colored fish the size of her slipper did a flip through the surface of the water as if in greeting. Not wanting to be caught staring at either Noemi or Imjin, Emrie turned her attention to the third girl. She was dressed in a shapeless laptevi that appeared to be high quality but was a garish rust color. And the girl sat so stiff she looked like she was trying to be another pole holding up the awning.

The girl stared back at her.

"I'm Brid. Your cousin."

"Oh, of course," Emrie said, caught off guard. She was unaware she had a cousin named Brid. And one didn't introduce oneself.

Noemi flicked a look of irritation Emrie's way as if she were the reason Brid had spoken out of turn and then introduced Brid Kanina Das, the Daughter of Omert Das from Kye-Boehlke, who by lucky coincidence had arrived on their doorstep moments before Imjin.

This must be the houseguest that Noemi had described as graceless, which seemed apt. Brid was . . . well . . . she looked strong . . . and tall . . . her hair was in four braids looped together around a bold, square face with large features and a down-turned mouth. She was about as opposite of refinement as could be said.

"Welcome, Cousin," Emrie murmured.

"Tea?" Noemi asked, her voice firmly pleasant. A matie brought over a tray holding cups and a metal pot so chilled it had frozen beads on its rim. Emrie received hers and let the sweet tea slide around her tongue, enjoying the silky lavender flavor and doing her best to stay in the background.

"It's lovely," Imjin said, holding up her cup. "Pol-Thiri's Tea Guild is exquisitely talented."

They settled into a bland conversation about tea and such. Emrie didn't look at Brid again, not wanting to encourage her rude behavior. When there was a lull in the conversation, Brid burst in a second time anyway.

"Why are we sitting here in this awful heat?"

Emrie winced. At least this time Brid's insolence couldn't be blamed on her.

Noemi's eyebrows shot up in disapproval. Brid must've caught the censure as she turned a shade of red worse than the color of her laptevi.

Imjin laughed, a slow, tinkling, high-pitched sound.

"Thank goodness," she said, sounding relieved. "I wasn't sure how to broach the purpose of my visit, and it is detestably warm today. Is it possible the sun favors Pol-Thiri even more than Gir-Tosaq? And the women of Pol-Thiri are so formal. Rules about who speaks and what topics are proper. Gir-Tosaq is less so. It's just easier."

"Of course, it is," Noemi said, her voice precisely polite even though Imjin had just roundly insulted her, their House, and Pol-Thiri. Emrie ducked back a bit more. Imjin Flaust in person differed greatly from what Emrie had expected.

Brid didn't seem to understand the tension and picked up Imjin's conversational thread. "Pol-Thirians *are* very formal. My father warned me. It's all blessings-this and ritual-that and no one ever means what they say. I'm not Pol-Thirian, though. What do you need? I'll help if I can."

"Tell us how we can advise you," Noemi snapped out, the more proper reply.

"Well," started Imjin as if she were oblivious to Noemi's growing ire, "I don't wish to marry the First Heir."

Noemi expressed no surprise by this pronouncement. If anything, she relaxed as if she'd expected it. Which meant what exactly?

"Then you shouldn't marry him," Brid said firmly. "Marriage is a personal choice in Kye-Boehlke. Isn't it the same here? If not, it should be."

"Yes, in Gir-Tosaq we take commitments seriously," Imjin agreed. "But it's more complicated than that, isn't it?"

They were both right. Marriage *was* a personal choice, but it was also complicated. Because while one married the person, one contracted into the House creating a permanent bond with every other member just as strong as that of blood. Thus managing marriage contracts between two people of different Houses was a difficult, tangled thing. Emrie couldn't imagine the complexity of doing so between city-oases.

"One mustn't give offense," Imjin continued. "Which is why I thought to approach House Das. One of the other Daughters of Pol-Thiri let it be known that Daughter Das was the First Heir's prior interest. I'm sorry to be forward," she looked to Noemi. "But if that's true, might you speak plainly?"

Emrie winced a second time, not sure if it was for Imjin or Noemi. The request was beyond intrusive and discourteous. There was no way Noemi could answer without breaking polite etiquette.

But Emrie could.

Maybe.

In fact, if Noemi had indeed anticipated this conversation, then this moment could be her reason for inviting Emrie. Which if Emrie was right, was a compliment in a backward sort of way. Emrie hesitated and then decided to go for it. Better to take the initiative and get chastised than fail in an expected duty.

"I'm so sorry," Emrie said, keeping her voice low and respectful. "Daughter of Gir-Tosaq . . . friend Imjin . . . you were misinformed. I can see how that might happen as such things aren't spoken of, but Noemi is promised to House Das. Also, there has been a long-standing agreement between her and the Son of a Fourth-ring House. When the time is right, he'll contract into House Das as her husband so that Noemi might someday become Head of House."

Noemi gave a solemn nod, and Emrie took that to mean she was pleased with the response. Thank the Tree.

Imjin puckered her lips. A crease appeared between her eyes as if she didn't like the answer. When she spoke, her voice had lost its cheer.

"Well, will you help me find someone else to marry the First Heir?"

"I—" Noemi started, but whatever she was about to say was cut off by a sudden movement at the entry to the Central Garden. The rug to the house swung open and Ahrens burst through.

Emrie hadn't even known he was in Pol-Thiri. By the irked look on her face, neither had Noemi.

"We have a guest?" he called out as he crossed the garden in wide, purposeful strides. That was Ahrens. He always had somewhere to go and did so with energy. He wasn't dressed for conversation but wore tight-fitting pantaloons and boots under a brown laptevi and overdress, fitted for being out in the desert. His hair was swept untidily but charmingly into a queue down his back and he had a healthy appealing glow that seemed to dare the raging sun to touch him. He also had white hairs, likely street dog, all over one arm, which meant he'd found an animal in distress and rescued it. Again.

Of the members of House Das, he was the one Emrie was closest to. He was only two years her senior and they'd grown up together. Which mostly meant him dragging her along in his wake and bullying her into helping him out of scrapes, but he was always cheery about it. Their father and Noemi now kept him so busy with Mining Guild business that Emrie rarely saw him outside of Petal Night. He winked. She grinned back as Noemi reluctantly led them through the formal greetings again. Likely, not only had Noemi not called for Ahrens, but Ahrens was inserting himself just to cause trouble. It was like him.

Imjin was also watching Ahrens and had the same expression of longing on her face Emrie had seen her use toward the now imprisoned Second Heir. Noemi indicated Ahrens should sit by Brid.

Ahrens stayed only a few minutes but spent it being his charming, rapscallion self. He listened with sympathy as Imjin spoke of her discomfort with her accommodations in the Sovereign's House and what an effort she was exerting to understand Pol-Thirian culture.

Ahrens opened his mouth to likely insert something indecorous, but Noemi cut him off. He must've finally taken the hint, as he excused himself and left.

At least, Noemi was now so annoyed with Ahrens that she'd hopefully forgotten about Emrie.

Imjin left not long after with a satisfied look on her face as if she'd found what she'd come for. Noemi sent Brid off with a matie to her new rooms. Emrie waited for her own dismissal, but it didn't come. Instead, Noemi stood and paced circles around the stone dais.

As it wasn't Emrie's place to remind her sister she was there, and it was safer not to be noticed, Emrie said nothing. Instead, she leaned over, putting her fingers into the cool of the water and making the fish swarm around her touch in colorful circles in the hopes of a treat. They hoped in vain as it was tradition that only her father and Noemi fed the creatures of House Das.

"That foolish, foolish girl," Noemi said, coming to a stop at the edge of the pond near Emrie.

"Father will send her home then?" Emrie asked, as Noemi appeared to be speaking to her after all. In truth, Emrie hoped he would.

"Unmarried? Not even he has that power."

"Brid's here to marry?"

"Brid?" Noemi returned to her impatient circling. "Brid, too, is a fool, but she isn't of whom I speak."

She meant Imjin then, which couldn't be good. Taking a minor risk just because she wanted to know, Emrie threw out another question, hoping Noemi was distracted enough to answer. "Is it true what Imjin said? Are you interested in marriage to the First Heir yourself?"

"Blessings, no. I'd like to live, Thank the Tree. Women don't survive long when too close to him."

Survive? Before Emrie could reply, Noemi came around the end of the pond and sank down next to her, taking her arm in a firm grip and speaking quickly.

"Forget I said that. I'm tired and not myself. I shouldn't have spoken so."

"Of course," Emrie said, taken aback by her sudden upset. "But what did you mean?" Then Emrie froze, waiting for Noemi to attack her for asking.

Noemi didn't. Instead, she gave a quick look around. When she spoke, she kept her voice low, just above a whisper.

"He lives in terror of being replaced. As long as he's the best option as the Sovereign's Heir, he knows he's safe."

"The First Heir?" Emrie asked, cautiously. "But no one can kill an Heir without breaking the Law of the Renoa. And what about the Second Heir?" Noemi never shared things like this with her. Ever. And it seemed important to understand. As if by bringing it up, Noemi was inviting her into this other world of the Firsts.

Noemi shook her head. "The Heirs can be killed. They just can't be killed directly. The Sovereign dislikes the Second Heir as do the Advisers. No one wants him to inherit."

Emrie nodded as if she'd known that, although this was the first she'd heard of the Sovereign disliking either of his Sons.

"It's his own children that are the First Heir's biggest threat. If the First Heir has a child, then there's another choice. And a valuable choice. Because, unlike the Houses, the Sovereign doesn't pick his Heir. So any child of the First Heir becomes the Second Heir, and thus should both the Sovereign and First Heir die, whoever controls that child, controls the Seat of Judgment. That is the First Heir's fear, and he solves this problem by not producing children."

"I see."

"No, you don't. He doesn't accomplish this by restraint or abstinence. He kills his mistresses the moment they show signs of pregnancy. Which both solves the problem of his being replaced and meets the criteria of the Law of the Renoa. A child is not an Heir until it's born."

"I see." This time she did. It made her want to shudder, but she stayed still.

"The First Heir will do the same to any wife he marries. Thus, every House has tied up any Daughter he has shown interest in elsewhere. Marriage to him equates to a very short life."

"That's awful," Emrie said, horrified but trying to keep her voice even to not halt Noemi's explanations. She'd heard nothing like this before. There were stories of incompetent Sovereigns, of course, Sovereigns in long ago history whose Judgments were unfair or those who could be manipulated. It wasn't something much discussed, and she'd never heard of Pol-Thiri having a truly evil Sovereign. Nor had she heard of someone blatantly working around the Laws of the Renoa. But that led to another disturbing thought.

"Everyone knows the Daughter of Gir-Tosaq is going to her death in marrying him, and no one is stopping her?"

"Her death was assured the moment she and her father committed to this expedition. She can't go home unmarried, she won't find anyone to take her place, and the First Heir already desires her. Foolish girl, she thinks she can escape this, but she can't and must not. Let's hope we are only one of many Houses that she approaches in search of help as the maties talk. It's bound to get back to the Sovereign's House that she was here, and if the First Heir learns she's trying to bargain her way out of a marriage contract, he'll kill her outright and blame whoever helped her."

And no one would stop him. Emrie understood that without it being said. He was the First Heir. He was accountable to no one but the Renoa. It was almost too appalling to be believed.

NINE

After too short a nap, Emrie spent the afternoon getting to know Brid. That went about as well as a Juju bird befriending a camel, but she learned Brid was a Third Daughter and a year younger than Emrie, which was surprising as she seemed older.

That night was Petal Night, and Noemi was her usual polite self at the dining table as if the morning conversation hadn't occurred. Only Emrie seemed to be feeling like the sand had tilted and the city-oasis was now sitting crooked. Or as if she'd had her first glimpse into the world of the Firsts.

Not surprisingly, Brid didn't perform well at the table. She was awkward when she accepted the opening platter. Uncle Otto's spouse, Uncle Vashir, helped her figure out where everything went on her plate and in which order to eat.

Thank the Renoa, Emrie wasn't forced to help. She used the meal to sneak a quarter of melon, a large sampling of duck, a sheaf of wafer bread, and an entire dish of apricot preserves into a satchel she had hidden in the folds of her laptevi. No one noticed, but she was an anxious wreck the entire meal.

Back in her own chambers, she had Mati Ereana bring her a bladder of water, explaining she had woken thirsty the night before. Once her maties were gone for the evening, she donned a rough-spun laptevi that she normally only wore for the Night of Deliverance Ceremony. She packed everything she'd stolen in the pail her father had given her and pulled her cowl over her head.

She didn't want to do this.

She would do it anyway, even if her hands shook like the rattling of leaves in a strong wind. Please, just let the Second Heir have thought to hide last night's water bladder.

She skirted the Renoa's Field without incident. The cooling caverns were bitterly cold, but she navigated them fine. The keys all fit their locks. The witchcraft didn't interrupt.

Too soon she was at the top of the stairs leading to the prison. She stopped there to listen for any sign that someone was waiting for her. The only sound was the noisy throbbing in her own chest.

That wasn't an excuse to run home, so she forced herself forward. When she entered the Second Heir's prison, it was as it'd been the night before. Pitch dark. Ghastly smell. No guards. No disturbances. The empty water bladder sat several paces back on her side of the bars as if he'd thrown it. For one moment, Emrie closed her eyes in relief, but that only made her aware of rags scraping against the stone floor. Panic forced her back several steps. She gripped the handle of the pail so hard her nails bit into her palm.

The shadow of him crawled toward her in a way less human and more one of Ahrens's dying dogs.

"Water?" His voice was more croak than words.

His desperation pushed past her terror to get her to move. She hurried to the same spot as the previous night and fell to her knees again to lay out his food, working as fast as possible to be done before he reached her. Only then did it occur to her that she hadn't brought him anything with which to eat the preserves.

"Water?" he said again, his voice louder if not clearer. She pulled out the new bladder and tossed it through the bars.

"Blessings upon you," he said in his rough voice. Emrie was strung so tight that the words were the screeching of a metal chair against a polished floor. He was too close. Close enough to make her shove the rest of the food through the bars so she could back away. He threw back his head and downed the water so fast it spilled over his face and down his chest. "More water?" he asked.

She had none, and as his desperation was evident, she got a sick feeling in her stomach. There wasn't anything she could do about it, and having left him his food, she started backward to flee again. But then she stopped herself. She only got to run like a chased gazelle once, and she'd already used that up. Her father was trusting her; he needed her to be valiant. She would not run again.

She forced herself to wait until he returned the bladder and solved the problem of the preserves by tipping the jar right into his mouth.

When she finally left, she took it all with her, leaving nothing behind.

***

"Is something wrong?" Brid asked Emrie the following morning as they waited in an antechamber of House Das for the norie bearers to bring a litter around.

No. Yes. Everything was wrong. She couldn't say that, though, and her mild dislike of her cousin was moving toward a strong aversion in the time they'd spent together. The morning's etiquette lesson hadn't gone well. Brid had questioned the "why" of every ritual and Blessing that Noemi tried to teach her, arguing that they were all ridiculous. Plus, she'd worn a shapeless and unsightly laptevi even though Noemi had sent maties with several lovely choices from the House Das storerooms. Noemi had gotten so frustrated that she'd directed Emrie to take Brid to a seamstress with instructions to find clothing Brid was willing to wear that didn't embarrass the family. While Emrie wanted to be pleased that Noemi had asked for her assistance, the truth was Noemi had given her the job because she didn't like Brid, either.

Since clothing was not Emrie's area of strength, she'd wanted to invite Keeli and Lianjit to come along. Only when she'd tried to carve the invitation, the witchcraft had bothered her nonstop and she'd given up.

"I slept poorly," she told Brid.

"You shouldn't let your sister bully you," Brid said in the dry way she had. "She isn't always very nice."

"She doesn't bully me," Emrie said with a sigh. She'd already explained several times the respect due Noemi and the roles within the House. Brid didn't seem to care.

"I won't let anyone bully me. Not ever. And I don't see why you should, either. The way you all live is impossible. Always taking orders and doing what you're told. I'm going to live how I like." Brid's face was scrunched into a frown. She towered above Emrie a good foot and Emrie had to look up to see her expression.

If she weren't so tired, Emrie wouldn't have replied the way she did. But she was tired. And afraid of having to go back to that prison tonight. And tired of being both tired and afraid. Plus, Brid had been maligning Pol-Thiri and House Das all morning. Emrie's words just came out and not in a sympathetic tone of voice.

"You act like the bird who flies to the feeding basin in hunger, but when the Head of House arrives with seeds, the bird attacks, and thus, the feed is lost and the bird goes hungry."

"I'm not like that."

"You're exactly like that," Emrie snapped back.

The door to the outside opened and a norie servant bowed to them, indicating the litter was ready. It was bedded in cushions with a rug-roof slung over the metal frame and gauzy brown fabric falling down the sides to keep off bugs. Eight matie bearers lined up along the poles to carry it. Emrie greeted them in a much nicer tone than she'd spoken to Brid and then ducked inside. Brid followed.

"You see me as hungry, like the creature in your story?" Brid asked once seated.

"That depends on why you're in Pol-Thiri." Emrie closed her eyes in the hopes it would keep Brid quiet. Which worked so well she nodded off into a nap.

She woke when the easy gliding motion of the litter came to a stop at Keeli's favorite seamstress. A norie servant pulled the curtain back for them to exit, but before Emrie could, Brid stopped her.

"You're right, and you're the first person to speak anything of sense to me in this entire city-oasis. I've been short-sighted. There's something I'm hungry for, and I'll try harder to follow the rules of Pol-Thiri until I have it."

"Well, that's good." Noemi would be pleased. Perhaps Brid wasn't as foolish as she seemed. On the other hand, it also made Brid seem like she was using the rest of them for her own aims. Which was a worse personality trait than just being obnoxious.

"If you're hungry, what is it for?" Emrie asked.

Brid frowned yet again. It seemed to be a habitual response for her.

"I don't think I like you enough to tell you."

***

By the time Brid was fashionably attired in a laptevi and overdress she hated but had agreed to wear, the hot, midday rains had arrived. The city-oasis was about to close down, and Emrie had succumbed to a raging headache. Back at House Das, she returned to her chambers for another nap but slept restlessly only waking to worry more.

That evening, her maties brought her a large meal all for herself which she stashed the majority of in the pail. She also stole a spoon and asked for six full water bladders. She didn't give an excuse for needing them, and the maties didn't question, Thank the Tree.

The bladders she tied two-by-two with string and hung over her shoulder. They were heavy. The strings dug into her neck, but it had to be done. As she walked around the edge of the Renoa's Field, she stopped at regular intervals to move them from one shoulder to the other, and by the time she made it up the stairs to the prison room, she was panting for breath.

The stench again hit her first, and she wrinkled her nose. He must've heard her coming as he waited on all fours in the spot she'd left the food the last two nights. That put him too near for her comfort. She didn't want to risk him grabbing her and holding her in place as a hostage until his guards arrived.

"Water?" he asked, not unexpectedly this time.

Because he was so close, she got a good look at him for the first time. Even though her lamp bleached all color, she could see his midnight hair was loose and matted. And while his profile was the same as she remembered, his face was rough in the shadows and unshaven. His laptevi and leggings were ragged and torn, and his feet were bare like a servant. And he was filthy. A street dog would be better treated than this.

As if he understood why she wasn't handing over the water, he slid backward. It should've been an awkward movement against the rough flooring, but he was graceful. Emrie was stuck by a fluttering lump of pity. That she knew of, he'd done nothing to deserve the treatment he was receiving.

Pity wasn't enough to make her incautious, and she kept a wary eye as she dropped to her knees. She placed the food first and then disentangled herself from the bladders, laying them out in a line on his side of the bars. He didn't rush over, as she half expected, but waited until she was done and had moved away.

"Drink them all," she said. "I must take the empty containers with me so that no one knows I've been here."

"No one will know," he said in that same cracked voice and then came forward to drink the first bladder as quickly as he had the night before, sloshing it down his front. For the second, he slowed, downing it without spilling. The third he sipped at only and then gathered it and the other three against his chest as if they were something to be protected with his life. Clearly, he wanted to keep them, and it would be better for him if he did, but it was too risky.

"No one comes," he rasped out. "Only the boy from before and now you. No one will know about the water."

"No one else comes?" Emrie asked, knowing she sounded foolish by repeating his words but too shocked to stop herself. She'd assumed she was supplementing what his guards gave him, not providing all of his nourishment. No wonder he was so thirsty.

"Turn the lamp away," he continued. "It hurts my eyes."

Emrie was still roiling with the ugly significance of his previous words. His brother had dumped him here and left him to starve to death?

In a practical sense, it was a way to kill the Second Heir without the First Heir being responsible. Especially if the First Heir didn't know for sure where his brother was imprisoned. Then she had another one of those odd, world-tilting moments of disconcertion. She wondered if her father had been wrong about the boy who'd been killed. Might that boy have been the one caring for the Second Heir and then been killed by the First Heir because he was the only one who knew where to find him? But if that were true, how had her father known?

***

The next several nights passed the same. She got good at sneaking away food and even made several trips to the kitchens to find a larger pail and items that might last the Second Heir longer. She never saw signs others visited. She even tested that by leaving a thread across the hall. For three nights in a row, it went undisturbed.

The Second Heir was entirely dependent on her, an eerie realization.

She took to covering the lamp with a gauzy scarf so that it created more of a warm haze than a glare in his eyes. To be safe, just in case he was trying to trick her into revealing herself, she tied a veil onto her cowl to hide her face. She also stuffed her nose with tufts of cotton.

Neither she nor the Second Heir spoke again as her leaving the food and water became a nightly ritual. One that she accomplished without trying to figure out the witchcraft.

But the caretaking was time-consuming, and the result of staying up half the night meant she slept in longer in the mornings. No one chided her for this. She attended a handful of etiquette lessons before Noemi told her she was released from the duty and commended her for whatever she'd said to Brid to improve Brid's demeanor.

Which was something, although Emrie doubted she deserved the compliment.

Keeli and Lianjit sent several invitations to join them on excursions around the city-oasis, but with Emrie sleeping half the mornings, her maties declined on her behalf. Since neither Keeli nor Lianjit came barging over to see what was wrong, they must have heard about Brid's arrival.

Then one night, as she finished putting out the Second Heir's food and water and collecting the empty bladders and bowls from the night before, he spoke again. Her mind was elsewhere, already thinking of how quickly she could hurry home and not paying attention to him until he was right next to her.

"I need a knife," he said, his voice smooth and even compared to before but still menacing.

Emrie jerked back with alarm, bringing her attention and her light right onto him. He flinched, covering his eyes with his hand. His hair was matted, his skin dirty and bruised-looking, and his face covered in a growing scruff. This close-up, he looked worse off than before rather than better.

"Why?"

"To cut my hair, of course." His voice held a mocking tone as if the answer was so obvious that Emrie was a fool to ask. "I need a Jeibel Knife for cutting my hair."

TEN

Emrie had never heard of a Jeibel Knife.

When Keeli sent an invitation to attend the enactment of one of the Sovereign's more creative Judgments, she made a point of rising early enough to go so that she could ask Lianjit. Besides, it was past time she introduced her friends to Brid.

They traveled by boat across the river to the Orchards, as nothing with deep roots that might interfere with the Renoa was allowed to grow within the city-oasis itself. Once there, the Judgment turned out to be a depressing one. It involved the halving of several orchard trees to resolve an issue between the Almond Guild and the Dairy Guild over a supply of hulls. Seeing healthy trees destroyed was more distressing than entertaining.

Brid behaved herself, and unexpectedly, Lianjit seemed to like her. The two of them spent the entire time discussing Barrack's Training. Apparently, in Kye-Boehlke girls weren't allowed to learn weapons and Brid was impressed that Lianjit had.

Emrie didn't get to ask her question until they were back at the dock of the city-oasis.

"A Jeibel Knife?" Lianjit said with interest in her voice. "That's not something that comes up often."

"But what is it?" Emrie asked. They'd just disembarked from a small passenger boat. The witchcraft had liked the river and made a nuisance of itself as they'd traveled, only stopping when Emrie was back on solid ground. She felt, and likely looked, uncomfortable rubbing her hands all the time.

"It's not a true knife, but a short sword," Lianjit said as the four of them walked toward where their litters waited near a warehouse run by Keeli's Guild. "The Rendering Guild used to employ them," Lianjit continued, "because they're wicked sharp. They're considered old-fashioned now, but people still own them. Your father likely has at least one. Some have names, and there are stories about them that go all the way back to the old Gods of the plains. Why?"

"No reason." A fat bug landed on Emrie's arm and she twitched it off, trying to appear as casual as possible. "Someone made a joke using the term and I wondered. What were the stories about the old Gods?"

"I don't remember. Something about requiring a blood sacrifice to bring balance into the world in the way the Renoa does for us now. And the Jeibel were used for ritualized suicide as well. Something like that."

"Sounds like the joke was in poor taste," Brid announced.

"It was," Emrie said faintly, rubbing her fingers against her sleeves even though they weren't tingling at all.

***

By the time the afternoon rains had come and gone and Emrie had found excuses to send her maties elsewhere, she'd worked herself into a frenzy of tension. He wanted to die? That's why he wanted a Jeibel Knife?

Suicide was forbidden.

She paced back and forth across her chamber, feeling like she was failing in some way that she couldn't define.

Nothing her father had said had prepared her for this. Keeping the Second Heir alive was supposed to mean food and such, not fighting against his own grisly desires. What was she supposed to do?

Not ask her father for help. That much she knew for sure.

Nor give the Second Heir a knife.

Eventually, she tired of pacing and went onto her patio to stare at the Renoa sitting in the middle of Its Field. The leaves were a brilliant sapphire blue in the descending light. The trunk was white with massive branches growing chaotic in every direction and every shape. One branch might make a sharp left turn, then corkscrew several times to end up facing the other direction, then split six different ways, two of those heading toward the edge of the canopy where It sprouted Its leaves. It made one feel small.

Emrie definitely felt too small for the problem in front of her.

Somewhere above her, two crows began a caw-caw conversation, and she wished there was someone, anyone that she could go to for advice.

Perhaps there was.

The Second Heir's life fell under the Laws of the Renoa. The Sages taught that through Its roots and the breezes that touched Its leaves, the Renoa understood everything that happened in Pol-Thiri. The Renoa might already know about Emrie's problem.

One of the crows gave a final cry to its friend and flapped away from the house. Crows were good luck. It felt like an omen. She would go ask the Renoa.

The footpaths through the Renoa's Field were twisting, turning, looping pathways of white flagstones hidden in the knee-high Sacred Grasses. They were called the Paths of Wisdom and Virtue and mimicked the shapes of the Renoa's branches. Navigating them prepared one to visit the Tree, and one always did so humbly barefoot and in a formal gait. Even though Emrie was impatient, she was careful to be respectful. Since the way was not straight, it wasn't a quick trip and when she reached the massive white trunk, the sun was slipping down behind the Houses of Pol-Thiri. She put her hand on the lowest rung of a silk ladder tied against the Renoa's trunk and climbed.

The ladder swooshed and the leaves whistled in a gust of wind as she made her way upward as if the Renoa was inviting her to ask what she needed. While the outside of the Renoa's leaves were a jewel-toned blue, from underneath they were pale metallic. The descending sun beamed underneath the canopy causing the light to reflect and bathe everything and everyone in a silvery glow.

Emrie paused part way up, basking in the moment's beauty and offering the Blessing-of-that-Which-Is-Life. There was nothing in, on, or above the earth as glorious as a Holy Renoa at sunset. That alone made her feel better.

But the echoing light also made this time of day the most popular to visit. She didn't want to either be in the way or be noticed, so after a moment of enjoyment, she kept climbing.

She stayed on the rope ladder until she was in the higher branches as was her right as a Das. Only the Sovereign and his Heirs were allowed in the crown, but the First-ring Houses could worship just below. She walked out onto her favorite thick branch, keeping her hand clamped to silk cording strung to help keep one's balance. She followed the turns and revolutions outward toward the canopy. A wild Juju bird called from above. She couldn't see it, so bright were the leaves in the light, but the sound reminded her of her father, which reminded her of why she was here and blurred her inner balance.

Once at her favorite spot, she lowered to her knees, pressing first her fingers, then her palms, then her forearms into the solidity of the smooth white bark. She whispered the five Blessings right into the Tree itself and then one thing more.

"What should I do?"

From somewhere in the distance, she heard the ritualized movement of cloth against bark as a priest worked varnish into the Tree. Down below she heard softly, softly a hand sliding down one of the silk lines and bare feet on wood. Time passed, but she was unaware as she was soothed into the listening.

What does the Second Heir need in order to live?

Emrie went still, feeling eerie and uncertain and not sure that the words weren't her own. This wasn't how the Renoa usually worked. Usually, it was just a feeling of being recognized, maybe appreciated, and then a new idea came to mind that hadn't previously occurred to her. It had never before offered words.

The words themselves felt like a question rather than a statement. Did the Renoa expect her to answer? How was she supposed to know what the Second Heir needed?

After several calming breaths, she turned her head to press her cheek into the cool of the branch and whispered so softly that barely a puff of air passed her lips.

"I don't know."

Perhaps the way to find out is to do as you've been asked.

"By giving him a knife?" She shuddered at the thought of her father's face if the Second Heir died by his own hand because she'd helped him. Or did the Renoa mean that if Emrie gave him a knife, he wouldn't use it? Seemed way too risky.

Emrie stayed where she was, toes, knees, palms, and cheek pressed into the branch until the sun was pulled behind the faraway mountains and the silvery light faded to dusky gray. The Renoa didn't speak again, and Emrie's thrill at receiving an answer turned back to uncertainty. It felt like yet another weight had been dropped on her shoulders, this one much heavier than the bladders of water she carried to him each night.

The Renoa seemed to expect her to figure this out on her own.

Eventually, she pushed herself to her feet to make her way down before it got dark. People did fall and die.

A wild Juju bird burst into its last song of the evening. Emrie looked back to where she'd been kneeling, at that one place where the branch was straight and thick. And then it hit her. The Renoa hadn't meant what the Second Heir had asked of her. The Renoa meant what her father had asked of her.

Emrie missed the next rung and had to grab tight and shift around to keep her balance. The Renoa thought that the Second Heir needed her to learn how to use the evil witchcraft?

Eleven

When Emrie had first realized that her father wanted her to learn to use the witchcraft, she'd been afraid. She didn't feel fear as she returned to her rooms, although she kept stumbling on her walk back through the Paths of Wisdom and Virtue as the idea was so startling.

It went against everything she'd ever learned. Disturbingly so.

What was more, the Renoa seemed to see her as responsible for the Second Heir in a way that felt much deeper than her father's instructions to care for him.

Maybe she should be afraid.

Back at her rooms, she downed half a bowl of chilled beets and squash to please her maties and packed the rest of her meal for the Second Heir. Then she retrieved the book on witchcraft from her mother's chest. Fear or lack of it, she was doing this.

The book wasn't heavy, but mimicking her father, she held it gingerly. The cover was cream, the pages wooden brown with silvery blue ink, and surprisingly, the words written in the orderly way of the scribes. She'd expected it to be a secret journal of sorts, not a true book from the Scribes Guild. She flipped to the back and then the front, looking for a Guild insignia, but there was none nor the name of any author.

She spent the rest of the evening reading. It wasn't easygoing. There were no stories nor examples of the use of the witchcraft nor explanations for what it was. The entire book appeared to be a treatise on mathematics with lots of phrases like vertexes, acute angles, radius of a curve, and transversal lines. She skipped forward to find diagrams and more numerics but nothing useful. Was it possible her father had given her the wrong book?

Seemed unlikely. She retrieved her writing materials and copied down ten of the most commonly used words. By the time she'd finished, she could hear the hoot of the night birds as if calling her to her duty. She couldn't bring the Second Heir a Jeibel Knife, but in a spark of good humor, she took along something else that might cheer him.

Once in the prison, she gave the Second Heir his food and then sat back waiting for him to ask after the knife. He didn't immediately, and as she watched him eat she got an eerie, deep awareness of how dependent he was on her. When he finished, he finally spoke.

"The Jeibel?"

"No." Her voice sounded funny to her ears from the cotton protecting her nose. "I brought something else instead." She held up a hairbrush with a smile, albeit one he couldn't see because of the veil.

"What am I supposed to do with that?" he asked, sounding every bit the Son of the Sovereign.

Emrie blanched. She'd made a huge mistake in teasing him the way she might Keeli or Lianjit or even Ahrens. She'd let her evening with the Renoa make her forgetful. He might be her responsibility, but that didn't mean they knew each other. He likely didn't even brush his own hair. She lowered her voice to a near mumble in an attempt to be conciliatory. "I can't give you a knife, you see. But your hair was bothering you, so I thought at least to let you get the mats out. I can do it if you like. You'll just need to put your head closer to the bars." Even as she said the words, it seemed a bad idea.

"I know how to brush my own hair." He sounded positively waspish. "Give it to me."

She handed the brush through the bars. He snatched it from her hand and pitched it against the far wall with a clatter.

"Next time bring me what I ask."

Emrie jumped to her feet, wanting out of there as fast as possible. She stopped herself, remembering her vow of not fleeing, and forced herself to walk sedately. So much for trying to please him.

The next day she dragged Brid to Lianjit's House. Lianjit had just returned from Barrack's Training and still wore pantaloons and a short laptevi with a leather harness over her shoulders meant to carry her practice sword, although it was currently empty. Her mother fluttered around offering Emrie and Brid sweet tea, checking that they had the most comfortable cushions in the House's formal chamber and then insisting Lianjit go douse herself in scented water to remove the stench of men. Lianjit ignored her and plopped down on a pillow.

"What's wherewith?"

"Vertexes and Transversal," Emrie said as soon as they had a break from Lianjit's mother. She handed over her list of terms.

Lianjit frowned. "Angles and lines? What're you up to?"

"Bettering herself," Brid said, which was what Emrie had told her on the way over. "She thinks she isn't smart compared to the rest of you." Brid's face was an image of stoic sincerity. There was no malice in the words, and yet Emrie flushed anyway. Why couldn't Brid just keep her mouth shut? Then of course Lianjit made it worse.

"You don't need to be. You're First-ring."

"Thank you for the confidence in my intelligence," Emrie muttered, which made Lianjit laugh.

"Look, I'll help you if you want, but you have nothing to prove."

Emrie didn't like that, either, but since Lianjit spent the next hour teaching her the beginnings of geometry anyway, she forgave her. Once Emrie was back home, she tried again to read the witchcraft book but found none of her new knowledge helped. Even if she had a basic idea of the difference between an acute and obtuse angle, the words of the book stringing the various concepts together might as well have been written in the clucks and screeches of Barn Guild animals. After several hours of getting nowhere, she skipped past the explanations to stare at one of the diagrams. The page was covered in dots like stars, with lines between them outlining what could very well be a constellation if she were looking at a book on the night sky.

No help there. She rubbed her fingers on the edge of her laptevi, feeling discouraged just because she'd been so hopeful. Then she caught what she was doing and stopped with her hand resting on the Juju birds stitched along the edge of the fabric. That made her think of her father and her duty. She had to figure this out. She touched the book with her other hand. Maybe she should compare it to the sky after all. Tracing the lines in the book made her fingers tingle, and before she could react, the witchcraft jumped away in a lightning bolt movement that reverberated up her hands and into her arms.

She leaped to her feet, frantically rubbing her hands against her front. The jump hadn't hurt, but it was a different startling feeling than usual. The same sense of alien presence, but this time it was as if it had gone elsewhere, leaving a recoil and a feeling of emptiness shooting up her bones.

Once the witchcraft was finished, she returned to the book, and what she saw startled her all over again. So much so that she rubbed her hands a second time even though they didn't tingle.

"Blessed of the earth, air, water, and sun." One line in the book had disappeared.

She touched the page with the tip of her fingernail, feeling for the carving. It was still there, but the ink was missing.

She clutched the edge of her laptevi, wrinkling the fabric in her excitement. She'd done it. She'd accomplished something using the witchcraft. But then a creeping, itchy feeling wiped out her pleasure. It felt about like the scuttle of a night critter caught suddenly by light in a darkened room.

She'd practiced the forbidden witchcraft.

She only let the feeling stay a moment, brooming it away as best she could. There was no time for second-guessing. This was her duty. It was what she'd been told to do. Now she needed to figure out just what it was she'd accomplished.

As she smoothed out her laptevi under her hand, in sharp contrast to the yellow fabric, she noticed a line of silvery blue the exact length of the missing ink from the book.

The witchcraft had moved the ink to the stitching?

Was that what witchcraft did? It moved things?

Well, that could be useful.

Emrie spent the next two hours trying to determine how she'd done it and failed. She traced the space where the line should've been on the page repeatedly. Then she traced where the line now sat and traced them simultaneously, but nothing happened. She tried both carving and inking a line on fresh paper and then tracing that. Still nothing.

Regardless, she refused to be anything but pleased with herself. This was progress.

***

Deriek pushed himself up from where he sat against the wall of his prison, the sound of what was left of his laptevi scraping against stone overly loud to his ears. The light from his single window was strong at the moment, and he could see the sad state that was himself and his surroundings clearly. His prison contained him, a drain in the floor in one corner to relieve himself, nine empty water bladders, and that window.

Since his recovery from near death, he'd taken to staring at it endlessly. When he slept, he dreamed of climbing to it, jerking off the bars, and escaping this hole of hell. It was all he ever dreamed about.

Craving was a funny thing.

One of his earliest memories was of his mother telling him tales of her people. Wild tales of talking birds, deer with wings, and goats that climbed the Renoa to snack on Its leaves, always with a moral to them that his mother wanted him to understand. Her most repeated story had been about a giant in love with a flying squirrel that had eluded him until he killed it.

From the deepest cravings of the heart come the most catastrophic hate.

He knew it to be true.

He'd been wrong in his list of things occupying his cell. There was a fifth—the brush the girl had given him in some attempt to mock his situation. He hated her, too, in a bloody, violent way.

By the fineness of her hands, the culture in her voice, and the high quality of the food she brought, she was connected to an inner-ring House. He'd tried rummaging through his memories to place her, but there were too many possibilities and his mind was battered and chipped.

He rose to his feet and collected the hairbrush. The handle was metal and cool to the touch.

His mother's people had another story. Of a clever lynx caught in a fur hunter's trap. Rather than bow to the hunter, it had chewed off its own leg, freed itself from its trap, and bled to death an arm's length away. There was honor in controlling one's own ending.

He flipped the brush over and then tossed it into the air, surprising himself when he caught it with all his old dexterity. He was not a lynx, but somewhere buried beneath the grime, he must still have cleverness left to him.

The girl was soft. He'd been wrong to frighten her. If she was willing to bring him things, then he needed to try harder to pull himself together and use her softness to his advantage.

***

Emrie grinned the entire walk to care for the Second Heir. She hadn't worked out how she'd made that line move, but she'd accomplished something she'd have considered impossible before this day, and it was a marvelous feeling.

"You're late," the Second Heir said in a snooty tone when she arrived. He sat just beyond the spot where she always left his food, still a dirty, ragged dog of a person but now ramrod straight with all the supremacy of his lineage in his posture. Emrie noted the change with relief. The Renoa had been right. Just studying the use of the witchcraft had improved him.

She laid out his food, putting down a mat first and then placing on it a dish of sweet potatoes and peppers roasted in cinnamon and paprika. Hopefully, he'd like it. She had.

"Aren't you going to apologize?"

"My apologies," Emrie said automatically, but his annoyance was laughable. Her arrival time was always more haphazard than scheduled.

At least he was speaking to her. That seemed another good sign.

Once his meal was set, she sat back to study him. He had a good face behind the scruff and dirt and ornery expression. Foreign, of course. Whereas Pol-Thirian males tended to have a square jaw and strong bones, his face tapered to a defined chin below a straight mouth and sharp nose. She couldn't see his eyes clearly and the lack of light bleached all color, but they were dark and tilted down at the corners in a way that would've made him look sad if his brow hadn't been so fierce.

She smiled at him, a useless gesture as she was veiled with her cowl pulled low. The smile shifted the cotton in her nostrils, making her nose itch. She rubbed at it and then pushed several of the water bladders through to his side of the bars.

"You offered to brush my hair," he said, almost condescendingly.

"You seemed offended by my offer." She kept her own tone even to avoid antagonizing him. It echoed in her head a bit thanks to the cotton. If witchcraft was a tool to move things, the first thing she was going to do once she figured it out was move the odor of this room somewhere else.

He held something up for her to see, the brush he'd thrown across the room the night before.

"I changed my mind. As a Son of the Sovereign of the blessed land of Pol-Thiri, I believe I'm allowed."

It was the longest string of words he'd said to her so far, and there was an odd tone to his voice. As if he were not just being regal but mocking her a bit as he did it? She wasn't sure. She finished laying out the bladders of water, uncertain of the best way to answer. When she finished, she sat back on her heels and kept her voice even yet again.

"Very well. I'll brush your hair if you like."

He tilted his head in a quick nod. As if he had been testing her and discovered something he approved of.

What did he expect to learn from her willingness to comb his hair? Her family Status was the only thing she could think of. In that, she hadn't given away much. Lianjit would never have groomed him. Neither would Noemi, but Keeli would have. A willingness to help had more to do with personality than Status.

He gave the brush a push in her direction. Emrie retrieved it, and they both moved away from the food, him turning his back. His hair was long, almost to the floor, and heavier than expected. Heavier than her own which fell to her knees when loose. She ran her fingers along the bottom third, doing her best to separate it into manageable chunks.

There was an odd intimacy to sitting there with him in the bubble of washed-out light. As if she were doing something deeply personal. Almost intrusive. She used to help Mati Dechta brush Noemi's hair when she was little, but other than that she'd touched no one's but her own. And no one touched hers other than her own maties and her father when he tugged her braids.

He made no comment or complaint or encouragement but just sat there, his spine autocratically straight. She wondered what he thought of depending on her. She wasn't about to ask. He wasn't someone who invited either questions or conversation. Or intimacy, for that matter. If he thought of her at all, it was probably as a matie.

She worked the tangles, gently loosening small sections, using the brush and her fingers to free them strand by dirty strand in a rhythm that wasn't unpleasant. The witchcraft gave a tingle at one point but subsided again before she could rub her fingers, almost as if it raised its head like a gazelle scenting the wind only to then drop back to the more mundane task of napping when nothing of interest appeared. Yet another curious new experience.

"It's no use," he said after she'd been at it long enough for her fingers to tire.

"Perhaps if I do a little each night . . ."

"You'll need to cut it. Bring a knife next time."

"I'm not giving you a knife. Jeibel or otherwise." It had to be said.

He swiveled around, pulling his hair out of her hands. The light flickered in his eye as if reflecting an inner irritation he must be feeling. He gave her a long and steady look, and she wondered if he'd had the same sense of her having stepped over a boundary by touching him or if he was angry because she'd refused him the knife. Either way, she backed away from him and the bars.

"Then bring rope as well," he finally said.

"I won't let you hang—"

"To bind my wrists," he said, sounding exasperated. "To ease your fears. To convince you to cut my hair. The vermin keep coming out of the dark to pull at it."

***

Emrie woke the next morning to a hand jostling her shoulder. She sat up with a start and looked blearily around as neither Mati Ereana nor Mati Sarta would do such a thing. She'd stayed up extra late working on the witchcraft book but learning nothing additional, and it'd been close to dawn when she'd put it away. The Second Heir had rattled her. How was she supposed to have known there were rats in his prison and that they liked hair?

"I need to talk to you," her brother said from where he perched next to her on her sleeping dais. "I need you to deliver a letter for me."

Emrie stared at him blankly, trying to wake up.

"Come on, little sister. You know you've missed me."

"I have," she admitted, rubbing at her eyes. And it was true. Ahrens always brought a vitality to House Das when he was around. But his rose-brown hair was loose and his overdress had an untidy, up-all-night, doing-something-disreputable look to it. What was more, he smelled of the sweet, herbal smoke of the Jemmy Pipes men passed around the back rooms of public halls. Her smile faded. It couldn't be a good thing that he's shown up here needing help.

"You swore to Father you wouldn't gamble anymore."

He stiffened. "I haven't—"

"Are you going to tell me you didn't spend the night playing Kopi-Far for money?"

"No, I—"

She made a rude huffing noise and threw back the blankets to get up. She adored her brother, but she wasn't naive about him.

"Okay," he said. "I'll admit it. I was playing Kopi-Far. But at the Sovereign's House. I barely lost anything. And I wasn't there to gamble. I was there to deliver the note myself. I failed, and that's why if you would stop throwing accusations at me and listen, I'll explain what I need you to do." He ran a hand over his head and caught a strand of hair in a sapphire-encrusted ring.

For the briefest moment, Emrie was reminded of brushing the Second Heir's hair last night. She put the thought away.

"Who's the letter for?"

"Imjin Flaust."

Oh no.

Ahrens's story turned out to be so, so typical for him. As Emrie had noted on Imjin's visit, he'd indeed caught her eye. Such a match was impossible, and he'd made that plain enough to Imjin to cool her ardor. However, Ahrens was still Ahrens, and so several seven-days ago, she'd talked him into sneaking a letter out of the Sovereign's House and delivering it to one of her father's servants hidden in the city.

"You aided a spy?" Emrie said with disgust. It was just like him to end up in the middle of such a thing.

"His name is Montali, and I didn't give the fellow anything useful," Ahrens replied with a surprising amount of defensiveness for him. "Just a note from Imjin."

"Did you read the note?"

"Of course. I insisted it not be sealed. I'm not a fool, Emrie, regardless of what Noemi says. The letter was a list of items Imjin needed and a glowing description of the First Heir and Pol-Thiri."

Which sounded good, but there were ways to pass secret messages in very bland, unnoticeable manners. Hadn't she tried to do the same when writing to Aunt Poercha?

Ahrens explained that he'd delivered the letter as requested and thought the matter done. Then yesterday afternoon, he'd been stopped in the streets by the same fellow asking Ahrens to take a reply to Imjin. This letter was also bland. Ahrens said it wasn't addressed to anyone or signed and spent most of its lines complimenting the beauty of the reader.

"I can't get close enough to her to deliver it," he said. "Apparently, she was incautious in approaching other Houses and now the First Heir keeps her surrounded by him and other women and no one else. But tonight is the start of TreeFall Watch and Imjin will attend the banquet after. I was thinking of mentioning to Noemi that you'd like to go. She's certain to let you take her place, and then you can pass the note to Imjin. But you can't tell Noemi; she'd never approve."

"No, she wouldn't." Emrie meant it as a warning, but he threw his arms around her as if she'd just agreed to help him. He used to hug her like this all the time when they were children, and she softened into him automatically.

"Thank you, thank you, thank you," he said in a passion-filled voice that was so him.

Emrie laughed against her better judgment and hugged him back. Ahrens, even at his worst, was hard to resist. He had too good of a heart.

An hour later, Emrie sat on the Breakfast Patio, sipping sweet tea, trying to think of what she would say when she approached Imjin at the TreeFall Banquet, and resisting an urge to lay her head down and go back to sleep. She propped her elbow on the table, rubbed her fingers absently when they tried tingling, and stared into the distance.

Out in the Field, petitioners walked the Paths of Wisdom and Virtue and one woman in an ornate brown laptevi wandered near the patio. Her cowl was up so Emrie couldn't see her face, but watching her formal glide from one foot to the other with a pivot at the turns was relaxing. Emrie's eyes closed. Behind her lids, she saw the woman's walking and pausing and then walking again. A rhythm not unlike breathing or tracing her finger on that line in the book.

Emrie jerked to awareness as if shaken once again by her brother.

What if it wasn't about tracing the line?

All those words she'd taken to Lianjit had been about how the lines formed other things—turns, corners, angles. She'd been a fool not to see it before. She dropped her cup and ran back to her suite, startling Mati Sarta who was tidying up. Emrie apologized profusely. Then the moment she was alone, she rushed to retrieve the yellow laptevi and the witchcraft book.

The first thing she noticed was that the angle at the end of the now blank line in the book and the angle of the embroidered Juju bird's wing were the same.

With a giddy sense of excitement, Emrie traced both, starting and ending on the far side of the angles. Just like before, the witchcraft jumped and recoiled taking the ink with it back to where it was supposed to be.

She whooped out loud in an indecorous show of joy.

This was it. This was the secret of the book. Or at least it was the beginning of the secret.

She spent the rest of the morning feeling like she'd just happened upon the blossoming of a hundred-year flower. She played with moving around lines etched in parchment onto objects in her suite that held the same shaped angles. She had plenty of decorated items to choose from and the length of line between the angles seemed to make no difference. It was so easy. The recoil settled into just a springing tingle as if with each try the witchcraft were figuring out how better to launch itself more gracefully from her touch. As if it too were learning.

An odd realization, but it seemed just as right as realizing the Renoa wanted her to do this.

As fun as this was, it wasn't all that useful to move ink between two places that her hands touched. When she tried to move the line without tracing the second location, the witchcraft didn't show up. She went back to the book to look again at the diagram that had made her think of the night sky. That diagram was simple. Just a series of lines and angles. But on the following pages, the diagrams made complete circuits, and some had curves and loops and such.

She pulled out two pieces of parchment and carved and inked two blockish outlines of Juju birds. She put a pot of kohl in the center of one and traced it. The jump happened the moment she touched her finger to the second Juju bird, taking the pot of kohl with it. Emrie jumped to her feet, laughing so loud that Mati Dechta showed up to lecture her on decorum.

But she'd figured it out. The witchcraft moved things centered within identical patterns.

TWELVE

reeFall was one of the four events of the Holy Renoa that divided the year into the Seasons. The official start of TreeFall was hard to predict as the Renoa lost Its leaves and twigs and bark when It liked, and once that happened, everyone was too busy collecting the Renoa's sacrifices to celebrate or give thanks. So as soon as the priests said the Renoa was readying itself for TreeFall, the Houses of Pol-Thiri did as well.

Emrie had forgotten about TreeFall, or not forgotten exactly as she'd been aware that the afternoon rains had petered out and the winds had taken over, but with everything else going on, she hadn't given it much consideration. She kept dozing off while her maties dressed her in her ceremonial clothing.

Her laptevi and overdress were pure white and whisper-soft with a sash of blue embedded with hundreds of tiny sapphires around her waist. She hid the letter for Imjin in an inner pocket.

Her father led the family through the Paths of Wisdom and Virtue, the going slow as they mixed with other Houses traveling to and from the Tree and the priests. Everyone was dressed in white and blue finery creating a human replica of the Tree itself. As they got closer, they were serenaded by reed chimes singing from the Renoa's branches for the new season.

House Das stopped at a wooden altar under the canopy. There, her father left a TreeFall sacrifice on behalf of the Mining Guild, a sack full of gems. One by one, the rest of the family left smaller, more symbolic sacrifices along with the traditional Silent Offering. When it was Emrie's turn, she kneeled and placed a vase of costly perfume on the wooden dais. Then she bowed her head and made the Silent Offering, the offering of one's heart, which was to sacrifice one's ego by admitting to the Holy Renoa one's most inner desire. Emrie had planned to whisper something about the Second Heir, but in the moment, with the sound of the chimes and the feel of the surrounding people, that didn't seem right. Instead, she silently mouthed that more than anything she wanted to honor her House and the Renoa Itself.

Once the rest of the family had finished, they went to one of the many gongs set at the edge of the canopy. Her father and a priest performed the ceremony of turning over the responsibility of the gong to House Das. Halfway through the ceremony, Brid nudged Emrie. Emrie replied with a frown meant to discourage conversation, but Brid leaned in to whisper in her ear anyway.

"Do you want to know what secret desire I offered to the Renoa?"

"You aren't supposed to tell. Not if you want the Renoa to help."

"But I need *you* to make it happen," Brid insisted.

Not what Emrie wanted to hear. Especially if Brid's desire was Ahrens. Their father would never allow it, even if Ahrens for some crazy reason was interested.

"You must help me. And Lianjit and Keeli, too," Brid said.

"We'll talk about it later."

That seemed to satisfy Brid. She stepped back.

The rest of the evening went easier than expected. After the gong had been turned over to the first of the requisite nories who would stand in watch for the start of TreeFall, her father led her and Ahrens through the flagstone maze to the Sovereign's House. Their own maties met them at the edge of the Paths to help remove their ceremonial overdress and change into more lively colors. Everything else was similar to the Ceremony she'd attended before but outdoors. She spent most of it at the fringes, too tired to attempt socializing.

She spotted Imjin about halfway through. Imjin greeted her with two kisses on each cheek in a way that must belong to her own people as it was odd for Pol-Thiri.

"My friend. My most excellent friend," Imjin said, and then described how much she adored everyone in House Das. Emrie did her best to respond just as enthusiastically while slipping the note into Imjin's hand.

The conversation and evening should've ended at that point, but Imjin didn't keep the note. She handed it right back. Emrie straightened, her exhaustion at least temporarily banked at the realization that the paper was folded differently. It was a different note.

To make things worse, Ahrens disappeared so she couldn't rid herself of the thing.

This was why she knew better than to get involved in Ahrens's endeavors; they were never as easy as he said.

When she got home, she let Mati Sarta help her into bed, but then the moment Emrie was alone, she got back up. A hazy glow still came from the banquet at the Sovereign's Courtyard, lighting the Field. She wouldn't be able to sneak over to the Second Heir soon. She went to Ahrens's suite instead.

He wasn't there. Emrie settled onto a cushion in his sleeping chamber to wait.

As the night passed and Ahrens didn't return, Emrie piled up several more of his cushions to make herself comfortable and rest her head. She didn't mean to fall asleep, but once done, she slept hard. She only woke when she became overly warm as someone had covered her in blankets. She pushed them aside to be hit full in the face by the morning sun. A loud in-and-out draft of snoring came from somewhere behind her.

No.

It must be the following day entirely. Dread hollowed out her chest. Not only had she not rid herself of Imjin's note, but she'd failed to fulfill her duty to the Second Heir. He'd gone hungry, and it was her fault.

She was going to kill Ahrens.

She woke him with a rough shake of his shoulder same as he'd done to her. He sat up sputtering and then looked at her balefully as if she were in the wrong for invading his space. She dropped the letter on his blankets.

"I want no more part of this. Don't ask me to help again."

***

Emrie spent the day feeling a rotten mixture of irritation at her brother and guilt for falling asleep that made her short-tempered. It didn't help that a letter from Aunt Poercha arrived with an invitation to visit. Emrie wrote back, thanking her and blaming her need to postpone on Brid.

When she snuck out that night, she brought blunt-nose shears and a heartfelt and humble apology that the Second Heir deserved but she didn't want to give him. Just once, she wanted someone to apologize to her.

Which was all about her brother and not the Second Heir.

The Second Heir waited for her as he had on her last few visits, seated with legs crossed, spine straight, and chin tilted up. Emrie laid out the mat and placed his food on top. He didn't rush for the food or water as he'd done in the past when hungry.

"If you meant to punish me for my unkind words, you used a cruel way to do it." His voice was smooth and controlled and haughty. "Badly done, girl."

Emrie pressed her fingers to the rough stone floor, grounding herself in the feel of the grit against her skin. He was right, but his tone irritated her. He'd never once thanked her for her nightly offering, and now he seemed to think it his due? Which, as the Son of the Sovereign and her responsibility, it might be, but he wasn't in a place to make demands.

"Gratitude is a featherbed," she quoted softly. "Indignation, a bed of nails."

He shifted his shoulders, leaning menacingly toward her.

"You want gratitude? I'm extremely and enthusiastically grateful you deigned to return tonight. You realize I had no way to know if you would or if I was being left to perish after all. If I offend you in the future, would you do me the kindness of informing me in the moment so that I can make my apologies and not have to spend an entire day wondering if I'm about to die?"

If he'd shown even a tad of humility, she would've felt for him. If he'd shown a whisper of something other than spite. If he'd sounded like he truly had feared for his life. Any of that, and she would've caved and apologized. But he was trying to scare her and realizing that, she wasn't afraid at all.

"I thought you wanted to die."

"Does the person who pays you know you failed in your duty?"

"I'm not paid." His words struck true, though. Her father had instructed her to come every night, and she hadn't done so. She took a deep breath to calm her irritability. "I'll cut your hair if you like. I brought shears." Very dull shears as that seemed a better idea than a rope.

He shifted as if trying to study her.

"You're not entirely a river muritt, are you?"

"Of course not," Emrie snapped back, her skin flushing hot. Muritts were docile rodents known for sitting unbothered while predators ate them. It was a horrible, offensive thing for him to say.

"Why didn't you come last night?" His tone changed, still sharp but with the addition of something else she couldn't identify.

She didn't want to talk to him anymore. The comment about the muritt *stung*. She did so anyway.

"It was TreeFall Watch. I couldn't come until the festivities at the House of the Sovereign were over, and the banquet went very late. I . . ." She hesitated a moment because regardless of how provoked she was feeling, her own honor insisted she admit the truth. "I fell asleep."

"I see." His mouth relaxed, and he gazed in her direction in a cockeyed way.

She knew he couldn't see her as she wore her veil, but his stare made her uncomfortable. "I *am* sorry. I wasn't trying to punish you. I don't even remember what you said to me the night before, rude or not."

"Neither do I. But considering all the unsavory things that went through my head, I figured I must've offended you."

Humor. That was it. An unexpected, and from what she knew of him, uncharacteristic, humor. She had no idea what to do with it.

"I don't offend easily," she murmured.

"Nor do you scare."

"I scare." The turn in the conversation was causing her not a small tangle of nerves. "You should eat."

He picked up the wafer bread and tore off one end with an effortless grace. They sat in silence for several minutes while he dined, the tension between them gone even if Emrie had no idea why. Since it'd be rude to watch him, Emrie distracted herself by trying to think of a way to remove the odor from the room with the witchcraft. With the change of the Season, she'd better do something about his ragged clothing as well.

"My hair?" he asked smoothly when he'd finished.

She nodded, and he turned around like last time. She adjusted the light so she could see and then also like last time, pulled a chunk of hair through the bars and ran her fingers over it. It was easier to focus on the hair than the person beyond.

The worst of the tangles and mats were down his back. Above his shoulders was still a mess, but not so bad. She took the shears and sawed back and forth just above the ridge of his shoulders. It was work, but the first hunk came loose, and she dropped it to the ground.

"You aren't my brother's creature, are you?" he asked after she'd been cutting for a while. He spoke as if they were just two normal people having a friendly conversation.

"I'm not." She tensed, waiting for him to ask her name or who had sent her. He said nothing more, and she returned to cutting. The silence became companionable again. Intimate, like last time, but she felt just a tad less of an intruder. Maybe it was silly, but she wanted to do a good job of his hair. She took her time, working small chunks and trying to make it even. The witchcraft didn't bother her at all.

"I'll die one way or the other," he said, still in a genial tone.

The shears went heavy in her hand. She put them down to study the back of his head. He'd said the words as if it didn't bother him. Testing again?

"My brother has been pushed too far. He won't allow me to walk free."

Emrie lifted the shears to even up one side but said nothing. This was dangerous talk. He was dangerous.

"I have riches of my own. My mother's jewels and those gifts I earned while with her people. They're hidden where my brother can't find them. I'll tell you how to get them in trade for a Jeibel."

Emrie shuddered. When she spoke, she did so softly to the back of his head. "I already told you I'm not bringing you a knife."

"You aren't to be bought then, Piara?"

"Piara?"

"I have to call you something, and it would be rude in our current circumstances to ask either your Simple Name or your House Name." She could almost hear a smile in his voice, as if he was amusing himself at her expense.

That pushed Emrie right back into irritation all over again. He was one of those people, like her brother, who seemed to know just how to get under her skin.

"I think you like being rude. And no, I definitely can't be bought. Don't try that again."

THIRTEEN

I t took Emrie two days to discover that adding loops to her outline of a Juju bird made the witchcraft move from one place to another continuously, even once she removed her fingers. It was as if the loops tied a knot at each end of the lightning bolt, keeping the tension in place. Then all she had to do was drop something into the center of the first Juju bird pattern, and it appeared at the second location. Directing this process toward scent was tricky, but the more she wafted in incense with a fan, the more the witchcraft seemed to understand what she wanted, learning again. An eerie thought, but one she wasn't about to question as long as it kept working.

After several more days of practice, she figured out how to draw in scent from a distance without a fan. She practiced that, partly for the revenge of it, by hiding a carved parchment in Ahrens's sleeping chamber and filling his space with the scent of rotting wildaberry.

The next step was figuring out a place to send the horrible smell of the prison. The most obvious was the river. So when Lianjit sent a note asking Emrie and Brid to meet her at Keeli's house because she had exciting news, Emrie suggested a different plan. The Barrack's Field was next to the river, and Brid had been angling to see it for some time. Emrie suggested they meet Lianjit there instead.

Before leaving House Das, Emrie collected two of the decorative rocks used to top potted plants and etched a Juju bird pattern onto each. She linked the patterns together and tested it with the witchcraft. They worked just like the parchment. One she placed in an inner pouch of her laptevi. The other she hid in her wooden chest for later.

At the Barrack's Field, Lianjit was surprised to see them but not upset. She offered to show Brid around the various practice arenas. Emrie used the time to stroll out to the river.

With the death of the Season of Water, the river was subsiding. Already its edges were a swampy, mucky mess that smelled like days-old dead fish and attracted too many insects. A stone path had been cleared through the muck, and Emrie followed it, batting bugs out of her way and wishing she had something to stuff up her nose now. She stopped where the muck turned into a slimy pool and offered the Blessing-of-the-Water. Once done, she tossed the carved rock into the pool where it sank out of view.

This was going to work. It was an excellent idea. Definitely not muritt-ish at all.

When she returned to join Brid and Lianjit, she found that Lianjit hadn't been able to contain her news until they reached Keeli's house.

"Her father's letting her get a sword," Brid said before Lianjit had a chance. Lianjit gave Brid a friendly elbow in the side, which Brid ignored. "A real one. That she'll carry whenever it pleases her."

"That's wonderful," Emrie said, thrilled for her friend.

Lianjit stepped in front of Brid but in a way that was more prodding than offended. She might have done the same to Keeli when she got motherly on them. It rubbed Emrie the wrong way. Her friends weren't supposed to like Brid.

"It's commissioned to the Guildmaster of Sword himself," Lianjit said. "Mother's against it, of course, but Father's having none of her interference. He says it's time."

"It is time," Emrie agreed, trying to put as much support into her voice as possible.

Once at House Portsri, they were escorted to Keeli's chambers. The space, like Keeli herself, was decorated with colorful trinkets and silk drapery and twice as many cushions as should fit. Lianjit repeated her story, and they all joined in her excitement.

"I have news, too," Brid announced after Keeli had handed out tea and biscuits. "Or at least a request. About my Offering at the Renoa."

"It's bad luck to speak of an Offering," Keeli chided.

"I told her," Emrie said, but that was all she could get out as she'd just taken a bite of a biscuit, and it had a lime center so tangy her eyes watered.

"You alright?" Keeli asked.

Emrie nodded.

"This isn't just a wish," Brid continued. "It's a goal. My goal. The reason I came to Pol-Thiri. The Renoa has put the three of you in my path to help."

Emrie took a big gulp of tea to clear away the taste, which hadn't been bad just unexpected.

"They tell a tale," Lianjit said, "of the Sovereign in Cur-Alkorashi giving his Renoa his desire to end a bad series of attacks by the River Nomads. He received the exact plan of how to beat them. And it wasn't like he kept that to himself. He told his Advisers and his Barracks' Captains. To this day we study his maneuvers."

"Half those old tales aren't true," Keeli said.

"But the Renoa does speak," Lianjit argued.

Emrie stole two biscuits for the Second Heir while no one was looking. Just imagine what they'd say if she told them *her* story. But of course, that was impossible.

"It does speak," Brid said, and then in that way she had, she burst out with what she wanted. "Everyone thinks my family sent me to Pol-Thiri to contract with a husband. But it didn't happen like that at all. I ran away. I told my father I was going to do it, and then I did. He wrote to warn House Das I was on my way, but I would've arrived regardless."

"But why?" Lianjit asked.

"To find my mother. My father won't tell me who she is." Brid's face colored but with defiance rather than embarrassment.

For a moment, Emrie's dislike of Brid subsided into sympathy. These things happened, of course. The children of uncontracted relationships were raised in the House of one of their parents as lower members of the family. They didn't inherit, well, except in situations like the Second Heir's, but other than that, along with the disharmony should one parent be married to someone else, it wasn't a disaster. Children, regardless of exact parentage, were valued.

Both Keeli and Lianjit looked to Emrie as this was a House Das matter. Emrie hesitated, not sure what to say.

"Were the Das in Kye-Boehlke unkind to you?" she asked carefully.

Some of the color faded from Brid's face. "No. That's not the point. The point is that I want to know, and I have a right to know."

Emrie tried again. "Perhaps your father had a reason for not telling you."

"Meaning my mother might be of inferior Status. I thought of that, and I don't care. I still want to know." Brid spoke too loudly as if she wanted to make sure every word was heard. "I got here by myself. I paid the Nomads to take me, and it was *awful*. I'm not going home without an answer. Someone here knows who she is."

Most likely Emrie's father.

It was hard to criticize Brid for wanting a mother when Emrie had never known her own. She knew the feeling of wondering what her mother looked like, sounded like, smelled like. And at least Emrie had Noemi to compare. Brid, it appeared, had no one but herself. At the same time, there was something critical of House Das in Brid's tale that made Emrie cross her arm over her chest and clench her teeth together.

"Here, here," Keeli said. "Can't you see what a true child of Pol-Thiri Brid is? Is not that the level of determination and . . . and . . . grit . . . that we're all supposed to be made of?"

"It's true," Lianjit said.

Emrie glanced to one then the other. Grit? It was an odd word, not one she'd ever heard Keeli use before. That Brid lacked thoughtfulness and manners didn't mean she had grit.

"Tell us the entire story of your mother," Keeli urged.

"Yes, do tell," Lianjit agreed.

Brid launched into her tale, which was rather simple. As part of the trade of the Salt Guild which functioned under the Mining Guild, Brid's father had gone to live in Kye-Boehlke and contracted with a local woman. On one of his visits home, he'd met Brid's mother and Brid had been the result. This had all occurred during the last Status War, and her mother's House had come out poorly. To protect the child, she'd sent Brid to be raised by her father.

"Well, we know when and where you were born," Keeli said. "Let's find out which Houses lost Status in that war. Lianjit can ask at the Barracks. I'll see what I can get off of gossip. Emrie, you check your family's history as Brid's birth might be recorded there. All three of us will help."

Emrie curled her hand into the sleeves of her laptevi, rubbing her fingers against the fabric. She didn't want to get involved in Brid's problems. No one asked her either way.

***

That night, Emrie brought the Second Heir fresh clothing. Before stepping out to let him change, she placed the second stone in a corner, touched the carving of the Juju bird, and told the witchcraft to attract the odor and send it out to the matching stone she'd left in the river. Then while he changed, she went exploring any other passages off of the hallway to prove she wasn't too afraid to do it. Was that grit? Doing things you were afraid of? It didn't feel like it, mostly because she wasn't afraid. Not even when the hallway led to a stairwell going up, which led to a locked door that must be to the Sovereign's House.

Once back with the Second Heir, she removed the cotton from her nose.

No odor.

She grinned to herself. Maybe grit was success.

Now that her initial goal was accomplished, she couldn't help but notice that the temperature in the room was dropping with the season. Warmth would have to be her next project as she didn't want him to suffer more than he already was. She finished laying out his food, including the two lime biscuits.

He picked one up and tasted it.

"Mmmm . . . These are good."

"I'm glad you like them," she replied politely.

"Who's your favorite Sage?" he asked as if trying to get her to engage with him.

"Jeminina."

"She of the single-petaled flower?" He put a hand to his chest in mock horror. "Who only wrote one book, and it was all blossomy metaphors and proverbs?"

Emrie pressed her lips together and kept her attention on his food. She liked metaphors and proverbs, but of course, he'd think such things silly. Lianjit, who was no muritt and definitely had grit, only read treatises on war.

"Who's yours?" she asked.

"Feytur the Prolific."

He lied. No one liked Feytur.

"He who wrote so many books, no one could possibly read them all and half make no sense."

"I've read them all." He sounded all stuffy and superior, but as if he were doing it on purpose to entertain himself. Or her.

She sniffed loud enough that he'd hear. He lied again, but that he was doing so was a good thing and made it hard to be offended.

"Bring me one of Feytur's tomes so I have something to do other than wait for your return each day." He spoke seriously now.

"I will." But then she felt a tinge of regret for giving in so easily. On the other hand, it was her job to care for him, and his request was neither a burden to her nor unreasonable. Being agreeable didn't mean one lacked grit.

"Piara, I thank you," he said, pronouncing each syllable so she'd noticed his gratitude. That was something, at least.

The next day she went to the Marketplace even though that was one of the few places the witchcraft still reacted unasked. She purchased a volume of the writing of Sage Feytur and the largest blanket she could find. Once home, she collected the book on the witchcraft and laid out the blanket on the floor. It was meant to cover a sleeping dais and would be large enough for the Second Heir to wrap himself in many times over.

Her first objective was to determine whether stitching patterns in fabric worked just like carving. It did. Next, she tested whether moving heat worked like moving scent by placing a carved rock on top of the furnace box the maties had brought into her room as the season cooled. That also worked, so she linked the carved rock to a pattern in parchment to see if the difference in materials mattered. They didn't.

Even better, she discovered that the single pattern in the rock could transfer heat to more than one stitched pattern in fabric as long as the patterns were close to the same size. Since she had no way to hide or heat a large boulder carved with a Juju bird, she would need to stitch multiple small patterns to cover the entire blanket to match a small carving.

It was slow going. Even stitching all afternoon, she didn't get very far, and then Brid interrupted to prod her into searching the family histories for birth records. Brid's birth wasn't recorded in Emrie's copy of the family lineage. The histories in her father's private library were more complete, but Emrie could visit and Brid could not. At Brid's bidding, she checked. Most of the histories were on the doings of the Mining Guild, but she found her own birth and her mother's death of a wasting disease. No mention of Brid at all. When she told that to Brid, Brid acted as if it were Emrie's fault. Typical.

The Second Heir was pleased by the book she brought him that night and wanted to discuss various passages with her, much like her father did with the family on Petal Night. It was flattering. She wasn't as schooled or well-read as he, but twice she made him laugh. The next night she brought him a copy of Sage Jeminina just to prove she wasn't ashamed of the things she liked. They read it together, and he mocked it from page one to the end, but his humor was directed at himself more than her. He made no more comments about muritts, and every day, he seemed better than the last. Her work with the witchcraft was doing its job.

It took Emrie another five days of stitching to finish the blanket. Once done, she drew a pattern in chalk in one of her back rooms and a matching one in the hallway just outside the Second Heir's prison so that she could use the witchcraft to take it to him rather than carry it.

When she handed it over, he thanked her so profusely it was clear he wanted her to notice. Then he engaged her in a long discussion on the obligations created by gifts, went over the pros and cons of becoming indebted to anyone other than the Renoa, and told her the story of three hungry dogs who gifted a dead rat back and forth between each other so many times trying to avoid being indebted that the rat fell to pieces. He was an excellent storyteller.

The next night, he was waiting as usual but this time with the blanket folded into a thick square so he could sit upon it.

"I would speak to you of this blanket, Piara," he said, his voice full of the canny amusement that had become his normal way of speaking to her.

"What does Piara mean?" she asked.

"It's from an old story of my mother's people," he said. "I'll tell it to you sometime. But not today. You may call me Deriek." He bowed his head as if bestowing a gift upon her.

"I can't do that," she replied, flustered by the invitation. She put out his food without looking at him.

"But you shall. Who's to know you broke etiquette? And who's to care? Not me."

She still couldn't do it. Not even her father called the Sovereign's family by their Simple Names. "You're pleased with the blanket?" she asked, trying to act normal and hide her reaction. "I purchased it at the Artisan's Marketplace."

"You're pleased with the blanket, Deriek?" he corrected with a sly glance in her direction.

She ignored that. She knew trouble-causing when she heard it.

"Deriek," he continued in a high voice as if pretending to be her. "I've a secret I must ask you to keep. A very grand one. So secret that my life and my family's Status depends on it. Deriek, will you keep my secret?"

He knew.

If he hadn't been so clearly teasing, this truth would've terrified her, but instead of fear, what fell on her shoulders was a heavy resignation. She went still, waiting for him to get whatever he was about to say over with.

"What can I, the most generous and powerful Second Heir, do for you, Piara?" he answered as the snooty version of himself.

Then he spoke in the unnaturally high voice. "Dearest Deriek, it turns out I have the witchcraft. I'm willing to use it to keep you warm during the season when the sun softens, but I need you to not tell anyone. I need you to promise."

"On one condition," he continued, back to being himself. Then he looked straight at her as if he could see her in the dark behind her veil. "Piara, what is my condition in keeping your secret?" The corner of his lip twitched and even in the low light she could see crinkles around his eyes. He was enjoying himself.

A smile crept over her own mouth even as she stood up. How could she be afraid if he was smiling?

"I'm not calling you Deriek."

"You just did," he said, sounding delighted.

"I—" she started, stopped, and then threw up her hands in defeat. She hadn't called him Deriek. She really hadn't, but he wouldn't let her win, and at least he didn't seem scared by her use of the witchcraft, which is what she would've been if their situations were reversed. "I'm leaving now."

"I was wrong to call you a muritt," he said merrily. "You're not a river creature. You're a desert panther, invisible until it lands on its prey."

The splotchy, ragged, thin-to-starved-looking panthers were the ugliest cats of the desert. Calling her that was far from a compliment.

"I'm neither," she said, turning to leave. She forgave him the insult, though, because he was laughing. A genuine laugh, too. There was something warm and inviting about it that was out of place in this dank prison.

Just before she was too far away to hear more, he called out. "I do promise not to reveal your secret, my little Piara. I absolutely do."

***

Deriek had long since taken to staying up at night so he'd sleep during the day. Otherwise, he stared too much at the window. It was like a nail pricking his flesh just enough to be constantly aware of the hammer poised above. The pain sent him into rages and then depression and then a calm so empty that sometimes he'd dig his nails into his arm to make sure the hammer hadn't struck and he wasn't dead.

Today, though, sleep eluded him. He considered distracting himself with one of Piara's books but couldn't bring himself to move from where he was wrapped in the blanket. Instead, he watched the walls turn from black to gray, feeling his sense of powerlessness pulled up with the sun. He held off staring at the window as long as possible. He told his eyes to shut, his body to roll to face the other direction. Neither obeyed, and he wanted to scream.

But he didn't. The one thing his little Piara had done for him was help him control his tongue. She scared too easily if he didn't. Or at least she pretended to scare.

No, the fear was genuine.

As was the deference, but she'd be far from the first person to latch onto him as a boot-scrubber only for him to find out he was being played.

He couldn't see her as one of those, either. She lacked guile.

The window above him filled with light beaming across the cell, one side to the other. He stared at it, a moth to its flame.

Artlessness and witchcraft. Piara was an interesting combination.

Most of what he knew of the witchcraft came from a book he'd read in Vin-Yonekur. It'd been vague on specifics and treated the witchcraft like a wild thing to be tamed into submission, not a metaphor that fit his little witch. Until he had a better understanding of what she could do, he could see no way of using it for his gain. A perpetually warm blanket was intriguing and convenient but not useful in achieving his goal.

But the witchcraft *was* a sign she wasn't what she seemed.

She wasn't a First, not with her tendency to obey. Sending someone ignorant and innocent might be a clever way to exploit his own weaknesses. It was hard not to like her.

What if she also was being used by someone? To gain his trust, make him weak?

If so, it was working. He wasn't pushing her nearly as hard as he should be.

The more he lay staring at the window, the more it seemed likely. What other reason would there be to pick someone so guileless out of a population of people raised on scheming?

She didn't know that was why she was here, though. It'd be obvious if she did. Nor did it benefit him to have her know. He'd continue to be cautious with her, keep her talking, and see what showed up in terms of opportunities.

Fourteen

Several days after the Second Heir called her a panther, Emrie settled on the Breakfast Patio to work on her next strategy for improving his life. She wanted to provide him a bath and had been experimenting with the witchcraft whenever she could to accomplish that. It was slow going. And she was tired again. She'd stayed out late too many times these past nights reading with him.

She gazed toward the Renoa and yawned before offering a quick Blessing of That-Which-Is-Life for guiding her in the right direction.

A gentle wind smelling of baked bread and spices wafted around her. On the Paths of Wisdom and Virtue, a woman in a brown laptevi and overdress paused at a corner in the flagstones. Watching that same woman had been what helped Emrie to realize the witchcraft needed angles. Emrie relaxed forward on the table, taking a sip from her tea as she watched the woman pace. Her fingers traced a pattern on the side of her cup. The witchcraft reacted like an overeager puppy, making Emrie smile. Was it a bad thing that she felt a sense of affection for the alien presence? That it seemed to have a friendly, willing personality?

Then the oddest thing happened. Emrie became aware that the witchcraft wanted to reach to where the woman walked. To the Paths themselves.

Which was strange. The witchcraft had only ever connected to patterns Emrie traced, and she'd never done anything with the flagstone.

House Sersi.

The name popped into her head unbidden. The color of the woman's dress was distinctive, and Keeli had more than once commented that House Sersi, they of the Soil Guild, were the only ones able to convince the Dye Guild to provide such a staid hue for formal dress.

Sersi was Eleventh-ring, and this woman, who walked with the bearing of someone of responsibility, would likely be their Head of House. Emrie watched her turn a corner. The witchcraft flared again, and Emrie gasped. The woman continued walking in the distance.

It wasn't the flagstones the witchcraft was reacting to. Or not exactly. The woman was using the witchcraft herself.

Which was so shocking Emrie pushed herself to her feet.

She didn't know how she knew it, but she did. That's why her own witchcraft was so —she stumbled trying to find the right word—interested, maybe?

Emrie needed to speak to that woman.

***

The next day, she let Brid talk her into going to Keeli's house. The excuse was the promise of attending a minor Judgment by the Sovereign, but really Brid wanted to talk about her quest. Emrie agreed in order to feel Keeli out about House Sersi.

They ended up not viewing the Judgment as it was an ugly one. A Son of the Vineyard Guild was to spend a day tied to a post with his mouth propped open for having lied and cheated another Guild. Not fun to watch.

Instead, they stayed at House Portsri, but as Keeli's mother and sister had visitors, they ended up on the roof.

"I'm so sorry," Keeli said for the millionth time as the afternoon winds had come early, and they were being buffeted about. "Mother's guests never stay this long."

"Yes, but did you find anything for me?" Brid demanded from where she sat next to Keeli in a ring of cushions. She tucked the hem of her laptevi over her knees to hold it in place against the winds.

"The roof is lovely," Emrie added to hush Brid's rudeness. She pushed at her cowl which kept blowing up into her face but didn't sit down herself. Instead, she stepped to the back to stand against a water cistern as a block. Lianjit took a place on the tile floor.

"I discovered," Keeli said to Brid, "that no one likes to discuss loss of Status. Not even my sister who does little else but gossip."

"Did your family lose Status then?" Brid asked, proving how rude the question was.

"Of course not," Keeli said as if affronted.

Lianjit snickered. "My father said that after a war, every family claims they gained Status. The Houses who don't are those who can't because they moved down an entire ring. Only the Firsts and the Heads of Houses know the truth of it all. Why don't the rest of us study recent history?"

"Then that's why you don't," Brid announced. "No one wants lesser Sons and Daughters to get involved. So, they just don't tell you anything."

Emrie, Keeli, and Lianjit all stared at Brid.

"Well considered," Lianjit said slowly, and Keeli nodded in approval. Emrie reluctantly agreed. The Status Wars weren't wars in terms of swords and spears and ranks of fighters throwing themselves at each other like the battles with the River Nomads. Nor was it the same as the Barracks' nories dealing with the crimes and skirmishes that happened in the outer-rings. Status Wars were about scheming and politics and who-owed-who and who lost control of their Guilds. Deaths were accomplished by poisons or daggers in dark corners. *Swords for strangers, poisons for friends*, was a children's saying.

That everyone except for the First of each House was kept intentionally in the dark about such things wasn't something Emrie'd considered before.

"It won't be as easy as I thought," Keeli said with a sigh.

Brid's entire bearing tightened. "Well, try harder."

Keeli laughed. "Yes, we'll have to."

The conversation continued on, but Emrie stayed out of it, wishing she had the luxury of laying bare her own struggles. After a while, the topic changed to Lianjit's new sword. That distracted Brid, and Emrie caught Keeli's eye and beckoned her over to the edge of the roof. Luckily the winds had died down.

Pol-Thiri spread out before them in a wide jumble of white buildings, blue tile, roof cisterns, and lots of vining plants dying back with the season. It was still beautiful.

"What do you know about House Sersi?" Emrie asked, being as blunt as Brid.

Keeli shrugged, unfazed. "Related to Brid?"

"Maybe." Emrie hadn't planned to use that, but it was a good excuse. For all Emrie knew, the Lady of House Sersi could've birthed a child Brid's age. Besides, Brid owed Emrie for being so difficult. "Likely it's nothing, and Brid gets intense so easily I didn't want to ask in front of her."

"She has no tolerance for hindrances," Keeli said as if it were a compliment. "But to go back to your question, I don't know all that much. The Head of House is a woman. She's devout and has a strong connection to the Dyers Guild."

All of which Emrie knew.

"Should I visit her?" Keeli asked.

The words were said kindly, almost too kindly, as if Keeli didn't think Emrie could do it herself. Which was just her being motherly and thoughtful, but Emrie bristled all the same.

"I'll do it, but what should be my approach?"

"Whatever you want. They are what . . . Ninth?"

"Eleventh." Emrie had double-checked with Aunt Calys. "I need a reason for being there."

Keeli shrugged. "They're Soil Guild. You're Mining Guild. If you visit an Eleventh-ring family linked to your House through guildwork, they'll think you're examining them in a search of a husband."

Emrie's rejection of that was visceral.

Keeli grinned and nudged her. "You don't have to actually be courting. It's a game. But I'm glad you're helping Brid. I get the feeling you don't approve of her."

Emrie shifted to look out over the city. "Sometimes Brid's a bit much," she finally said. The wind picked up again, plucking at her braided hair and rustling the surrounding plants.

"She's passionate, isn't she," Keeli said, sounding admiring again. "Nothing about her is superficial. It's refreshing."

"Refreshing." Emrie couldn't match Keeli's enthusiasm.

Keeli grinned a second time. "Let's find her mother and get it over with. Then things will go back to normal. She isn't taking your place you know. Not with us and not within your House."

***

"I have a question for you," Emrie said that evening to Deriek, who she was only calling by his Simple Name in her own head. She'd decided Keeli was right. The quickest way to end Brid's annoying quest was to get it over. Once Brid had her answer, she'd return to Kye-Boehlke. "Were you tutored in recent Pol-Thiri history?"

"Yes." He said the single word cautiously. Possibly the first cautious thing he'd done since she'd started caring for him. He sat as always on his folded blanket. His empty containers of food were pushed to one side.

"Do you know if there was a Daughter who birthed a child outside a marriage contract seventeen years ago during the last Status War?"

"That's a very specific question," he replied. "Why exactly?"

"I have a friend searching for her mother." She hesitated and then decided to be relatively honest. It wasn't like he had anyone to tell. "Her father told her that the mother of her birth came from a family that lost favor in the war, and that was why he'd raised her instead of her mother."

Deriek tapped out a one-two rhythm on his thigh as he considered.

"To the best of my recollection, her mother wouldn't be First-ring. The birth of a child to one of them that was then given up would be well-known. With the shrinking size of the First-ring families, they hold tight to their children." He made a flowery hand motion pointing to himself as an example. "The Second through Fifth-ring families are in similar situations, if not quite so precarious. A handful of them lost Status in the war. Everyone with ties to the Masonry Guild, of course. Even with that, I'd argue your friend isn't starting with the right questions."

"What would the *right* questions be?"

"Who doesn't want her to know and why? What is it that makes owning the connection impossible?"

"Her mother was married to someone else?"

"Maybe, but it would seem odd that her father wouldn't admit that."

Yes, all of that had occurred to Emrie originally. "What else?"

Now his lips quirked up and his voice lightened. "I can't answer that. Perhaps the witchcraft will tell you. That's what it's for, isn't it?"

The witchcraft? She lifted her face in his direction with both a sense of confusion and eagerness. "What do you know about the witchcraft?"

"Nothing. But you do. And we're talking about you here, aren't we?"

It took her a beat to get what he was saying. And then she jerked to her feet and took several paces backward, insulted. He thought she was *Brid*? How could he think she was Brid? She wasn't Brid at all.

"Or not," he replied.

Fifteen

Everyone knew that if one rubbed two pieces of wood against each other fast and long enough, one could make heat and smoke. Emrie had seen it done any number of times. That point of friction where the two sticks touched was what both Keeli's and Deriek's words felt like. Deriek hadn't even meant to insult her. He'd just understood the story wrong. She should be able to let it go.

She couldn't.

And how could Keeli imply Emrie was jealous?

She wasn't. At all. There wasn't anything to be jealous of. Brid was a nobody and a rude nobody at that.

Only Emrie wanted to be seen for who *she* was, not in relation to Brid. Which made no sense as Deriek had never met Brid. But there it was—Brid's existence took some indefinable thing away from her.

Emrie was worrying herself about it the next morning when a breathless Mati Sarta came rushing to find her.

"The First Daughter of House Kolera arrived to see the First Daughter Das as part of a previous arrangement. But the First Daughter isn't here. She went out this morning with Mati Dechta."

"Oh, mercy."

Emrie jumped to her feet. It was unlike Noemi to make such a mistake.

"We can't offend the Daughter of another House. I'll greet her and come up with an excuse." Which wasn't how she'd like to spend her morning but at least she knew Taspin Kolera. Emrie hurried to where Taspin waited in the Central Garden. The garden's dais has been rearranged for the Season of the Air to face away from the pond, with ribbons attached to the edge of the awning. Taspin sat under it wearing a crisp pearl-pink laptevi. She didn't rise for Emrie, but as a First, she wasn't obligated to do so.

"All honor and Blessing of the Holy Renoa to the Daughter of the revered House of Kolera who we of House Das hold in highest esteem." Emrie continued with the greetings, saying everything just so. Taspin responded in kind. When they were finished, Emrie waited for Taspin to invite her to sit, but she didn't. Brid would've sat anyway.

"Noemi is unwell?" Taspin asked in her drawling tone. "The maties seemed in such a stir I thought something must be wrong."

Emrie shifted her stance in the hope Taspin would notice she'd like to sit.

"Not wrong." She kept her voice calm and easy. "The maties worried of offending you. Noemi was called away on guildwork. Please forgive her and accept my humble company instead."

"These things happen," Taspin said with a wave of her hand. "But it's not me in need of entertaining. We were summoned to visit Imjin. I thought to collect Noemi on my way. Might you attend in her stead? It would be quite the misdeed for no one of House Das to appear."

"Of course." The words came out automatically. Emrie'd never be so ill-mannered as to refuse.

"Hurry, then. You must change your overdress. We're late already." Taspin stood.

Emrie rushed to her chamber and had Mati Ereana help her change. She'd never been invited to the Sovereign's House for a social visit before. Taspin's excuse for coming by was strange, too. House Kolera was *closer* to the Sovereign's House than House Das, not the other way around. It was the one she snuck under each night to reach Deriek.

Once they'd arrived at the Sovereign's House, they were shown to a patio facing the Renoa. The sun had been blocked by a purple and blue canopy edged in ribbons, and under it, Imjin lay on a cushion as if asleep, her eyes covered by a linen cloth. In the background, a matie piped out a slow melody on a whistle.

Imjin did not appear to be waiting for their arrival. Emrie looked to Taspin. What was going on here? A second matie removed the cloth, and Imjin sat up.

"Oh," she said, sounding delighted. "I didn't realize you'd come to visit, Friend Emrie, how is your darling brother?"

Imjin didn't give her time to answer, instead sending a matie for tea. The room filled with movement as more maties arrived to rearrange the cushions around Imjin and bring in a table and tray. The one playing the whistle stopped.

"Please sit," Imjin said. "I suppose you'll want formal greetings?"

"Not if it displeases you," Taspin said while taking the cushion next to Imjin. Emrie sat on her far side. It was an insult toward Taspin and herself to not perform the greetings. Imjin had been in Pol-Thiri long enough to know that.

Imjin began a conversation about various boys of the inner-ring Houses. Emrie slipped in Noemi's regrets but, other than that, stayed silent and let Taspin talk. Surely this wasn't why Taspin had brought her here?

Then the rug to the interior of the Sovereign's House was thrown open in dramatic fashion and the First Heir stepped out.

Emrie couldn't help it; her mouth fell open. Taspin straightened in her seat, giving the First Heir her full attention. She seemed more pleased than surprised to see him.

"Cystel," Imjin said, her voice sour. "Blessing of the Renoa. Have you come to join us?" That Imjin used his Simple Name was shocking, but it didn't seem like she'd invited him in advance. Which meant what? That Taspin had somehow? To get Noemi into his presence? Emrie wasn't good enough at these kinds of games to know.

The First Heir settled onto a cushion with barely a glance at the three of them. It was the closest Emrie had ever been to him, and she plastered on a smile to hide her alarm. He was a big man, broad and muscular, and much older than Emrie, Imjin, or Taspin. She could see only the barest resemblance between him and Deriek. The shape of the forehead, the length of the nose, and the same thin lips. That was it.

Or at least as much as she got with a quick glance. She wasn't about to stare.

Imjin poured him tea, taking her time about it while sighing several times. The First Heir downed it in three gulps. An uncomfortable silence settled around them. Luckily, as the Daughter with the least amount of Status, Emrie's role was to stay in the background.

"What brings you to my patio today?" Imjin finally asked, sounding irritated.

He studied his empty cup. "I'm here for the flowers of this House to grace me with good luck, good fortune, and beauty." His voice was deep and off-rhythm somehow like a dancer who lacked the skill to follow the drum.

A wide, pleased smile spread across Taspin's face, but not so Imjin's, who rolled her eyes in a way that reminded Emrie of Lianjit. Emrie kept her face straight even though the compliment was awkward and graceless. Maybe if he'd smiled when he'd said it or at least glanced up. There was something emotionless about the words, as if he'd memorized them to have available for this moment. None of which eased her genuine fear of him.

The conversation ground on with Imjin casting displeased looks at the First Heir, Taspin giving him her full attention, and the First Heir focusing on a trail of insects crawling their way across the patio.

He only stayed a few minutes, and when he stood, he stepped over to the insects, grinding his boot into their trail, killing several dozens of them and disrupting the rest. In doing so, he relaxed. Those familiar-looking lips turned up in the corners, and he finally appeared pleased to be there. Emrie was deeply grateful he was unlikely to ever look in her direction.

"Such a disappointment he can't stay longer," Taspin said once he was gone. Imjin made an ugly noise deep in her throat, and Emrie kept her opinions to herself.

Not long after, Taspin and Emrie left as well. Taspin's goal must have been the visit with the First Heir, although what she'd hoped to accomplish was beyond Emrie's ability to guess.

"Just a moment," Imjin said. She whispered instructions to a matie, and the girl fetched a folded note. "For Noemi," Imjin said. "To thank her for a kindness she did me."

Imjin placed the note in Emrie's hand and then leaned in close to double-kiss her on the cheek and whisper into her ear, "Give it to your brother instead."

***

Emrie was going to murder Ahrens. But only if the First Heir didn't find out he was in contact with Imjin and do so first.

She loved her brother, but had he no sense at all? She considered shredding the note and forgetting its existence, but if she did that, she'd need to read it first to make sure it wasn't important. If she read it, she'd be dragged deeper into Imjin's mess. No. She'd deliver it and give Ahrens a lecture he was likely to ignore.

The moment she arrived home, she went in search of him but was stopped by Mati Dechta. "Your sister requests your presence."

Emrie nodded her understanding and tucked the note as deep into her pocket as it would go. If she was right about Taspin's intent to cause problems, then Noemi was about to reward Emrie for attending in her stead.

She found Noemi in her chambers, sitting on a cushion with a stylus in her hand and several piles of parchment scattered across her writing tray. The moment they were alone, Noemi turned on her.

"You foolish girl, what were you thinking?"

Emrie darted a glance at her sister's face, which was stiff and cold and not pleased at all. "I went in your stead," Emrie said and then licked her lips when Noemi frowned. "It seemed the honorable thing to do."

"Have you ever known me to miss an appointment?" Noemi's voice rose. "To fail our House's honor? Have you?"

"No, but—"

Noemi put the stylus down so hard it slammed against the stone table. Her eyes were narrowed with a stark line between them.

"I absented myself on purpose. Imjin has made a mess of things, and I'm keeping my distance."

"I'm so, so sorry," Emrie said quickly. "I didn't know. Taspin said—"

"Don't be a dimwit. Taspin is a Kolera. House Kolera hates us. She paraded you through the streets like a memorial to the Renoa for every House in the city to see. Half the balconies facing the Sovereign's House are filled with watchers. I doubt there's an interested party in Pol-Thiri that doesn't know my sister spoke alone with Imjin Flaust of Gir-Tosaq."

Emrie felt like one of the bugs the First Heir had scattered. She'd known none of this. She couldn't have known.

"We weren't alone," Emrie said, trying to defend herself just a little. "The servants were always there and Taspin. And the First Heir."

For a moment the room went still as if Noemi needed a moment to digest her words. Her eyes tightened even more as she stared at Emrie. When she finally spoke, her voice was low. "The First Heir joined you?"

"He seemed bored?" Emrie replied carefully.

"He wasn't." Noemi jumped to her feet. "I have to tell Father."

Then she was gone, leaving Emrie standing there unsure what to do. Eventually, Mati Dechta came by.

"Child, go to your rooms. It does no good to hold vigil here."

"I was foolish," Emrie replied.

"We know." Mati Dechta said it in a way that made Emrie feel like she'd not just disappointed her sister but the very walls of the House.

She left Noemi's rooms, going next in search of Ahrens. As she did, what burned within her was that same rubbing, damaging friction that she'd felt after Deriek had thought she was Brid. She'd have done whatever Noemi wanted if she'd just known what that was. How was she supposed to have known?

She found Ahrens hunched over a record book having to do with salt exports, and all her hurt and frustration focused on him. She dumped the note onto his book.

"You're going to end up causing problems. For yourself and for House Das. The First Heir is evil, Ahrens. Stay away from him and Imjin."

He gawked at her, eyes wide and blinking innocently.

"Look, I've read every one of the notes. They're harmless."

"Notes? How many have there . . . No, don't tell me. I don't want to know."

"I won't tell you, then." Ahrens shrugged and turned back to his book.

Sixteen

The Second Heir's prison seemed particularly gloomy that night. The walk up the final stairwell had a dampness that reminded Emrie too much of the gray frustration she'd felt all afternoon. How was she supposed to see the danger or know what to do if no one gave her any information?

She arrived at the prison, her feet dragging on the stone floor, reluctant to speak to Deriek. She was not in the mood for yet another difficult person.

He sat cross-legged on the blanket as had become his habit, and she laid out his meal without speaking.

"Did you figure out a bath for me yet?" he asked.

His gratitude was slipping. It was she who'd mentioned to him several nights prior that she was devising a bath, but of course, he'd turn it into something she owed him.

"Almost. Tomorrow." She finished and rose to her feet to go. She didn't feel like reading with him.

It struck her then that if she wanted to understand what she'd done wrong and how the hidden power structures in the world of the Firsts worked, the person most likely to tell her was right here.

She dared not ask.

"What's wrong, Piara?" he asked softly.

"Nothing. And stop calling me that." It was a knee-jerk response. She'd grown to like the nickname. It was something special she had all for herself. It also felt good to be the difficult one for once. The problem, though, was that he seemed to like it when she stood up to him. When he spoke, he was back to teasing.

"I'll stop if you'll say, 'Nothing, Deriek.' Although I won't believe that nothing. Your fists are clenched and usually you lay out my meal in an exact line."

His food was all shoved together in a pile. "For all that is wood and worthy, do you have to be observant, too?"

He chuckled.

It didn't help her mood, so she said the one thing she figured would shut him up. "Tell me why your brother locked you in here."

"How could you not know?"

She glowered at him for that. Of course, such knowledge would be common knowledge to everyone but her. Since he couldn't see her expression anyway, she gave up and sat down, relaxing her hands in her lap just so he'd notice.

"Tell me."

"What do the rumors say about my brother?"

She sighed but played along. "That you are the best of friends, but also the opposite. That he's afraid of being replaced."

Her lamp sat between them, and by its hazy light, she could see his lips tilt up. He did a half-lidded thing with his eyes. He didn't deny her, though, and curiosity got the best of her irritation.

"Is it true?"

"Yes. Do the rumors say why?"

"They don't."

"Thus, I have a single clue as to your identity," he said cheerfully. "Although I'd assumed as much already—you're not a First."

Meaning that all the Firsts of Pol-Thiri knew this already? It fit with what Brid had said about who learned recent history. Which was so unfair.

"Please, tell me about your brother, anyway."

"Since you asked politely, I suppose I will." His grin widened. "Since the day of my birth, he's wanted to kill me, just because he cannot. You see, I'm better than him at every aspect of life, family, sword, and court. He knows it. I know it. Everyone knows it. It makes him crazy. But as an Heir myself, I'm not easily killable, and as I'm careful to never beat him in a way that proves my superiority, he has no reason to challenge me directly. To take action otherwise would be to admit the truth of his own shortcomings, and he lacks the ability to do that."

He seemed to expect her not to understand what he was saying, but she did. What he'd just described was the truth of the unstated. Sage Jeminina even had a proverb about it, and Deriek's family didn't have a monopoly on such things. Her situation was not dissimilar. There was no question of who held the skill and talent and beauty in House Das. The difference was that Noemi also held the Status.

Emrie looked to Deriek. "The First Heir took no action until the Daughter of Gir-Tosaq arrived and preferred you to him."

"Yes, that seems to have pushed him over the edge."

"And do you want her affections?"

"No, I believe I don't."

Silly as it was, Emrie was glad.

"From what I've heard, she doesn't want the First Heir, either." Saying the words out loud made her wonder if that wasn't part of Imjin's attraction for the First Heir. That his interested was in antagonizing her.

"They say . . ." Emrie hesitated. She wanted more, but she also didn't want him to think about where she was getting her gossip from.

"Call me Deriek," he said with a humorous, calculating look in his eyes, "and I'll answer to whatever 'they' say."

Emrie still hesitated, but only for a moment because she wanted to know. "Deriek, they say the First Heir is so afraid of being replaced that he murders his mistresses rather than let them bear a child of his. And they say he'll murder the Daughter of Gir-Tosaq if she marries him. Is that true?"

"Yes." Deriek said the word so easily, so casually, it was a painful thing.

"How?"

"How does he do it? He strangles them and dumps them in the river. And not just his mistresses. He also kills any woman who attracts our father's attention, including his own mother. And likely mine."

Bile burned the back of Emrie's throat and she shuddered. "No one stops him?"

"No one dares. He chooses girls of little value. He pays their Houses richly to keep the balance. And he's First Heir."

SEVENTEEN

They said that back in the early days when the Renoa's canopy was too small to climb and worshippers sat on the ground with their backs to the trunk, the Renoa gave the priests two Laws for the good of the people—That which is freely given must be freely returned, and that which is taken by force must be returned five-fold.

People being people, the way to enact the Laws became complicated. How did one compensate five times a murder? How did one return a gift that was consumed? How did all of this function between family members and friends so closely tied that every interaction incurred a natural debt? To help Its people solve these problems, the Renoa created the Seat of Judgment, chose the First Sovereign to figure it all out, and added a third Law—That which is called of the Renoa can only be struck down by the Renoa.

Emrie knew the three Laws of the Renoa. Everyone did. They were the first words she'd learned to read and the pledge recited as part of most Ceremonies. The First Heir was riding between the first and the third Law as if they were donkeys, him with one foot on each back.

Emrie had also been taught the Renoa never broke Its own Laws. Its branches were fixed. So what did it mean that the Renoa had given responsibility to Emrie for the person second in line to inherit? Somehow this was all related to her responsibility. She wanted to know more.

Hoping to please Deriek, she put her efforts into conjuring his bath and picked a night to surprise him with it. She had the maties leave her one of the large basins used to carry the potted plants around the house. Into it, she placed fresh clothing and everything else he'd need. Then late that night she used chalk powder to draw a giant Juju bird around the basin. She was excited to show Deriek what she could do.

When she arrived at the prison, she handed him a thin rug and told him to unroll it within his side of the bars of the cell.

"What are we doing?" he asked.

"You'll see." It was hard to hide how much she wanted to please him with this. And that was separate from asking him more questions about his House.

Once he had the rug in place, she put her arm through the bars and touched the stitching. The witchcraft, as if as eager as her to show off, leapt for the chalk pattern back in her chambers. Between one blink of the eye and the next, the bathing tub and all its contents were before her.

Deriek scrambled out of the way.

"You could've warned me," he yelped.

"I brought you a bath," she said, unable to keep the glee of success from her voice. He'd reacted just as she'd hoped. "You'll have to unpack it. And here, place this stone at the bottom so I can fill it with water."

"The stone fills with water?" He sounded genuinely curious.

"No. You'll see."

He took the stone, and she reached into her pocket for a second one. It was much smaller than the others she'd used, palm-sized, square, and flat. This was one of her more ingenious ideas, and she and the witchcraft had practiced quite a bit to figure out how to make it work. She ran her finger over the pattern she'd carved and the sound of burbling water came out of the tub. She'd linked four patterns together. A stone currently sitting in the bottom of one of the bathing basins of House Das, the stone in the tub, the stone in her hand, and the stone she'd dropped into the river's muck. The one in her hand worked to start and stop the water moving between the others. The last she'd use to rid the tub of the dirty water when Deriek was finished.

"Well done," Deriek said, and maybe it was her imagination but there seemed to be awe in his voice.

Emrie flushed with pleasure. "I'll go sit outside. Call for me when you're finished, and I'll make the water leave."

"Just so."

She took a seat on the floor around the corner to listen to him bathe. He let out a sigh of contentment when he first got in and then made a funny-but-rude comment about her scented soaps. Even that pleased her, and she had the rather uncomfortable thought that the two good things in her life at this exact moment were him and the witchcraft.

It was an unexpected truth. Startling because she hadn't seen it coming. But it *was* true. Somehow, growing out of their conversations and daily visits, she'd come to like him. As a person. Perhaps even as a friend.

She hadn't meant it to happen. He should be someone so distant from her life that he didn't seem real, her sacrifices for him part of her loyalty to the Renoa and her House, not anything personal. But he *was* real, and different from how she'd originally thought of him. He was still pretentious and could be cutting, although he directed his sarcasm more at himself than her. Even when he mocked her and such, he was never truly unkind. Or at least not since the beginning, and she forgave him that as he hadn't been in good shape and she'd been busy being terrified. Since then, they'd developed a routine between them that felt every bit as comfortable as the one she had with Keeli and Lianjit. Maybe even more comfortable. She'd never touched their hair or prepared a bath for them. She'd never glowed at one of their compliments, either.

That thought led to the next natural one—outside of this prison any such connection was impossible and dangerous both for herself and her House. Nor had she forgotten the darkness she'd seen within him. It was still there. He just hid it better now.

Even with all that, she liked him, admired him even, and that was a rare and special thing.

He called out that she should return, and she found him standing next to the tub in his new clothing, his hair hanging lank around his head. He gave it a shake like a dog and then ran his fingers through it several times before turning to grin at her.

Emrie froze. Maybe it was the smile. Maybe it was seeing him clean and normal. Maybe it was the previous realization that he was no longer just her responsibility and duty. Maybe it was that the ends of his hair curled where they hit his shoulders, and she wished she could touch those curls that she'd created. Either way, what vined and grew through her was a deep-rooted embarrassment.

"I should've remembered a brush," she muttered.

"Alas, you aren't perfect," he said, his voice full of jest. "What a relief for the rest of us."

Emrie's face went red, and she was so, so glad he couldn't see behind her veil. She turned her attention to the stone in her hand and touched the pattern to send the water out to the river. Again, the witchcraft seemed eager to perform, and the tub was emptied faster than her traitorously full heart. She needed out of here before she did or said something she'd regret.

"Tell me about the witchcraft," he said, folding the damp towels into exact squares and placing them in the tub's bottom.

"There isn't much to tell." She glanced toward the exit door.

"Does it hurt you?"

"Hurt? No."

"How does it work?"

She hesitated, tucking her hands into her sleeves.

"You don't want to tell me."

"I don't." But of course, she wanted to tell him. She wanted him to see all that she'd learned and be impressed with what she could do. And she wanted to hear him laugh. His genuine laugh, the warm human one rather than his amused disdain. She wanted to understand him, because even if she liked him, she did not understand.

"I don't know. I'm just figuring it out, and it just works." Emrie took a step backward.

"I've made you uncomfortable," he said with a sigh. "I apologize. But don't leave. Stay for a while." He strode over to his usual place and beckoned her to hers. "Cleanliness has made me feel social, and you're the only one I have to bestow that gift upon. How is your friend in search of her mother? Any luck?"

Emrie's insides gave a little turn at him wanting her company. The wet of his hair gleamed, and Emrie's fingers twitched against her will. She reminded herself that she was his only option, that his desire for conversation wasn't personal, that thinking otherwise was a terrible idea. She answered anyway.

"My friend has had no luck so far. But she's determined."

"Determination is always a good quality. How about this? If you ask me nicely and call me by my Simple Name, I'll let you pester me with questions about my sordid history."

It was the single thing he might offer to get her to stay.

Which he likely realized. Emrie sat. "Fine. Deriek Costa Valiyard, Second Heir to—"

"Cheating," he said, his voice soft, teasing, and there was his smile again. "But I'll let you win. What do you want to know?"

"Why does your father not want you to inherit?"

His smile faded.

"I'm sorry," she said quickly, not wanting to ruin his mood.

"No. Don't be. You surprise me is all. A witch who performs miracles but doesn't know how. A girl with soft hands and a well-trained voice, who knows nothing of politics but wants an answer to the question everyone has spent my entire life trying to convince themselves doesn't exist."

He placed his palm on his thigh and began tapping out a rhythm with his fingers. He didn't look upset about her questions, though, more thoughtful.

"It starts with a story. I've always liked stories, don't you? This one's about a Sovereign, one with a problem. Everyone says he was a decent man. An honest Judge when in the Seat, dedicated to the Renoa, loyal to Pol-Thiri. But his problem overrode all that, and thus he solved it in the same creative manner he employed between the Houses and the Guilds and the disagreeing parties that came before him. You see, he had a son whose head was filled with demons and not the type that could be expelled with prayers to the Holy Renoa or treated with elixirs. These demons had the child pulling legs off rodents at two years old and skinning puppies at four. Everyone offered reasons for this. They said the child was spoiled. They said it was a nanny who taught the boy to disparage the Renoa and look to the old gods. They said the Sovereign's wife was secretly a witch."

Emrie flinched.

He smiled, this one wry, before continuing. "Either way, the boy's deeds became more and more horrendous. The Sovereign's Son was a danger who should never sit on the Seat of Judgment, but there is no way to involuntarily remove the inheritance from an Heir once born. So the Sovereign took matters into his own hands. He took a concubine, a foreign girl no one cared about."

"Your mother."

"Indeed, my mother." His gaze was unfocused, settled somewhere on the bars between them as if he were seeing the story unfold. His fingers still tapped an easy rhythm. "Cystel enjoyed killing. No creature was safe, and my father thought he'd never be able to resist murdering the helpless newborn that I was. Especially when my father impressed on Cystel that should my father be forced to pay recompense for any more dead dogs or servant's children, he would disinherit him in favor of me."

"But that can't be done. It's the one thing Sovereigns don't get to choose."

"True, but Cystel was nine. He wouldn't have known any better. My father planted the seed and waited for Cystel to kill me in some gruesome way that would force the Renoa to take action against him, rid Pol-Thiri of a potentially dangerous Judge, and free my father to produce another Heir."

Emrie gasped out loud.

"Don't feel badly on my account," he said, still tapping out a rhythm on his thigh. "I've lived with the fact that I was conceived to be murdered by my brother for a very long time. You have to admit, it's an elegant solution to an impossible situation."

"It's horrible." The words burst from Emrie's mouth with all the hurt and outrage he should've been expressing.

"That, too." He quirked his lips up.

"But your brother didn't kill you."

"No," he said, still with a voice full of good humor and calm acknowledgment. Tap, tap, tap. "My mother got to him first and explained the Law around Heirs and the rather small pieces the Renoa left behind of the person who broke it. She put fear into Cystel, and Cystel didn't kill me. He hates me though, and wants to kill me more than he wants pretty much anything else on this side of the Salt Sea. But he can't. Or at least he can't do it with his bare hands as he'd like."

"And your father?" Emrie asked, somehow knowing this was going to get worse rather than better.

"My father's obsession is the continuation of House Valiyard. Thus, he and I and Cystel are stuck in a rather ugly triangle. If either Cystel or I kill each other, we both end up dead, my father produces another Heir, and House Valiyard holds onto the Sovereigncy. Should we not deign to kill one another, Cystel someday inherits and uses the Seat to destroy our name along with Pol-Thiri."

Emrie saw the last leg of the triangle. "Or your father could kill Cystel, let the Renoa exact punishment upon himself, and then you'd inherit."

"Correct. But he won't do that."

"Why not? Maybe not right now, but what about right before his natural death?"

"Well, that's a possibility, but not likely. Partly because my brother won't be easy to kill at the best of times, and my father is already not the man he once was. Partly because should my father have decided on that path, he would've prepared me. There exists an entire library on the proper training of an Heir to the Judgment Seat, and I'm banned from it." The cheerful tone of his voice belied the pain of the words, but Emrie heard it anyway. The darkness he hid.

His tapping stopped.

"My father sees me as unworthy of the Seat of Judgment. He blames me for my mother ruining his plans. He hates that my blood is diluted by that of Vin-Yonekur. Most of all, he has any number of times asked me to goad my brother into killing me, and I always refused. He sees me as disobedient and disloyal."

The pleasantness in his voice never wavered, but she could see how false it was and her own heart slumped on his behalf. Emrie's hand gripped the stone in her pocket, and the witchcraft reacted as if questioning what she needed. Then she had another thought. One she couldn't ask him but would like to. What was her father doing involved in this mess?

Eighteen

The gongs for TreeFall struck on a morning Emrie was sitting on the Breakfast Patio watching Lady Sersi walk the Paths and trying to come up with a reason to approach her without it looking like she was courting. Not approaching felt like procrastination.

It had been several seven-days since Deriek had admitted the truth of his situation. Since then, he'd told her a new story every night. He said they came from his mother and the people of Vin-Yonekur. One was about a lizard at war with a hawk and another about a leopard whose spots turned blue when it got too close to the river. Each story had a moral that he made fun of but told her to take to heart. He seemed to have an endless supply of stories. She took to leaving as early as possible to be with him and staying as late as she dared.

It was, all over, a dangerous situation.

Usually, it was Lianjit who was prone to infatuations. Once or twice a year, she met a boy at Barrack's Practice she couldn't stop talking about. Two years ago, Emrie had taken a turn when one of Ahrens's friends caught her eye. Ahrens had been oblivious. At first, his friend had been as well, but then the boy started encouraging her and even once escorted her to the Marketplace. It'd been fun and awkward and nerve-racking. Right up until Noemi had noticed and pointed out that the boy was middle-ring and only after her for her connections. That had flattened Emrie's feelings entirely.

This thing with the Second Heir was like that. A crush. It too would pass.

She hoped.

When the first gong rang across the Field, it made the tea in Emrie's cup slosh over the lip, splashing her fingers and forcing her to put Deriek out of her mind, likely a good thing.

A string of equally loud gongs followed, and the ground and the house and everything else trembled. She dropped her cup to the table, tossed off her slippers, and bolted for the

Field to help with LeafFall. Lady Sersi, ahead of her, had her laptevi pulled up with both hands as she leapt over the grassy dividers between the Paths. This was the single moment each year when formality and etiquette got set aside.

The Renoa's leaves lost their silvery blue sheen the moment they hit the ground, and the leaves with sheen were the most useful. From the first gong, until the last leaf fell, the people of Pol-Thiri rushed to catch them.

Emrie arrived to see a leaf twirling and dancing its way down between the branches. She lined up underneath so that it settled on her palm. She breathed the Blessing-of-the-Air over it and then since the first leaf one caught was considered blessed, she sent a quick prayer of gratitude to the Renoa for Deriek's improvement. The leaves kept falling, and she collected as many as she could. The Paths of Wisdom and Virtue filled with running bodies as those nearest hurried out to help.

When Emrie's hands were full, she ran to one of the wooden caskets filled with oil. Once preserved, the leaves would be turned into dyes and inks and elixirs and other such commodities.

An increasing crowd of people lifted their hands and swayed like trees themselves as the Renoa bestowed Its Blessings on them one fragment of itself at a time. It was beautiful. And fun to see all these normally serious people hurrying about. Noemi arrived with Aunt Calys and her husband. Then the two uncles, Ahrens, and Brid, even though this wasn't her Renoa. Emrie never saw her father, but he would be here somewhere as well.

At times the leaves fell so quickly it wasn't possible to collect them all or to avoid stepping on those on the ground, and soon there were so many people that they were bumping into each other. Still, it was a joy. Even the Houses that disliked each other worked together for TreeFall. By the end, her arms ached, her feet hurt, and she was pleasantly exhausted.

That night she decided to be the one to tell Deriek a story for once. To tell him of her day. The Sovereign's House didn't participate in TreeFall, so likely he'd never experienced it. When she arrived, he was sitting bent forward with his forehead in his hand.

"Are you alright?" she asked as she'd never seen him so before.

"Fine," he muttered.

She laid out the food she'd brought. He waved her off when she tried to urge some lemon-honey tea on him and the most divine roasted squash covered in date sauce.

"It was LeafFall today," she said. "The most glorious LeafFall I've ever attended. Did you ever watch LeafFall or BarkFall or BranchFall from the Sovereign's House?"

He picked up a piece of wafer bread, bypassing all the delicacies.

"Deriek?"

He didn't respond and hadn't looked at her once since she'd arrived. It was unlike him. "Is something wrong?"

"No. Just go. I'm tired." He gave a half-cough behind his hand.

"Are you certain something isn't wrong?" she knew she sounded worried, but she couldn't help it. And not just because she'd picked up an infatuation. He was still her duty. "I'd help if there was a problem."

He looked up then. Abruptly. So much so that she felt pinned by his fierce gaze. "Like the hawk ignoring the chattering wren, maybe I just don't feel like socializing with empty-headed young girls at this exact moment. Has that not occurred to you?"

Emrie flushed, stung, and took several steps backward.

"I see." But she didn't. If something was wrong, she needed to know.

Then she had another thought. The Renoa had said to do what her father asked. Her father had asked her to learn the witchcraft, but she hadn't come up with a new way to use it. Not since his bath really. Not since she'd gotten distracted by worrying about her infatuation. If this lack was causing his sudden change, then she needed to learn more of the witchcraft to make him better once again. It was time to force herself to go to House Sersi.

***

The note Emrie carved to Lady Sersi was flowery but simple, offering a Blessing on the House and requesting an invitation to visit. A reply came back immediately. Much too soon, Emrie was on her way.

She wouldn't court House Sersi. She'd be polite and noncommittal and bring up Lady Sersi's morning devotions to see if it might open the conversation to the witchcraft. As Emrie walked over, she practiced several approaches to avoid thinking about how badly she didn't want to do this.

House Sersi was not quite inner-ring, and thus it was smaller than what Emrie was used to. The walls were still white, the front door carved wood, the hallway inside strewn with fine carpets.

She was shown to a small courtyard with a raised dais for receiving guests. There waited no less than fifteen women, all staring at her.

Emrie faltered for a moment, thought of Deriek again and that she *had* to do this, and searched for the Lady of the House. Lady Sersi stood up.

"Welcome, Daughter of Das."

Up close, Lady Sersi had a square, kindly face, her piles of braids woven with the silver of age. She had small wrinkles around her eyes and mouth that appeared to be from too much smiling. All of which was encouraging. Still, there was no way Emrie could bring up the witchcraft in front of all these people. While she and Lady Sersi went through the back and forth of a greeting ceremony, Emrie hunted for an excuse to get her alone.

Once done, Lady Sersi invited Emrie to sit in the circle of women. Emrie did and complimented the House and the proffered food and the cushions and all the other expected things. She was starting to think she might manage the situation without embarrassing herself when the rug to the interior of the house was pulled aside and a boy joined them.

Not what Emrie wanted to happen.

"Lanka Sersi," Lady Sersi said, introducing him with not a small amount of maternal pride, "First Son of House Sersi. Lanka, please join us."

He was tall, and his hair was braided but messy as if he'd just removed a cap. His face was too long to be handsome, but he had blunt intelligence in his eyes. He also looked unhappy to be there.

Emrie knew how he felt. A flush of heat so strong she wished she had a fan worked its way up her chest and neck. She knew the other women saw it. There was a general murmuring and several of the women flashed her approving smiles. They thought she liked him, although she was actually mortified. Keeli had said nothing about the Sons of Houses being paraded for her inspection.

Lanka sent her a disapproving glance as if he'd looked her over and found her unappealing. Which should've been insulting, but Emrie was relieved. Maybe this wouldn't be so bad.

"Our Lanka is very dedicated to the Soils Guild," one woman said, her voice full of admiration. "So dedicated we have to pull him away from the beds by force or he forgets to eat. He doesn't just maintain the soil of the growing fields, either, he's working with the Growers Guild to experiment and provide richer flavor in our foods."

"That's impressive," Emrie managed to get out.

"He attends Barrack's Practice every morning," another woman said, eager to get her compliments in. "He's very strong."

"And devoted to the Holy Renoa," a third added.

Emrie wanted to curl up and die. Lanka Sersi turned stony. At least he wasn't enjoying this either.

"Lanka, tell her about the growing beds here at the House," another woman said.

"The most valuable soil is kept here where it can be watched over," he said almost curtly.

"House Sersi is very dedicated," Emrie murmured.

Several of the other women launched into descriptions of how right Emrie was. Lanka shot his mother an annoyed glance so blatant there was no way a single person present didn't miss it. Lady Sersi excused him not long after. As he left, Emrie got an idea of how to get Lady Sersi alone. Emrie turned to face her.

"I'd love to see the beds where you grow the soil. There are some here at the House?"

"But, of course." Lady Sersi rose to her feet with a pleased smile. No one else moved, which was what Emrie had hoped would happen.

The Soil Garden was four to five times the size of the courtyard she'd been received in. It was open to the sky and had water running from one side to the other, but not on the ground. Instead, it ran in canals between rows and rows of white-bricked beds.

"The larger growing beds are nearer the river," Lady Sersi explained. "These are the experimental beds where we are mixing different feeds for the worms."

"Worms?" Emrie asked as if she were interested while trying to figure out how to work the conversation around to where she wanted it to go.

"Worms being underground creatures that dwell among roots, they live closer to the Renoa than any other creature but birds." She dug her fingers into the nearest bed and lifted a handful of soil. It appeared light like cotton, and she stirred it with her opposing index finger to show Emrie. "See? A worm."

It was small, four times the width of a sewing needle and twice as long with a pleasant blue color.

"Impressive," Emrie said, hoping that was an appropriate compliment.

"These worms are the pride of House Sersi," Lady Sersi said, her voice composed. "It's the best we have to offer."

Oh no.

Exactly what Emrie didn't want to hear, but rather than a sense of panic, what hit her was disappointment. Lanka hadn't liked Emrie at all so any encouragement on Lady Sersi's part meant she was only interested in Emrie's Status.

Since Lady Sersi was being upfront, acting like a decent person, and Emrie had little left of pride to lose, she decided to speak plainly.

"I requested this visit for a reason other than seeking a marriage contract."

Lady Sersi frowned. Emrie placed her hand on the edge of the nearest planter, nervous. The dirt inside wasn't still. The soil murmured with the soft rustling of the creatures below.

Emrie removed her hand. "I've something to ask you. I'm going to trust you, and I hope you understand I offer you the greatest of respect in doing so." That all came out well.

"Of course, Daughter Das."

Emrie took a deep breath. "I see you sometimes, in the Renoa's Field. I see you walking the Paths."

"We owe our lives to the Holy Renoa," she said simply. "Are you also devout?"

"Of course," Emrie said quickly. "But that's not it. I see you out there and something happens."

"I see." There was no inflection in Lady Sersi's voice as she said the words, but that seemed to hint at an invitation. Or at least enough of one that Emrie felt buoyed.

"I feel it. You do something other than perform devotion." Emrie hesitated, but then decided in for a paw, in for the whole dog. That was something Deriek had said as part of one of his stories. "I feel it in my fingers."

The sound of the worms rustling filled the space between them. Emrie swallowed audibly. "Will you tell me what you are doing when you walk?"

"No, dear." Lady Sersi said it with all the motherly bearing of Keeli. "Have you told your father?"

It was such an about-face to what had seemed Lady Sersi's previous encouragement that it took Emrie a moment to respond. Also, her father was the last person she could approach. He'd already made himself clear on this topic.

"About seeing you? No. I've told no one."

"Thank you, dear, your discretion is appreciated. But I meant have you told your father about your fingers? Is House Das so diminished that such goes neglected?"

She was asking why Emrie hadn't had the witchcraft removed yet, but Lady Sersi had said it in such a way as to insult House Das, which made Emrie stiffen.

"It's not that. There's a plan. Of course, there's a plan, but it hasn't been implemented yet. And my family is under a great deal of stress. I don't want to burden them."

Lady Sersi crossed her arms over her chest, looking unconvinced.

"I see. Child, you need to speak to your father about this, not me."

"Of course, I do. But I also want to understand. Is what you are doing also witchcraft and—"

Lady Sersi shook her head, a mother remonstrating a naughty child.

"You mustn't speak so. It's dangerous and not helpful. But no. It's not that which you mentioned. It's guildcraft, and I won't speak of it to you. You need to go to your father. He'll know just how to get help for you with yours."

It was such a frustrating answer and Emrie didn't want to give up. Guildcraft was a term used for the work and creations of the Guilds. Emrie'd never heard it linked to anything witchery before.

"Are you saying guildcraft is also witchcraft, because—"

"Not a word more." Lady Sersi's voice hardened, and she put her hand up to cut off Emrie's words.

But Emrie needed to know. To help Deriek. Because Lady Sersi did understand what they spoke about, and Emrie had no other options.

"Consider well," Lady Sersi continued, "that you've given me something to use against you."

Which startled the breath right out of Emrie.

"Use against me? What do you mean?"

Lady Sersi said nothing. Just looked at Emrie as if she were being very, very stupid.

Which made things suddenly, uneasily clear.

"You're saying you could use my questions to force me to marry your son?"

She smiled. It wasn't motherly or even friendly this time. It was the smile of a Head of House.

"He has little interest in marriage to you, but in terms of the balance of the branches, I won't forget that the tree bends my direction."

Nineteen

One of Deriek's stories had been about a child who'd found the prettiest little rabbit down by the river. The child chased the rabbit until they were both lost to the child's caretaker. The child hadn't worried, not with such a glorious rabbit in sight. The rabbit led the child into a swampy area of the river where the rabbit hopped from tuft of grass to tuft of grass, keeping out of the muck. The child tried to do the same but was too heavy and sank into the mud and was eaten by a giant eel. That child in the moment it realized its mistake was how Emrie felt after leaving House Sersi.

Lady Sersi was a First. She'd be just as involved in the Status fights as the other Firsts. Why had Emrie overlooked that? Because she'd seemed nice?

Emrie'd been a fool.

Again.

And she hadn't found a new way to help Deriek.

She decided to tell him. He already knew about the witchcraft, and if he didn't have any ideas on what Lady Sersi had said, maybe he'd at least think her problems humorous and cheer up that way.

When she arrived, he wasn't in his usual spot.

"Don't be difficult tonight. I've had a horrible time of it today."

No response, not even a whisper of movement or the sound of him purposefully trying to remain motionless to scare her.

Fear tickled the back of her throat. His cell felt empty. As if he was gone.

She put the pail down and lifted the cloth from the lamp to shine it from one end of the cell to the other. The door of the bars was shut as always. The rug she'd used to move the tub was still rolled up next to the stone for the odor.

"Deriek, this isn't funny."

Still nothing. She stepped closer to the bars, trying to get her small light to reach the back corners. His blanket had been strewn haphazardly across the ground. And there, finally, she spotted a dark shadow against the back wall, unmoving.

Emrie grabbed the bars of the door, shaking it so it rattled.

"Deriek? Wake up."

Silence. She remembered suddenly his talk of his life being worthless and his earlier request for a Jeibel Knife. What if he'd hurt himself? What if it was too late? She was trapped on her side of the bars, and he his.

The panic of it hit with a thud as if a book or a brick had been thrown from the sky to land square on her chest. This could not be happening. He belonged to her. She'd improved his life. She'd become his friend. She'd learned to use the witchcraft to the best of her ability. She'd done everything she could think of.

That last thought interrupted her panic, and she got an idea. The Renoa had implied the witchcraft was supposed to help. She knew how it could.

She rushed to the rug and shoved it through the bars, laying it out flat and smooth. Now all she had to do was figure out how to create a pattern on her side large enough to hold herself. The pattern she used to bring his pail of food and water was too small. Experimenting with the witchcraft had shown her that it would cut off anything that hung over the edges of the pattern.

She had nothing with her to draw a new pattern. No chalk or thread or paint. For a moment, she considered laying out his food in a shape on the floor, but that wasn't a creation and she'd never once felt the witchcraft respond when she'd laid out his food before. She held up her hand, staring at her fingers which tingled not at all, and begged for help from That-Which-Is-Life.

Use your life.

The words made no sense, and she was pretty sure they'd come from her own frantic mind rather than the Renoa, but then she had another thought.

Emrie shoved off her overdress, a shock of cold pushing through the thinner fabric of her laptevi. She ignored it and felt around for the sapphire brooch pinned at her waist. She used the pin to prick her finger and then dabbed the blood on the ground to draw a pattern. It wasn't easy. Each prick provided so little blood that she spent more time squeezing the injury and pricking additional fingers than she did drawing, and it hurt. But when she finally connected the end of the pattern to the beginning, she knew it would work. The witchcraft tingled, excited, concerned, searching to know where she wanted to connect. Emrie stepped into the center and traced the pattern with her sore, battered fingertip, and the witchcraft leapt away. One moment she was bent over her bloody pattern, the next she was on the blanket.

There wasn't time to think of what she'd just done, let alone feel a sense of pleasure or accomplishment. She rushed over to Deriek and gave his shoulder a hard shake.

"If you're playacting, I'm going to kill you." When he didn't respond, she tangled her fingers in his hair and pulled.

He moaned.

Relief the width of a thousand rivers flooded her body. He wasn't dead.

She ran the light over him. He lay hunched over his middle, his arms underneath. She tried again to push his shoulder, putting the lamp down and using both hands and all her strength. This time he fell sideways, and she went with him, landing half on top. He moaned again. It turned into a weak hacking cough. His skin burned as if he sat outside at noonday. He was ill.

"Why didn't you tell me?" she choked out.

Because he still wanted to die.

In that moment, it felt like he was standing in front of that door with the rug half-pulled. "I won't let you do this," she said loud enough that the sound echoed. "You're mine and you'll live."

There wasn't time to return to House Das and beg Mati Dechta for the Renoa-blessed ointments and medicines she kept for illness. Even if there were, going to Mati Dechta would require an explanation she couldn't provide. If she were going to keep him from pulling that rug back all the way, she had to heal him now. At once. With witchcraft.

She grabbed the warming blanket, draping it over him and herself. She tried to pull him up so that he rested against her, but she wasn't strong enough, so she laid down behind him, sliding one arm under and one arm over his body. He was so hot it felt like hugging a furnace box filled with branches fresh-shed from the Renoa. She pulled aside his laptevi to touch his skin, wrapping him in her arms and, she hoped, her witchcraft. She whispered the five Blessings aloud. One to the sun. One to the air. One to the water. One to the earth. One to That-Which-Is-Life. Then she traced a pattern on his bare flesh. Both hands at once, hoping the witchcraft would understand that she wanted to move the illness and not anything else of importance.

Her fingers skimmed the solid feel of his skin. She traced his ribs, feeling the outline as she built her pattern.

She whispered as she touched, "Live, Deriek. I insist you live. Live, Deriek."

Her words became a pattern all of their own, and the oddest thing happened. The witchcraft didn't jump. It settled. As if her fingers were pushing past his skin and tissues and deep into his self.

"Live, Deriek. I insist you live," she chanted. She sensed somehow the illness—fat red splotches of angry inflammation that didn't belong. She told the witchcraft to circle them and send them to the rock she'd left buried in the river where they'd do no harm. It worked, but there was a lot of illness and as she pulled it out, the empty holes refilled with more angry splotches. The witchcraft couldn't keep up. Her eyes filled with tears at the futility.

"Please, help me."

An image popped into her mind. Of the Renoa Tree in the Season of Water, the thick branches, the wide trunk, the afternoon rain falling onto Its vast canopy. She saw what looked like her own pattern of a Juju bird made up of the turns and crisscrossings of the branches, the long tail of feathers was her favorite branch. She felt the pattern call to her through the witchcraft. She called back, and suddenly under her fingers, Deriek was flooded with the Tree's own heart blood.

"He must live," she said, changing her chant in the hopes the Renoa heard.

What felt like hours passed as Emrie removed the illness and the Renoa filled the gaps. Vaguely, she was aware of chilled air on her back, her fingers cramping as they continued to build pattern upon pattern upon pattern on his chest, her lips going stiff with the repeated words.

At some point, the Renoa's heart blood slowed. Her fingers stilled. Her hands fell limp. She was too exhausted to make even one more pattern, but his chest rose and fell. He was alive.

"Thank you," he whispered, his voice as hoarse as it had been when she'd first met him. "But you shouldn't have done that."

***

Deriek lay in the dark for a long time before he had the strength to right himself. He felt weak as a new calf and when he pushed himself up, his arms trembled. He needed more sleep, but he could feel the girl shivering behind him, and he couldn't let that be.

When he'd recovered enough strength to do so, he spread the warming blanket before them and half carried, half rolled her onto one side. He lay down next to her and pulled the blanket around to enclose them both. It was the best he could do.

He should be furious with her. He'd made a choice, and she'd taken that from him, just as every other person stole his choices at every step of his life.

In the moment, all he could manage was a grudging appreciation. Which made him frown as he wrapped his arms around her and pulled her back against his chest, ignoring a ripple of cold as he did so.

He had no idea what she'd done, but she'd burned herself into him somehow, healing him and giving him strange visions of climbing in the Renoa. And, if she was real, making him realize what a gift she was.

It wasn't a new thought. He'd fought it often enough lately as he'd found himself unable to press her too hard for information.

He enjoyed their nights together. She was intelligent and thoughtful and funny. She saw his humor for what it was, which very few people ever did, and she only let him push her so far.

The room was dark, her lamp long since faded. Lying next to her still form, it was apparent she'd paid for her actions. He couldn't hold her generosity against her.

He turned his head to rest his cheek against her hair. She smelled of flowers, and he was reminded of being a young child and watching his mother's maties pour steaming, scented water from a jug to rinse her hair. His mother hadn't ended up being real, rather just one more person using him for her own aims. He smiled darkly at the thought.

With the tilt of his lips, something else moved as well. A tiny shift. One that wouldn't have been noticeable if he wasn't laying so still and so tired. He was aware suddenly of the beat of her heart against his chest, the feel of life under her skin where his hand cupped hers, the slow rise and fall of her breath. And he adjusted his own to match.

Such a small thing. So innocuous. So unexpected. He gripped his arms around her, holding her tight. She sighed, and the sound seemed too loud. He was suddenly too warm. Too close to her. Too defenseless.

He'd never even seen her face.

For just a moment he considered the possibility, the what-if of letting this moment seed and sprout and entwine them both in its branches. He released one hand to push back her veil. He traced the angle of her jaw, the slant of her cheekbone, the curve of her nose and lips. Learning the look of her by touch.

What if he were a normal member of Pol-Thiri society? What if he was allowed a life and House? What if he wasn't standing on a broken tree limb ready to drop from underneath him at any moment? What if he hadn't been betrayed so many times before?

What if she never betrayed him?

He thought of the window, high on the wall. This moment was a voice telling him there was a ladder he couldn't see but if he climbed it anyway, he'd find the bars disappeared.

He pulled back from touching her face. Bars didn't disappear. Everybody lied. Everyone used him. He had to protect himself, and the best he could hope for in this situation was endlessly staring at the sky until the sun went away and he was left facing the dark again and again and again.

***

Emrie woke with a start. The ground under her was hard, but she was comfortable anyway. She could hear Deriek breathing, so he was still alive. At some point, they'd reversed their positions, and he was now behind her; two birds wrapped in a nest of warm blanket. No one had held her so since she was a child. The closest she could think of was years ago her father pulling her against his chest at the edge of the fishpond to keep her from falling in at her excitement over watching the fish, but this wasn't like that. This was different.

Good different.

His breath came in a steady rhythm against the back of her neck. His body warmed hers at every point where they touched. There was a strength in how he held her that made her feel secure and grounded. He smelled like the Sacred Grasses of the Renoa's Field in spring. Life and renewal and the newness of a morning. Or perhaps he smelled like the Renoa Tree itself.

She'd be happy to lay pressed up against him for the rest of forever.

His fingers twitched where they were wrapped tight around her middle. He was dreaming. She wondered if he dreamed of her.

The motion also reminded her that she *couldn't* stay forever. Letting herself think these things or enjoy his nearness went against everything she knew and understood.

She pushed back the blanket to look outside. The room was still dark, but the barest of shadows on the wall said dawn was coming. She still had to get around the edge of the Renoa's Field and back home before there was too much sunlight to give her away. She eased away from him.

Her lamp had died at some point, but even without it, she found the rug. She centered herself on it and touched the embroidered pattern. The witchcraft answered in its now-familiar way. It asked, with a sense of concern, where she wanted to go. To the blood pattern on the other side of the bars? Or to the chalk drawing in her own rooms she'd once used to move the tub?

Emrie wouldn't have thought there was enough chalk pattern left for the witchcraft to find, but the offer was clear in her mind. With deep thanks to the witchcraft, she chose the chalk and her room.

TWENTY

Maybe it was her exhaustion or maybe the faded pattern, but this time the jump wasn't smooth. Emrie arrived in the chamber that held her clothing with a shove, as if the witchcraft pushed her forward between the shoulder blades to keep her going. She fell to her knees and would've sat there recovering only she heard booted, limping steps coming from her sleeping chamber. Since she'd barely spoken to her father outside of House functions, and she couldn't remember the last time he'd entered her rooms, this couldn't be good.

Emrie pushed herself up, made a halfhearted effort to straighten her laptevi, and stepped forward.

"Father." Her voice was hoarse and raw from her hours of chanting.

He stopped his pacing and looked her over top to bottom. His lips were down-turned in disapproval, but that was normal.

"Is something amiss?" she asked, clearing her voice as best she could.

"I don't want to know what you've been up to this night, is that clear?" He placed a hand on the metal post of her sleeping dais, wrapping his fingers around it like it was a sheathed sword.

"Yes, Father."

"My Second Daughter seems to have taken it upon herself to demean our House in every way."

Emrie took a step back at the vehemence in his voice.

"I'd never do that."

"You deny that you publicly aligned yourself with the Daughter of Gir-Tosaq?" The words were as much threat as question.

Emrie wanted to argue. To insist it'd only been that one time, and it'd all been Taspin's fault. But surely Noemi would've told him all that already. She ducked her head.

"I'm so sorry. I didn't mean to bring dishonor."

"That's not the worst of it, is it?" he said as if she hadn't spoken. "You courted the Son of an Eleventh-ring House that is tied to both the First Adviser and even more so the Seventh Adviser. Both of whom saw your actions as House Das trying to undermine their own relationships." He didn't quite shout the last words, but it was close. She could see the outline of the tendons in his wrist where he gripped the canopy post.

"I didn't do any of that," she whispered.

"You deny you went to House Sersi?" He spat the words.

Emrie took a second, tentative step backward.

"Do not leave this room."

"I wasn't . . . I just . . ." She couldn't find the words to explain, and her whole body trembled. Gods, what had she done? Keeli hadn't warned her about any of this, and she'd had no idea.

"You deny it?"

"I went there," Emrie answered quickly, trying to pacify him. "But I told Lady Sersi I wasn't courting. I wanted to talk to her, and I didn't know anyone would think anything of it. Noemi kept telling me I was too young for courting, and that no one would take me attending banquets or such seriously."

He didn't look appeased. "Why for all that grows did you go to House Sersi?"

Emrie hesitated. She'd told Lady Sersi she wouldn't betray what she'd seen and even more, her father had made it clear he didn't want to know about the witchcraft. She went with the next best explanation.

"I went for Brid."

"Brid?" He spat the name as if it tasted bad on his tongue. "Pray tell me what Brid needs from House Sersi?"

"It isn't what she needs. It's that she made a request of Keeli, Lianjit, and me. She came to Pol-Thiri in search of her past. The mother of her birth, to be exact. We thought House Sersi was a possibility."

Emrie wouldn't have thought it possible for her father to get any more upset, but he did. The gauzy canopy over her sleeping dais rustled with the tension in his hand.

"You fools. You entire group of fools. This is why no one trusts Seconds."

"That's not fair. If there were reasons we shouldn't have searched for Brid's mother, no one told us."

Her father rushed her. One moment she was standing in the middle of the room, trembling at his anger but also wanting to defend herself and her friends who hadn't meant harm. Then he was there. Hand raised. Palm open as it connected with her face.

Emrie flew sideways, knocked off her feet. Her head slammed to the tile floor.

For a flicker of a moment, the room went dark as if the lamps had all been gutted. She scrambled trying to figure out what had happened. She briefly considered she might be back with Deriek, curled under the warming blanket in his embrace. Only she wasn't warm and fat tears pooled behind her clenched eyelids. She heard the off-cadence thuds of her father's footsteps coming closer and memory returned. The air in her lungs went wet and heavy, like a blanket doused in water, and she sobbed just once to clear her throat enough to breathe.

No one had hit her before, never. She wanted to tell her father that. To remind him she'd always been a dutiful child. She'd rarely even been scolded, and when she had, she'd fallen all over herself in apology and determination not to repeat her error. How could he not remember?

She heard the rustle of cloth and then felt a hand on her hair giving one braid a tug. She cracked an eye to see him sitting on the floor next to her. It would've been hard on him to get down. His hip didn't bend well, and he rarely sat on anything except benches.

"Emrie, I'm sorry," he said quietly. "I shouldn't have lost my temper. I shouldn't have struck you."

Emrie pressed the heel of her fist into her chest, fighting to hold herself together. His apology made everything that much worse. He knew who she was and hadn't cared. She clenched her eyes shut again. The tears leaked out the edges and her nose dripped. She kept her head down and shifted so she could cry into her sleeve. She didn't want him to see her face.

"You've been a good daughter helping with your project, but our family is in danger, and confusing the situation by courting or asking awkward questions on behalf of our houseguest makes for more danger. I tell you with certainty that Brid isn't the Daughter of House Sersi nor any of the other Houses of the Rings. She is Das. Her or you or your friends suggesting otherwise hurts all we've worked for."

Emrie said nothing, but in a weird, distant way, she finally felt the sting where his hand had connected. Slowly, slowly the entire left side of her face burned.

"Do you understand what we are fighting for?" His voice increased in intensity. "What we stand to lose?"

The throb wasn't just about her face. A matching bruise beat a sore spot on her insides, too. If Brid's secret was so important, why hadn't he warned her? Why didn't any of them ever think to include her?

When she didn't answer, he continued, "We're in danger of losing Noemi." His voice changed again. His words were protective, anxious, and proud. A father speaking of the daughter of his heart.

And that was the answer to her questions. Her father was fond of her, but only in the same way he was fond of his birds and fish and tame gazelle. It was another slap. Another truth. Emrie opened her eyes. His gaze was on her, intense, focused, but it wasn't for her own value. He wanted to impress upon her Noemi's. The hand that had struck her was on the ground beside him.

"The First Heir wants Noemi," he continued. "He has for years."

"Thus, Imjin's to be sacrificed instead?" The words were soft, unforceful, and she wasn't really talking about Imjin.

"Would you see your sister dead?" he snarled back, the anger returned as if Emrie were the enemy. "All of us gone? The House given to another?"

"Of course not, but—"

"Then pray daily to the Renoa that the Daughter of Gir-Tosaq accepts the First Heir and gives us time." He took a deep breath to calm himself and lowered his voice. "Already the First Heir envisions plots by those trying to help the Daughter of Gir-Tosaq escape him. Do you see, Emrie, why you must remain quiet, unproblematic, available when needed, and otherwise outside of what Noemi and I do?" He reached over to tug on her braid again. He used the same hand that he'd hit her with. "Please, Emrie, trust that what we ask of you has purpose and is for all our benefit. You've always been a good Daughter."

She didn't want to hear it. She didn't want him to pat her head but rather pull her into his arms. She wanted him to tell her she was valued, too. That he cared about her future and talents and promise. She wanted him to trust her, the way he did Noemi. He'd never even explained his purposes with Deriek, just given her the charge.

She didn't know how to say that and doubted that if she did, he would hear her anyway. There was one thing that he had to know, though, and she said it carefully, not wanting to antagonize him more.

"Brid won't give up her search. Maybe if you spoke to her, told her who her mother was . . ."

He looked pained at that and ran his hand, not the one that had hit her, over his shorn head.

"I'll ask Noemi to have a word."

***

Emrie pretended nothing was wrong when Mati Sarta and Mati Ereana came to her sometime later. She said she'd tripped in the dark and slammed into the metal edge of her sleeping dais to explain her bruise. She laughed at her own clumsiness for their benefit, then let them dress her and send her off to the Breakfast Patio.

The birds sang as usual, but the sound hurt her ears. She was starving after her night healing Deriek, but the food had no luster. And the tea was too chilled; she had to send a matie for an overdress as she couldn't stop shivering. While she waited, she stared dully at the Renoa while not having any idea what she should think or feel or do now.

So, of course, Brid showed up.

"You told Noemi I was looking for my mother. Why?" Brid's brow was furled, but not in anger, rather as if she were trying to undo a complicated knot. Did everything have to be about Brid?

Brid sat down across from her.

"What happened to your face?"

"I tripped," Emrie said in a monotone.

"Sorry to hear it. I'm glad you told Noemi about my quest."

At least Emrie didn't have to explain about her throbbing cheek. Having been polite about it, Brid seemed much more interested in her own issues. As usual.

"I'm not angry with you," Brid continued. "Noemi is going to help me. She thinks it's a delightful task. Those were her exact words—a delightful task."

Which made no sense at all considering what her father had said.

"I see." Emrie rubbed at her forehead, too tired to think about it. She listened while Brid chatted about how wonderful Noemi was beneath her stiff exterior. When Brid finally left and Mati Dechta returned with Emrie's overdress, Emrie still couldn't quiet her soul-deep chill.

"You were foolish again, child," Mati Dechta said, examining her cheek.

"Not intentionally."

"That's the inherent definition of the word foolish."

Emrie looked down at her lap.

"You will heal. Now go walk the Paths. Offer penance for your foolishness. Find balance. It will make you feel better if nothing else. The walls of the House still stand."

Emrie nodded with no intention of following orders. But then once Mati Dechta was gone, Emrie took off her sandals, left the overdress behind, and walked onto the Renoa's Field anyway.

With all three parts of TreeFall over, the Renoa was laid bare, a massive twisting of raw white wood striking skyward. Almost no one but the priests went into It once It shed Its leaves and bark and excess branches, and Emrie didn't make a conscious decision to do so herself. But walking the Paths of Wisdom and Virtue felt right and that was where they led.

She didn't climb far, settling on a lower branch that was wide enough for an ox and cart and thus much safer. She hadn't the energy to take a proper devotional pose either and instead curled on her side, pulling her knees into her chest, tucking her bare toes into her laptevi, resting her injured cheek against the cool, smooth wood, and pulling her cowl over her head.

She didn't want to think about her father anymore, and she didn't feel up to thinking about Deriek, but her mind drifted around those topics anyway. She let it wander as if she were walking the branches around and up and out and back. She remembered the conversation ages ago with Deriek about Brid. He'd said that the interesting question wasn't who Brid's mother was, but why a person would want to hide that information.

Why did her father want to hide it?

If her father knew the truth of Brid's birth then it seemed likely Noemi did as well, which meant Noemi wasn't helping Brid but playing some kind of game.

It all came back to Brid.

Why would her father be so bothered by Emrie's questioning of Brid's parentage that he erupted so brutally? Because that was what had caused it. Not the mishap with Imjin or that Emrie had visited House Sersi. He'd been angry at both, but it was Brid's quest that had caused the violence. Brid was important.

Emrie pictured him speaking, heard his voice again almost as if he were there. *I tell you with certainty that Brid isn't the Daughter of House Sersi nor any of the other Houses of the Rings. She is Das. Her or you or your friends suggesting otherwise hurts all I've worked for.*

Emrie repeated the words several times, mouthing them to herself. He'd given something away there. He'd suggested Brid was entirely Das, meaning her mother was a member of House Das as well as her father. For that to be true and for Brid to have been born in Pol-Thiri, then Aunt Calys would've had to have birthed her, which seemed unlikely. Aunt Calys was much too old. Even more, if Brid was Aunt Calys's child, why the explosion from her father? Such a truth might be embarrassing or hurtful, but it wouldn't be dangerous.

The second possibility settled over Emrie like a gentle falling from the branches above as if there were still leaves to drift down and cover her. Her father had said Brid wasn't a Daughter of any of the other Houses of the Rings. Is she also wasn't fully part of House Das . . .

Only four types of people weren't part of the rings—the priests, the Sages on the rare occasion there was one, the River Nomads, and the family that lived in the single House within the Renoa's Field itself.

Emrie shoved herself up, staring aghast past the bareness of the branches to the city-oasis beyond.

It seemed crazy. Ridiculously crazy. It was probably wrong. She'd never been good at puzzling through the doings of her father.

It also explained everything.

If Brid was a Third Heir that her father had hidden away since her birth, then Emrie, by admitting to the search for Brid's mother, had been working to leak the secret.

Was it possible then?

Brid and the First Heir had the same oafish, bluntness about them, and they looked alike, tall and square and all Pol-Thirian.

Emrie turned the idea over, trying it like a key in every lock she could think of, and it fit.

Which still proved nothing.

But then she felt a small murmur of assent come from the Renoa itself. Not a sound, not a feeling, but a sensation. Bark against skin. Brief, but real.

Yes.

Twenty-One

When Emrie returned to House Das, she felt less in balance than when she'd left. She didn't know what to do with what she'd been given and wasn't even sure she was meant to do anything. The Renoa hadn't given any instructions or even asked any questions this time. It almost felt as if It just wanted her aware of the truth.

There wasn't time to do more than recognize this as a matie waited with a message that she was to attend Noemi. Emrie wanted to refuse, but manners overcame the desire. She found Noemi in her private garden.

Noemi appeared not to notice her or perhaps she was ignoring her again, so Emrie walked over to stand in front of her, forcing Noemi to look up. Her gaze went straight to the bruise on Emrie's cheek. She raised her elegantly arched eyebrows in disapproval. Then the look was gone and when Noemi spoke, her voice was practical.

"The Renoa was a good choice. It makes you appear devout and that can't but help the situation. Yes, Father told me what happened, don't look so miserable. I won't yell at you, although I've no doubt he did. If it helps, he once yelled at me for doing something foolish as well. Sit down, Emrie. The world isn't ending this very moment. You aren't so important that this can't be fixed. Father and I have decided on a course to do so."

There was a metal bench with an amethyst-colored cushion opposite Noemi. Emrie took it, not sure if she should be relieved or alarmed.

"There's only one way to solve the mess you created with House Sersi. You must court in earnest."

Emrie shot to her feet, definitely alarmed.

"I said, 'Sit down,'" Noemi said in a tone so mild it made the command all that much more forceful.

Emrie sat. "I have no desire to marry yet."

"Neither do I," Noemi said, sounding unsympathetic, "and yet we both must. House Sersi isn't a good match for us, but there are any number of other families that will do.

Not that you should pick immediately. The more boys you consider the better. It will decrease interest in your visit to House Sersi. You understand you can't contract out of House Das, correct? Whatever boy you marry will contract into us."

"You said I was too young to court." This was not a conversation Emrie could take passively.

"Girls have married younger. It's just not expected yet."

Emrie wasn't against marriage entirely. She just wanted to be her own person first, have her own place in the family, and she didn't feel either at this exact moment. "I have no desire to marry right now, and I'm supposed to get to choose for myself."

Noemi gave her an exasperated look. "You made that choice when you undertook your trip to House Sersi."

"Can't I just pretend to go courting and then change my mind and not marry at all?"

When Noemi spoke, it was as if she were speaking to a small child. "To choose one boy over another is expected. We all have our preferences and that's understood. For you to consider a string of boys for courting and then not marry at all sends the message that you find them unworthy. It's insulting to their Houses."

"How would I ever know something like that?" Emrie argued.

Noemi sent her an aggravated look. "By paying attention to how all the other girls go about life, Emrie. That's what I did."

Emrie's cheeks flushed at the rebuke, making her bruise ache that much more.

Noemi must have taken this as Emrie conceding because she reverted to her practical tone. "You'll need to visit twenty Houses at least. I'll have Aunt Calys arrange the first three or four so that our closest allies are remembered. If you have thoughts on boys who interest you, ask me about them, and don't go visiting without checking first. Do you understand?"

Emrie nodded. She hated it. She wanted to cry again. But she understood. She had no choice.

***

She'd forgotten Deriek's food. Emrie didn't realize it until she went to pack for that night, but it was true. She'd been so focused on saving him the previous night that she'd left his pail on the wrong side of the bars and too far for him to reach. He was going to be furious.

Or worse, sick again with hunger. It was the perfect horrible ending to the worst day of her life.

When she arrived at the prison, he was seated in his spot and looked his normal self, straight posture, dark hair curled on his shoulders, and a tilt to his lips that said he noticed she was taking careful note of his health. He stood up so that they faced each other, the bars between them. She was hit by a need to tell him what had happened. Every ugly bit. She'd beg him to listen and put his arms around her the way he'd held her the night before. She wouldn't even mind skipping the conversation part.

Of course, that couldn't happen. It was just the infatuation getting involved. Her goal should be feeding him and learning why he hadn't told her of the illness. No, not why he hadn't told her, that she could guess. But the why behind his desire for death.

She didn't do it, though. Instead, she just stood there.

"I'm healthy again, as you see." He used an overly cheerful tone as if daring her to contradict him, and his smile was too wide. He shrugged back his shoulders which parted his laptevi along a jagged tear.

She didn't remember ripping his laptevi.

"I'll bring fresh clothing tomorrow," she said.

"And will you fix this as well?" Again, his voice was quick and friendly. Too quick. He pulled back the two halves to show her his chest.

She leaned forward in the dim light but saw nothing of note.

"I'm going to come in there."

Before he could respond, she went to the pattern she'd made in blood, being careful to pull the lamp and pail in close to her body. The rug she'd used last night was still in place and the witchcraft moved her with an effortless delight.

He gave a shocked intake of breath at her arrival. That would've pleased her at any other time, but in the moment, she couldn't find the energy to feel anything at all.

"That's how you did it," he said, sounding impressed.

"Necessity forced me to learn a new skill."

"Well done." He smiled, a genuine smile that included both sides of his lips, indentations around his mouth, and a sparkle in his eyes. Emrie's heart tripped in response. Which she couldn't let happen. She turned away and placed the pail in front of his usual spot. Then she took her lamp and held it up to investigate the skin behind his torn laptevi. A needle-thin line followed a pattern up and around, making the outline of a Juju bird on his chest. No, not one Juju bird but two, facing each other. Right where her fingers had traced.

Until that moment, she hadn't considered how she'd healed him without stitching or painting or placing chalk down first. She'd just done it and had been too overwhelmed by other things since then to give it thought.

It appeared the witchcraft had dug the patterns it needed itself. The scars, if that was even the right word for them, reminded her of parchment after characters had been carved but before it had been inked. She reached out to trace one.

"I marked you," she said, aghast.

"Yes, you did." His voice went raspy. His skin was solid and warm under her fingers, but not with fever this time, rather a healthy, male heat. The witchcraft gave a slight flare as if asking what she wanted, and she flattened her hand against one of the birds.

Deriek grabbed her wrist, pulling her away. "That's enough, Nitsya." His voice was rough and his grip firm.

"I'm truly sorry," she said quickly. It felt just like the moment of realizing she shouldn't have visited Imjin or that she'd accidentally treaded on the secrets of Brid's parentage. She'd had no idea the witchcraft could create patterns itself. It'd never done so before. "I didn't mean for that to happen. If I'd known, I'd have brought ink with me or something else that would come off. Does it hurt?" She glanced at him from the corner of her eyes, trying to see if tonight's humor hid a fury. All she saw was the usual mask of amusement that seemed to be his default.

"It doesn't hurt," he said easily enough. "It's nothing. Don't bother yourself. Just don't do it again."

"I didn't mean—"

"And that's enough of that as well, Nitsya." He slid one hand down to take her by the elbow. "Come then, sit. And please tell me that's my food as I'm famished. I was unable to reach the pail you left last night."

He was acting as if everything was normal, but it wasn't. Nothing was.

"I'm so sorry for that as well. Here let me set it up for you." She fell to her knees next to the folded warming blanket and pulled off the lid of the pail, but he swiped it from her with his effortless grace.

"I'm capable of doing this myself now that there are no bars between us."

"Oh, of course," she said, adding flustered to the growing pile of sickening emotions she seemed unable to rid herself of. Her earlier wish to curl up in his arms seemed foolish.

She took several deep breaths trying to calm herself and get the situation under control. She was doing neither of them any good by being an emotional ninny.

"Thank you for the food, Nitsya," he said politely and took a seat. He patted the spot next to him. The warming blanket was more than large enough for them both.

"You're welcome." Emrie hesitated and then sat. "There's something I need to ask you."

He chose a dried berry from the pail without unpacking the rest and popped it into his mouth.

"You want to ask why I'm calling you Nitsya rather than Piara?"

"Not that, no."

"Come now, you're a curious creature. You want to know." He was teasing her just as he always did.

She should've enjoyed it. She couldn't.

"Truly I don't care—"

"The name Piara is from an old story of my mother's people. About a pet mongoose. I'll tell you the story if you insist."

"I want to ask you about last—"

He spoke louder, right over the top of her. "You see there was this family." His voice took on the cadence of his storytelling. "One morning while picnicking out beyond the Orchards, they came upon an injured mongoose. The family was too kindhearted to leave the creature to die, so they emptied a basket of food, wrapped it in linen, and took it home, determined to help it, and then train it as a pet."

He was avoiding her question. She didn't have it in her to push him and caved to allowing him to control the conversation.

"You see me as kindhearted."

"Not exactly." He laughed, took several more bites of food, and then gulped down some water. He seemed to have recovered from last night's ordeal even if she had not, and his spirits were high, possibly because she'd done something new with the witchcraft. She should be grateful for that. She was, but she was also just worn. She sat back and let him tell his story. It was a distraction if nothing else.

"Mongeese are intelligent animals, you know. More than most give them credit for. They're venerated in Vin-Yonekur in the way the Pol-Thirians have stories of the clever crow. This tale thus is one of warning. The family took the beastie home. They fed its hunger and healed its injury and kept it in the family's garden. This would be a lower-ring family, you understand, they'd only have the single garden."

"My House has one garden," Emrie lied, just to be a part of his storytelling. It felt good to do so. Releasing something she'd been holding onto too tight.

He snorted in mock disbeleif.

"So Piara is a beloved family member then," she said, teasing him back just a little because she knew that wouldn't be it. His stories rarely ended well.

"Not exactly," he said again, with a cocky grin. "Once the creature was healthy, it found their home an excellent place to live. It discovered the kitchen, opened the cupboards and casks of food to help itself. At one point in the tale, I believe it gets very much drunk on the family's wine. It liked the softest of places to sleep, so it rearranged the First Daughter's finery, digging a hole right into her favorite rug, ruining several good laptevis, and building a nest. Nothing they tried broke the mongoose of its bad habits or helped instill good ones. Basically, the family's kindness led to their lives being taken over and rearranged by an untrainable mongoose named Piara."

"I see." And she did. The minuscule amount of good humor he'd dragged out of her disappeared. He saw her as a pest. A creature of little value and no importance. Well, it wasn't a new designation. Her father and Noemi saw her the same way. So did Keeli and Lianjit at times. Deriek had even chased her out of his prison with such words. Emrie stared toward the far side of the bars trying to find an ounce of rebellion at such a designation, an ounce of grit. She came up empty.

"And what is a Nitsya then?" she asked, trying to keep a stupid tremor from her voice. "A cockroach with its own tale?"

If he caught her hurt feelings, he ignored them. His pleasant tone didn't waiver. "A deer actually, and yes, it has a tale, although you'll have to wait until I decide to rename you something else before I tell you. But never fear, Nitsya is a beautiful name."

"I'm sure it is."

He turned serious then. The cheer disappeared as if it had indeed been as fake as it had originally seemed. He straightened and looked at her square. He'd only done that a few times, and it always felt like a glimpse into the person he truly was.

"I know you want to drag out of me more sordid details of my family life and my choices and why last night—"

"I don't want to." She choked the words out from the depths of her misery. "Really, I don't want to. I have to."

"You think you have to," he agreed quietly. "But not tonight. And not tomorrow night. Maybe after that. You're exhausted. I'm hungry. Let's just leave it for a bit. Let us pretend to be friends. And just to be clear, I don't see you as a Piara. You've more than earned yourself a better name. If you are offended by Nitsya, then I'll change it. Or you can pick your own. I'll call you whatever you like."

It was the nicest thing he'd ever said to her. Better than his being impressed by her use of the witchcraft or showing his gratitude for the things she'd brought him.

"Thank you," she whispered, feeling yet again like she might cry, if for different reasons. He was the first person all day long to think of how she might be feeling or notice just how tired she was.

He reached over and took another biscuit. She studied his hand as he flipped the biscuit around before popping it with a snap into his mouth. It differed from her father's. His palm was narrower. His fingers were strong and wiry, and clever and kind, like the rest of him.

"We are friends," she said. "So I'll leave my questions if that's what you desire. But just for a few days. And I like Nitsya just fine, too."

TWENTY-TWO

It was several seven-days before Emrie brought up her questions again with Deriek. That was partly because he kept asking her not to and then filling their time together by entertaining her so well that she wished she never had to return to House Das. And partly because she needed some space to work through all that had happened already. Her life felt like a sapling on low ground when the first of the rains hit, the river rose, and anything that dared to grow too close got flooded.

Aunt Calys set up a visit with a Second-ring House to go courting. It went about the same as her uncomfortable visit to the Sersis, only this time, Aunt Calys was with her, the boy seemed as keen as his mother on impressing her, Emrie said nothing that might be misconstrued as an offer, and there was no talk of the witchcraft. Two days after that, she and Aunt Calys visited another House, and that miserable experience almost felt routine.

Emrie avoided her father. He'd struck out some piece of her that wouldn't fit into its original place, and she had no idea what to say to him or even what to think. When she saw him at Petal Night and listened to him read the words of the Sages, he seemed a stranger. And she'd developed a slight obsession with other people's hands. She couldn't stop staring at them.

As for Brid, Emrie tried to be nicer to her. If it was true that Emrie was being kept in the dark about what was happening around her, then that was a thousand times truer for Brid. As the Sovereign's Daughter, she was also due a certain amount of respect. She was Deriek's sister, and Deriek was Emrie's friend. Plus, Emrie still was unsure what she was supposed to do with the information she now had. Tell Brid? After the disaster with Lady Sersi, she didn't feel inclined to share anything with anyone. Not without knowing the bigger picture of what was going on first.

At the same time, Brid settled into her life at House Das in a way that grated. Emrie heard Brid chatting to the maties, following Noemi around, and singing to herself in a gruff but upbeat voice. It was unfair that Brid was so happy.

Even the weather reflected Emrie's unsettled mood. The winds abated and the air cleared, but it left behind the utter stillness of the morning frost. The sun, refusing to be forgotten even in its season of rest, melted away the frost, and the afternoons were pleasant as long as one wore a heavy overdress. The maties moved the birds and plants indoors, and the furnace boxes were replenished with this year's droppings from the Renoa.

Emrie used the chill as an excuse to stop going out. Keeli sent an occasional invitation, but neither she nor Lianjit came to visit. Perhaps Brid kept them informed of Emrie's doings as she called for a litter most days. Emrie didn't ask. She felt odd about leaving House Das as it seemed likely that Noemi and her father were having her watched. How else could they have known about Lady Sersi?

She wasn't used to being so morose, and her own grim mood wore on her until she realized she'd have to try harder with Deriek. On the evening she decided to confront him, she used the witchcraft to go to his prison, as had become her habit.

"I'll never get accustomed to your mode of travel." He sat wrapped in the warming blanket. They'd taken to sitting side-by-side every night, and she went over to join him.

"It's freezing down here," she replied. "Are you warm enough?"

"I'm perfectly warm, but you're shivering." He swung the blanket up and around her and then reached over to enclose them together. Her insides warmed faster than her outside. It almost felt like an invitation to ask him personal questions.

It was the closest she'd been to him since the night she'd healed him. Their arms brushed and her knee pressed comfortably into his thigh, both of which she liked way more than she should. There was such a strength about him, even locked up and helpless as he was. It was getting harder and harder not to notice.

"Why do you want to die?" she asked in a blunt-like-Brid way to distract herself.

"Are you certain you want to know?" he asked with a quirk to his voice. "Because I've had a remarkably pleasant time lately. Less the cold and that I'm locked up, of course. Plus, you won't like my answer."

"I think you'd better tell me anyway."

He looked away, exhaled, and then when he spoke it was by rote. As if he'd practiced what to say and had been waiting for her to force the issue, which was likely correct.

"Because my death is the only way for me to win."

He was right; she didn't like his answer at all.

"That makes no sense."

"My entire life is bound by waiting for my father to push Cystel and me to kill each other. If I kill myself, I take that from them both." He shrugged as if the entire thing was of no consequence.

"That also makes no sense."

"It's like this. If I die not by my brother's hand, then it forces my father to either sacrifice Pol-Thiri to Cystel or do the one thing he has always rejected—kill Cystel himself. Either way, my father loses."

What he seemed to be saying was that if he died at his own hand, then House Valiyard would be finished.

That was his goal?

She didn't just dislike it; she couldn't understand why he did. At the heart, it was an ugly form of revenge.

"Your father loses, but you *don't* win. You end up dead."

She reached under the blanket to touch the back of his hand with her own as if the contact might unlock a little of the mystery that was him. It was a very forward thing to do, and she half-regretted it immediately.

He did the last thing she expected and turned his hand over, lacing his fingers through hers like a warp and weft in a way that was both reassuring and anchoring. He squeezed her fingers playfully before answering.

"Your Sage Jeminina of the Single Petal wrote that death is but a releasing of a leaf, that the life of the tree is in the branches and trunk and root. What is the loss of one leaf as long as the tree still stands?"

She'd always found that saying by Sage Jeminina comforting, but it felt different sitting here, feeling the growing, thrumming awareness of him centered where their hands touched. She didn't like the idea of him being gone. It wasn't amusing or clever or a win.

"You aren't a tree." Her voice was breathless because his touch was such a distraction. Then she had another thought, a disturbing one. "What if there's a Third Heir?"

"That would be convenient, but there isn't," he said with a dry certainty.

"But what if there is?"

Deriek shifted her direction as if to look at her through her veil. The blanket fell back, and he raised his free hand to fix it. For just a moment she felt as if he were poised to hit her, and she flinched. He reached over slowly, carefully, and pulled the blanket up on her shoulder, brushing the back of her neck with his knuckles as he did and leaving little tendrils of something that felt like cold but wasn't running along her skin. When he spoke, he went serious again for a moment.

"Is there talk of a Third, Nitsya?"

She wanted to tell him. She even opened her mouth to do so before her brain caught up with the many reasons she could not.

"I once heard someone joking about it."

"Recently?"

"No."

He put his free hand down, away from her, almost reluctantly, and drummed his fingers against his knee.

"I've heard no rumor to suggest so. My brother wouldn't allow it for one thing. He took care of his own mistresses and having learned the lesson of me being born, he'd do the same for any woman who became pregnant by our father. Our father, to my knowledge, has invited no one to his bed since my mother anyway. But they say . . ." His drumming paused.

"What do they say?" she asked, curious. She'd heard no suggestion of a Third herself.

"They say Cystel's mother died after several stillbirths."

Meaning the First Heir had somehow arranged the deaths of other siblings? But just as she thought it, a chill ran down Emrie's spine.

"Someone could've stolen a child away and raised it in secret?"

He gave a shake as if ridding himself of the idea. "Unlikely. My brother is thorough about these things, and it's more likely he found a way to kill his rivals without breaking the Renoa's Law. Even if I'm wrong and a child was saved, it wouldn't solve all problems. If a Third Heir exists, then my father will want Cystel and I to kill each other all that much more."

But it also meant there were options. Emrie straightened with a sudden excitement. Maybe this was why the Renoa had told her about Brid. She put all that energy into her voice and was the one to squeeze his hand this time.

"You must fight your father. Let me help you."

He jerked his hand free from hers as if her words had hurt him. "How would you help me?"

"If there is a Third—"

"If there is a Third," he said, his tone now sharp, "I could trick Cystel into killing this other sibling of ours, and then my father would either have to kill me or allow me to inherit."

Emrie sat back, both seeing his logic and startled by it.

"I didn't mean that."

"I didn't think you did." The words were harsh. Harsher than he'd spoken to her in a long time. Then he sighed and dropped his shoulders as if forcing himself to relax, to let go of whatever darkness had taken over.

"Alright," she said, slowing her voice and speaking with more caution. "Maybe not that, then. But I could help you by freeing you from here. You could run away to Vin-Yonekur. You liked Vin-Yonekur, I think. Your stories are all about there, and you speak of it with fondness. I'll help you go there."

Something within him stirred, not a movement exactly but a run of jagged emotion under his skin as if he were physically pained. Emrie couldn't tell why and wished she were still holding his hand. This time she didn't feel confident nor forward enough to reach out.

"That doesn't work, either," he said, almost tiredly, and rubbed at his brow. "My mother tricked me into going to Vin-Yonekur before. My father retrieved me anyway, and those I left behind there don't want me back. Besides, I'm too old now to foster, and I have no Guild association nor skills for a Guild. I could join the River Nomads, I suppose, or become a norie guard, but could you see me as either? And even should I decide to do so, my father would just bring me back as none of that absolves the role he created me to play. What I truly want, what I've wanted for a long time, is to stop being everyone else's pawn. Even yours."

"I'm not trying to make you my pawn, Deriek."

"Let it go," he said so softly she could barely hear the words. "I told you the truth of my situation. Now please, just let it go."

TWENTY-THREE

Emrie couldn't let it go. It pricked at something deep within her; the same something that had made her determined to do a good job of caring for him and had pushed her to keep learning the witchcraft even though it hadn't worked at first. He was her duty. And even more than that, what happened to him mattered.

He mattered.

And not just because of his family standing or connection to the Seat of Judgment. If he were to walk into a room, people would stop to watch. When he spoke, people would listen. She listened. He knew things. He had wisdom and knowledge and a clear view of the world that she envied.

That he would throw it away rather than fight for it, fight for Pol-Thiri, was wrong. Apart from everything else, including any personal feelings she might have, she couldn't let him do so.

However, she also knew better than to tell him. If their two tempers ever collided, he'd run right over the top of her.

As the days went on and they fell back into their routine, she didn't bring his situation up again but neither did she stop thinking about how to change his mind. How could she help him see that his plan was just a grisly form of revenge? That there were other matters of importance?

What does he need to live? That's what the Renoa had asked.

She'd thought the answer was learning to use the witchcraft but with what she now knew about Brid and the rest of his family, she wondered if there was something more. Something larger that she was supposed to do for him.

She was sitting in her room picking seeds off a toasted wafer bread thinking about it when Mati Ereana arrived with a message from Lianjit. Her sword was finished. Would Emrie and Brid like to accompany her to the Swordsmith's to collect it? Emrie'd barely managed to read the note when Brid burst in.

"You have to go. Everyone thinks something's wrong with you." Brid was dressed in peacock blue laptevi, not unlike something Emrie might wear, with gold embroidery at the cuffs and hem. Her hair was done in braids twisted and pinned with colored threads to match, just like Keeli always wore hers. Brid had caved on fashion after all.

"Of course, I'll go. Lianjit is one of *my* best friends."

It wasn't just that, though. Aunt Calys had suggested another courting visit for that day, and the Swordsmith's was the better choice. She pasted on an agreeing smile and asked Mati Ereana to arrange a litter for them. On the way over, Brid informed her of the various ways Noemi was working on finding out the truth of her mother. Emrie kept her mouth shut.

The Lord of the Guild of Swords in Pol-Thiri had a workshop in one of the outer-rings near the northern edge of the city-oasis. It was a functional type of place with walls of dirt-streaked beige. They met Keeli and Lianjit inside. Brid immediately fell in love with everything about the workshop and demanded the Guildmaster answer her questions and show her his forge and workroom. He obliged. Emrie hung back, not all that interested in the tour and even less interested in watching Brid enjoy herself. She finally left the salty metallic smell of the place for the hallway outside. Keeli followed her.

"Everything is well at House Das?" Keeli had an older sister look on her face.

"House Das," Emrie said evenly, "is the epitome of jasmine-scented cushions and polite conversation about the proper size of raindrops."

Deriek would have enjoyed that. Keeli only gave her an odd, confused look.

"Brid thinks you're unhappy."

"She's wrong," Emrie lied. She didn't want to talk about it. She didn't like that Brid was gossiping about her, either.

"My mother says you're courting."

It'd only been a matter of time until one of them found out, yet Emrie was unprepared to answer. She hesitated, and Keeli picked up the thread of conversation.

"You've been open enough about not wanting to marry yet. Has that changed?"

"No," Emrie murmured.

Keeli sighed in an I-thought-so kind of way. "They tell us a marriage contract is supposed to be our choice, but it's not true, is it? If it makes you feel better, remember that day we sat up on the roof in the wind because my mother had company? She was visiting with a boy she likes for me. The Third Son of House Hru. He's willing to join our House if Kairin gives up the role of First Daughter and marries so that I take her role.

It needs to happen as Kairin is a terrible First, and neither she nor my brother are right to inherit. My opinions are irrelevant to the matter, of course. You see, I understand about families saying we have freedom but then taking away any choice but what is best for them in the name of House honor. Does Noemi have a boy picked for you?"

"She doesn't," Emrie replied, and then because she genuinely wanted to know, she asked a question herself. "Are you happy with your situation?"

Keeli shrugged. "I haven't decided yet. The boy seems pleasant enough."

It was a very Keeli way to look at things.

"You'd be an excellent First." And it was true. Keeli would.

The others joined them to move to the next room, leaving the conversation hanging, but Keeli gave her arm a supportive squeeze as they followed the Guildmaster.

They were shown into a long room with a variety of tables, each holding a clutter of tools. At the nearest, a man in a vivid tangerine laptevi polished a knife with a cloth. The moment Emrie looked at him, the pads of her fingers tingled. He was using the witchcraft.

The small arcs of energy in her fingertips were interested in what he was doing, similar to what had happened when she'd seen Lady Sersi. Emrie pulled her hands back into her sleeves, rubbing frantically on the inner lining and telling the witchcraft to settle. The man put the knife down on the table. He didn't look at her but smiled invitingly at the Guildmaster. Emrie didn't think he'd noticed her reaction, but she'd been aware of his. He'd been making patterns with his cloth on the knife. His witchcraft had been bringing something to him and adding it to the metal.

She didn't know how she knew that, which was a weird feeling all on its own, but she did. Her witchcraft did.

The Guildmaster dropped an affectionate hand on the shoulder of the second man and introduced him as a principle in the Sword Guild, the lord of a Twenty-eighth-ring House, and the finest Polisher he'd ever met.

Lianjit picked up the knife he'd been working on and held it up to the light. It shined pale blue and silver.

"No one gets better color than Pol-Thiri's Sword Guild," she said in admiration.

Using the witchcraft to do it?

It'd never occurred to Emrie one could *change* a thing with the witchcraft.

It'd also never occurred to her that someone might use it openly as he had.

The Polisher left them to go to a cabinet in the back and return with Lianjit's new sword. Emrie watched him closely, but he did nothing else to give hints about the witchcraft.

The sword shined with an even more unearthly silver and blue than the knife. The hilt was wrapped in hide with an uncut sapphire fitted in the pommel and figures of leaping foxes carved into the handguard. It was a beautiful weapon. A smile bigger than the Renoa's Field widened across Lianjit's face.

"My father says it's the finest sword he's ever seen."

"It is," Brid insisted.

"I agree," Keeli said, and then they each took a turn holding it.

When it was Emrie's turn, Lianjit handed it over with the tip facing the floor and still Emrie nearly hit her own leg taking it from her. It was heavier than expected for such a graceful thing, and it had an odd expectation of power to it. As if just by gripping it, she had courage. For the first time in her life, she regretted not attending Barrack's Practice with Lianjit.

What Emrie didn't see on the sword were any patterns of the witchcraft. Even the foxes weren't in a patterned arrangement, and her own witchcraft showed no interest in the blade at all. She handed it back. There were no clues as to what the Polisher had been doing.

***

When she returned home, Ahrens was waiting for her.

"I need your help." He stood in the hallway just outside her room, a hip cocked as he leaned against the wall.

She walked around him.

"No."

"You don't understand. It's important." His face had a pleading look on it, a calculated one, and when he smiled at her, he used too much teeth.

No matter how much she adored him nor how charming he could be, she was not getting dragged into another one of his undertakings. Emrie pushed aside the rug to her rooms.

"If it's important, do it yourself."

"I can't. I need to get a message to Imjin—"

Emrie stopped and turned around, the edge of the rug still in her hand. "Don't get involved, Ahrens. There's so much more going on than is spoken of in the city-oasis, and Father and Noemi are working on it."

"Both of them would happily sacrifice Imjin if it got House Das more Status. But is that what matters the most? What about this girl's life?"

He was right, of course. Sacrificing Imjin was no better than sacrificing Brid to save Deriek. But neither was it as simple as Ahrens portrayed.

"If not Imjin," she argued, "then the First Heir will take Noemi. What about that?"

"I don't believe it," Ahrens said. "It's just what Father says to make all their scheming seem less ruthless. Stopping the First Heir's lusting after Noemi was the point of her promising a marriage contract to Hurra. No one, not even the First Heir can break that against Noemi's will. If she's in danger, then she needs to formalize the contract."

Ahrens pulled a silk scarf out of his pocket. It was sun yellow with small red disks strung around the edges in two layers so that they tinkled and clattered against each other.

"I need you to give this to Imjin tonight at the Hall of Guests. I've already arranged for you to take Noemi's place again. Imjin will understand the message, and even if you get noticed, you won't know enough to do any harm. It's just a gift. An item made in Gir-Tosaq that you saw in the Marketplace and thought she'd enjoy."

"Ahrens, are you courting Imjin yourself?"

Ahrens laughed. It was, all things considered, a reassuring sound.

"Of all that is green and good, no. She'd drive me batty in a season. But that doesn't mean I'm willing to let her be sacrificed." He dropped his voice. "I'm going to get her out of the Sovereign's House and out of Pol-Thiri." Ahrens pressed the scarf into her hand.

Pretty much what Emrie'd suggested to Deriek that he'd refused. Which made it hard to reject Ahrens.

"The problem," Ahrens continued, "is that the First Heir has her isolated. But you've already visited them both, and the First Heir didn't object. It'd be natural for you to bring her a gift."

"It's been too long since my visit." And Noemi would never approve, not to mention their father. But Ahrens was acting for Imjin's good, and Emrie respected that. Besides, she got an idea of an easy way to pass the scarf that would be no risk to herself.

"Fine, I'll do it."

***

Emrie attended the Ceremony of the Thousand Gratitudes with Ahrens since their father had business elsewhere and would arrive late. The Hall of Guests was just as splendid as she remembered. She was greeted by several girls her age, sisters to the boys she'd courted. She now knew enough about their Houses to have a decent conversation even if there was a sense of avarice in it all. Not that they were unkind, but none of these girls had spoken to her on her first visit.

She saw Taspin in the distance once, but Taspin didn't approach or even look in her direction. Apparently, Emrie had served her purpose there as well.

The witchcraft remained absent, although that was probably because, with the drop of the weather, the cooling grates were not in use this time. Which was another interesting question that she hadn't considered for a while.

She used the socializing to encourage the Sovereign's maties to come by often with the trays of food and drink. Each tray had the Sovereign's emblem engraved on it, the twisting, turning branches of the Renoa. As she collected her food, she ran her fingers over the emblem in one specific area that made a pattern similar to her Juju bird.

Imjin was up on the dais again, sitting by herself and looking bored. The First Heir prowled around her. Every once in a while, a matie with a tray approached each of them. It wasn't until the fourth time this happened that the tray used was one Emrie had prepared. When the matie held the tray down for Imjin to inspect, Emrie touched a stone in her pocket, sending Ahrens's scarf from where she'd left it sitting in her chamber amidst another pattern.

Imjin startled, glanced to the First Heir, and then snatched up the scarf and hid it in the folds of her laptevi. Perfect.

Then, as if in unison, forty or so of the hundreds of other guests all looked sharply up and directly at Imjin as if they were aware of what Emrie'd just done. Not a single person turned in Emrie's direction, Thank the Tree, and it was all over as fast as it had happened, but those that had looked had been aware of the witchcraft. Just as Emrie had with the Polisher and Lady Sersi. Which meant what?

And then she realized one single person was staring at her after all. Emrie let him approach, keeping her face as calm as possible under the circumstances. Ahrens stopped in front of her, his expression way more delighted than she would've liked.

"I know your secret."

"And do you also have a secret?" She kept her voice calm, cautious. At the same time, excitement bubbled within her.

He chuckled and dropped a hand on her shoulder.

"Nope. It runs in our mother's side of the family, though. It skipped her, but Father had high hopes for Noemi for the sake of the Guild. She didn't get it, but when you started acting odd, I couldn't help but wonder."

Emrie's excitement flattened, and she shrugged off his hand. Once again, her family had left her ignorant.

He'd said something else of note as well. Witchcraft worked for the sake of the Guild?

Witchcraft was witchcraft unless it was used by the Guilds and then it was guildcraft? That's what Lady Sersi had implied, too.

It was such a First way of thinking of things.

"You know how it works? This guildcraft?" she asked.

"Gods of old, no. That's why I need you."

Not what she wanted to hear. He glanced toward Imjin and the First Heir.

Twenty-Four

Emrie took what she'd seen to Deriek. She was tired of feeling ignorant. She wanted answers and trusted him not to be cruel about how little of the world around her she understood. She found him sitting in the back of his prison again and took up a stance above him, one hand holding the lamp, the other on her hip.

"You need to tell me what you know of the truth of Pol-Thiri."

When he spoke, his voice was wary. "I've told you everything I know."

She ignored that and grabbed his hand, pulling until he gave and unfolded to his feet.

Only then did she release him to retrieve his pail and a cushion she'd brought for them to share.

"What exactly are the Guilds?" she asked.

"The Guilds?" He seemed surprised. "Why are you questioning the Guilds and why are you so upset? What's happened?" He settled down on one side of the cushion, leaving space for her, but she wasn't ready to sit.

"Everything happened," she said, and it came out more dramatically than she'd intended. She told him what she'd discovered without admitting that the witchcraft she'd used in public had been in the Hall of Guests. She couldn't hold still while she spoke and paced around his cell, making circles just outside of their shared light. Deriek watched her and didn't interrupt.

"It's all a lie," she finished even more agitated than when she'd started. "Every House and every Guild must have someone with witchcraft or guildcraft or whatever one calls it as it must be the same thing. Which makes no sense. If it's so common, why not just admit it and be done? Why not admit all the old stories are wrong?"

"Secrets create a power unto themselves. As do their revealing." He sounded amused.

Which was so far from what she felt she was suddenly suspicious.

"Did you know?"

"That people keep secrets and are rarely what they profess themselves to be? Yes."

"Don't be difficult. I meant the witchcraft and you know it."

"Sorry." He didn't sound apologetic at all. He sounded like he still found this funny. "I didn't know before you told me, but having learned, it makes a certain amount of sense. Come. Sit. Your pacing is making me tired." He shifted over so she could have half the cushion.

She dropped down next to him just because he'd asked. He turned so her knee rested atop his thigh. Made her want to shiver with pleasure, but she forced herself not to get distracted. She needed answers and he must know something of use.

"Has it always been like this?" she demanded. "Are the stories of the glory of Pol-Thiri and the Blessings of the Renoa all lies? Is it all just witchcraft?" That was the heart of what was bothering her.

"They aren't lies to those who believe."

"You're being intentionally inscrutable. Please, I want to understand."

He quirked up one corner of his lips, the pale light in front of him illuminating more shadow than anything else.

"Inscrutable. I like that." He tapped her knee with two fingers in that way he had. "My inscrutability wasn't intentional, rather a quote from Sage Baliyea who wrote endlessly about expectations conquering experience. But that's not a fair answer. I will say that I've been in the branches of the Renoa, and I've seen the beauty of Pol-Thiri, and both are real. I don't know where the divide is between the Renoa and this power of the Guilds you have seen, but I think likely there is a divide and it may not be on the Renoa's side. People are inherently selfish and ambitious."

"That's a terrible way to see the world." It didn't come out as forcefully as her previous words. His touch was softening her ire. It struck her that he enjoyed touching her as much as she liked him doing so. Really, he'd reached out to her much more than she had to him. It was a delicious realization, one that should leave her afraid. Right now, she was going to enjoy it.

Acknowledging that made what she'd discovered about Pol-Thiri not so bad. As if *he* were the stabilizing force in the windstorm of new realizations.

"It's even worse in Vin-Yonekur," he said with a shrug.

"In what way?"

"Its Renoa is the youngest of the seven and has the least influence on Its people. The Houses of Vin-Yonekur have been waging a Status War for fifty years straight. The Seat of Judgment has changed hands nine times in those years. Vin-Yonekur is unstable at the centerline and that allows for greed and avarice to rule the city in a way we don't see in Pol-Thiri where our Renoa has a steadying influence. Not that we don't have our own hunger for power; myself being the center of such." His lips twisted into a mocking smile.

Emrie said nothing, not liking this line of joking. She leaned toward him, shifting just enough to press her entire leg against the solidity of his.

For just a breath he stopped drumming and then when he began again, the rhythm was a hair quicker. As was the beating of her heart. She wasn't embarrassed, even though she should've been.

He cleared his throat. "Have you seen any witchcraft outside of work done to support a Guild?"

"I haven't looked." It hadn't occurred to her to do so. "But I will."

He relaxed his hand on her leg. Instead of tapping, he caressed back and forth with his thumb in a way that made it hard to concentrate on anything other than where he touched. It was like the entire universe settled down to just this one place, this one moment, just the two of them. She'd felt nothing like it before and almost wished he'd stop talking so that she could just feel.

"I'm only guessing here," he said slowly. "But perhaps each Guild works in its own sphere, employing the witchcraft in a way only they understand. That would make sense. The Guilds are notoriously jealous of their trades."

It took a long pause for her to catch up with what he'd said, so focused was she on the slow slide of his thumb. But once she did, it caught her attention. Regretfully.

"Then what am I?"

"As a witch?"

She nodded and leaned farther into him.

"Well." He lifted his hand to make a flourish as if amused by something, but when he spoke his voice was pensive. "I'd say that you're someone with power but no binding loyalty to a Guild and thus no holds on what you do with your skills other than your own conscience." He paused. "You, Nitsya, are unbound and thus threatening. Especially, I think, to me."

***

Was this what it felt like to love? Emrie spent the next morning feeling like she walked not on the ground but just above it. The warmth of the sun radiated not from the sky but from the center of her chest.

It eased the betrayal she felt at what she'd learned. All her distress. All her worry. And if Deriek was right, the witchcraft was common.

She would go to the Marketplace to look. A visit there wouldn't be suspicious should Noemi or her father be watching her outings. Also, it was a distraction from having to think of all the reasons falling in love with Deriek Valiyard was a terrible, foolish thing to do. She called for a litter and was heading to the door when Brid came rushing over.

"You're going out? You never go out."

"I'm just headed to the Artisan's Market."

"I'll come along. I need a word."

Emrie nodded as if she didn't mind. It was odd to think of Brid and Deriek as siblings. She couldn't imagine two people more unalike in appearance or temperament. Where Brid was tactless and abrasive, he was gallant and thoughtful.

She and Brid settled into the litter, and the nories carried them smoothly forward. Emrie turned her gaze outward, watching the people of Pol-Thiri walking with their baskets and carts and occasional donkeys. It was hard to focus on them or Brid, as her thoughts slipped to how Deriek liked to touch her and how now more than ever she had to find something for him to live for and how she was doing something very much ill-advised by making this about her but would not stop.

"You are ignoring me, and I have something important to discuss," Brid said.

Emrie sighed and glanced over. "My apologies."

"Accepted." Brid shifted awkwardly in her seat. "Now you're looking at me like I forgot to braid my hair this morning. What's wrong with you?"

"Forgive me my inattention," Emrie replied, withholding the half-dozen cutting things she'd have liked to have said, most of which she'd learned from Deriek.

Brid fidgeted with her hands, twisting her fingers in her lap. Her broad face had a scowl on it. The litter bearers came to a halt and settled them onto the ground. Emrie sighed a second time and reminded herself that Brid was due honor regardless of how Emrie felt about her.

"What is it you wish to discuss?"

One of the nories drew back the curtains for them to exit. As he did so, Emrie was hit by an awareness that someone was using witchcraft. It was as if the presence within her hands understood what she was here looking for and was excitedly tugging on her sleeve and pointing her in the right direction. She glanced around, trying to catch the source.

"Lanka Sersi," Brid said.

The feeling had a directionality to it, but it was coming from the opposite way of the Marketplace. Emrie exited the litter and turned to where workers from the Clay Guild were using buckets and cloths to wash down the outer wall of a neighboring House. A woman stood on a ladder halfway up the building, her hand and cloth pressed into the wall, her entire body leaning into the circles and swipes of her cloth.

She was the one.

The witchcraft really was that common.

Emrie couldn't tell how the woman was using her witchcraft. The wall, like all walls, was solid white. Was she making it white? Emrie wasn't sure.

"Did you hear me?" Brid demanded. "I wish to speak of Lanka Sersi."

"I know the name." Emrie continued studying the woman on the ladder. Was it possible the pattern was in the woman's cloth? The Polisher had been using a cloth as well. Maybe that was it. Emrie would have to try something like that herself.

Brid grabbed Emrie by the arm, pulling her around so Emrie was forced to look at her.

"I want to contract with him."

"What?" Emrie turned her attention to Brid in confusion.

"I want to contract with Lanka Sersi."

Emrie furrowed her brow. The Soils Guild boy with the square, callused hands of hard work who hadn't liked her and whose mother knew Emrie's secret?

"I didn't realize you knew him."

"I know him. I want him. I want him more than I want to find my mother." Her voice was so filled with longing that it was painful to hear but not in any sympathetic way. Did Brid have to overshadow Emrie in this, too? Was Emrie not allowed to treasure her feelings for Deriek without being eclipsed? Emrie began to walk. Almost immediately her witchcraft alerted her again. A man in a stall was working on the embroidery of a slipper. *That* required the witchcraft?

"It all started," Brid said, and thank the Renoa she had the sense to lower her voice, "with Keeli mentioning you'd gone to House Sersi. You started acting strange, so I visited them as well to see if you'd learned something you didn't want to tell me."

"I would've told you anything relevant," Emrie snapped back. "That I said nothing meant I learned nothing."

She caught the feeling of the witchcraft yet again. The distraction was a relief. She didn't want to listen to Brid wax on about falling in love.

The witchcraft wasn't close by this time, so she couldn't place where it came from nor any other details. Her own witchcraft reacted only with a slight tingle. It was almost as if Emrie's becoming aware meant that the witchcraft no longer needed to point its finger. Or at least that was what it felt like. It occurred to her that where she'd felt the strongest witchcraft the first time had been the fountain. The water must be moved somehow similar to what she did with Deriek's bath. Possibly the cooling grates under the Hall of Guests function similarly. It wasn't just that the Guilds used the witchcraft, it was that the entire city-oasis did.

Brid waved her hands dismissively, oblivious to anything but her own interests. "Forgive me for being less than believing. No one in Pol-Thiri speaks the full truth. And you're Das."

That was just rude.

"I would've told you about House Sersi if I'd thought it'd help you find your mother." Which since it was a lie proved Brid's point.

"You should've told me regardless, but it doesn't matter. I went, Lanka and I met, and we've been meeting ever since." Brid stopped walking and Emrie was forced to stop as well. "When I first arrived in Pol-Thiri, everyone treated me as if I were here to catch a husband. Keeli and Lianjit and even you all thought I was after Ahrens. Don't frown like that, I know you did. Lianjit even admitted it, and Ahrens didn't help as he's always so nice to me, but I never was interested in him. I never thought to marry for years and years. But now I do."

"I don't know what to say." Not that Emrie needed to say anything as Brid didn't allow her to do so.

"You must help me," Brid continued. "Tell me what I have to do to get your father to agree to the contract. Lady Sersi says her House can't let Lanka contract into House Das. He's to be the next Head of House so I'll have to join them, and I can't do that without your father's permission."

Emrie laughed in the mocking, superior way Deriek liked to use. Of course, Brid was going to not just tell Emrie of her romance but demand assistance. Then again, if Emrie was right about who Brid was, her father was more likely to let Emrie marry into House Sersi than Brid. Her laugh died in a rather uncomfortable flash of insight. What happened if an Heir contracted into a House through marriage and then inherited the Seat of

Judgment? What happened to that House? Would that House become de facto the new House of the Sovereign?

Emrie came to a dead halt causing someone behind her to stumble and then give a mild curse. Brid kept going.

This could be what her father was working toward.

If Brid was the Daughter of the Sovereign, the Sovereign could take her from House Das whenever he chose. But if Brid contracted with Ahrens, then her ties to House Das would come first.

If that was her father's goal, then he hadn't hidden Brid away just to keep her alive, but to use her to take over Pol-Thiri on behalf of House Das.

Maybe.

Yes, her father was as scheming as Ahrens had said, but he wasn't diabolical. Was he? Even with everything that had happened, she didn't want to think of him that way.

Brid stopped walking and turned back, giving Emrie an impatient look.

"Lady Sersi says the balance between you and her falls in her favor and because of that, you'll be thrilled to assist me in convincing your father to let me make the contract. Those were her exact words. Thrilled to assist. What's more, I insist upon it."

A sick roiling churned Ermie's stomach. There was the next problem of course. Emrie couldn't deny Brid what she wanted. Nor could she tell her father what was going on. Or explain any of it to Brid. In another flash, she saw the likeness between Brid and Deriek. It wasn't in their appearance or their personality. It was in this shared, bloody determination to get their own way.

***

"I have a problem," Emrie said to Deriek that night.

"I'm here for you," he said, holding open his blanket in invitation. "Like the flower waiting for its honeybee or the thirsty plant, the rain, or the matie, his master. You might notice I've no other options."

It sounded like something his brother might say, although Deriek filled the words with a mocking irony that the First Heir had lacked.

"You're in a mood, aren't you?" She'd hoped to return to where they'd left things the night before.

"Of course not."

She dropped down next to him, letting him draw the blanket around them both so that she was surrounded by his warmth. She inhaled the living earthiness of the Renoa that still clung to him and relaxed for the first time since learning the truth of Pol-Thiri and Brid. This was what she'd been waiting for all day.

He tugged the blanket tight. "Are you planning on telling me your problem or were you simply making an observation?"

He *was* in a mood. She should try to figure out why, but for once her situation seemed more urgent.

"Someone found out my secret and is blackmailing me."

"They know about me?" He sounded pleased by that rather than horrified, but it was likely meant to irritate her.

"Not you. Me. My witchcraft."

"I see." He sat back and turned his head in her direction, but all she could see was the vague motion, not his expression as the lamp needed a new wick and its glow barely reached their knees. When he spoke, his tone was still light. Too light. "What does this person want of you to keep quiet?"

"She wants me to convince my family to let my cousin marry her son. But I can't. I mean, even if I tried, it'd never work. The Head of our House will never agree and none of the other Firsts will go against him. My cousin is too important."

He cocked his head as if in interest. "What does your cousin want?"

"She says she's in love." Emrie threw all the frustration she felt at that truth into her voice. Especially as Brid seemed the least likely person in Pol-Thiri to even understand what love was. She gave a quick glance in Deriek's direction to check his reaction to her usage of the word, but he was looking straight ahead.

"A sentiment that always causes complications," he said as if stating a timeless truth. "What do you want?"

"To never have met this horrible person or let on about the witchcraft. I thought I could trust her."

He reached over and put his hand on her knee, the same spot it had rested last time, and she took that as a good sign. The warmth of him sank through her clothing, and for a moment, everything outside of that one spot disappeared yet again. Maybe she was wrong, but she almost thought she caught a smile as if he were testing her reaction to him and pleased by her response. As if he was as affected by her as she was by him.

When he spoke, his tone didn't change from airy and sarcastic. "Trust. You've fallen victim to that pit of deception humanity calls trust."

Emrie really, really wished that he would take this a little more seriously.

"I trust you."

"My apologies. It won't end well for you."

She gave him a shove with her shoulder. Not a hard one, just enough to tell him he was being obnoxious. To almost anyone else doing such a thing would've broken etiquette and been inappropriate. With Deriek, it felt just right.

"You aren't very good at this tonight."

He shrugged. "What is it you expect me to do? Pull out a handy sword and battle this woman to the death on your behalf? Would that satisfy you?"

Emrie studied his profile. She couldn't see either his eyes or his lips. Just the outline of his nose, the molding of his fierce brow, and the scruff of a long unshaved jaw. It occurred to her then that she might have misinterpreted him. He wasn't being obnoxious. He was being defensive. That was the meaning of his moodiness. Being difficult was one of the few defenses he had.

She couldn't see the purpose of his behavior. She wasn't attacking him.

"I want you to care," she said softly, trying to break through to him.

"You think I don't care?" His voice rose with the question.

"Tonight, I don't know what you think." Emrie kept her tone easy as if he were some kind of feral creature she didn't want to scare off. "My cousin has a will of iron. My father will never agree to the contract. If I get outed as a witch, I'll end up in front of your father, who at the very least will cut off my hands and ruin my House."

Deriek rose abruptly, leaving her sitting alone in his blanket. It was such an unexpected move that she stared at him.

"Deriek, is something wrong?"

"Never." He paced just far enough away that she couldn't see him but could feel his passage back and forth. "In Vin-Yonekur, they tell a tale of a River Nomad so ferocious that he killed all that came against him. No Barrack's soldier was strong enough to beat him, and it was feared his raids would reach the Renoa itself. Until, that is, a promising younger Son copied the Nomad in every particular. The boy left his home. He practiced his sword, learning the ways of the river and adding its fighting arts to the ways of the city. He practiced day and night for years. He traveled, visiting every city-oasis, fighting in every battle he could until he was the greatest swords master that ever lived. Then one day he came face-to-face with the Nomad himself and killed him. But when he returned triumphant to his former life and House, the Renoa rejected him. *You have become that which you sought to destroy.*"

"What a horrible story." Nor could Emrie see how it related to her problems with Brid or his change in demeanor.

"I know. That's why I told it to you."

"By way of warning?"

He stopped near her. He was no longer mocking, but his voice held a deep intensity.

"Because it's a legitimate fear, Nitsya. You have resources. You are wealthy. You are a witch. You are more than clever enough to exploit others' weaknesses. But don't be like Tenkiantemir, the boy in the story."

Emrie swallowed, confused. "You think I'm going to destroy my cousin? Or this woman?"

"I don't know." His words were abrupt, sharp. "Who do you think is in the most danger?"

"Me," she said honestly, but he refused to look at her.

***

Deriek paced his cell for a long time after Nitsya left. The restlessness was building again. It'd disappeared after she'd healed him. He'd felt more himself, the darkness had relaxed, the window had become just a window. Now it was returning. She was making it return.

He spun around, landing in the first position of the First Dance of Swords. Even in the dark, even out of practice, his muscles remembered the precision of the movement and the balance of his weight over his feet. It felt good. Releasing. He shifted his stance wide and spun left, his sword hand dipping as if parrying.

She was slowly, brutally, falling in love with him.

He could see it in the tilt of her head, the catch in her breath, the way she touched him whenever she thought he wouldn't mind.

Which mirrored how he'd been treating her.

They were both in trouble. The realization had been creeping up on him for days, but he'd known it for sure when she'd arrived this night so certain he'd help her.

Which meant her betrayal was coming.

He felt its approach like the daily creep of morning light into his prison. Torturous. Unavoidable.

He relaxed into the dance, letting his body do what it knew best.

He'd lied to her tonight. He'd done it intentionally. The woman who knew of the witchcraft was unlikely to do more than make demands. She would realize that should Nitsya go before the Seat of Judgment, she'd be open about herself and the witchcraft and the connection of such to guildcraft and the Guilds. Nitsya had manners but no guile; her mix of practicality and candor worked as a defense against people like this woman. He'd bet every one of his mother's jewels that no one, most of all the Guilds, and thus this woman, wanted the truth of guildcraft brought into the light.

None of that had occurred to Nitsya.

Neither had the fact that *he* had no loyalty to the Guilds. And while he'd given up trying to puzzle out Nitsya's identity, he knew enough about her that a few carefully worded questions to his father's sycophants would give him her name and House in no time at all. He'd have to be free to ask those questions, but if he asked Nitsya to free him, she would.

Then all he'd have to do was corner her Head of House. If Deriek threatened to take the tale of his captivity and her witchcraft to his father, he'd have her House under his thumb and be able to employ them one and all as he pleased.

That connected to the situation with his father and brother. To a resolution that his brother had tried and failed at several times—get control of one of the Houses and force them to sacrifice a minor member into doing the killing of the Heir and taking the Renoa's repercussions on themselves. A time-honored tradition in Vin-Yonekur. The Renoa there had never failed to react in such a situation.

He was Nitsya's biggest threat.

She didn't see it. Nor did she see that he'd been parsing her words and making some pretty solid guesses as to what was going on. She missed it not because she wasn't smart enough; she'd proved herself plenty clever. But even though she'd let drop she was the Daughter of a Head of House, she'd never learned to see the world through a political window.

It was both her weakness and one of the things he found appealing about her.

Deriek came back to a neutral stance, his hands in front of him as if he were holding a sword perfectly balanced between him and his opponent. He would not use what he knew against her.

He should.

He should take whatever advantage he could.

But he would not.

He lowered his imaginary sword to the ground. What would it look like if she didn't betray him? If what they had between them was given a chance to become something more? Did he even know?

He thought of his mother, the way she'd smiled at him and told him he was the most important thing in the world to her. He'd been devoted to her, even after she'd had him kidnapped and sent from Pol-Thiri. He'd ached and cried, that young boy that he'd been, running away and getting himself caught in an effort to return to her. He'd been determined to go home until the moment he'd learned she'd sent him to Vin-Yonekur hoping he'd win the Seat of Judgment there.

Then there were his friends in Vin-Yonekur. Those he'd thought of as the closest friends of his life, who'd turned out to be doing the same.

He moved into the Second Dance, using the entire cell. Even in the dark, he knew where his boundaries were.

But Nitsya was not political.

For a moment, he paused in the swing of his arm and cadence of his feet as a dark humor rose in his chest. If Nitsya didn't betray him, she'd do the opposite. She'd open up to him entirely. She'd tell him the truth of all she knew. She'd name names. She'd give history. She'd behave in the exact way that would save her from the woman attempting to blackmail her over the witchcraft.

She'd be honest.

The difficult, restless feeling he carried under his skin could see it happening. Could see himself trusting her, loving her. He didn't know if that was a good thing or not.

TWENTY-FIVE

Deriek had made her cry. It hadn't been a lot of tears and Emrie'd wiped them away quick enough, but she hated that it'd happened at all.

Deriek had said she had cleverness and could use the witchcraft to solve her problems, but he'd made her feel as if the opposite was true. He was just trying to distract her, keep her from prying too deep into him, but it didn't matter. It still hurt.

To make things worse, the next morning Noemi sent for her just as the sun was being pulled from its rest, to warn that Taspin Kolera had been asking after her. Noemi questioned at length whether Emrie had somehow encouraged this.

Of course, she hadn't, but Noemi didn't seem to believe her.

She left Noemi, only to then be caught by Mati Dechta who lectured her on causing difficulties for her sister and her House.

From there, Aunt Calys appeared, letting Emrie know she'd planned a courting visit for early afternoon. The boy was excited to meet her.

Emrie went to the bathing rooms to soak and hide for a while. The basin she chose was tiled in blue and deep enough to tread water with a fount at one side and a drain at the bottom keeping the water fresh. In the warmer season, doors on two sides opened to an enclosed patio allowing fresh air. With the doors closed against the cold, the room had a heavy humidity to it made worse by the volume of potted plants sharing the warmth. It fit her mood.

Of course, this was also the place from where she'd stolen water for Deriek's baths.

She sent the maties away and rested her forehead against the lip of the basin, feeling like the plants were all leaning over her, about to fall inward. She had no desire to engage in a battle against Lady Sersi and Brid. What she wanted with all her heart was to discover a way to save Deriek.

There was a rustle of plants and Emrie looked up, expecting to see one of her maties. Ahrens walked in instead.

"I'm bathing," she shrieked, ducking farther underwater.

"So noted," he said, grinning unapologetically. "I need to talk to you where no one will overhear, and this seemed the ideal location."

"Couldn't we have done it while you were in the baths?"

He chuckled. "You'd never have agreed to meet me."

Not true. Anything was better than this.

"I need to talk to you about Imjin," he continued.

Of course, he did. "Go away, Ahrens."

"You need to help me get her out of Pol-Thiri. I can't do it myself and something bad is going to happen. She wore red yesterday, which means she's afraid for her life."

Emrie paddled over to the side of the bath to grab a linen towel and then wrapped it around herself as best she could in the water as it tangled in her cloud of loose hair. Ahrens sat down cross-legged on a cushion meant for maties.

Emrie felt for Imjin, but she had problems of her own.

"Please, go away," she said, trying to sound more assertive.

Ahrens acted as if he hadn't heard. "We've tried everything to get close to her. Montali's afraid that if we don't do something soon, she might take action of her own, and then the First Heir will kill her. I need you to use your witchcraft to get her out."

"I can't do that. I don't know how. And who is Montali?" She knew immediately she shouldn't have asked. It had been meant rhetorically, but by Ahren's sudden eager expression, he took it as encouragement. He looked right at her, his eyes innocent and owlishly wide.

"I suppose it's time to tell you the truth of it. Can I trust you to keep my secret?"

"Never mind. I don't want to know—"

"Montali is Imjin's brother," he said, right over the top of her. "He's the one that sent the letters and the scarf. He's the one who's been trying to help her. And . . ." Ahrens leaned forward, his voice deepening with a sudden urgency. " . . . I love him."

Emrie looked up at Aherns with narrowed eyes. He sounded tortured by this truth, but she was learning to be wary. He'd never before mentioned love or courting or anything like that in her hearing. Declaring such a thing now seemed suspiciously well-timed.

"Does Father know?"

"Of course not," Ahrens said, "he'd never approve."

True. Noemi had once said that their father had been against Uncle Otto contracting with Uncle Vashir because of the progeny issue, but Father hadn't yet inherited House

Das back then and hadn't been able to stop it. And now, of course, there was the need of tying Brid into the family and Ahrens was the only option. Ahrens couldn't have picked a worse time to find love. If, that was, he was telling the truth.

"Father hasn't mentioned you contracting with anyone else, has he?"

Ahrens laughed, and it seemed genuine. "I'll never inherit House Das. It'll go to Noemi, as it should. You'll be the one to marry, hopefully to someone fertile, and have lots of little Das to repopulate the family. I'll go to Gir-Tosaq with Montali. The problem is that he won't leave while Imjin is in danger, and neither of us can get close to her. Thus, you're going to help us using your skills. I told him all about you."

"He knows about my witchcraft?"

Ahrens made a dismissive wave of his hand. "I tell him everything."

That convinced her he was telling the truth, because her use of witchcraft getting out didn't just hurt her, it hurt their entire House. Ahrens was too smart to risk that.

"It wasn't your secret," she argued. "Under the Law of the Renoa, you now owe me, not the other way around."

"Absolutely," he agreed. "I'll give you anything you want. But first, you have to help free Imjin. For me. And Montali."

Emrie rubbed at her forehead feeling cornered. She didn't want to get involved, and it seemed so unfair that both Brid and Ahrens got to find love and fight for it while the best-case scenario for her heart was that no one ever learned how she felt. Still, he was her brother. She couldn't walk away, although even if she got Imjin out that wouldn't help Ahrens with the problem of their father's permission.

"I don't know how to do this. It won't be as simple as the scarf." Or the actual moving would be simple enough. She'd do it just as she did her visits to Deriek, but it wasn't like she could just stroll into the Sovereign's House carrying a large blanket and ask Imjin to step into it. "I'll have to figure out a way to get to her."

Ahrens reached over and tousled the top of her head, pushing her half underwater as he did so.

"You're the best sister ever. I can't tell you how grateful I am, and just wait until you meet Montali. He's very upright and devoted. You'll love him."

***

Emrie decided not to tell Deriek about Ahrens cornering her. She wanted to. She'd gotten into the habit of telling him her problems, and if anyone was likely to know how she could get to Imjin, it would be him. But telling him would give too much away, and she didn't want him to know she'd let herself be coerced by yet another person.

That night, she brought along a much larger lamp than usual as she'd forgotten to ask Mati Ereana to change the wick of her usual one and it was unusable. The lamp made the room so bright she could see the ceiling for the first time, which was much higher than she'd realized. It felt like standing at the bottom of a giant hole. A giant hole under the Sovereign's House.

The Sovereign's House . . . there was a door from here up to the Sovereign's House. If she could figure out how to use the witchcraft to unlock it, she'd be able to reach Imjin from down here.

Deriek sat against the wall again. He opened the blanket wide and smiled as if he were glad to see her. Apparently, whatever had been bothering him had released its claim. She slid gratefully in beside him and pestered him into a story. He told her a long-winded tale of a giant that accidentally squashed a flying squirrel under its heel.

It was an entirely satisfying evening.

The next morning, she pulled out the book on witchcraft to hunt for ideas on locks. She didn't come up with anything. Nor did she find clues as to what the Polisher or woman from the Clay Guild had been doing, either. The book was still gibberish to her.

She tried asking the witchcraft while touching a pattern, but it didn't seem to understand. Communicating with the witchcraft was like yet another door and lock. When she had the pattern correct, the key fit, the door cracked and there was space for a brief rapport. But if she didn't have the pattern, then the door remained closed.

Over the next couple of days, she made a point of going out with Keeli, Lianjit, and Brid, hoping to watch for more witchcraft. Away from the Marketplace, it was harder to find.

Instead, she learned it was common knowledge that Imjin was held prisoner by the First Heir, and everyone wanted to know how the Renoa felt about it. Were the First Heir to do such a thing to someone from the rings, he'd owe recompense, but when the insult was between the city-oases themselves, it became complicated. Which was interesting, but not helpful to Emrie.

Neither was encouraging Brid to talk about Lanka to learn more about House Sersi. Brid had nothing but compliments for all of them.

One good thing happened on the Brid front. Noemi came up with a plausible story for Brid's birth that distracted Brid entirely. According to Brid, Noemi said that Brid was Aunt Calys's granddaughter. Apparently, Aunt Calys had given birth to a child outside of her marriage contract. That daughter had been raised by the girl's father and everyone pretended she didn't exist in order to spare the feelings of Aunt Calys's husband.

It could be true, but Emrie doubted it was, even when Brid started spending her afternoons with Aunt Calys.

This was fine with Emrie. When she wasn't working on trying to find a solution for Imjin, all she wanted to do was think about Deriek. She got the feeling he was waiting for something from her. She didn't know what it could be, and it wasn't concrete enough of a feeling to question him. Perhaps she was wrong. Maybe the cold and the short days were making him feel too confined. As the Season of the Sun's-Rest settled in, she gave him a second blanket, added rugs to his floor to keep his feet warm, and whenever she could get away with it, used the witchcraft to send him pots of hot tea during the day.

She was asleep in her piles of rose-scented blankets late one morning when Mati Ereana prodded her awake.

"What's wrong?" she mumbled as her maties had taken to letting her sleep as she liked unless she instructed them otherwise.

"Your father wishes your company in the Central Garden."

Emrie sat up. Her father wasn't usually at home late morning, so something must be going on.

"Of course, I'll come."

When she arrived, he sat alone, and not on the dais by the pond. An area had been cleared in the field where the gazelle grazed. Rugs had been laid and iron benches with cushions circled a blue-flamed fire pit. Her father sat on a bench feeding a gazelle out of the palm of his hand.

All of which meant what? Brid becoming impatient and approaching her father about Lanka seemed the most likely disaster. Emrie's legs went quivery with sudden anxiety.

She followed a stone path across the Garden's field and stopped before the fire pit. It was filled with carefully cut and cleaned slices of the Renoa's branches that put off enough heat to make her want to remove her overdress. Her father offered her a formal greeting. She replied in kind. It was all so ordinary that Emrie clamped her hands together to hide that he was making her nervous. She remembered too well their last private conversation.

He nodded for her to take the seat opposite his. The gazelle wandered off.

"Do you ever wonder about the life of our ancestors before the Renoa?" he asked, gazing off into the distance.

"No, father." Was that the correct answer? She went warm, then hot. Sweat beaded on her brow.

He rubbed at his jaw, and Emrie's gaze followed the motion of his hand. He waved Emrie closer and held up something for her to take. Another book.

"Your favorite Sage, yes?"

The book was Sage Nya. And while it appeared to be a lovely copy, she couldn't see that she'd done anything worthy of reward. Also, Sage Nya wasn't her favorite Sage.

"I was wondering something," he said almost casually.

It was such an unusual way for her father to speak, that she sat forward on alert.

"Yes, Father?"

"I need a certain someone moved to a place by the river. Supposing I gave you just the right key, to unlock just the right lock, could you determine a way to move this person without letting him free or giving away your identity?" Again, it was all said easily, coolly as if he was asking her to retrieve a basket of bread from the maties or place a potted plant in a different room from where it currently resided.

She hesitated because there was nothing casual about this. Nor would she need any key, although her father wouldn't want to know that. Even more, she didn't want to move Deriek without knowing where he was going.

"When?"

"The Night of Deliverance."

The Night of Deliverance was the shortest day of the year. It was the night the Sacred Grasses of the Renoa's Field were burned so that their ashes might encourage the coming of the Season of Soil and regrowth. It was a seven-day away.

"Inside of Sage Nya's book," he said, still too casually, "there are two keys. The first is to a barred gate you know of. The second is to the room where this person must be transported. The direction is written in the book. You may visit there in advance to prepare. The location is innocuous, and no one will think twice of you visiting. I'm trusting you with the rest of it. You must make the transfer with no one discovering you were involved."

"I—yes, Father."

But her father *intended* something. With everything she knew of Brid and Deriek, there was no avoiding that truth. Plus, her father had previously told her he didn't have a key to Deriek's door. Her father had lied.

Which was so much worse than him just not telling her things. If he'd lied about this, what else was he lying about?

He rose to his feet, wincing as he did so. The cold was hard on his hip.

"Our problems are ending. Once you've taken care of this last item, your duties will be complete and you may write to your Aunt Poercha. I'd like you to stay at home, though. Invite your aunt to come here." And then he smiled, which he rarely did.

The hairs on the back of Emrie's neck rose in alarm. Fear crowded out all her other worries. Fear of her father. Of his lies. Of what he intended for Deriek.

He stood, kissed the top of her head, and tugged on a braid of hair just as he always did, but instead of patting him on the arm, Emrie ran her fingers over the embroidered pattern on his sleeve.

It wasn't planned. She had no goal. If anything, it was a desperate impulse based on her own fears of touching him too directly. The embroidery wasn't a Juju bird, either, but a series of off-kilter rectangles joined edge to edge with loops at the inner corners. The witchcraft settled right into the pattern.

He stepped back. "You've always been a good Daughter, Emrie. I recognize that."

Emrie nodded, shaking inside, and then listened to the retreating thump-thump-tread of his uneven gait while keeping her gaze on the blue fire. She now had a way to use the witchcraft to find out what he was planning.

TWENTY-SIX

If the witchcraft could transfer objects and odors and heat, it should be able to transfer sounds as well. Provided her father didn't change his laptevi, she could use the pattern on his sleeve to listen in on his conversations. Doing so was a betrayal of him, etiquette, and Emrie's own honor. She would do it anyway.

She made several practice attempts, asking the witchcraft to bring her sounds from other places in the House. It worked. She spied on Mati Dechta lecturing one of the junior maties on decorum and then used the rug in the prison to listen to Deriek, who was so noisy he must be dancing or moving around or something. She'd imagined him sleeping all day, but he wasn't.

Once she had the witchcraft transferring sound, she crawled onto her sleeping dais and pulled the blankets over her head to listen in on her father. She pressed a small cloth embroidered to match his sleeve to her ear, and with her eyes squeezed shut and a knot in her chest, she traced the pattern.

Immediately, she heard the clunking bell of an ox, a woman calling out that she had prunes for sale, the bark of a street dog, and then the raucous voices of men laughing. Emrie startled and glanced around her room half-expecting to have been transported by the witchcraft to the streets of Pol-Thiri.

The sound settled into a more regular rhythm of voices and conversations as if her father had joined a gathering. He spoke, telling someone he had an invitation to play Kopi-Far. That got Emrie's attention. Even more so when he went through formal greetings and the person who answered had the dull, arrhythmic voice of the First Heir.

They weren't at the Sovereign's House, she didn't think. Her best guess was that they'd met in a Tea Hall.

Tea Halls were men's places. No woman of Status would ever degrade herself with entry. They were meant for gambling, smoking Jemmy pipes, and overindulging in brishka. It was the last place she'd expect to find her sedate, responsible father.

Another proof she didn't know him at all.

Two other people joined them, neither of which Emrie recognized by voice. The group conversed about the measurements of the river depths, the annual harvest of clams, and other such Guild business. It was about as interesting as listening to Aunt Calys discuss courting. A musician piped a tune on a whistle, and Emrie struggled to separate the conversation from the music.

Someone entered Emrie's room, and she stopped the witchcraft and hid the embroidered cloth under her blankets.

Mati Sarta checking on her. Emrie had expected this and gave a story of being overtired and wanting to rest. A few minutes later, Mati Dechta showed up. Emrie pretended to be sick while Mati Dechta checked her over and went in search of a foul-tasting concoction that Emrie had to down before she was finally left alone again to spy on her father.

She lost nothing for the distraction. Her father and the others were playing Kopi-Far. Emrie tried to pay attention, but Kopi-Far was a long game and boring at the best of times. It took all afternoon for them to finish, and Emrie was only half paying attention by that point. It was the sudden absence of sound that caught her attention. Then she heard her father's voice.

"Sire, I've come this day to offer you your heart's desire."

Emrie leaned into the cloth. Her father had to be speaking to the First Heir, and the First Heir's heart's desire was to kill Deriek, wasn't it? This couldn't be good.

"Speak, Fourth Adviser," said the First Heir, "and impress me. I have gifts all the day long. I weary of them."

Emrie's heart raced.

"I'll be plain," her father answered. "You want the Daughter of Gir-Tosaq to give up her games and move forward with the marriage contract. I believe I have a way to encourage her."

What? Ahrens wouldn't like this.

The First Heir gargled out an ugly laugh which gave Emrie chills.

"Perhaps I tire of the girl and her games."

"Perhaps you do," her father said. "But then, what better way to end things than with a contract? She's very beautiful."

There was silence, and Emrie wished she could see them. What were they doing?

The First Heir spoke, his voice slow. "What is this power you have? Give it to me and I'll command the contract."

"Alas," said her father, sounding more submissive than she'd ever heard before. "It isn't something that can be gifted, and better that should hands be soiled, they be mine."

The First Heir made a humming sound as if considering, it was the most honest emotion she'd ever heard from him.

"No gift can be freely given. What is your demand in trade?"

"Once the Daughter of Gir-Tosaq accepts your courting, I want an Heir of the Sovereign for House Das."

Emrie gasped and then pressed her free hand to her mouth to suppress the noise even though she didn't think they could hear her. But Deriek? Her father's plan was to marry Deriek into House Das? To whom? Noemi? Herself? Noemi was already promised with Hurra.

"The Second Heir is dead," the First Heir said with finality. Then he paused. "Or do you know otherwise?"

"I've heard rumors. Specifically, I've heard rumors that he sees his life as valueless until his elder brother is contracted. Once that is accomplished, he might reappear. Rumors being what they are, they could be wrong. It's a risk I'm willing to take for the opportunity to align my House with yours."

The First Heir chuckled, deep and ugly. "Even if he isn't dead, Deriek won't agree to the marriage contract."

"I believe I have a way to resolve the issue of assent as well. All I require is your agreement and the Renoa's Blessing."

Silence again. Much too long of a silence for Emrie. Deriek would hate this.

"Fourth Adviser, you seem very much convinced my brother lives."

When her father spoke, his words were mild. Suspiciously so. "The best part of Kopi-Far are the final gambits. The greatest win requires the greatest risk."

The First Heir laughed again. It was a laugh of superiority. Of delight. Of someone who thinks they know something someone else doesn't, and she knew then that the First Heir would take the deal. The laugh said he thought her father was foolish, and the First Heir's next words confirmed it.

"You do realize, Fourth Adviser, that I just beat you in Kopi-Far."

"That I do, First Heir Valiyard. That I do." Her father's voice while even and calm and on the surface submissive, held its own superiority. He also thought he was going to win. Emrie'd bet her life on it.

But not Deriek's.

The two men came to an agreement. They said the binding words of contract.

Emrie heard the uneven steps of her father walking away and then the noise of the larger room. She put the cloth down and told the witchcraft to relax. What had he said? Exactly? Because in a binding contract, the words mattered. *Once the Daughter of Gir-Tosaq accepts your courting, I want an Heir of the Sovereign for House Das.*

He hadn't named Deriek. He'd said an Heir of the Sovereign. That had to be intentional. Her father wasn't foolish with words. It could be that he intended to force Deriek to marry her and use her time caring for him as weight to get him to agree. But it seemed much more likely he intended Brid to marry Ahrens, and then to have Deriek and the First Heir kill each other.

This hadn't previously occurred to Emrie, but if Brid wasn't a child born into House Das at all, if her mother was from some other House, then her father would need this agreement to complete the marriage contract.

On the other hand, convincing Brid to do something she didn't want to do wouldn't be easy and as far as Emrie knew, her father had no leverage over Brid. Her father likely realized this as well. He very well could intend to pair Emrie and Deriek and then have the First Heir kill Brid.

If that happened not only would Emrie get Deriek for herself, but she'd end up the wife of the Sovereign.

TWENTY-SEVEN

The next day, Emrie took a litter to the location carved into the back cover of the book. Her father needed to see her following his instructions.

Everything about this felt hideously sick-to-her-stomach wrong. She was the bird before the bird feeder that she'd once described to Brid. The Head of House wasn't looking, and she could steal the seeds to appease her hunger but every single one of them was spoiled.

She wasn't ready to contract.

She did want to be free to love Deriek in the demanding, difficult way Brid loved Lanka and the heart-pained way Ahrens wanted this boy Montali. It was just too soon, too fast. She wanted time to enjoy loving him, not rush into romance like Brid and Ahrens seemed to be doing. She wanted to uncover all the mysterious bits he hadn't yet let her see. She wanted it to happen in a normal setting where they were just Emrie and Deriek without all the darkness and the politics and his suffering hanging over their interactions. And she wanted him to want that, too.

It would never happen if he was forced into House Das. Time and again he'd made it clear how much he loathed being controlled. If a marriage contract happened because he was compelled into it, he'd end up hating her.

Her norie bearers took her litter to a squat, dirty line of buildings near the docks. The area was noisy with an uneven, ringing beat of someone hammering on metal. The clanging rattled the inside of her ears.

One of the nories went inside and returned with a man in a drab laptevi and overdress. He introduced himself as being of the Carters Guild, those who moved goods around the city-oasis, and said he'd been warned to expect her and that the holding room for her item was prepared. He bobbed a lot while speaking in that way some people had when trying to show their submissiveness. Maybe it was her imagination, but his movements seemed in rhythm to the banging on metal.

The building inside was empty, but that was to be expected during the season the sun rested and the river shrank. The Carter showed her to a series of smaller chambers, each fitted with steel locks.

"For our more delicate and valuable transactions," he said with a bow before one. Emrie used her key to open the door.

The Carter followed her inside, extolling the protections of the room from thieves. Emrie looked around, only vaguely listening to him. At least here the clanging was quieted.

The room was square and plain with no windows and only the single door. Emrie motioned for one of her nories to lay out a huge mat she'd brought along. It had a Juju bird already embroidered into it.

"My article is precious, and I don't want it marred by the stone floor," she explained to the Carter. "Or stolen."

"Of course not," the Carter replied. "Whatever you leave will be secure. No one can access this room except the holder of the key."

Emrie nodded, her thoughts still focused elsewhere. She couldn't allow her father to set up either Deriek or Brid to be killed.

She stared down at the key in her hand, a burning, red fire building within her at her father for doing this, for not being who she'd always thought him to be. Keys, keys, keys. She held so many keys, but not one fit any of the locks she faced: Deriek, Imjin, Brid, her brother, this unknown boy named Montali.

Montali.

She'd been so absorbed with the problem of Deriek and Brid that she'd missed something. Something huge. She needed to get home.

***

"Montali is in danger." Emrie cornered Ahrens in an alcove of Has Das. It was his turn to pay attention to her.

Ahrens rolled his eyes. "He's not. No one knows who he is."

"You're wrong," she insisted. "Listen." She told him of the conversation she'd overheard, the threats against Imjin, and what their father wanted in return for forcing Imjin to marry the First Heir.

"He knows where the Second Heir is hiding?" Ahrens asked, sounding surprised even if he'd missed the relevant part.

"Yes. And what Father holds over Imjin must be Montali. If Montali's life were in danger . . ."

"Imjin would cave." Ahrens's face dropped, his charm and cheer disappearing in a single moment. He rubbed at his forehead, and Emrie had to duck sideways to avoid being elbowed in the face.

"Father knows who he is," she said, thinking of how he'd known about her visit to Lady Sersi. "Father always knows. He's probably been using you to monitor Montali this entire time."

Ahrens said a very obscene word. "I'll send Montali into hiding. He won't like it, but he'll agree to protect his sister. What else?"

She hadn't thought past warning Ahrens of the danger, but he was right to ask. Montali was just one key. Guaranteed her father also knew about Lanka Sersi. Which *did* then give him something to hold over Brid after all.

"We have to get Imjin free. Then, Montali and Imjin will be safe." If Imjin disappeared, her father's agreement with the First Heir would be broken. Deriek, Brid, and Imjin would be out of danger. "We have to act fast. It's going to happen on the Night of Deliverance."

"Can you free her by then?"

Emrie hesitated. It would be taking a tremendous step, a massive leap. Sure she'd helped Ahrens in the past, but she wasn't someone who plotted. Noemi was. Her father was. She was just a Second Daughter. And yet, she already had some ideas, and she had the witchcraft to help.

"I don't have it all figured out, but to start, I need to get her a message that no one else can read. I can give you the specifics of what it needs to say. And then the Second Heir—"

"If we want to toss Father's nose in the air and force him to leave Imjin and Montali alone, we should find the Second Heir and take him with us. He'd make an excellent husband for Imjin."

Emrie took a step back, startled into silence. Ahrens was right. He was completely and utterly right. Imjin was the solution to everything.

Deriek wouldn't like it.

Twenty-Eight

She took her time bringing it up. She gave Deriek his food and then sat with him under the blanket, keeping her attention on the dark and trying not to fidget while she waited for an opening. He seemed in no hurry, eating in a measured way.

"You're excited about something," he finally said in a voice that was tinged with a knowing humor. No mocking, though. It gave her hope.

"Not excited. Anxious, maybe."

"I won't like it then." It wasn't a question. Trust Deriek to get to the heart of the matter.

"Probably not." Emrie glanced to the side to catch his expression. The corner of his lips curled up. He was pleased although she had no idea why. She twisted her hands together in her lap.

"Just get it over with, why don't we."

"Alright." But then she hesitated, and they sat there a moment longer. He took her hand in his like he'd often done but instead of linking fingers, he turned it over, placing his thumb in the middle of her palm and pressing down, making her fingers relax.

"Nitsya, you can tell me anything, you know."

She could. She knew that. Telling him wasn't the problem, rather his reaction when she did so.

"My family has decided it's time to take you from here. I've been told to move you."

"I see."

"Deriek, what if there's a way to get what you wanted? To extricate you from this place and your horrible situation?"

There was a long moment of silence as if he were weighing out how he should respond. When he spoke, the humor was still there.

"Tell me the all of it. What's going on?"

"My father trusts me. He'd never expect me to help you, to free you."

"I see." Deriek went still, and there it was again, as if he were waiting for something from her, as if he had some sort of expectation of what she was going to say. So she told him. All of it—Imjin, Montali, Ahrens's plan for them to leave. She didn't give names other than Imjin's, nor mention her father or Brid.

"You can leave Pol-Thiri with the Daughter of Gir-Tosaq. You'll marry her and contract into her family. Considering the way your brother has treated her, the balance is already tipped. Surely, her House will take you without your father's release. That will make you a member of the House of the Sovereign of Gir-Tosaq with a life and a position there that no one here can touch. You live." Emrie waited for him to explode, to tell her it was all foolishness.

He didn't.

"Nicely done. I applaud your creativity." He dropped her hand onto her thigh and reached over to tear off a corner of wafer bread, his movement jerky, almost violent.

"What are you thinking?" she asked.

He pushed the blanket back so that he could tilt his head up to the ceiling, stretching the back of his neck. But rather than fly into a rage or anything like that, he relaxed back down and took a drink from a bladder of water and said nothing.

"Deriek?"

"You missed the moral of Tenkiantemir's story. Does the Daughter of Gir-Tosaq know of your plans?"

It wasn't the direction Emrie'd expected him to take, and he was right, she didn't understand how the story related to this situation.

"Regarding you, not yet." Emrie explained about Imjin being kept isolated and how Emrie was going to contact her using the witchcraft. Deriek listened without commenting, his gaze away and beyond. "Will you agree to it?" she asked, somewhat desperately.

Again he didn't answer for a long time. "I believe I won't."

"Please, Deriek," she pleaded. "I don't want you to die."

"You don't want?" he snarled, the change in his temperament so sudden she startled. Then he jerked away from her, dropping the blanket to the ground. The cold rushed in, chilling Emrie's skin.

Here was the reaction she'd been afraid of.

"Is that so wrong?"

"It is." He flung himself to his feet but didn't stomp off into the dark as it seemed he might. Instead, he turned to look up at something high on the wall. The window perhaps. When he spoke, his words were filled with that mocking he was so good at.

"You want me to move to a different city-oasis and become a pawn yet again, a hanger-on to the Sovereign of Gir-Tosaq, living on the goodwill and at the sufferance of a girl I found petty and self-involved."

"Because it's the better option." Emrie rose to her feet as well.

"Well, it's the better option for you anyway." He laughed, an ugly, scornful sound.

"Yes, for me," she said, irritation at him rising in her breast. His laughter was just rude. "But for you as well. You don't end up dead."

"You act as though I haven't considered this upside. You think you know better than I do what I need. You likely even think you have tender feelings for me that justify you enacting your will on mine. You don't want to save me. You want to be my savior."

"That's not true." She stepped in front of him, unwilling to let him speak so. He knew her better than this. "You're intentionally twisting everything around so I'm your enemy."

"Aren't you my enemy?" he asked, his voice building. The words spilled from him like a tipping barrel, faster and faster as if he'd held them in for so long they couldn't be repressed. "Do you truly believe Tenkiantemir spent all those years learning and training and warring in order to save his people? Or did he do it to *become* the hero that would save his people? There's a difference. And you, my dear Nitsya, have spent much time trying to prove to me what a good, kind, thoughtful person you are. Your words, this plan, your very demeanor show that it wasn't for me at all, was it?" He dropped his chin so that he was staring down at her, his eyes dark flames. "It was all to convince me, your family, perhaps the entire city-oasis, that you are someone worthy. A hero yourself. To earn yourself a name."

"You're wrong," she snapped back. His words didn't make her tremble and quake as they once would have. They lit the tinder of something deep and angry inside her instead, something she hadn't even realized was there. "How dare you say such things to me."

"I'm not saying it. You are. The tone of your voice proves I'm correct. I won't play this role in your game. I won't go to Gir-Tosaq. I won't be forced to act against my own will."

She held his gaze, smoldering. Of course, she wanted to be a good person. But she wasn't trying to hurt him in order to achieve that. For all that was wood and worthy, she was sacrificing her own happiness with him to save him.

But anything she said at that moment he'd attribute to more of his skewered view of her. That realization fed the hot flickering flame in her chest, fanning it into something larger, scorching, furious. How dare he.

He was wrong about one more thing, too. She could force him if she wanted. He was the one who'd pointed out that she was both clever and a witch.

***

Emrie was so enraged at Deriek that her first thought after leaving the prison was to let him rot for what he'd said. No one, not even Noemi had ever said such hateful things to her. The moment passed, and with it arrived a recognition that she was acting like him rather than herself. He'd let the darkness he carried rule his tongue. He'd attacked her because he'd felt attacked himself.

She knew this about him. He'd done so any number of times before, if not to such a degree. And she couldn't retaliate with the same. Anger didn't help. Anger made everything worse. She tried to bank the worst of it, only somewhat successfully.

She didn't know what to do. She still didn't have enough keys for all the locks in front of her, especially if Deriek was actively bolting doors closed. Her fuming did give her an idea of how to get a rug to Imjin, though. She needed to get through one real locked door, and her father was a man with access to many useful keys.

Since that problem had a solution, she handled it first.

The Juju birds' cage had been moved indoors to a sunny room just down the hall from the kitchens. The next morning, Emrie rose early and waited there for her father to come to feed them. He didn't look surprised to see her but greeted her as usual and then invited her to join him while he scattered the seeds. The birds went wild with chirping. It was all so normal that for a moment Emrie had a wild hope that she'd misunderstood everything. That he wasn't plotting against Deriek. That he was still the noble father she'd always believed him to be. Then, her anger gave her a shove in the back to remind her of everything that had happened.

He made his obeisance to the birds and then to the Renoa out in Its field. She kept her voice low when she made her request, respectful.

"I need something if I'm to move—"

"Don't speak plainly."

She ducked her head to acknowledge his words. She lowered her voice even more. "If I'm to fulfill my duty," she said, just loud enough to be heard over the birds. "I need my assignment, my person, to go above ground. It doesn't have to be outdoors. And it must be close to the holding place as it will be hard for me to get him there. I explored the halls and there is a locked door that appears to lead upward. Do you know where that door goes? Do you have a key?"

"I know of that door. I can procure a key, but the door leads into a servant's hall of the Sovereign's House. You mustn't be found in the Sovereign's House."

"I won't be," she assured him, putting lots of sincerity into her voice.

He turned away from her to face the cage. When he nodded, she saw the motion via the back of his head. She'd gotten what she wanted, but she hadn't been wrong. He really was plotting to use Deriek.

She watched him as he added a few more seeds to the feeders of his beloved birds and had another thought. The Renoa had asked her what Deriek needed in order to live. She'd thought the answer was obeying her father in learning to use the witchcraft, but that had been short-sighted. There was no way the Renoa was working with her father to dismantle the House of Valiyard. There was no way the Renoa wanted Deriek to die as part of her father's plotting.

Maybe what Deriek needed was someone who saw his value and had the ability to save him from her father and force him to do that which he did not want. Maybe that was the Renoa's point. She thought then, back to the conversation between Keeli and Lianjit about grit. She *could* force Deriek into safety. She *could* save him. Not from anger, but because she knew herself to be the person who held the responsibility for his life.

TWENTY-NINE

When Emrie next visited Deriek, he refused to speak to her. Apparently, their argument wasn't over, but since she didn't want to give away what she was thinking, she let it go and returned to her rooms. He would hate her just as much for sending him off with Imjin as he would if forced to marry into House Das. It was a price she had no choice but to pay.

She began to prepare, and it felt good in the same way learning the witchcraft had felt good. As if she was accomplishing something of importance.

Ahrens gave her another scarf with bangles around the edge. If Montali had followed instructions, it would somehow tell Imjin to lay the scarf where it wouldn't be noticed by anyone but her and then check it often for a note to appear in the center. Emrie embroidered a Juju bird into the scarf and then had Ahrens arrange for her to attend the Hall of Guests the following night. That worked out perfectly as Noemi was ill yet again. Their father used the opportunity to give Emrie the requested key.

The evening went smoothly. Once again, a number of people noticed her witchcraft delivering the scarf, but this time Emrie paid attention and made careful note of who they were. She recognized several, including Lady Sersi.

The next afternoon, she carved a letter to Imjin. It took her three tries to get the note right, and in the end, she kept it simple. If the Second Heir, Deriek Valiyard, were to accompany her out of Pol-Thiri, would she be willing to contract with him? She instructed Imjin to write out her answer and place it on the scarf.

Emrie figured out how to get the witchcraft to sense when that had happened, which for some odd reason it seemed to like. Not long after, it brought her back a small piece of parchment with an oversized "yes" dug so deep that the ink leaked through the backside.

When she told Ahrens that Deriek would join them on their exodus, Ahrens hugged her and told her she was brilliant. In return, she impressed upon Ahrens how difficult Deriek was likely to be, and that he'd have to be taken to Gir-Tosaq as a prisoner while he got used to the idea. The entire time she could just hear Deriek's voice making it clear how he felt about this. She had trouble sleeping.

It was still the better choice.

She and Deriek kept their distance. She brought a second cushion for herself and took to sitting with him in silence while he ate, everything she wanted to say curling and struggling within her, the loneliness of it.

She embroidered another rug with a large Juju bird and used the key from her father to hide it in a storage area not far beyond the underground door to the Sovereign's House. She sent a note to Imjin telling her where to find it. A day later, Imjin wrote back that she had the rug.

Emrie gave Ahrens the directions and the key to the room by the river. She'd transport Deriek and Imjin there, and then it'd be easy enough for Ahrens and Montali to collect them and flee the city-oasis before her father even knew it'd happened.

To keep anyone from noticing how preoccupied she was, Emrie made her daytime activities as inconsequential as possible. She asked Aunt Calys to set up another courting visit. She, Keeli, and Brid journeyed to the Barrack's Field to cheer Lianjit when she earned a tassel to decorate her sword scabbard.

She traded several more notes with Imjin through the scarf, telling her which night to lay out the rug and what to expect. On her last night with Deriek, she picked food items she knew he preferred and laid them out for him as she used to do. She knew very well he disliked it when she played the servant to him, and maybe that was part of why she did it. She almost preferred his anger to his silence.

"It's a feast for the Night of Deliverance," she said and left it at that.

She returned to her room and paced, checking the rise of the moon way too often, waiting for it to be perfectly aligned over the Renoa. It wasn't the Night of Deliverance, although Deriek would have no way of knowing. That was a full day away. Tonight was his deliverance, though. It was the night he left Pol-Thiri.

When the moon was set, she sent a note to Imjin and received an immediate response that she was ready. Emrie went to the chalk markings in her back room, but before crossing into the pattern, she sent a prayer to the Renoa that Imjin wouldn't be difficult, that Deriek would find the destiny he was meant for, and that maybe, someday, he'd forgive her for what she was about to do. Then she stepped into the center of the Juju bird and bent to touch the lines of the pattern.

Emrie's first impression when the witchcraft deposited her on Imjin's rug was that she was outdoors. The second was that someone was standing almost directly in front of her, holding up a blindingly strong lamp.

"Turn the light away."

"I'm assisting you," a high, delicate, annoyed voice said. Imjin's voice, Thank the Tree.

They were in the same upper-story patio where Emrie and Taspin had visited. She and Imjin were alone, but Imjin stood with the lamp held high and a doubtful look on her face as if she didn't quite trust Emrie.

For her part, Emrie had no idea what to say to this girl who would hopefully become the-boy-she-loved's spouse.

Imjin had followed instructions and dressed Pol-Thirian. She wore a plain laptevi of green, had one satchel at her side, and her hair was in braids.

"Your hair color might give you away," Emrie said, grasping for something to fill the space between them. "You'll need to keep it covered once you're freed. You'll remember to do that?"

"I'm not an idiot," Imjin replied. "You *can* get me out of here, right?"

"Of course," Emrie tried again. "I'm just nervous—"

"And you think I'm not?"

"I didn't mean to imply that." Emrie tried to sound both soothing and confident even though she felt neither. "All you have to do is stand in the middle of the pattern. The witchcraft will move you to a secret room. Once you're there, step back against the wall. I don't know what'll happen if you're still standing on the mat when I send Deriek over. I never practiced that."

"The witchcraft could hurt me?" Imjin asked, sounding suspicious.

"You won't even be aware of it." Or at least she didn't think Imjin would.

"How long will I be alone?"

"I don't know. Not long. But the Second Heir will be asleep, and he's likely to stay asleep for a long time. You'll have to wait with him until your brother comes to get you. That might not be until daylight, I don't know his exact plans."

"There's an awful lot that you don't seem to know."

What a rude thing to say, and it wasn't as true as it used to be. In realizing that, Emrie glared at Imjin much as she had Deriek when he'd taken what she felt for him and turned it into her wanting to earn herself a name.

"Just step in the pattern."

Imjin did, giving Emrie a nod that was either insulted or anxious, Emrie couldn't tell. She touched the pattern, and the girl, the lamp, the satchel, and that problem disappeared.

Before Emrie left, she took a moment for several deep breaths. She didn't want to be angry with Deriek the last time she ever saw him.

Once she was ready, she sent herself through the witchcraft to his prison. She arrived to the sound of his snoring. Mati Dechta's sleeping draft in the pudding had worked.

She got the work part over first. To make moving him easier, she pulled the rug she used for his bathing tub right next to him. It took all her strength to roll, push, and then arrange him inside the Juju bird, and it brought her back to the night when he'd been so sick. He felt the same heavy limpness.

He lay on his side, his hair falling forward in thick chunks that hid the lines of his face as if behind a curtain. Emrie pushed them out of the way, running her fingers through the silkiness, loving the feel of the strands that she'd cut herself. She tucked them gently behind his ear. This was it. The last time she would touch the warmth and goodness that was him.

Emrie curled up beside him, not ready to say goodbye. It wasn't close enough. She leaned forward, pressing her forehead into the side of his head, burying her face in his hair. He smelled like himself, part underground thing, part warm living thing, and still a bit of the Renoa. Emrie rested her lips against his cheekbone.

"Please understand that I'm trying to help you," she whispered right into his skin. Her eyes pooled with tears. "Don't be too angry with me. You need to live. You deserve to live. And I want you to live. Deriek Valiyard, I think even you want to live."

THIRTY

Illness wasn't common in Pol-Thiri, and when it happened, it was usually brought on by the River Nomads. Not that the River Nomads made the people of the city-oasis sick on purpose. It was said that since the River Nomads rejected the gifts of the Renoa, they were inherently out of balance and thus more prone to attacks from the unnatural world. When that happened, they flocked to the nearest city-oasis for help and spread their problems to the general populace. This, of course, was in their periods of peace, when their Gods were not demanding they attack the people of the cities and destroy the Renoas.

Deriek's illness had been an oddity, but not unusual. Being locked away from the elements for too long could knock one's internal rhythms off balance as well.

All of which was why Emrie was unalarmed the next morning when Mati Sarta and Mati Ereana woke her with word Noemi was sick. Also, Noemi seemed to make a habit of feeling ill whenever she wanted out of a social engagement.

When Emrie's maties said her father wanted her to attend Noemi's rooms, Emrie's first thought was that her actions of the night before had been discovered. That led to several moments of panic. But no. If it were true, her father would've come for her, not announced that there was a problem by sending maties. She got up and hurried to attend him. To do otherwise would be ill-mannered and thus suspicious.

Noemi's suite had always had a formidable air about it, one about accomplished goals and hard work. Right then it was eerily silent. Only her father and Mati Dechta were present. Both stood near Noemi's sleeping dais. Noemi lay to one side, tucked under silken blankets and propped on bright pillows. Maybe it was just in contrast to those pillows, but her face held no color at all. She was truly ill.

Emrie's father turned to her, his face equally pale. "Were you sick a seven-day ago? The day you spent in your room sleeping?"

"I was tired only." Emrie glanced back and forth between Mati Dechta and her father, not sure what it was they wanted from her. Mati Dechta nodded as if she'd expected the answer but didn't enjoy hearing it.

Her father frowned. "You haven't been sick since?"

"I don't believe so," she said carefully, trying to parse out his words.

"It wouldn't have mattered if we'd caught it earlier," Mati Dechta said, her tone low but with a firmness behind it Emrie hadn't ever heard directed at her father before. At Emrie, yes, but never him. "There's no cure," Mati Dechta finished.

Her father gazed steadily at Emrie. "Can you cure your sister?"

"What's wrong?" she asked, still carefully but with rising alarm.

"Come," Noemi breathed. "See." She struggled with her blankets, pushing at them until Mati Dechta helped and then lifted the hem of her sleeping shirt so that Noemi's belly was exposed.

Emrie moved closer. There was a small black line on her belly. As if someone had inked her.

"What is it?"

"Placr Beetle," Noemi said, her voice weak. "It's the poison of a Status War."

Swords for strangers, poisons for friends. Emrie blanched, all the blood of her body draining the way the water had when she'd emptied Deriek's bath. Noemi couldn't possibly have been poisoned.

"It's usually a swallowed poison," Mati Dechta said. "Although it's deadly to the touch as well, just takes longer. It makes the person sick almost immediately, but then festers, moving with the rhythms of the body until it rises to the skin after six or seven days."

"A seven-day?" Emrie asked with a jerking glance at her father. She and Noemi would've gotten ill about the same day. No. That wouldn't be right. She could see what must've happened. Noemi would've gotten sick the day after her father had conversed with the First Heir.

Emrie forced herself not to look at her father in horror. His dealings with the First Heir had gotten Noemi poisoned? The anger she'd felt when arguing with Deriek flared and flamed in her chest again. This time she squashed it. There wasn't time to let her emotions rule. She could blame her father later. Right now, she had to rid Noemi of that ugly black line.

This she could do. She would save her sister and force her father to see who she really was. "I'll need some ink and a brush."

Mati Dechta went to fetch Noemi's writing materials. When she returned, Emrie dipped the stylus in the ink and drew her Juju bird on Noemi's belly, encircling the black mark. She was aware of her father watching her, judging her use of the witchcraft.

The pleasure of accomplishment rose within her. For once, the responsibility was on her shoulders.

She finished her drawing and reached with a single finger to touch the pattern. The line of illness on Noemi's skin reminded her of one of Lady Sersi's prized worms, but darkened and lifeless.

In the background, she heard her father offer the Blessing of the Sun and follow that with the Blessings of the Earth, the Air, the Water, and finally That-Which-Is-Life. After a moment, Mati Dechta joined him so that together they repeated the Blessings in sync and in rhythm over and over again. There was something right about the cadence of their joined voices, something that fit into Emrie's self, two acknowledging hands on her shoulders while she worked on a difficult problem. She traced the pattern and felt the witchcraft settle into Noemi, just as it had Deriek. Eagerly. Determined.

Again she didn't see, so much as feel, Noemi's inner self. Emrie closed her eyes and sank onto the sleeping dais, keeping one hand circling.

It was the same experience but different. Instead of angry red blotches, she found a tangle of the blackened line, almost as if the piece on Noemi's skin was a broken tail or a snippet of snarled yarn that had gotten loose. The tangled ball moved and twisted, growing itself and pulling parts of Noemi into it.

She directed the witchcraft to remove the whole thing and knew immediately that wasn't possible. Doing so would take too much of Noemi with it. Instead, she asked the witchcraft to pull one loose fiber of the ball and send it out to the river where the rock she'd left there would now be buried in dried mud. It worked. But even as she rid Noemi's body of that single bit of line, another strand slithered into its place.

Just like what had happened with Deriek.

Emrie and the witchcraft went to work, calling out to the Renoa for help.

***

Deriek awoke in the dark knowing he'd been drugged. He recognized the grogginess and how far away the tips of his fingers felt from the joints of his arms. It took a while for the drug to dissipate enough to reconnect the extremities of his body, his anger, and his memory. Nitsya had drugged him and moved him while he slept.

She'd done it.

She'd betrayed him.

Just as expected.

This new place was dark, but the darkness was different, too silent. Funny that the small window of his former prison had had a sound to it, but it had. In this place, there was no window. No possibility of hope or escape.

For the moment.

There was another person with him. It took him a long time to recognize this even though she was not quiet at all. She was breathing hard and fast. Fearful. And it wasn't Nitsya.

Deriek sat up, which brought the breathing to an abrupt halt. He ignored that and the girl who would be the Daughter from Gir-Tosaq. He stretched his arms out, feeling the crack and stretch of his body unwinding. He was weak, but not as bad off as the last time he'd been drugged. He rolled his shoulders, swung his arms in the familiar opening movement of Tenkiantemir's Fifth Dance of Swords, and then stood up, noticing again how different he felt without that window staring down on him.

The black energy within him roared, demanding release.

From the deepest cravings of the heart comes the most catastrophic hate.

Betrayal was a shared blade, and Nitsya had swung first.

THIRTY-ONE

The Renoa said no.

Emrie woke to crusty tears in the corners of her eyes and the lingering effects of crushing failure. She was in her own bed, although she had no recollection of getting there. Heavy rugs had been drawn over her windows, but cold light slipped through a crack at one edge. She could smell the acrid scent of what remained of the Sacred Grasses after the annual burning, the aftermath of the Night of Deliverance. The odor would last for days; it always did.

She lay unmoving, staring at the sliver of light and letting the scent attack her. It stung the nose and throat in the same way a screeching bird frayed the ears.

The Renoa had said no.

She and the witchcraft had picked apart that knot of poison all day. She'd sent her pleas to the Renoa as her father and Mati Dechta chanted in the background. She hadn't worried at the Renoa's absence at first—it hadn't shown up immediately for Deriek either. But the longer she'd worked, the more worried she grew. Then, after hours and hours of trying, when Emrie was nearing exhaustion, the Renoa had softly but firmly whispered into her inner ear.

No.

Emrie sat up, pushing back long strands of hair that had come loose from her braids and tangled around her face. She heard the pad-pad of her maties in the next room, meaning they'd been waiting for her to rise. When they entered, their faces held no encouragement. Mati Ereana helped her to dress and Mati Sarta brought a tray of food, which Emrie picked at before announcing she would return to Noemi's chambers.

The charred smell of last night's burning was stronger there than in Emrie's chamber, as if it were drawn to the site of her failure. Her father stood at the edge of the sleeping dais as he had the day before. Mati Dechta sat at Noemi's side as if she'd never left. Noemi's sleeping tunic was pulled up, the lines of ink on her skin smeared and four of the insidious black marks now on her belly.

"I'll try again," Emrie whispered.

"No," Noemi replied. Her voice was slow and rough. "Too much risk. House Das needs you now."

Gods of old, no.

A sob rose in Emrie's throat, and she pressed a hand to her mouth, her eyes watering. Mati Dechta pinched her on the arm in remonstration.

It wasn't just Noemi that she'd failed. It was all of them. The entire House. She wished, oh, how she wished, she could talk to Deriek about what'd happened. Ask him why he thought the Renoa had rejected her and beg him to comfort her.

Mati Dechta nudged her. "You should go, child. Your sister will be cared for to the best of my abilities. You are needed elsewhere."

Emrie stood and left the room, taking swift gulps of the sour air until she became lightheaded. How could this be happening? How could she have failed? This one thing. This one vitally important thing. Why had the Renoa rejected her?

Had Deriek's awful story about the boy who'd gone after the River Nomad been correct after all? Had the witchcraft turned her into someone the Renoa no longer recognized?

No. The Renoa hadn't rejected her. That was the wrong word for what had happened. It just hadn't given her what she'd wanted.

Her father followed her out and told her to accompany him to his inner sanctum where he closed the wooden door and then turned to face her. He looked gaunt with exhaustion, and in that moment, Emrie could feel no anger toward him. When he spoke, she heard the awareness of what he'd done in his voice.

"There'll be no hunt for Noemi's killer nor seeking recompense from the Sovereign. I know who did this and there's nothing we can do."

"The First Heir?" She couldn't help a pinch in her voice.

"I wasn't vigilant enough. We've lost on this front . . ." His voice shook. There was so much pain in it that it broke through Emrie's own misery. He turned away as if he wanted his suffering for himself alone.

If he'd turned toward her, even the smallest amount, she'd have thrown her arms around him and comforted him. Forgiven him. Asked him to forgive her. Shared the burden. But he didn't. Etiquette and his own reticence wouldn't allow for it.

"There's still you and Ahrens to protect," he continued. "I can give you until the next Ceremony of the Thousand Gratitudes to prepare to be seen in public."

There wouldn't be a Ceremony until the odor from the Night of Deliverance wore down, but Emrie understood what he was telling her. He wanted to make sure she knew the appalling, ugly truth of how her own life was about to change.

Which led to another thought.

The First Heir must have poisoned Noemi because when her father had made that awful contract he hadn't specified which member of House Das was to marry an Heir. He'd meant Emrie or Ahrens, but the First Heir must have assumed he meant Noemi.

That was her father's error. That was why the First Heir had poisoned her sister.

Her Father gave a shake as if pulling himself together.

"We must show a strong front. We must not be broken. The other matter . . ." He glanced at the solidity of the shut door. "The Second Heir . . . Leave him where he is. I'll find someone else to care for him. Those plans are on hold."

It was the single thing he could've said to jerk Emrie's attention away from thoughts of Noemi.

"I already moved him." Even with everything else, she had this item, tiny compared to what had gone wrong, where she hadn't failed.

The room went quiet, and Emrie counted the swords on the wall to keep from letting her expression or anything else betray her secret. Her father didn't look at her.

"I'll send someone to deal with it. Go about your days as normally as possible. I spoke with Ahrens earlier—"

"Ahrens?" Emrie cut her father off for the first time in her entire life, her voice high. "He's home? Here? In the house?" He should've collected Deriek and Imjin yesterday morning. Ahrens should be long gone.

"Yes. He left Noemi's room right before you entered."

***

"What happened?" she asked without preamble. She'd hunted Ahrens down in his rooms. They were alone, and she didn't bother to lower her voice. "Where's Deriek?"

He shook his head, long and sorrowful.

"They won't leave."

"Deriek? You and Montali were supposed to make him. I warned you he'd be difficult, but you said—"

"I mean Imjin and Montali. They refuse to leave Pol-Thiri. They say their father made Imjin contract before their Renoa to stay here."

"But you had a plan to return to Gir-Tosaq." Imjin had said she'd marry Deriek there.

Lines of despair framed Ahren's usually cheerful eyes and mouth. He pressed a balled fist against the wall and then leaned his forehead against it. He smelled like the burning of the Grasses which meant he must've represented House Das last night.

"*I* had a plan." The words sounded like they mangled his throat on the way out. "Montali never said a word against it or told me he couldn't or wouldn't leave. And Emrie," he pushed away from the wall. "I think it's because something's wrong in Gir-Tosaq. Really, really wrong. Montali won't talk about it, and he tells me everything."

Emrie's ire rose even more. *Montali tells Ahrens everything* seemed to only be a correct description of their relationship in Ahrens's imagination.

"What happened to Deriek?" she demanded.

"I have them hidden. They're safe and will stay safe, but I have no idea what to do now."

"Deriek is with them?"

Ahrens turned to look at her.

"Deriek?"

If he wasn't several hands taller and broader than her, she'd have physically shaken him. "The Second Heir," she shouted. "The person with Imjin. Locked in that room. Meant to return with her to Gir-Tosaq. Where is he?"

Ahrens gave her an irritated look. "He attacked us and left. Sprained Montali's wrist in the going and left me with a bruise on the back of my head." He turned to show her the back of his head, but Emrie didn't care. She'd *told* him to be cautious and to expect Deriek to be difficult. His excuses fell flat and left her heart skipping in fear.

"Do you know," she asked, hating that she had to ask, but not knowing what else to do. "Can you find out . . . please . . . if any bodies have been found that might match the description of the Second Heir?"

Ahrens's eyes widened in surprise, but he shook his head.

"We would've heard if someone had killed him. I'm sorry but I can barely provide for Imjin and Montali. I have to figure them out first. The Second Heir is on his own."

***

The rest of Emrie's day was long with the exhausted feeling of being pulled in the two separate directions of her sister's illness and Deriek's disappearance. Neither of which she could do anything about other than accept her own helplessness. She spent the afternoon with Noemi, wanting to do something comforting, like crawl into the bed and wrap her arms around her sister. Noemi had other ideas, insisting Emrie retrieve her writing materials and then dictating instructions on the Guild and the House and who Emrie should contact about what problems. Emrie did as she asked, listening but writing almost nothing down.

That night, she went in search of Deriek. Or not in search exactly. She couldn't find a way to do that, but she figured out how to check that he lived. She retrieved the cloth she'd used for listening to her father, redid the pattern as a Juju bird, and asked the witchcraft to give her sounds from the patterns in Deriek's flesh. What it brought wasn't sound, or at least not in a normal sense. It was like when as a child one stuck one's fingers in one's ears and then spoke or swallowed or tapped one's foot. She could hear the steady rumble of a heart and the rasping of air entering and exiting a body as if the patterns were carved on the inner layer of skin rather than the outer.

He lived.

She sagged onto her bed in relief.

It was a temporary relief.

Nothing she'd done changed his situation.

She kept the cloth to her ear, making sure one breath always followed another until she couldn't stay awake any longer.

The next day she waited for her father to show up demanding to know what she'd done that had allowed Deriek to escape. It never happened. Apparently, her father didn't care enough to tell her Deriek was gone.

On the third afternoon after her failed healing, Brid arrived with a tea tray.

"I know Noemi is ill."

Emrie had given little thought to Brid, she who was at the center of everything. Forced to see her now, healthy and hale and with a stubborn look on her face, felt unfair.

"Noemi told me, but I figured it out days ago. Noemi says I'm to help you. Mati Dechta says I should stay by your side."

Emrie said nothing. Resentment accomplished nothing, and Brid was unlikely to notice either way.

Brid deposited the tea tray on a stone table and sat.

"Noemi says you need help."

"I heard you the first time," Emrie muttered.

"She wants me to receive visitors and attend the Hall of Guests with you and help you keep up with the guildwork as everyone knows you're terrible at it."

"Noemi said that?"

"No. But everyone knows." Brid poured a cup and shoved it Emrie's direction. "And I'm to make you go to the Marketplace today so everything appears normal. Which is silly as nothing is normal, but I said I'd do it."

"You are very kind." Emrie looked toward the hall beyond her chamber. She wished Brid was the kind of person to understand her look as a hint to leave so that she'd stop listing out the ways Noemi thought her incompetent. All of which Emrie was well aware of.

"I'm not kind. I want something."

"What do you want?" Emrie asked, but she knew the answer.

"Lanka," Brid said as expected. "Once you become First Daughter, you'll release me from House Das so I can marry him. Lady Sersi says I must give you time to adjust to Noemi's death. I'm tired of waiting, but I'll do as Lady Sersi says. In the meantime, I'm going to tilt the balance between us my direction."

Emrie picked up her cup of tea, feeling an irrational desire to throw it at Brid. What an insensitive, brutish thing to say. Still she kept her voice calm. "You can't move the balance enough to gain that boon."

"I don't have to," Brid said. "I told you. I figured out Noemi was sick on my own. I went by to visit her when you were there with your father and Mati Dechta. I heard them chanting. I saw what you were doing, and I'm not stupid like you think I am. I know what I saw. I know your secret and I know your father knows. You and he will buy my silence by freeing me from this thrice-cursed House."

Emrie tightened her hand on her cup so hard, the porcelain gave a crack. Regardless of who Brid really was, Emrie wished she'd never been born.

***

It took two days more for the news of Noemi's illness to become common knowledge. How it got out, Emrie didn't know. The first person to show up to give condolences was Taspin. She asked after Noemi and then fawned all over Emrie. It was a disgusting display that Emrie took without letting her dislike show. Brid kept her mouth shut as well, pointing out afterward that Taspin was half opportunist, half leech. Which coming from Brid was quite the insult.

Over the course of the next seven-day, the women of the other Houses visited. Aunt Calys handled most of them but insisted Emrie be present. Keeli and Lianjit came with their mothers. On their way out, Keeli gave her a quiet hug and Lianjit squeezed her hand.

Whenever possible, Emrie listened in on Deriek not yet being dead. Every moment with that cloth not pressed to her ear was spent certain he was already gone. Every breath and beat of his heart filled her with a wrenching fear that it would be his last. It was a torture she couldn't stop inflicting on herself, one that left her wrung like twisted cloth.

Noemi's skin turned yellow. More and more black lines covered her torso and then her arms and legs. She stopped taking anything but tea. Their father came and went, checking on Noemi whenever he could, looking as drawn as Emrie felt. Mati Dechta never left Noemi's side.

It was during all this that her father sent a matie to remind her she would be attending the Hall of Guests that night. Both he and Ahrens had business beforehand, so she was to take Brid along as company. It was a suspicious arrangement, but Emrie couldn't see anything to do but agree. Noemi selected her clothing and instructed her on what she should say, repeating the same words over and over, not seeming to remember she was doing so in a way that hurt to hear. Emrie's brilliant, beautiful, proud sister was wasting away to nothing. When Noemi ran out of breath, Mati Dechta took over, keeping things as normal as possible.

Emrie dressed slowly for the Ceremony, dreading that night as much as she had her first one.

Her laptevi was in a lavender so pale it almost looked blue. It was fitted in the bodice and then fell in pleats to the floor. The cowl draped low to show off the graceful line of her spine, and she wore a silver chain with one large sapphire that hung between her shoulder blades. Mati Serena did her hair in a complicated swirl of braids and knots with matching lavender threads. A woman's manner of dressing, not a girl's. Noemi was forcing Emrie to make a statement. Brid wore a laptevi in orange.

The moment they entered the Hall of Guests, Emrie was surrounded by people and Brid was pushed to the side. Emrie forced a pained smile and let Keeli's vapid elder sister chat at her. Next, came a string of the boys she'd courted and more of Noemi's friends.

Brid was dogged, keeping as close to Emrie as possible, like a guard. Emrie tried to act agreeably and not say anything too foolish, but everyone wanting her attention felt surreal.

The First Heir entered, and Emrie had to turn away, so deep was the hatred she felt for this man who'd poisoned her sister. But she had little energy in her for hatred and as quickly as it struck, it flared out. She just wanted to go home to listen for Deriek.

Then, as if the thought of him were the conjuring itself, she looked up and saw him. Right there. In the Hall of Guests.

Her heart burst into a wild, uneven beat. Her skin flushed, and she blinked several times just to be sure she was awake.

He was thirty paces from her, a familiar half-smile on his lips, chatting with a girl in sunset pink. It'd been so long since she'd seen him in light and color that the beauty of him snatched the breath from her chest, leaving her to gasp painfully to catch it back.

She wanted to run to him but held back. He wouldn't recognize her, and she'd learned the hard way about acting without thinking. Brid pressed between Emrie and an Eighth-ring girl to ask if she was unwell.

"I'm thirsty," Emrie managed, to rid herself of Brid.

He was dressed in green-black and looked so elegant her knees felt weak. His hair hung free, resting at his shoulders just as she'd cut it, but combed back and tidy. His face was smooth now that he'd had access to a razor, the change emphasizing the sharp line of his jaw narrowing to his chin. She would've liked to touch his skin to feel the difference. She could even mark the spot above his cheek where she'd whispered her pleas for him to live.

"The Second Heir has returned," she said softly.

"Showed up just today," a Third-ring boy announced. "They say he's been hiding with the River Nomads until the Daughter of Gir-Tosaq left."

"I see," Emrie said, but she didn't. It made no sense. He'd fought against her suggestions that he solve his problems some way other than death. He'd gotten angry when she'd pushed him about it. Yet here he was.

For her? Was that possible?

She made a small noise in the back of her throat, a keening of hope. The way he held himself, relaxed but waiting, the way he tilted his head, the way he tapped two fingers against his thigh, everything about him was so familiar. So hers. She waited for him to turn and meet her gaze, for their eyes to lock and the knowing, the familiarity to happen. He was Deriek. She was Nitsya. Of course, he'd recognize her.

Deriek continued speaking to the girl as if he were enjoying the conversation. He bowed in a courtly, graceful way that made his hair brush forward along his face. A gray jealousy grated up Emrie's chest. That hair was her doing. That he was alive was because of her. He belonged to her. The entire room should be able to see it. Why wouldn't he look at her? He led the girl to the dancing rings.

The conversation around Emrie continued. One boy speculated on the trials of living with the River Nomads. A girl admired the Second Heir's style of hair and wondered if the rest of the boys would copy it.

Deriek wasn't as relaxed as he was trying to portray, though. He glanced around the room, casual about it as he danced, trying not to let anyone notice what he was doing. Almost as if he was searching for someone.

But not for her. Deriek was the most observant person she'd ever met, and she was openly, blatantly, staring at him. He seemed to be carefully *not* looking her direction. Which meant what?

That he couldn't stand to do so.

Pain, equal to being hit by her father or failing to heal Noemi, struck Emrie dead center. She fought not to double over with the blow of it.

She had no right to it. She'd known the repercussions of the choice she'd made. Something within her cracked anyway.

The dance ended. Deriek led the girl back to her friends, and only then did he turn Emrie's direction. He didn't catch her gaze but looked past her as if he wanted to direct her attention. She followed the look.

He stared at a girl in orange. A girl who frowned as she awkwardly plowed her way through the crowd toward Emrie carrying a goblet. His sister. Brid.

What had been cracked before broke so suddenly even the witchcraft reacted, shooting its jolt of lightning up her arms in horrified recoil. Emrie wanted to fall to her knees. To run from the room. To hide so no one would see her heart shattering like glass on a cold tile floor. She wrapped her arms around her waist to hold the pieces together.

There was something much worse than knowing he couldn't forgive her.

She saw no surprise in his gaze as he watched Brid. He'd known who he looked for. He knew who Brid was. *It won't end well for you,* he'd once said when Emrie'd insisted that she trusted him. He'd told the truth.

The something worse than facing his hatred was realizing it had all been a lie. That he'd figured out the secret. That he'd used her to turn the entire situation his own direction. That it was over.

Two days later, Noemi died.

Thirty-Two

The worst of the seasonal cold broke, and the sun lost its smudginess and hardened in the sky. The Juju birds' cage was moved back outdoors, but when Emrie went out to the Breakfast Patio each morning their raucous calling for attention had been culled to two lone birds. The rest had died of Placr Beetle poison found in their feed. It was much debated if Noemi or Emrie's father had been the intended recipient as normally her father fed them.

Emrie didn't doubt the First Heir had gotten who he'd intended. Like Brid, he wasn't as foolish as he seemed.

Emrie took a seat at a table, watching dully as the remaining birds hopped from branch to branch within their barren cage. She couldn't bring herself to offer them or the Renoa any Blessings.

Deriek had made no move to speak to her since the night she'd seen him. Nor had he approached Brid. Emrie had made no effort to warn her father that Deriek knew the truth. Brid still had no idea what was going on around her. It almost felt like Emrie was back to the beginning when she'd been oblivious to the never-ending wranglings going on around her.

Life went on.

Mati Dechta arrived to deliver tea, fresh-baked wafer bread, and warmed honey.

"It's chilly this morning. You should go indoors."

The sluggish cold reflected how Emrie felt inside. She chose a bread.

Mati Dechta left without saying more. The entire House was worried about her. The day prior, Aunt Calys had suggested it was past time she wrote to Aunt Poercha. Underpinning the conversation had been an insistence that Emrie step up to her duty to House Das rather than wallowing in the unseemly grieving for Noemi that was drowning her. How Aunt Calys knew about her need for Aunt Poercha, Emrie didn't bother to ask.

Brid pestered her daily, too, but not about Lanka. She also seemed to think Emrie was on the verge of collapse and kept bringing her every luxury she could think of. Apparently, Brid did have a kind side. Just as likely, Brid was working toward her own self-interest.

Emrie heard the sweep of the rug to the House being pulled aside but thinking it was Mati Dechta yet again, didn't turn to look. The two Juju birds tweeted and chirped a sad little song, and she heard the thump-slide of her father making his way across the patio. He didn't stop to feed the birds but made his obeisance to the Renoa and then took a seat opposite her.

His head was freshly shorn and the matie who had done the job had nicked him above his ear, leaving a scab. The crags on his face had become canyons, and the end of his beak of a nose was red as if he'd been rubbing it. That he was suffering should've made her want to reach out to him, but an ugly part of her felt he deserved it.

When he spoke, his voice had lost the desperation of the days they'd watched Noemi dying and was again the same stern sound as always.

"You are now First Daughter."

"I am." It wasn't hard to say. She'd practiced just to be certain she could speak the words without a tremor.

Perhaps her practiced confidence offended him because he looked away before speaking. "There's something of what we must speak."

"Of course."

Whatever her father had broken when he'd hit her had scarred. Who knew why that was. Perhaps it was realizing Deriek, too, had used her. Perhaps it was seeing her father for who he was. Perhaps it was because when she'd finally gone to the Renoa to ask why It wouldn't help her heal Noemi, she'd received no answer.

The maimed part wasn't in the same shape as before and would never go back, but she no longer needed it to. Her father had lost the right to be her judge.

"The Second Heir doesn't know you are the one who cared for him?"

"I don't believe so, no." She lied easily enough, waiting for him to get to whatever plot he'd come up with next. He had no choice now but to involve her.

"And your relationship with him, he'd have positive feelings toward you? The balance is weighted in your favor?"

"It's hard to say," she said carefully, not wanting to be caught unawares. "He's not an easy person."

"A situation has arisen."

"With the Second Heir?" She wanted to ask him about Brid, but she didn't. She didn't think he'd tell her the truth.

"With the First." He sat with his back to the rising sun and without the Renoa's canopy to filter it, a ray of light shone into Emrie's eyes, leaving her father in shadow. "You've heard that the Daughter of Gir-Tosaq has disappeared? Likely her people have snuck her out of the city and are hiding her along the river until the waters rise and she can return home. The First Heir needs a replacement for her, and quickly, as he's been made to look foolish. He has indicated an interest in you."

"Me?" Emrie's voice squeaked in surprise, and she shifted so that the trunk of the Renoa blocked out the blinding light. "How does he even know who I am?" The one time she'd met him, he'd been intent on killing insects.

"Everyone knows who you are, Daughter of Das." Her father sounded impatient. "Do you understand what will happen if you marry him?"

"Of course, I do," she snapped back. "Why me?"

His brows drew together as if he found her quick tone disrespectful. Emrie didn't care. "First, the Sovereign's health hasn't been good for a long time, and it's becoming hard to hide that. Which pressures the First Heir to marry. While you didn't inherit the depths of your mother's beauty, you're attractive in your own way and taking you from House Das leaves us bereft of a First Daughter. Second, he has tired of troublesome girls and wants someone biddable. Everyone knows you are so."

"I see." Another hit. Another truth. The First Heir's interest wasn't really about her. The First Heir wanted to continue to punish House Das and thought she'd be easy to manipulate.

"Our greatest protection for you and our House is your relationship with the Second Heir. You must use it. You must court him. You must convince him to contract into House Das." He dropped a fist on the table. The bones of his knuckles showed white.

Her only outward reaction was to settle deeper into her seat. She didn't fear her father hitting her. She saw through him too well. His entire last statement would be a lie. He wouldn't be encouraging her to court Deriek to bring him into House Das. Deriek would need the Sovereign's or the First Heir's permission to do that, which he was unlikely to receive since her father's agreement with the First Heir was over. Unlike Deriek running away to Gir-Tosaq, should House Das take him without permission from his House, there would be a heavy price to pay, a Judgment. A simpler solution to protect Emrie from the First Heir would be for Emrie to quickly marry someone else.

More likely, her father wanted her to plant herself between the two Heirs. To become the next person they fought over. The person they killed each other over. Then her father could present Brid to the world to inherit, somehow married to Ahrens.

But her father had miscalculated. Deriek wouldn't fight for her. He had his own goals. Even hurting as she'd been in the Hall of Guests, she'd read him easily. There was no way she could've mistaken the calculation and cunning and pure knowing in his countenance while he'd stared at Brid. She didn't know when he'd figured out that there was a Third Heir, but it must've happened long before she'd drugged him and set him free. *It won't end well for you.*

The way she saw it, her father wanted both Deriek and Cystel dead with Brid Das as the Sovereign.

Deriek must want to pit Cystel against Brid and claim the Sovereignty for himself.

Cystel wanted Deriek dead and Emrie to be his bride.

Other than Lanka, Emrie had no idea what Brid wanted.

What do you want, Nitsya?

She'd spent so much time letting other people answer that for her. They'd given her titles and names and roles to play. The good daughter, the obedient sister, the girl with the witchcraft, a muritt, a leopard, Piara, Nitsya, the Second and now First Daughter.

What do you want?

The answer came to her like the shaking of the earth under the city-oasis that happened in the Season of the Soil, like a jump of the witchcraft.

She looked at her father, keeping her face schooled and relaxed, trying to give nothing of her thoughts away and knowing she wasn't as successful as she liked. She wanted Pol-Thiri to be what it was supposed to be. She wanted her House to feel like they weren't endlessly under attack. She wanted Deriek to live without death hanging over his life or a Seat just out of his reach. She wanted Deriek to forgive her and acknowledge that he hadn't just been using her, that something had sprouted between them, and that it was young and tender but still alive.

She looked past her father, staring toward the naked white tree in the distance, an awareness settling over her. She couldn't have everything she wanted, but she could see a way to fix some of it. She knew her father. She knew Deriek. She thought she knew enough of the Sovereign and the First Heir.

It wouldn't be easy, and she couldn't see how to make it happen just yet. Even if she figured that out, she might fail. But she'd proven that she wasn't a person who gave up just because a thing was hard.

For all that grew under the sun, it'd be right to try. She was good at trying. She did have grit.

All she had to do was rid the world of the First Heir.

***

Emrie sent Brid off on an errand the next morning and invited Keeli and Lianjit to visit. As much as she'd prefer to take care of the First Heir by herself, there was no way she'd succeed alone, and Keeli and Lianjit were also Second Daughters who'd been much overlooked.

To do them honor and guarantee privacy, she had the maties set cushions under an awning near the Central Garden's fishpond. When Keeli and Lianjit arrived, they both seemed confused by the formality but neither questioned it. Lianjit's expression was neutral, and Keeli's was curious but cautious.

"Is something amiss?"

Other than her sister's death?

Emrie didn't say that. Instead she poured them each a cup of tea. They wore their cowls down and Keeli had glittering emerald threads in her braids. Emrie wondered absently if witchcraft had created the sheen.

"I need your help," Emrie said, feeling nervous even though she'd practiced her opening. "There's something I must do and things I must learn in order to do it. It won't be easy."

"What's going on?" Keeli asked.

There was a sudden shock of movement and black wings from above. All three of them looked up. One of Pol-Thiri's clever crows settled on a pole of the awning. It might've been coincidental as the maties threw scraps out to attract birds, but Emrie hoped it was a sign. She took a deep breath and began.

"Back in the Season of Water, I started to have trouble with my hands." She told them the story as it had happened, holding nothing back—the witchcraft, her father, Deriek, the Sovereign's problems, even Brid's role and true parentage. She was honest about her own success and multiple failures. She admitted how dangerous the First Heir was and that she feared him.

By the time she was done, the sun had been pulled much higher in the sky. But also the air felt lighter, the world warmer. The crow stayed the entire time, listening, and neither of her friends looked at her as if they were surprised by what she'd accomplished. Which had to be one of the greatest compliments she'd ever received.

"Brid looks just like the First Heir," Keeli said as if considering the matter. "I can't believe I didn't see it before."

"This entire time, we've been befriending the next possible Sovereign. Can you imagine what that'll do to our reputations should she inherit?" Lianjit asked.

"This is too important to let it be about us," Keeli replied with a chiding nod in Lianjit's direction.

"And it's *if* she inherits," Emrie said. "But that's what I want to happen."

"She'd make an interesting Sovereign," Keeli continued. "Emrie, I know the two of you don't get along, but she does have a strong sense of justice and is bluntly honest."

It was true, barring her blackmail over Lanka, Brid was principled.

"I'm hoping," Emrie said, "that if I present the Sovereign with Brid and show him she is his daughter, he'll kill the First Heir himself so that she can inherit and carry forward the House of Valiyard with honor."

"But even if the First Heir dies," Keeli argued, "Brid won't inherit next, the Second Heir will."

"Not if Deriek refuses to take the Seat. He doesn't truly want to be the Sovereign. He thinks he wants it only because he hates his father." She could picture the expression on Deriek's face if he heard her second-guessing him, but she was right. He didn't want to be Sovereign. He'd shown no interest in the doings of the city-oasis other than when she'd brought them up. He didn't seem to like politics or even the peoples of the rings. He wasn't ambitious that way. Not really. He was meant for something else. A role tied to the Renoa perhaps. A Sage, maybe. He just hadn't realized it yet, and she was going to have to convince him.

"The Second Heir is a quitter," Lianjit said. "He's never stood up for his people."

Emrie let that go as she didn't want to expose Deriek too much by trying to explain.

"The challenge is getting the four of them together—The Sovereign, the First Heir, Deriek, and Brid. I can't do that alone."

"I can handle Brid," Keeli said.

"I can't handle the First Heir," Lianjit added quickly.

"He's the biggest problem," Emrie admitted, although deep inside she wasn't sure that was true. Deriek, too, would be hard. "If the First Heir's interested in me already, I was thinking I could court him. I just don't know how to do that."

"You courted all last season," Keeli said, the words half question.

Emrie tried to add in a bit of humor. "Mostly Aunt Calys has been courting on my behalf, and I've been sitting quietly trying not to embarrass myself. I'm terrible at this kind of thing. Keeli, you are good with people and I'm good at learning. Will you teach me?"

"I suppose I'd better," Keeli said.

"Then I could lure him away," Emrie said.

Lianjit leaned forward. "That only works until we have to capture him. Neither of you knows how to use a sword, and while I'm good, he's bigger and better."

"Yes," Emrie admitted. "We'll need more help. I was thinking Ahrens. He has a friend I can pull in as well. I have something they both want that I can hold over their heads."

"That," Lianjit agreed, "gives us more options."

Up above them, the crow took off, flapping for the open sky.

***

It'd taken Deriek less than a day of freedom to discover her real name, and he hadn't been surprised by it. House Das was known for being cunning and conniving. That his brother had poisoned her sister made everything fall into place.

He'd recognized her the moment she'd entered the Hall of Guests just by her bearing and the way she'd tilted her head as she looked around. Everything about her was exactly as he'd pictured, fine-spun and poised. A heron, not a hawk.

In that moment of recognition, he'd wanted to ring her slender neck. Every ounce of burning fury he'd built up focused in on her and her treachery.

By the time she'd noticed him, he'd had himself under control.

She'd stood there staring at him in such a straightforward way that only someone blindfolded would be unlikely to notice. Which his brother was not. Her putting herself at such risk had scared him badly enough that he'd then given away his own plans to surprise her into pulling herself together. It was the only thing he'd been able to come up with to do.

He blamed himself for that. He blamed her even more.

Her "cousin" had been as easy to spot as she had, and while he'd had a moment of shock at the clear likeness to his brother, the truth of the matter was that he wouldn't have looked twice at the girl if he hadn't known the secret. Deriek had since learned the girl's schedule, found her connection to House Sersi, and ingratiated himself with them.

What was not going well was that his father saw his return as an acceptance of his ill-fated purpose and had been calling for him daily to discuss it. Deriek blamed Emrie Das for that as well, irrational though it was.

Deriek waited until the maties were gone from his rooms for the night and the surrounding House as silent as it ever got. He rose from his sleeping dais, thinking about how to get Brid Das to trust him, and dressed to go out. He'd once been exceptionally good at strategy. This should be easy.

He told the norie guards at the exit of the House that he was going to Gennant's Tea House just as he did every night, but then he turned neither that direction nor toward the open desert. Instead he hid his ornate overdress in an alcove so that he wore only a nondescript laptevi. He covered his distinctive face with his cowl and walked around the inner circle until he reached House Das. He stepped into its shadows to stare at the wooden entry door, carved with birds of prey.

Gods of old, he hated her. Hated her more in these last weeks than he did his mother or his father or any of his friends from Vin-Yonekur.

He wanted to bash the door down. Raid this place that belonged to her. Destroy the memory of her making him hope.

Her door had become another window. Another barrier to haunt him.

This was supposed to be easy, but it was not. He was supposed to be free, but he was not.

THIRTY-THREE

Emrie dressed especially well for the next Ceremony of Gratitude. She wore a ruby laptevi that had been her mother's, with a cowl so fine it appeared as if fire cascaded down her back. She rode in a litter to the House of Guests alone. Brid had been left behind as this was the night Emrie courted an Heir.

Just not the one her father was expecting.

Using the witchcraft to travel, Emrie, Keeli, and Lianjit had been meeting nightly to prepare. They'd worked out the details of their plan, Keeli had taught Emrie what she knew of courting, and Lianjit had insisted both of them learn to properly hold a sword to avoid looking incompetent. The swordwork hadn't gone well, but it had become the fun part of their nights.

They'd decided not to bring in Ahrens until they were sure the First Heir was hooked, although Emrie discovered where he had secreted away Montali and Imjin. They were staying in an unused wing of House Das. Which was both audacious and risky.

When Emrie arrived in the Hall of Guests, she was immediately mobbed. She didn't look at the Sovereign's dais, not even a glance to see who was there and who wasn't. That had been Keeli's first rule—let the First Heir approach her, which if what her father said was correct, he was likely to do.

She spent the first half the evening chatting, occasionally dancing, practicing the little tricks Keeli had suggested and feeling awkward. She wasn't likely to get good at courting or acting natural with strangers. It kept her distracted enough that she didn't break Keeli's second rule—do not under any circumstances look for or make eye contact with Deriek Valiyard, regardless of how badly she wanted to do so.

She'd just finished dancing with a Sixteenth-ring boy when she let her gaze wander to the Sovereign's dais. She spotted Deriek right away, but kept her eyes soft and unfocused, looking instead to his older brother who was standing arms crossed staring her direction. Their eyes met. He stepped down from the dais.

Even Keeli hadn't thought it would be this easy.

The drummers started up new beat, and Emrie's heart pounded in fearful sync to the rhythm. She was doing this.

The First Heir stopped in front of her, and she forced herself to raise her gaze from his boots. His eyes were dark pools of nothingness. No emotion, no energy, no acknowledgment that he was looking at a fellow child of the Renoa. To make it worse, everything about the way he stood, feet apart, hips braced, hands flat at his sides, was threatening.

She should've started studying sword years ago.

The drumming got louder. The woodwinds' melody joined in.

"Daughter of Das." There was no pleasantness in his voice, just that odd off-rhythm tone.

His eyes slanted down like Deriek's, and she focused on that rather than on the fact that he'd killed her sister.

"First Heir Valiyard." She was scared enough to sound just as docile as he thought her to be.

They proceeded through a formal greeting while the surrounding people pretended not to be watching with avid curiosity. She wondered what her father thought. Perhaps this was what he wanted to happen anyway.

"A flower as fine as you deserves as worthy a setting. Would you honor me by joining me on my father's dais?" His tone belayed both the compliment and that this was anything but an order.

"Yes." Her voice quavered, and his dead eyes flickered with interest at her fear.

Once on the dais, he positioned her on a cushion where everyone could see, Imjin's same cushion, and then ordered a matie to bring food. He said nothing more to her, leaving her in order to pace the dais, a hulking, brooding, monster of a man. Emrie's tension rose and ebbed the nearer and farther he moved from her, and it seemed he liked that as well.

But the truly terrifying thing was how impersonal it all felt. The matter of her future had been settled in his mind just because she'd said that single word of agreement, and he no longer needed to think of her beyond making sure everyone noticed his conquest.

Then in one moment when the First Heir was farthest away and she could breathe a little easier, someone came up behind her. She couldn't see him and didn't turn to look but knew who it would be.

"What are you doing?" Deriek whispered against her ear, his voice tight and sharp.

She shivered at the warmth of his breath down her bare neck with a badly timed rush of joy. He smelled of the Renoa, but instead of being mixed with a musty underground tang, he wore a scent of some type. Something warm that made her think of the winds of LeafFall. Even as she noticed, she looked to the First Heir. He'd been engaged by someone else and his back was turned in her direction. Deriek was not stupid when it came to his brother.

It was also a good sign that he'd approached her. Keeli had thought he might. Neither of them had expected it so openly, but Emrie's father would be pleased.

"What I must," she said firmly.

"He's only after you because he saw your interest in me. We must speak. Set it up so you can come to me, Nitsya."

Relief flooded through her body, making her want to sag backward against him. He would never speak so unless he still held a space inside himself for her. But it was too soon to claim it. They weren't ready, so she kept her voice even, almost impersonal.

"You once said that you'd tell me the meaning of Nitsya when you were ready to call me something else."

"I—"

"Don't you think it's time? My name is Emrie."

Even without looking, she could feel his frown. "Send me one of your witchcraft rugs."

"Not yet."

***

The First Ceremony had gone so well that Emrie, Keeli, and Lianjit decided there was no need for dragging out the courting, especially as "courting" was a complete misnomer for what had occurred. The next step was bringing in Ahrens and Montali.

Emrie cornered Ahrens and said she'd tell their father the Flaust siblings were living in House Das unless he let her speak to them. Ahrens caved immediately. He was just as easy to bully as she was.

At first glance, Montali looked just like his sister, delicate with an attractive prettiness of features. He was only slightly taller than her as well, but where Imjin simpered, he just looked plain old unhappy. That didn't improve when Ahrens introduced Emrie.

"I've come to make you a trade," she said.

Montali shrugged his shoulders in an uninterpretable foreign way. For a moment, she reconsidered trusting him. Once she laid out the plan, she'd be giving him and his sister a power over herself.

"Tell us, Sister," Ahrens said loudly, with a sideways glance at Montali to say he thought Emrie foolish. "We're waiting."

Unfortunately, there was no better option than to trust them. She outlined what had happened and her current goal. That led to questions, which she answered honestly, only holding back what was unrelated or too personal.

Ahrens glanced regularly at Montali as if for his reaction. Imjin appeared shocked. Montali kept a stony expression on his face and asked the most questions. He wasn't the type of person Emrie'd have ever put with Ahrens, and she was gambling on Ahrens's affections being returned in equal measure by the stiff, pouting boy. She turned to her brother.

"I'm now First Daughter. If you do exactly what I say, help me capture the First Heir, and remain silent about what you know until he's dead and Brid takes his place, I'll give permission as First Daughter for you and Montali to contract, bringing Montali into House Das. Even against Father's wishes."

Ahrens's eyes lit at that, but Montali's narrowed.

"You say your Renoa spoke to you, specifically telling you this cousin is an Heir?"

"I wouldn't say the Renoa speaks," she replied. "But It gave me the knowledge, yes."

He made another one of those shrugs that she couldn't interpret. "You had this happen before?"

"A message from the Renoa? Yes."

A look, yet again uninterpretable, passed between him and his sister. It was Imjin who broke it, turning to Emrie with a sigh.

"He's going to help you whether or not you invite him into House Das. If a Renoa revealed that this is what It wants, there's no way my brother will refuse."

"It's true," Montali said, displeased.

Ahrens threw his arms around Montali, who softened at the touch and leaned his head against her brother's shoulder. Watching them, Emrie was overcome with a rather unfair jealousy. But at least they'd agreed to help.

Thirty-Four

Time was such a funny thing. There were moments of Emrie's life that seemed to drag on forever. Her childhood seemed a lifetime ago. The days after Noemi's death had felt like years. Then some moments did the opposite, occurring so fast there wasn't time to think. Or perhaps that was just her nerves over what was to come.

The First Heir approached her within moments of her arrival at the next Ceremony and brought her to the dais. Just like last time, he prowled around showing no more interest in her than he would a potted plant.

After she was settled, she made a point of catching Deriek's eye. At the first safe opportunity, he approached, stiff, angry, his expression hard. Which she should feel bad about but took as hopeful. Before he could say a word, she pushed a scarf into his hands.

"Not tonight," she whispered. "Tomorrow night. After dark. Earlier rather than later."

Then once Deriek was gone, she called the First Heir over and managed to get out with only a few tremors that she was to attend Barrack's Practice the next day to admire Lianjit. Would he also be there?

"If the flower wishes to turn its head to see the sun, then, of course, I will be the sun."

Emrie looked down at her hands as if she were embarrassed by his compliment. In truth, it was so horrendous she felt an inappropriate desire to giggle. He didn't speak to her again, and Deriek kept his distance.

The First Heir was already present when she arrived at Barrack's Practice. Lianjit was in a different part of the field from him, and after admiring her friend, Emrie wandered over to where he and several other men were attempting to kill each other with poleaxes. The First Heir was by far the strongest of the combatants. He didn't hold back in his attacks the way the others did. Lianjit, who was a third his size, had been right to insist they needed help.

He handed off his poleax to a norie and came to Emrie's side. The exertion had roused him. His skin was flushed, and for once, his eyes were bright.

"Daughter of Das, flower perfumed and decked in finery, you grace me with your presence."

"I'm impressed," she said. "I've never seen a weapon wielded in such a way. How long did it take you to learn?"

"I'm gifted." He described his training and how he'd once used just such an ax in helping the nories drive off an attack from the River Nomads. The words fell out of him in an awkward jangle, and she had the oddest thought that in his own ungainly way, he was trying to impress her. That struck her as sad.

Not sad enough to keep her from edging them both away from his fellows and toward where she needed him to go. She complimented him as she did so, and he preened.

As soon as enough time had passed for Lianjit to be in place, she touched a carved stone in her pocket to send her to where Ahrens and Montali waited. Then she strolled over to an area shaded between buildings, bringing the First Heir along with her, him still talking about killing River Nomads. She mentioned she was feeling overwhelmed and asked him to escort her back to her litter.

"As the flower wishes."

"You're too kind."

He never noticed the rug laid out in a narrow place between two buildings. They stepped onto it together, and Emrie touched the carved stone once again. The next moment they were in Deriek's old cell with Ahrens, Montali, and Lianjit poised with swords and a large blanket which they tossed over the First Heir's head. The battle that followed wasn't as brief as Lianjit had hoped, but it ended with the First Heir bound in the blanket and ropes.

Emrie and Lianjit returned to the Barrack's Field to be seen and then returned to their Houses in the normal way. It all worked so perfectly that the ride back to House Das felt excruciatingly slow in comparison. Once home, she ate an early lunch with Brid to keep herself distracted. Then Keeli and Lianjit arrived with news that there was a Judgment about to happen on a middle-ring House involving a Daughter getting caught stealing and having to give up the best of her wardrobe to an outer-ring House. That kept their afternoon occupied and in such a way no one would think to consider them part of any plot against the First Heir. It wasn't until evening that they parted again to rest for what would come next. Emrie had a hard time staying still, and Brid finally asked what was wrong.

"Noemi's birthdate is tomorrow," she replied, which was true.

It was barely dark when Emrie started getting everyone into place with the witchcraft. Ahrens, Montali, and Lianjit with the First Heir, Keeli hidden in Emrie's rooms so she could collect Brid. Then it was time to send the witchcraft in search of the scarf she'd given Deriek. She hadn't told the others, but this was the part that would either make or break their plan. And her.

She used the scarf to listen first and heard the tread of someone pacing. That felt about right, so she sent herself to him, arriving in a well-lit room. She was in a sleeping chamber and the space was bare. Just a simple dais covered in a mattress and blankets. There were no plants, no rugs on the floor nor fabric on the ceiling. If this was his room, he lived like an ascetic. He was dressed like one, too, in an unadorned laptevi and pantaloons all in darkest green, same color as when she'd first seen him in the Hall of Guests.

There was something so familiar about him that she wanted to rush over, throw her arms around him, and bury her face into his chest in relief.

Based on his expression, he wouldn't welcome her doing so. She remained where she was and offered what had to come first in a voice she hoped was friendly.

"I'm sorry I tricked you and drugged you. I know you hate me for it. I was willing to live with that if it meant you also lived, but I've changed my mind."

"Why are you wearing a sword? Are you planning on attacking me?" His lips twisted as if with humor, but his eyes were hard.

She wore a sheath down her back in the same way Lianjit always did. It held a practice sword, and Lianjit had impressed upon Emrie any number of times that the sword needed to stay put. It had also been Lianjit who'd wanted her to carry it. She said it made Emrie look a little less dewy-eyed.

She grinned, hoping to encourage Deriek's sense of humor.

"I won't attack you. If I tried, you'd have it out of my hands before I got it free of the sheath. I'm not someone meant to carry a sword."

Deriek didn't take the bait. Instead, he scowled.

"What did you do to my brother? And don't tell me you know nothing of his disappearance. Is your father behind this?"

Of course, he'd given the credit to someone else, and her humor was not the best approach, but she refused to let him get under her skin. This couldn't be about her.

"I forgive you for that." She stepped out of the pattern and went to the doorway to peek outside. The room beyond seemed equally plain as this one. "My father instructed me to court you. Everything else I've done has been of my own volition."

He crossed his arms over his chest and didn't move, but his gaze followed her and his voice was filled with contempt.

"Do tell. What have you done?"

Emrie answered easily, soothingly. "I need your help. I need you to take me to your father."

"I need you to answer the question," he snapped back.

There was one other doorway off of his sleeping chamber and she went there, peeking through to a dressing chamber. Checking her surroundings was another suggestion of Lianjit's, who'd worried Deriek would have nories waiting to grab her and ruin everything. The room was empty.

She went to the scarf, picked it up, and tucked it into her pocket.

"You told me a story once," she said, softening her voice even more, "of the Renoa of Vin-Yonekur and how one day a goat went to visit. Seeing the people in the Tree, it climbed as well, going higher and onto thinner branches than anyone thought possible. Fearing it would fall, the priests hovered beneath with outstretched blankets to catch it. They even encouraged it to jump to them. But when it finally fell, the Renoa twisted and turned using its canopy to slow the descent and the goat landed unharmed on its feet."

"Your 'cousin' is the goat?" he said, his voice gone flat.

She sighed and offered him a weak smile.

"I'm the goat, and I need you to hold the blanket not knowing what I will do or if the Renoa will help."

"That's all foolishness. What are you planning, Ajnee?"

"Ajnee?" She knew this one, and it wasn't likely meant as a compliment. Ajnee was the title of one of the Old Gods, the Lady of the Morning who pulled the sun from its sleep with a silken noose and forced it to rise. Still, he wouldn't have used a nickname if he didn't have some spot, small though it might be, that looked beyond the darkness that surrounded him and saw her.

She stepped forward. One step, then two until she was so close she had to tilt her head to look at him. Emrie became aware of how alone they were. Not in a bad way, but in the way they'd been in his prison. Just the two of them. No one else. His dark anger. Her need to help him. It was all so familiar.

"I'm afraid that if the goat or the Renoa tells the priest what will happen, the priest won't hold the blanket. I thought I was doing the right thing by sending you to Gir-Tosaq. I did everything I could to keep you alive and make your life as bearable as possible. I lied for you. I kept secrets and betrayed my family. I broke every rule of etiquette and society; I learned to use the witchcraft for you. You think I want you to be my pawn, but what I really want is for you to be whole."

"What you want is for me to trust you after you betrayed me." His voice stayed flat. He looked beyond her rather than meeting her eyes, building an invisible wall between them. "What if instead, you trusted me? What if you helped me with my plans?"

"Deriek . . ." Emrie lifted her hand and touched it to his laptevi so lightly she could barely feel the fabric. The witchcraft aligned with the marks on his chest as if it, too, wanted to reach out to him.

He flinched but didn't back away.

"Any plan of yours ends with Brid dead," she said softly. "But you aren't your brother nor your father. Deriek, if you were, you'd have killed your brother long ago in some devious way that wouldn't antagonize the Renoa. Like he tried to do to you." Deriek was honorable. The most honorable person she'd ever met, and she put every bit of her belief in that truth into her voice. "Deriek, you don't want to murder anyone, and you've met Brid, I think. She's innocent of your situation."

His face shuttered. He closed up, and his eyes became as dead as his brother's. As if the person she knew had disappeared.

"I have killed."

"In battle," she said, making a guess. "Not murder. Not family." She pressed on his chest hard enough that he was sure to feel her now. It was time to be honest. "You said I wanted to be your savior. That I wanted to earn my worth. You were right. Back in the beginning, when my father said I was responsible for you, I went to the Renoa and asked what I should do. The Renoa responded. It asked me a question, *What did the Second Heir need to live?* In my own weakness, I thought I was supposed to provide the answer. My caretaking might be your saving or my learning of the witchcraft. I even thought the Renoa wanted me to force you to live. I was wrong, and not just about the last."

She slid one hand up to his cheek, but he remained a statue staring over her head.

"I was wrong to want it to be about me. I was trapped. Deriek, I think you're the same. I think you're trapped by your own hatred. Your entire life has been centered around your father's choice, this one betrayal—"

"Many betrayals," he snapped. Under her hand, his jaw was clenched so tight she could feel his pulse.

"A series of betrayals," she said gently and stroked his skin, "that started with your father. It's all you can see, and you see it in everything. In everyone. You relive with every person, every day, what your parents did to you."

"What they created me for," he corrected.

"It keeps you from seeing beyond the darkness to ask why you exist for just yourself. But the Renoa sees. It's linked to you, to your House. It saved you in a way it wouldn't save my sister. I think when the Renoa asked me what you needed in order to live, It wasn't telling me I was to find an answer. It was saying *you* needed to ask the question. That you couldn't do so. That you were trapped in this darkness of hatred for the people that had hurt you."

He jerked back, knocking her hand away. His expression was terrible. Anger and anguish primed to explode into violence.

Emrie gave a jittery gulp. She couldn't help it. The last person who'd looked like that had been her father, and then he'd hit her. But this was Deriek, and so she put her hands back on his chest, curling her fingers to clutch the fabric as if to hold him to her. She tried to smile reassuringly, tried to get him to see that he wouldn't scare her off with his bitterness and fury.

"You're afraid, I think. You're afraid to hope there is more. But Deriek, I think you hope anyway."

***

The darkness within Deriek rose until he envisioned wrapping his hands around her neck and choking out not just her words but her life. How good it would feel. How final. She knew nothing and thought she knew everything. Just like everyone else.

But then his imaginary hands weren't on her but on the door to her family's House. And then around the bars of that window in his prison, his hands bloody from scratching his way up the wall, one lost fingernail at a time as he'd searched out this girl Brid and watched Emrie throw herself at his brother and himself be battered by his father telling him over and over and over again that it was past time he fulfilled the purpose of his birth. Deriek was slippery in his own shed blood as he pulled backward against the unforgiving metal of the bars, screaming, yanking, raging.

As always, the bars were solid.

But Nitsya had little guile.

He couldn't look at her. He didn't want to see the sincerity brimming from her face, to be forced to recognize that every word she said she believed to be true. He didn't want her to be right.

Because she was that, too.

He'd thought of a thousand ways to successfully kill his brother and never gone through with any of them.

He liked what he'd seen of Brid. She was apparently his sister, and he didn't want her to be murdered.

His life had never had a purpose higher than escaping the current person trying to use him.

From the deepest cravings of the heart comes the most catastrophic hate. He heard the words in his mother's voice as if she were standing there in front of him instead of Nitsya. He pictured her; hair so dark it shined blue. Large, deep eyes that always seemed to see right through him. And a kind smile. Why, why, why? Why had his mother even given birth to him?

If you hadn't been born, you wouldn't have the chance to save your people. If you hadn't been sent to Vin-Yonekur, your brother would have killed you before you were prepared. If the window hadn't been barred, you'd never have turned to see the light of the girl. The words weren't his mother's. They were his own.

"I want to control my own life. Not be endlessly funneled to where someone else demands I go." He said it aloud, too loud, but not to Nitsya.

Not even the Renoa chooses the color of Its canopy nor controls the seasons that force It to drop and regrow Its leaves. That doesn't mean It lacks control.

Nitsya's hands still rested on his chest and he was suddenly aware of the lines she'd carved into his skin. They tickled as if someone were redrawing them with the tip of a bird's wing.

"I have nothing but hatred," he said to the surrounding room.

"You have me," she replied softly.

From the deepest cravings of the heart comes the most catastrophic hate.

"You *forced* me to hate you. Everyone I love forces me to hate them."

You choose hatred with your head, not your heart. This time the words weren't words but the rustling of a wind through branches. *Drop your leaves, child.*

"I don't want you to hate me," Nitsya said, her eyes wide. "Can't you just love me instead?"

He held onto the imaginary bars with both fists. He raged at the world that had birthed him to die, at all those who'd seen him as nothing but a pawn, at how much it all hurt. The rage burned so brightly he expected Nitsya to step back from the heat. She didn't, and so he released the metaphorical bars in one swift motion, letting go, falling, into her. He grabbed her hands where they rested against his chest, their fingers intertwining. And then he leaned down and with more desperation than passion, he kissed her.

THIRTY-FIVE

It wasn't how Emrie had envisioned her chat with Deriek going. When he kissed her, it was so sudden she didn't kiss him back. She didn't know how. She put her arms around him instead, and he let out a broken sigh as all the breath was expelled from his body at once. She had won. Him.

That acknowledgment was all there was time for. She let him go, grateful he'd chosen to trust her and hoping later she'd get to say everything else in her heart.

"Please," she said. "Will you take me to your father?"

He hesitated, drawing back but not away, his voice rough. "My test, I suppose?"

"More of a test of me," She bit her lip to keep from blurting the whole of it. He nodded, so she put her hand in her pocket and used a stone to transfer a note to where Lianjit waited and a second to Keeli, the signal that she was on her way to the Sovereign's rooms. They walked swiftly, Deriek moving with a determination that reminded her of how Ahrens went through life, forceful but reckless. Deriek hadn't entirely reached the end of the edge he balanced upon.

"Give me your sword," he said as they rounded a corner.

She started to pull the sword from behind her head as Lianjit had shown her, but he reached over and took it before she could.

"You really don't know what you're doing, do you? I was half afraid you were going to kill someone, but the worst this could give is a mild bruising."

"It's symbolic. And to make me look less a muritt." She tried to interject humor. "But if I can't bring a sword, neither can you."

"No. I don't think I should, either. Not even a symbolic sword." He shoved it behind a wall rug and took her hand, all business now. "My father has nurses attending him night and day. He'll be awake but resting in bed. I'll need an excuse to request an audience. The easiest would be a decision on my part to court you."

"My father would be pleased with that," she said and smiled. Doing this with him at her side felt so right.

They arrived at the Sovereign's sleeping chamber without issue. Deriek sent a matie with their request, and approval to enter came moments later. Once they were in, he dismissed the maties while Emrie looked around. It was the single largest sleeping chamber she'd ever been in and opposite Deriek's in all ways. Lavish and lush with one entire wall of massive wooden doors that must open to the Renoa.

The bed was in the center, covered in blankets and draped with indigo silk in the corners. The Sovereign appeared small midst the massive bed.

He waved a hand at them to approach. Deriek performed the formal greetings, introducing her. He was entirely respectful, not an ounce of mocking in his voice. Emrie stayed in the background until the formalities were finished.

"Why are you here?" the Sovereign demanded, regal even lying down.

Emrie turned to Deriek. "I need a moment. Stay with your father and don't interrupt." She gave him a pointed look and then let go of his hand to step behind the bed where the Sovereign couldn't see her. She laid out the gauzy scarf on the floor and used it to bring a larger coiled rug, the same one she'd used to trap the First Heir at Barrack's Practice. She unrolled it and used the pattern within to bring Keeli and Brid. Brid immediately started throwing out questions, loudly.

"Who's there?" the Sovereign demanded. "What is going on?"

Keeli snapped a hand over Brid's mouth and pulled her aside. Emrie nodded and brought Lianjit, Ahrens, and Montali with the First Heir propped between them to the room as well. The First Heir's restraints had been redone so that his head was free, but he was gagged. The rest of them wore plain laptevis with their cowls up and veils over their faces to disguise their appearances. Keeli had wanted Emrie to do so as well, but she thought she'd be more effective if the Sovereign could see her.

Ahrens and Montali deposited the First Heir on the bed next to his father. They had trouble keeping him there and Ahrens sat on his feet. The Sovereign pushed himself up.

"You will explain yourself. Immediately."

"What's going on?" Brid kept demanding even as Keeli shushed her. "Why is that man bound? How did I get here? No one warned me about this."

Emrie took a deep breath. "We are going to solve the problem of who inherits the Renoa's Seat of Judgment."

Lianjit pulled her silvery blue sword from its sheath and handed it to Emrie. Emrie took it, holding it point-up as Lianjit had instructed and being careful not to hit either herself or anyone else. She brought it down in a reasonably smooth arc to rest near the First Heir's head. This was partly for effect. Partly to make it easier to hand over to the Sovereign once he agreed to her plan. And partly because holding the sword tired her wrists, and Lianjit thought it'd look bad if she accidentally dropped it. There'd been no question as to which sword would be used.

"Explain," said the Sovereign. Up close, his skin had a dried-out, wasted look.

That didn't stop a small quaver in Emrie's voice when she spoke. "I will."

She dared a quick glance at Deriek. He'd stepped back so that he was just outside of the ring of people surrounding the Sovereign's bed and had an inscrutable look on his face.

"The First Heir can't inherit," Emrie said, going into the speech she and Keeli had prepared. "With deepest respect, it must be acknowledged that he's unfit. They say he kills his mistresses. They say he has no respect for the Renoa's Laws. For the good of Pol-Thiri, he *cannot* inherit. You, as his father, have the responsibility to kill him. You are ill. They say you won't get better." She gave another quick glance around. The room had settled, and they were all listening now. "You must kill him, and I'm willing to make a contract with you to get you to do it."

"You think you have something I want?"

"I know I do." Her stomach twitched like a snake having just been skewered by a spear. She wasn't good at these things. "First, Deriek will renounce his claim on the Seat. He doesn't want to be the Sovereign anyway."

She glanced at Deriek who was still watching her without expression.

"You know I'm right about this." She turned back to the Sovereign. "As part of his abdicating, you'll release Deriek from House Valiyard. He'll then be free to figure out his own life."

The First Heir struggled anew.

"Which leaves the Seat of Judgment with no Sovereign at all," the Sovereign snapped, his tone implying they were all idiots. At least he was listening.

"Second," Emrie continued, speaking faster as her nerves rose. "As First Daughter of House Das, I will release my cousin from our House so that she has no obligation to us, but only to you. Her name is Brid—"

"I don't want to marry into the Sovereign's House," Brid announced loudly. "I want to marry Lanka Sersi."

Emrie kept speaking. "Brid is the Daughter of House Valiyard. I don't know the entire story. Brid doesn't know, either. Perhaps nobody does." Which they'd been careful to add to protect her father, who did. "Brid was born in Pol-Thiri and snuck away to Kye-Boehlke to be raised there in secrecy so that the First Heir couldn't kill her. Now she has returned. She is the child of your blood. She is meant for Pol-Thiri. She can inherit the Seat of Judgment as a Valiyard, but only if I agree to release her from House Das. Because otherwise, when she inherits, and she will one way or the other, she'll do so as a member of House Das and House Valiyard loses the Sovereignty."

"This man isn't my father," Brid insisted. "My father is Omert Das. I'm the granddaughter of Calys Das."

"No," Emrie said, turning now to face Brid. "You aren't. They lied to keep you safe. Your mother was a daughter of Aunt Calys," she lied, "but your father is definitely the current Sovereign. You were hidden away as a baby and raised as a Das so that the First Heir couldn't kill you. The Holy Renoa told me so and you look just like the First Heir." Emrie turned back to the Sovereign. "Doesn't she?"

"How old is she?" the Sovereign asked, without glancing at Brid.

"She'll be seventeen when the rains start."

The Sovereign studied Emrie rather than Brid and so intently she was reminded of the First Heir's interest in the insects. Suddenly, the sword, even resting on the cushions, felt too heavy in her hand. She flushed warm and rather desperately wanted to blink and look away. Or run away. This was the Sovereign. To disrespect him was to disrespect the Renoa itself. Yet, she wouldn't back down.

The Sovereign looked away and then spoke with the finality of a Judgment. "She isn't my Daughter, and Deriek won't inherit. Cystel will be a poor Sovereign, but he'll inherit. The Seat of Judgment stays in House Valiyard through him."

"Look at her," Emrie said, her voice rising.

"I don't have to. My wife, Renoa bless her, died in childbirth over twenty years ago. While it's none of your concern, I'll inform you I had a single concubine who I never touched after she became pregnant. There's no chance, at all, that this girl is my daughter."

"But—"

"And no witch will use her craft to take control of my city." And then he yelled in full voice and with full authority of the Sovereign, "Nories. House Valiyard is under attack!"

For a long moment she just stared at him, a seeping disappointment settling over her. "I'm sorry to hear that," she said. Of all the millions of ways this could've gone wrong, and she, Lianjit, and Keeli had discussed many, this one hadn't occurred to them. The Renoa had been the one to tell her about Brid. Her father wouldn't have struck her over protecting a true orphan. Brid was a Valiyard. The Sovereign just preferred to lie than admit it.

Well, she had one other option.

Time slowed down as she gripped Lianjit's sword with both hands. The others would see this as a disaster, and they'd planned for such. Keeli and Lianjit would grab Brid and go to the rug so that Emrie could send them to safety. Ahrens and Montali would follow. She could hear movement behind her that was hopefully them preparing. She'd have to let go of the sword to use the witchcraft. She couldn't quite yet.

For the good of Pol-Thiri, the First Heir couldn't be allowed to inherit. Someone had to make the sacrifice and take the Renoa's punishment. Emrie raised the sword over her head, feeling the weight of it in her hands and arms. Ahrens called her name. There was more noise from behind her. She imagined the expressions of horror on their faces as they realized her intentions. She hoped Deriek would forgive her this as well.

She aimed. Lianjit had taught her just enough that she knew she hadn't the strength to remove the First Heir's head but this was still going to be messy and final. She started the swing and then closed her eyes. Lianjit's sword struck solid matter with a metallic reverberation that shuddered through her hands and arms and ripped the sword from her grip. She opened her eyes to see it spinning away and Deriek standing on the bed over his brother. His stance was wide, a sword that he must have taken from Ahrens or Montali a solid barrier between her and the First Heir.

"If I don't get to die, neither do you."

"What would you have me do?" Emrie asked evenly. "The First Heir can't inherit."

"Anything but this," he said just as calmly as if there weren't people yelling and chaos brimming around them and nories pouring in from several sides.

"Emrie," Keeli called, "send us out of here."

Without taking her eyes off Deriek, who smiled as if this was the most normal of moments, she touched the embroidery of her sleeve and felt the witchcraft leap. Ahrens yelled her name but it all seemed background noise to staring into Deriek's eyes. She told the witchcraft to take Ahrens and Montali away. It was too late for her and Deriek. At least they were together.

The nories swarmed them. Deriek tried to defend her, moving so fast he was more whirlwind than man and blade.

The Sovereign yelled, "Not him. Her. Take the girl, the witch. Beware her hands."

Deriek tried to get between her and them, but the nories wouldn't engage him and he was only one person against many. She didn't want him to get hurt, so she raised her arms in surrender.

"I failed at this as well," she said sadly, wistfully, as the largest norie she'd ever seen grabbed her hands, engulfing them in his.

The First Heir writhed on the bed, making a roaring noise through his gag. Laughter.

THIRTY-SIX

The giant norie dragged Emrie from the Sovereign's Room, his fists so tight around her wrists that she was sure to have bruises.

She'd never experienced a norie who wasn't gentle with her.

It was a stupid thought. An unimportant one considering that she'd just destroyed her life and her House. But focusing on the norie kept her from panicking. He'd taken her hands, but she was clever. What other than the witchcraft did she have to use?

Her voice.

"Brid Das is a Third Heir. Her father is the Sovereign." She told not just the giant norie but everyone else they passed as he dragged her through the halls of the Sovereign's House.

She must look and sound like a lunatic. Unmannered. Irreverent. She didn't care.

"Cystel Valiyard must not be allowed to inherit. He's a monster. He killed my sister. Everyone knows this to be true."

The norie took her down a set of stairs. To the cooling system? If they put her into Deriek's old cell, there'd be a rug there she could use to escape. No, she didn't even need that. All she needed was some time alone. She could use her own blood to escape. Then she'd find the others and figure out what to do next. She kept talking.

"He locked Deriek up in a prison. He meant to starve him to death. The Renoa helped me keep him alive."

The place they took her was not the cooling system. It was warm rather than cold. The norie tugged her into a small room with no windows and a single metal chair and table. Two metal boxes were attached to the table by leather straps. The norie pushed her into the chair. She began her tale from the beginning, trying to catch the nories' eyes as she spoke. Neither the giant nor his companions looked back. One of the nories undid the straps and separated each box into halves. The insides were carved in the shape of palms and fingers.

Now Emrie panicked. Her tongue twisted around her words but she kept talking anyway. She spoke faster and faster, her words near incoherent. Sweat dotted her skin under her clothing.

The norie holding her wrists forced each hand into a box, his face grim. She tried to fight, but he was too strong.

While the huge norie held her hands in place, another added cloth to fill in the space around her fingers and then closed the top of the box and redid the straps so that her hands were immobilized. The moment the giant let go, she jerked backward so hard it felt like she'd pull her bones free from her skin and muscle. The giant grabbed her again, forcing her back into her seat. More leather straps were used to bind her to the chair so she couldn't fight. She was trapped.

But it couldn't be over. She wasn't giving in.

She shut her lips, and the room went silent. So much so that the giant looked at her. Even brown eyes in a steady Pol-Thiri face, a queue of rose-brown hair down his back. Not a monster. A child of the Renoa doing his job against a dangerous witch that he believed had endangered his Sovereign.

Think. She knew what she knew, and the Renoa *had* told her that Brid was an Heir.

She relaxed against the bonds.

The nories seemed uncertain what to do now that she was restrained and quiet. She straightened. She needed to stop acting like a lunatic and become a Das. A First Daughter Das. Like Noemi.

"I'm afraid of you. Afraid of this. But I'm not lying. The Renoa told me to use the witchcraft to keep the Second Heir alive." She spoke clearly and precisely so that there could be no mistaking her words. "The Renoa told me that Brid Das is an Heir to the Seat of Judgment. I have one request. Please listen to what I ask and then go tell the Second Heir. Please."

THIRTY-SEVEN

The morning after Emrie was taken, Deriek stood with his arms crossed, his chin cocked, and his hip leaning against the wall of the chamber that held the Seat of Judgment. To the rest of the occupants of the room, he'd look as he always did when attending such events—bored and ill-tempered. On the inside, he was a mix of tension and exhaustion.

He'd come so close, so terrifyingly close to watching her die. It had been the single most horrific moment of his life. So much worse than anything that he'd been through before.

He wasn't about to let her be put in that position a second time. When Emrie had one of his father's nories bring instructions on what she wanted him to do, he'd agreed entirely.

In the room with him were the Advisers, Heads of Houses, and other Firsts of the inner-rings. Most sat on tiers of cushions around a central carpet embroidered in the likeness of the Renoa. The Seat itself was at the head of the carpet. It wasn't a true chair, but an oiled and polished gnarl of white wood that rose from the floor and curved over on itself to provide a back and armrests. A living root of the Renoa Tree itself.

His father looked frail in the large seat with the morning sun shining down upon him from the upper windows.

Cystel paced back and forth on the carpet, roaring about the indignities thrust upon him and making extravagant demands for justice that mostly came down to being allowed to torture and kill Emrie Das. Spittle marred the corners of his mouth and his face was a dull purple that matched the bruised color of his laptevi and overdress. His words were near undecipherable. A positive.

The nories had carried Emrie's tale far and wide, and several dozen Heads of House had come to Deriek during the early morning hours to make their bids and curate his influence in how they felt this day should work out. All of them he'd listened to. One of them he responded to. Lady Gai Sersi. Not that he trusted her, but what she had to gain was obvious and aligned with Nitsya's needs.

House Das was conspicuously absent.

That Deriek was present and not locked up just as tight as Emrie came down to the nories having a terror of harming an Heir. Cystel had demanded the nories capture him anyway.

As expected, his father eventually ended his brother's ranting and called Deriek forward. His father was always fair when it came to the Seat of Judgment. "Why did you bring that girl to my chamber? Did she ensorcel you?"

Deriek pushed away from the wall in a slow, relaxed motion as opposite of his brother's antics as possible. When he spoke, he kept his tone easy, amused. This could still go very wrong.

"I've never felt ensorceled. I don't believe she has that ability. I brought her to you because she called in the Law of the Renoa, and I felt I had no choice but to comply."

"She lies about the Renoa," his brother spat. Their father held up a hand. His laptevi fell back upon his arm showing lax wrinkled skin where once had been muscle. A fading man, who refused the responsibility of his own failures. For a moment, the old rage swelled in Deriek. He banked it; let it go.

Deriek worked his way around the tiers of people on cushions until he stood not on the carpet but next to it.

"My understanding of the story is thus," he said, launching smoothly into what Emrie had asked him to do through the nories—tell the truth. All of it. Not something that came natural to him, but he'd do his best. It was her greatest defense. "On the night my esteemed brother took a fist to me in the Hall of Guests, he also convinced the Third Son of the Fifth Adviser to capture me and lock me up. That boy brought me food and water for several weeks before disappearing. My understanding is that he was murdered." He glanced to the Fifth Adviser, who went pale. "In terms of ridding Pol-Thiri of an Heir without involving the Renoa, it wasn't a bad plan. I believe I was meant to starve to death with no one living having direct knowledge of my location."

Cystel began to sputter, but his father put a hand up again to silence him.

"How the Daughter of House Das realized my situation, I know not. Possibly the Third Son told her, but it seems more likely the Renoa did. I would've perished if she hadn't come nightly from thenceforward. This was done from her own goodness and I believe on command of That-Which-Is-Life. To be certain, one would have to ask her."

He gave a nod toward the audience. Several people shifted in their seats. "She's also the person who freed me when my situation became dire. The entirety of her actions created a debt on my side of the scale that when she showed up in my room last night, I was obligated to return."

More murmuring. Deriek wondered if Cystel knew that while their father sat on the Seat of Judgment, it was the people of Pol-Thiri that were going to make this decision. Their father was far from immune to public pressure.

"The charges of witchcraft are serious and upsetting," he continued. "They're also true. I attest to this—she used the witchcraft both last night and during the time she cared for me. I believe she did so under duress. I believe her when she says her instructions came from the Renoa itself and not any desire of her own. I saw firsthand her struggle to figure out how to use the witchcraft. I don't understand how this factored in with this girl Brid Das. I puzzled through some of what Emrie Das believed to be true and saw no proof of Brid Das's heritage beyond the resemblance between Brid and my family. But it could be true." He looked to Lady Sersi then, just a quick glance as this had been her idea. "If we want to know the truth, we must take Emrie Das, Brid Das, my brother, and I to the Renoa and ask."

Deriek smiled as if he couldn't care less what was decided. He backed away, but before he'd made it a step, the head of the nories, a behemoth of a man, raised his voice in an entirely non-norie way.

"The nories concur. Take them all to the Renoa."

"I concur as well," said Lady Sersi.

A murmuring arose as person after person agreed.

"Let it be so," his father said from the Seat of Judgment. "Organize the Field. Let the Renoa decide."

Deriek didn't relax a single muscle or give any signal that he'd even heard. Step one was done.

THIRTY-EIGHT

A single night in the overheated prison and Emrie understood the desperation for water that Deriek had displayed the first few times she'd visited him. The nories had locked her up and left her, and she'd spent the night in stifling heat, craving something to drink so badly her throat burned and her mouth hollowed out. The chamber stank of her sweat.

She'd slept a bit, slumped forward in her bindings, but only a bit as her hands itched inside the locked boxes. It wasn't even the witchcraft, just the heat. But it reminded her of the witchcraft so that she couldn't quite forget that she had been cut off from it. She would've cried in misery if there'd been any moisture in her body to make tears.

But she refused to see this as failure. It wasn't over yet. She wasn't giving up.

When the giant norie finally returned, she begged for water in a voice as parched as Deriek's had been. He took one look at her, muttered something she couldn't make sense of, and turned on his heel. When he returned, he brought with him not just a bladder but Mati Dechta. Emrie had never been so glad to see someone in her life.

"Please," she croaked out.

"My child. What have you done to her?" Mati Dechta raced over and threw her arms around Emrie protectively. The norie filled a cup and handed it over almost apologetically. Mati Dechta held it to Emrie's lips, and she gulped it down not caring that it spilled down the front of her.

"I'm okay," she said once her mouth was no longer so parched. She had to be. And Mati Dechta was calm, which she wouldn't be if Emrie was already condemned. "What's going on?"

"I've come to help you dress," Mati Dechta said with a glance at the norie. "I'll need to clean you as well. Your father says you must be presentable to go before the Renoa as the Daughter of the House. As a Das."

Emrie nodded, understanding that they couldn't talk.

But going before the Renoa . . . That could mean any number of things.

Mati Dechta brought in two more maties from House Das. One carried a bucket and towels, the other Emrie's white TreeFall laptevi.

Mati Dechta had a quiet argument with the giant over freeing Emrie's hands so she could change. Mati Dechta lost the argument, a first in Emrie's experience, for which the giant apologized not to Mati Dechta, but to Emrie.

"My instructions are specific. I cannot remove the boxes." But he did remove the straps holding them to the table so that Mati Dechta could lift them as needed.

"We'll have to cut everything and sew you into your formal dress," Mati Dechta said.

The giant norie moved to the far corner and turned his back.

Changing wasn't easy. Mati Dechta muttered the entire time about what a poor job she was forced to do because of the boxes, which was unlike her. She was usually quite reserved.

"You'll have to be careful, child. These stitches won't take much abuse." When Mati Dechta stepped in close to hold the sides of the dress together for the other matie to sew, she whispered something else. "Listen well, I come with a message from your father."

Emrie straightened.

"Hold still," Mati Dechta snapped as if Emrie were indeed that small child that Mati Dechta called her. Then she stepped in close again and spoke fast. "You've done well so far. The Second Heir has positioned you the best he could, and now you must trust the rest of us. You're to be tried under the Renoa with the three Heirs. The entire city-oasis is gathering to watch. When you speak, you must ask a question. You must ask how the very First Sovereign was chosen. Do you understand?"

"No."

Mati Dechta gave her a small pinch on her arm. "Don't tease, child. Do you understand?"

Emrie hadn't been teasing, and she didn't like not knowing the whole.

"I'll remember the question."

***

Emrie was too weak to walk, let alone lift the metal boxes. After a brief discussion, Mati Dechta bullied the giant into carrying her. Emrie tried to argue that it would make her look undignified, but Mati Dechta overrode her and told her to save her strength for when it was needed.

Two other nories helped him pick her up, and the giant apologized for manhandling her. He was growing on her.

Mati Dechta arranged the folds of her white laptevi, so they fell gracefully down the front and her sapphire sash gleaned around her waist. She'd redone Emrie's hair in a simple style and brought her braids around to fall forward over the dress. The boxes with her hands inside rode in her lap.

"Your father wants you looking young and vulnerable. Innocent," she said before leaving.

The Sovereign's House was empty as they passed through the halls, Emrie in the arms of the norie. When it was time to exit onto the Field, she pressed her eyes shut not wanting to see the crowds jeering at her. She couldn't so easily avoid hearing them. The movement and voices and the high-pitched sound of the bone whistles used to serenade criminals came from all directions.

The norie tried to be gentle, but it was an uncomfortable trip. She wasn't accustomed to being carried, and the corners of the heavy boxes dug into her midsection. She was about to crack her eyes to see how much farther to go when someone spoke right up against her ear.

"Look to me, Daughter of Das. Learn what it is you once asked me to show you. He said to call you Nitsya and you'd listen. All I ask is that you give away as little of my truth as you can."

Emrie shot her eyes open, but Lady Sersi was no longer there, and the crowd was as large and pressing as she'd feared. Nor was there time to look more or consider the message. They'd reached the Renoa. A metal dais intricately designed in wrought iron had been placed under the bare branches.

"You must stand on your own now, Daughter Das," the giant said in a deep and respectful voice.

Getting back onto her feet was only slightly less awkward than being picked up. The giant and a second norie guided her onto the dais. They took up posts to either side of her, supporting the weight of the boxes. It left her arms stretched wide but without the help, she'd have fallen.

People stood in every direction along the Paths in front of her, creating waves of living beings that serenaded her with unevenly pitched voices and whistles. She found Keeli with her House, a hand pressed to her mouth. Then Lianjit. Taspin, who was grinning. And one of the boys she'd courted. He had tears on his cheeks. She couldn't remember his name.

It all felt impersonal again, which if someone had warned her this was going to happen, was the opposite of what she'd have expected to feel, considering there was still a good chance she was going to lose her hands if not her life in the near future. Maybe she was too terrified to feel anything.

She saw her father, his face blank, his posture giving nothing away. But he wouldn't, would he? House Das spread out around him. Even the maties had been allowed to come. And Montali, holding Ahrens's hand.

The only person she couldn't seem to find was Lady Sersi.

The crowds parted, and a procession headed by the Sovereign's open-air litter made its way to the dais. The three Heirs walked behind it. Deriek glanced at her just once in acknowledgment, then kept his attention elsewhere. His brother watched her with dead eyes. Brid had a pensive, worried look on her face as she searched the crowds, likely for Lanka. She didn't seem to have any better luck finding House Sersi than Emrie.

The litter was brought onto the dais, but not set down. More nories joined those already holding it, and they lifted the Sovereign above the heads of everyone present. The Heirs lined up next to him. Brid still scanned the crowds.

The Sovereign began the Ceremony of Gratitude. Emrie had never heard the entire thing recited, just bits and pieces during the other Ceremonies. The Sovereign led, calling out elaborate Blessings, celebrating each one in flowery language. Priests standing in the lower branches of the Renoa repeated his words while lighting lamps. The people of Pol-Thiri copied the words a third time, sending them up to the Renoa. Rhythm for rhythm. Tone for tone. Each line said three times, growing in voice as the light of the lamps reflected off the pure white of the tree. The trumpet of sound rumbled through Emrie's entire being.

It wasn't a quick ceremony. As the sun lowered in the sky, Emrie tired and sagged against her bound hands. She still hadn't found Lady Sersi in the crowd. Based on Brid's continued looking, neither had she.

Then it was done. The Sovereign settled back and one of his maties rushed forward with a flask of water. No one offered water to any of the rest of them, and Emrie's thirst returned. There wasn't time to do more than acknowledge that fact as the First Heir used his father's pause to take over.

"We're here to judge the witch and the impostor," he yelled.

Like before, the priest repeated his words, copying his awkward cadence so that all might hear. Emrie flinched, but then she went back to watching Brid, whose face lifted in a smile as all her attention focused on one spot in the crowd. Thank the Tree for Brid's single-mindedness.

The First Heir continued. "Emrie Das is a witch. My brother confirms. Balance has been upset. I demand to perform the punishment."

A cacophony of bone whistles went off as if in agreement. Emrie followed Brid's gaze to where Lanka stood. He stared back at Brid, his expression just as intense as hers. Next to him was his mother.

"And I demand," Deriek started, and the priests copied his drawl to such perfection that Emrie couldn't help but glance at him because she loved that sound so very much. He continued. "That what I said be confirmed. Emrie Joleyn Das claims the Holy Renoa gave her the responsibility."

"Lies!" shouted the First Heir, not waiting for the priests to finish repeating Deriek's words. The First Heir's face was the same purple as his laptevi.

Emrie turned back to Lady Sersi, who met her gaze and nodded. Lady Sersi looked downward as if searching the ground. There were so many people it was hard for Emrie to see what she was doing. Lady Sersi leaned over to say something to her son, and Lanka stepped forward, using his height to clear the way. Now Emrie had a perfect view. It hadn't been the ground Lady Sersi studied. It was her bare foot. She used the tip of her toe to draw a line along the edge of the stonework of the Path.

And Emrie understood.

In that same moment, she realized that the Sovereign and every other person in visual distance were staring at her.

"Tell them," Deriek said.

Emrie had lost track of the conversation. "I . . . What specifically?"

The priests captured her hesitation, and she winced.

"Tell them about your visits to the Renoa."

"Alright."

Considering how many times she'd done so already, it should've been easy, but it wasn't. This time was the hardest of all. She kept it simple, as much for herself as because it was difficult speaking in short phrases so that the priests could repeat them. She told of the Renoa asking what Deriek needed to live and her desire to answer the question. The

Renoa instructing her to learn the witchcraft and that she'd thought the mere act of doing so had helped Deriek, but she'd been wrong. Thinking of Lady Sersi, she gave as little away about the witchcraft as she could. Deriek helped with that, asking her questions that led the conversation more toward him and the Renoa. At Deriek's prodding, she told of the Renoa confirming Brid was an Heir and of her then forcing Deriek to tell her the truth about his birth. She paused after that, aware that she'd just made the Sovereign look bad in front of his people.

She didn't have the courage to see what he thought of that, but the crowd went silent.

"Tell of last night, when you tried to kill the First Heir," Deriek said and his voice changed becoming softer, kinder.

She admitted she hadn't asked the Renoa for assistance in this. Her actions had been motivated by stopping the First Heir from killing Deriek, stopping Deriek from killing Brid, and in revenge for the poisoning of her sister. But still, it had felt like this was what the Renoa had wanted from her all along. She explained that the solution to all the problems had come to her all at once, and she'd decided from the beginning that if the Sovereign refused to do it, she'd raise the sword herself. The First Heir couldn't be allowed to inherit.

A murmur passed through the crowd.

"And that's pretty much all of it," she finished. "The Sovereign says Brid isn't his. The Renoa told me she is." And then, since it seemed to follow anyway, she inserted the question Mati Dechta had given her. "Has this happened before? How did the Renoa indicate who should be the Sovereign in the first place?" She didn't know the answer; it wasn't something she'd ever wondered or questioned.

The murmuring increased, but no bone whistles went off. Deriek turned to his father right as someone from below yelled out, "To the top."

"In Vin-Yonekur," Deriek said as if he were pondering the matter, although Emrie could tell it was faked. "When there's a question of who inherits, they do what was done at first. All petitioners climb the Renoa without ropes or ladders. The Renoa chooses who to help or hinder, and the first to the crown is the chosen one."

The Sovereign glanced at his Advisers. It was an odd thing to witness as if he himself were unsure of what to do. By the noise of the crowd, Deriek's suggestion was a popular one.

"Let it be done," the Sovereign said. "Let the Renoa decide."

***

Deriek bowed out of the competition. He wasn't meant for this, and Emrie was glad he knew it. After some discussion, it was decided to leave the ladders and rope already in place as they were. Because of the season, they only reached a quarter of the way up anyway. After that, Brid and the First Heir would be forced to find their way using the branches.

A gong sounded. The climb began. The First Heir was past the silk ladders and out on a branch before Brid made it halfway. She was snail-like slow, pausing with each step as if considering where best to place her hands and feet. While Emrie hadn't expected her to have the brute strength of the First Heir, this caution was odd. It almost seemed as if Brid was being slow on purpose. As if she were making room between herself and the First Heir.

If Brid was working with Lady Sersi too, that could be exactly what was occurring.

Because, clearly, Lady Sersi had shown Emrie the trick of her witchcraft for a reason. She wanted Emrie to do something. To stop the First Heir.

They all did. That was the goal of everything Deriek and her family and Lady Sersi had worked toward this day. Emrie had the power and held the duty.

Emrie looked at Deriek, but he wasn't facing her. Everyone was looking up. No, not everyone. Next to Lady Sersi, Lanka met Emrie's gaze. He didn't nod or do anything encouraging, nor did he look at her with disdain the way he had when she'd visited his House. He just held her gaze, steady, waiting.

There was a gasp from the crowd. Brid had made a misstep and slid backward but appeared to have caught herself just in time.

Just to see if she could use the witchcraft as Lady Sersi had suggested, she ran her toe over the pattern in the wrought iron at her feet. She imagined the usual sensation in her hands floating down her body and settling. In doing so, she felt a flickering. Her toes didn't tingle with the strength she was accustomed to. It felt more like trying to cut bread with a dull knife that shredded more than sliced or having a conversation through a very thick rug. But unlike that knife, the more she dragged her toe back and forth along the iron, the more even-edged the bread became. The door cracked. She felt her witchcraft hunt for and then find a pattern in the lines and swirls of the wrought iron that matched her Juju bird. The witchcraft was learning once again. She thanked it profusely, realizing in that moment that she'd never done so before and she should have.

Brid reached the end of the ropes and paused with one hand on a branch as if considering what to do next. She wouldn't know this Renoa like she did the one in Kye-Boehlke. She might never have climbed it before.

But Emrie knew it. She remembered where it was her witchcraft had connected when she'd healed Deriek.

Much farther up, the First Heir continued to ascend. He was now hard to see even in his dramatically colored laptevi. The lower branches blocked the view. Regularly, he disappeared only to reappear a few moments later. The crowd called out sightings.

There was no chance of Brid beating him without help.

Emrie needed to be that help. Even as she thought it, she felt the witchcraft reach from the pattern under her foot to that exact area of branches that she'd visited so many times in her life and from where she'd drawn strength before. A cold uncertainty twined around her, vining up her chest, her neck, her throat.

Should she help?

She could send the First Heir to Deriek's prison so that he was out of the way. That was likely what Deriek would want her to do. The First Heir would disappear, and even the others in the crowd with guildcraft wouldn't know that she'd been involved. Back in the Hall of Guests, they'd only been aware of the landing place, not the sending nor Emrie in the middle. She could even put him back in the tree later after Brid won. It would be considered a miracle of the Renoa. Brid would win the Soveriegncy.

But it wouldn't be over because the First Heir was not someone to accept defeat.

She could move him to the stone buried in the river's muck instead. Moving to a pattern so much smaller than himself would cut him to ribbons. He would die, and the Renoa would know she'd killed him. She would have to pay the price.

And Pol-Thiri would be left not knowing if he was still out there, to return at any moment.

Emrie could no longer see the First Heir, but the comments yelled by the crowd gave her some idea of where he was. The cries were in disapproval. They hoped Brid and not the First Heir would succeed. Or perhaps that wasn't it at all. Perhaps they just wanted to see the Renoa do something dramatic and watching two people climb wasn't exciting enough.

She'd been willing to sacrifice her life for the chance to free Pol-Thiri of him before, and nothing had changed. Not really.

She felt it then, a heady sense of power knowing that she held the future of everyone she knew right here in this moment. She, the overlooked girl, the one meant to stay in the background.

It was her choice.

Someone yelled that the First Heir was nearing the crown.

"But is it *right*?" she whispered aloud, looking up at the stark, bare loveliness of the Tree. Maybe everything that had happened had led to this moment. Maybe what the Renoa had wanted from the beginning was for Deriek, Brid, and Cystel Valiyard to come to this place, this choice.

What had she said to Deriek just the night before? *You're afraid, I think. You're afraid to hope there is more. But I think you hope anyway.*

It *was* right.

Emrie thanked the witchcraft and then explained she wanted something new. Not to move the First Heir out of the pattern made by the branches so far above. But to move him over within the pattern. A full body's length, so that he stood not on wood but on air. So that he would fall.

The witchcraft leapt with understanding. Emrie felt the shift as if she were there above in the tree with the First Heir, being shoved to the side.

In the same moment, there was a sudden heartrending crack of splitting wood. The Renoa shuddered, not once but multiple times, each accompanied by a thud like a beating on the largest drum in existence. The ground shook. The crowd screamed. Half the nories holding the Sovereign's litter were knocked off their feet. The litter tilted, sending the Sovereign sprawling. The smaller norie holding Emrie's arms in place jumped sideways to help the Sovereign, dropping her box-encuffed hand so suddenly that it swung sideways. An audible crack of fire shot up her arm, through her elbow, and into her shoulder. She screamed so hard it felt like she would shake the sky loose from the soil.

She saw three things before she passed out: The frantic expression of the giant norie as he caught her, Deriek racing in her direction, and a body clothed in vivid purple tumbling to the ground.

Thirty-Nine

The view of the Renoa had changed. It wasn't a huge change, just one missing wedge near the top of what was a monstrous edifice. But it was a dramatic change. An empty space through which light and the contrast of the sky could be seen where once had resided a massive curling branch.

The missing branch, Emrie's favorite branch, hadn't disappeared. It still hung there, half attached to the trunk, caught in the branches beneath it like a sad, half-dead animal. The priests were discussing what to do about this, and the Tree had been closed to worshippers.

Emrie'd spent the first days after the branch fell and the First Heir died drugged as she discovered firsthand that she had a very low tolerance for pain and having a broken arm set was unbelievably painful. Even once the worst of it was over, her arm was useless, aching and strapped with linen to iron bars from her elbow to her palm. But just the arm. And only to help the bone heal straight. No one was worried about the witchcraft for the moment.

Every morning she sat on the roof of House Das with her injured arm propped on cushions and herself wrapped in blankets, sipping at warmed tea, listening to the sounds of Pol-Thiri, and staring at that treeless wedge of space.

She couldn't bring herself to sit on the Breakfast Patio, although she'd heard that the two remaining Juju birds were building a nest, so there was hope that the numbers would be revived. She felt a need to be with the Renoa, though. A need to acknowledge that empty wedge of space.

She didn't know if she had killed Cystel Valiyard or if the Renoa had done it. Emrie's moving him with the witchcraft had happened in perfect sync with that branch dropping. Either way, the Renoa had taken the punishment upon itself.

The people of Pol-Thiri saw her as a hero, which had been fun at first when those of her House had lavished attention on her, and she'd both announced and celebrated the assistance of Keeli, Lianjit, Ahrens, and the Flaust siblings. Only her reputation hadn't waned. Whether this was because the people of Pol-Thiri believed her heroic or because it was a convenient way to see the turn of events, she didn't know. When she sat too near the Renoa's Field, those on the Paths of Wisdom and Virtue tended to wander her way a little too often.

And then there was Montali. It was he who'd started rumors about her arm breaking in the same moment the Renoa's branch cracked, confirming a sacred connection between her and the Tree.

Emrie found that embarrassing rather than flattering. Luckily, Keeli had witnessed the norie release Emrie and the swing of the iron box that had broken her bone so neither she nor Lianjit took Montali's story seriously. But the rest of Pol-Thiri did.

Even with Montali's rumormongering, Emrie was grateful for him and Imjin. They added a needed chaos to the somber House Das. Emrie and Ahrens had agreed to wait until life settled to have Montali contract in. In the meantime, her father invited the siblings to stay. Brid had moved out, declaring she wanted nothing to do with House Das and all the lies they'd fed her. Hopefully, she'd forgive them before she inherited the Sovereignty. Lady Sersi was working on that, and it was universally understood that Brid *would* be the next First Heir. Dogged, determined Brid had kept climbing as the Renoa had quaked and shook until she made it to the top.

Keeli stood up to her mother and refused to marry, telling her parents she would take on the role of First Daughter as she was better suited to it than her sister, but she wouldn't be compelled into marriage to earn the title. Her mother gave in. Emrie was proud of her friend.

Lianjit returned to Barrack's Practice to find that Montali had told everyone about Emrie's first attempt to kill the First Heir using her sword. It was determined that the sword had earned itself a name and was titled That-Which-Tries. Lianjit hadn't been pleased by this. She told anyone who would listen that a sword should only receive a name if it does something heroic when wielded by its actual owner. It was an endless topic of discussion when the three of them got together with Keeli arguing that the solution was for Emrie to keep the sword and the name. Lianjit didn't like that any better.

Barring Emrie still missing her sister and several unanswered questions about Brid, life had taken a turn for the good. So when Mati Dechta joined her on the roof, Emrie was unprepared for what she had to say.

"Your father has asked Deriek Valiyard to visit. To hear a story I have to tell."

"Deriek's here?"

She hadn't seen him since the day under the Renoa, but that wasn't unexpected. The First Heir's death had split the inner-ring Houses like a club on a melon. Deriek had been right that his brother had coerced several of the inner-ring Sons to capture him and lock him up. It came out that the Son of the Fifth Adviser had been murdered not by the First Heir himself, but by the Second Son of the Seventh Adviser. Not that the Son of the Seventh Adviser had known this, but he'd still had to take responsibility for the murder, and his House had lost Status and their place in the First-ring. And that was just the largest chunk of the rotting fruit. There'd been a line of creative Judgments issued forth from the House of the Sovereign. They said that some Judgments were from Deriek himself, even if it was constantly pointed out that Brid would become the First Heir once all proper Ceremonies were complete, not Deriek.

"May I bring him up?" Mati Dechta asked.

"You may," Emrie said, unable to hide how pleased and nervous she was to see him again. While Mati Ereana and Mati Sarta brought more cushions and laid out refreshments, Emrie used her uninjured hand to arrange the drape of her laptevi and pat down her hair. She had this irrational worry that everything had changed because of the things she'd said. Or perhaps even worse, that she'd invented what had happened between them only in her own head.

When Deriek arrived, he looked resplendent in the midnight green he seemed to favor. His hair was still loose, pushed back from his sharp face and curling at his shoulders, just as she liked it. He stopped in front of her and they stared at each other, both of them with smiles that were just a little crooked. Emrie began the formal greetings.

He put a hand up to stop her.

"Don't you think we've earned our way past all that?"

"Earned is an interesting word for it," she said carefully.

"You have a better one?"

"No."

He made an elaborate bow in her direction, ducking low and scrolling out one hand in a flowery way that made her laugh.

"My dearest Ajnee," he said in a teasing voice. "You have my sincerest apologies for not coming sooner. I thought it better to keep our connection quiet and having met my father and knowing the personality of your cousin, you can imagine how goes life day-to-day under the Sovereign's roof."

"Not well?" Emrie asked, knowing then that everything was alright between them. He'd always been so good at entertaining her.

"I almost feel sorry for my father. He's still insisting she isn't his, you know." He folded down onto the cushion next to hers. She would've liked to have shared a seat as they had so often before, but of course, that would no longer be seemly. She started to pour him a cup of tea with her good hand, but he lifted it away from her to perform the service for himself.

"I've been waiting for you to visit me," he continued. "I owe you a story and have the rugs you left in the Sovereign's House strewn about my chamber in case you decide to come demand it."

"It never occurred to me." But she was thrilled about this, too.

"Well, now it will."

Mati Dechta returned having shooed the rest of the maties off the roof. Deriek gave Emrie a questioning look. Emrie shrugged. At least, they were oblivious together. Mati Dechta came to stand before them both.

"Might I sit?" she asked. It was a first in Emrie's memory, and looking at Mati Dechta closely, there were circles around her eyes and frown lines around her mouth. She'd shouldered Emrie's care over the last weeks. Just as she had Noemi's. Just as she always did. She *was* House Das in many, many ways.

Emrie nodded.

After she was seated, Mati Dechta spoke. "The Head of House Das has asked me to tell you a story. It's an old tale. One that if you'd both known would've changed recent events. Although perhaps it's better that you did not. If there's one thing that's clear, it's that the Renoa works as it will."

"I suppose this is about my father?" Deriek asked, his tone still joking.

"Yes." Mati Dechta gave him a reproachful look as if telling him to reign in his humor. "But more so your mother." Then she looked to Emrie. "And yours."

And that got both of their attention. Emrie, warily so.

Mati Dechta turned to her. "You know that your Uncle Otto used to accompany the river caravan deliveries when he was younger? He and your father have never quite got along. It was better if one of them was kept out of the House."

"I didn't know," Emrie replied.

"It was Uncle Otto who found Costina, Deriek's mother. She was an Eighth Daughter in a First-ring family of Vin-Yonekur."

"And she was wild," Deriek added, his tone still light. "She ran away from home if my understanding is correct."

"She did, but she wasn't wild," Mati Dechta corrected. "She was determined to live her life as she saw fit."

Which sounded like Deriek himself.

"You knew her?" Deriek asked, and this time he sounded genuinely curious.

"Otto found her in Ter-Ramachat. Ahrens inherited his skill for bringing home strays from his uncle." Mati Dechta smiled as if in remembrance. "But yes, your mother lived in House Das when she first came to Pol-Thiri, so I knew her. It was her idea to attract the attention of the Sovereign. The truth of the First Heir was already known, and the probable solution seemed to be a concubine. No one anticipated the Sovereign's plans or that Costina's child would be born with death hanging over his head. None of us, not Otto nor Emrie's father, Brunau, nor especially your mother, would've gone through with it if we'd known." She looked at Deriek then. "Or perhaps Costina would have. She loved him at first, you see."

Deriek had gone still watching Mati Dechta, his head cocked to one side, his eyes straight.

"You don't speak as a matie," he said evenly. "Who are you?"

Emrie looked between the two of them while they stared at each other. Mati Dechta ruled her sphere of House Das, but Emrie'd never heard her speak like this to anyone but Emrie and Ahrens. Something was off here.

"I'm Mati Dechta. But that's not what you're asking, is it?"

And then Emrie knew, and if the revelation wasn't so jarring, she would've been pleased by beating Deriek in doing so. There was one other person who'd been included in this story of Deriek's mother but hadn't yet been named. Emrie saw the moment Deriek got it. He stood, breaking his eye contact with Mati Dechta, and moved to take the seat on Emrie's injured side, to protect her. In the movement, she could feel his anger stirring, the memory of the darkness that still shadowed him. This time on her behalf.

"Continue the story," Emrie said so softly the words were barely audible.

Mati Dechta nodded. If she knew Emrie had puzzled out her secret, there was no sign. Noemi had been like that, too, hard to read if she so chose.

"It didn't take long for us to learn of the Sovereign's plans, and the next bit you both know." She spoke to Deriek. Perhaps it was easier for her to tell the tale if she didn't have to face Emrie.

"From the moment you were born, your mother made sure the First Heir understood the repercussions should he harm you. She protected you best she could, living on the fringes of the Sovereign's House, trying to undo a situation that we'd unintentionally created. I ask no forgiveness for this. Nor for what those of us of House Das did next." She sent a quick glance Emrie's way.

Emrie said nothing.

Mati Dechta continued. "I could say it was with, if not the approval, at least the knowledge of the Renoa, and that's true. Brunau wouldn't have agreed without asking. It was frankly the only thing that persuaded him to let me do it, and it took us years of waiting to go through with it. The First Heir wasn't old enough at first. And then I became pregnant with Emrie."

In flashes so quick they felt like the flap of wings, Emrie was hit by the emotions of it all—fury and hurt and betrayal and a well of empty longing that would never run dry. This woman spoke so easily, so calmly, about something that should be so painful.

Emrie hid her reaction by staring at the Renoa. Crisp and white and damaged against the blue sky and the unfolding yellows and reds and browns of the desert mountains beyond. She didn't need the Renoa to confirm to her that what this woman she'd known her entire life was saying was true. Nor did she need to ask if Noemi had known, because, of course, she had.

And yet still, pieces were missing.

Deriek leaned forward, toward Mati Dechta, his voice not angry but cold and accusatory. "You seduced Cystel and produced a girl child you named Brid."

Mati Dechta stiffened at his tone, but Emrie was grateful for it. He was putting the focus on himself, providing Emrie space, being her defender.

"I did a horrible, despicable thing," Mati Dechta said, challenging him right back. "But the Sovereign was faithful to his dead wife other than your mother, and Cystel Valiyard killed two of his mistresses during the time I was pregnant with Emrie, and he wasn't yet a man."

"Then to keep Cystel from knowing of the child that you conceived, you pretended to die," Deriek mocked.

"I pretended to let him poison me. We then sent most of the remaining family of House Das out of Pol-Thiri. No one could know the truth if Brid were to be safe. And not just from the First Heir." Mati Dechta threw back her shoulders as if daring him to argue with her and in that moment Emrie could see it. Not just the resemblance to Noemi but to Brid as well. The stiffness and the defiance of it. "A Sovereign and two Heirs," she continued, "neither of which were right. That's all that stood between the Seat of Judgment and a new Soveriegnty. So, Brid went with Brunau's cousin to Kye-Boehlke. Otto, Brunau, and I stayed here to keep anyone from killing either you or Cystel until Brid was old enough to fight for the Seat."

Deriek snorted in a droll disbelief. "To fight as a Das."

Her mother's eyes flashed in annoyance. "Do I not deserve anything for my sacrifice? Does not my husband and our House?"

"Why are you telling us all of this?" he asked. It wasn't an answer to Mati Dechta's question.

"Because you'll discover it on your own," she snapped. "Or at least Emrie will." She pursed her lips then and turned her attention to Emrie. "The people of Pol-Thiri will remember the witchcraft, and regardless of the good it did, witches aren't to be supported. My sister must come to bind it. My twin sister. One look at her and the whole of it will be out. So, I've told you. And you'll guard the secret for now. The Renoa has spoken, but there are still only two Heirs between House of Valiyard and a civil war."

Which was a reason to tell Emrie all of this, but not Deriek. The only reason to include him was if today was the start of a new game, a new plan. And her mother had even given away a clue as to what it was.

There were only two Heirs between House Valiyard and a new Sovereignty. If one of them contracted into House Das . . .

It shouldn't have been a harder blow than realizing Mati Dechta was her mother, but it was. It was also the thing that pushed Emrie past being able to keep her reaction hidden. Anger hot and ugly flashed through her.

If Brid was born of Emrie's mother, then Brid had never needed to contract into House Das. Her father's deal with the First Heir had always been about Emrie and Deriek. She could see it so clearly.

She hadn't been sent to care for him for either his need or the witchcraft. Her father could have had any number of people keep Deriek alive with food and warmth and such. Her parents had meant to trap him into House Das by using her as bait. They'd used her secret of the witchcraft to tie them together. To build a bond that her parents could then exploit. They were still doing it.

She looked at Deriek, saw the knowledge of this in his eyes.

"You are who you are," he said, his lips quirking up at the corners as if in amusement. "None of this is your fault." He meant it. She knew that. It didn't stop her fury.

Deriek shifted as if he were going to distract her mother again, give Emrie more space, but Emrie didn't need it. It was her turn.

"Do you love us at all?" she asked, banking the anger just barely. "These children you produced—me, Ahrens, Brid, even Noemi? Or are we just tools to increase the power of House Das?"

"I sacrificed for the good of us all," her mother said not sounding remorseful at all.

It wasn't the right answer or even an answer.

There was a sound from behind them, and Emrie turned to see her father. He must've been there the entire time. He made his way slowly, unevenly around the cushions to stand beside his wife. Deriek moved in closer, taking Emrie's injured arm onto his lap.

"Both your mother and I love you," her father said quietly. "You claimed the Renoa had spoken to you, and we believed it. The Renoa has spoken to no one in House Das for many years. You've always been a good Daughter, Emrie. If the Renoa trusted you, then I felt we had to as well. It was never just about Brid." He reached over as if to tug on her hair, but she flinched, and he placed his hand on her shoulder instead.

There was a time Emrie would've fallen all over herself in pleasure for such words, but he also hadn't answered the question.

She looked at Deriek, saw his strength, and leaned into it. She wouldn't let her parents beat her with their betrayal. Or control her future or his.

Deriek smiled as if saying he knew how she felt. She nodded back and reached over with her good hand to touch her father on the sleeve. He would hear her this time.

"I *am* a good Daughter. I'm a good sister, too, and I trust the Renoa will end up with the Sovereign It wants. So Deriek won't be joining House Das. He stays as Second Heir until Brid has Heirs of her own. Valiyard Heirs. Because I'm in no hurry to marry and I am better than you. I care for my House and the good of my family members, even Brid, more than I care for power."

FORTY

The first thing Emrie did upon arriving in Deriek's room was insist he find a cushion big enough to share. He did, collecting a huge one from his sleeping dais.

"Large enough for you, Ajnee?" he asked with a grin.

"Yes," she said and then took exactly one-half for herself. It was her first visit, and there was an opportunity for awkwardness here that she was determined to avoid. "I like it better when you call me Nitsya. Plus you owe me the story of the name."

He sat down next to her and pulled her splinted arm onto his lap, unfolding her fingers to touch the pads one by one. "Can we keep the endearment Nitsya between ourselves? It's possible that someone other than me knows the story. We wouldn't want to destroy my reputation for being aloof."

Emrie elbowed him. They'd already decided that what was between them needed to remain private for a while. And not just to stop her parents from using it. They needed time to grow.

"Your reputation is already shattered," she teased. "Now tell me my story."

"You aren't going to be kind about this are you?" He sighed, pretending to be much put upon.

"Not a chance."

"Fine. There once was a deer named Nitsya who lived in Vin-Yonekur." He slipped into the wonderful sway and rhythm of his storytelling. "Vin-Yonekur having more grazing land than Pol-Thiri, this wasn't an unusual thing, but this doe was. Unusual that was. So much so that even the Houses of the inner-rings would make trips out to ogle her. She had wings, you see. Great plumed wings of blue and green."

"Some swordsman isn't going to chop them off to help her with her vanity, will he?"

Deriek gave her a look of mock affront and leaned over to whisper against her ear, making her shiver.

"I told you. This is a lovely story. Embarrassing for me, but lovely." He sat back up. "Everyone wanted to see this doe. And when she lost a feather it was treated with the greatest of reverence, like a product of the Renoa itself. But the challenge with a winged deer is that she's hard to keep contained. The farmer that owned her gave her his best field. He brought her treats and care. He slept in her barn and brought her into his house when it was cold. He dedicated himself to pleasing her in every way that he could."

"Sounds good to me."

He wrinkled his nose at her. "The doe named Nitsya agreed with you. As many times as she roamed, she always came back. The farmer thought it was because of the quality of his field and the care and the honor of being so revered. But he was wrong, you see. The doe appreciated the honor and the care, but it was what she felt from her farmer that became a tether stronger than rope or iron or even witchcraft. His love bound her like nothing else could. She lost her desire to leave him."

Emrie grinned. It was the perfect story. Almost.

"The way you tell it, I'm the farmer and you're stuck tethered to me. But I don't want to be the farmer. I want to have the wings."

He curled her injured arm against his chest, pressing it against his heart and then touched his lips to hers, gently, softly, tenderly. "Too late, Nitsya," he murmured right into her skin. "You gave the wings to me."

***

Thank you so much for reading Feather & Blade! If you have a moment to help out a newbie author, please consider leaving an honest review in one of the usual spots. It really does help.

If you *really* liked the book and want to receive notices for my upcoming book releases plus a free novella set in the world of the Renoas—with several fun tie-ins to Emrie's Tale if you can spot them—here's a link to come join my monthly newsletter: https://tinyurl.com/354z8rhh Happy Reading! ~Rachel

About the Author

Rachel Taylor Thompson lives in the central coast area of California with her husband, daughters, and a truly ridiculous number of animals (including but not limited to horses, rabbits, chickens, cats, a guinea pig, a bearded dragon, bees, and various wild animals that endlessly steal everyone else's food). She started storytelling after she and a group of friends played the game Two Truths and a Lie and not a single person guessed that "I'm writing a book" was her lie. Since her friends had so much faith in her, she decided to go for it. To hear more about her books (and animals) head over to her website: www.racheltaylorthompson.com.